A PLUME BOOK

THE DOCTOR'S WIFE

ELIZABETH BRUNDAGE is a graduate of the Iowa Writers' Workshop and winner of a James Michener Award. Her short fiction has been published in *The Greensboro Review*, *The Witness*, and *New Letters*. She lives with her family in Massachusetts.

Praise for *The Doctor's Wife*

"What Elizabeth Brundage has done with *The Doctor's Wife* kept me up two nights—the first was the one in which I read it, and the second was the night when I kept trying to argue with her. 'He wouldn't do that,' I wanted to say—but yes, he would. He would almost surely do all that. And so would she."
—Dorothy Allison, author of *Bastard Out of Carolina* and *Cavedweller*

"*The Doctor's Wife* is certainly a tense and compelling psychological thriller, but it's more than just a page-turner. In her dark depiction of small-town intolerance, Brundage invites us to question . . . our engagement with the world. My favorite (and truly the darkest and saddest) line of the book is the very last."
—Ruth Ozeki, author of *My Year of Meats* and *All Over Creation*

"Elizabeth Brundage has exquisitely captured the tension that resides at the crossroads of self and society. *The Doctor's Wife* encapsulates not only our uncertain, conflicted times but the maddening, endearing, fascinating contradictions of the American moral construct. This novel is as politically pertinent as it is a page-turner."
—Meghan Daum, author of *The Quality of Life Report*

"*The Doctor's Wife* is a full meal of sex, danger, and small-town paranoia which I greedily devoured."
—Laurie Fox, author of *The Lost Girls*

"Elizabeth Brundage's prose reveals an honesty, clarity and grace uncommon for any novel, let alone a debut, and her insights consistently surprise and astonish . . . *The Doctor's Wife* is a novel to savor, praise and share."

—David Corbett, author of *The Devil's Redhead* and *Done for a Dime*

"Steeped in psychological suspense, compelling and compulsively readable."

—Bookreporter.com

ELIZABETH BRUNDAGE

The Doctor's Wife

A PLUME BOOK

PLUME
Published by Penguin Group
Penguin Group (USA) Inc., 375 Hudson Street, New York, New York 10014, U.S.A.
Penguin Group (Canada), 90 Eglinton Avenue East, Suite 700, Toronto, Ontario, Canada
M4P 2Y3 (a division of Pearson Penguin Canada Inc.)
Penguin Books Ltd., 80 Strand, London WC2R 0RL, England
Penguin Ireland, 25 St. Stephen's Green, Dublin 2, Ireland (a division of Penguin
Books Ltd.)
Penguin Group (Australia), 250 Camberwell Road, Camberwell, Victoria 3124, Australia
(a division of Pearson Australia Group Pty. Ltd.)
Penguin Books India Pvt. Ltd., 11 Community Centre, Panchsheel Park,
New Delhi – 110 017, India
Penguin Books (NZ), cnr Airborne and Rosedale Roads, Albany, Auckland 1310,
New Zealand (a division of Pearson New Zealand Ltd.)
Penguin Books (South Africa) (Pty.) Ltd., 24 Sturdee Avenue, Rosebank,
Johannesburg 2196, South Africa

Penguin Books Ltd., Registered Offices: 80 Strand, London WC2R 0RL, England

Published by Plume, a member of Penguin Group (USA) Inc. Previously published in a
Viking edition.

First Plume Printing, December 2005
20 19 18 17 16

Copyright © Elizabeth Brundage, 2004
All rights reserved

Title-page photograph © Brian Cencula/CORBIS

Ⓟ REGISTERED TRADEMARK—MARCA REGISTRADA

The Library of Congress has catalogued the Viking edition as follows:

Brundage, Elizabeth.
The doctor's wife : a novel / by Elizabeth Brundage.
p. cm.
ISBN 0–670–03316–2 (hc.)
ISBN 0–452–28691–3 (pbk.)
1. Physicians' spouses—Fiction. 2. New York (State)—Fiction.
3. Physicians—Fiction. I. Title.
PS3602.R84D63 2004
813'.6—dc22   2003065773

Printed in the United States of America
Original hardcover design by Francesca Belanger

For Scott, Hannah, Sophie, and Sam

Goosey Goosey gander,
Whither shall I wander?
Upstairs and downstairs,
And in my lady's chamber;
There I met an old man who wouldn't say his prayers;
I took him by the left leg
And threw him down the stairs.

—MOTHER GOOSE

The Doctor's Wife

Prologue

The memory starts here, in my apron pocket, with the gun. I remember holding it. It felt good, cold. And inside my body it was hot, blistering hot, and I took the gun out of my apron and started walking across the kitchen floor and it came to me that I had memorized every squeal in those old wood planks and I went to the cellar door, which was laughing blatantly in my face, and I got my hammer and I started whaling on that door thinking, Fuck you, you assholes, fuck you a thousand times and fuck all your mothers! And I hacked away at that door like it was some kind of live animal, and then it was open, it was broken, it was striated, and there was wood all over the place, and chipped paint like all the pieces of my heart, and I helped myself to the darkness beyond it, and I rumbled down the stairs in my work boots, into the cold stink of the cellar, and I grabbed him. I said, Get up, you've caused me enough fucking trouble, and he shook in my grasp, like a child, he shook, and I could see in his face the reckoning, I could see he was sorry, he had come around, he had come full circle, and I knew somehow that I was responsible for that, I had done that and it made me proud. I yanked on him and he in his weakened state cowered and I could feel the temptation to do it right then, I could feel it, I had to work at suppressing it. I wanted it to be over, I wanted him to be somewhere else, buried deep in the ground where no one would ever look and in the spring it would be covered with flowers and those lovely fluffy dandelions that you can blow into a thousand pieces. I used to do that when I was little and I used to wish for things but I never got what I asked for and now, in retrospect, when I consider my unrelenting devotion to Jesus, I have to say that I am sorely disappointed.

They find me on the ground, drooling in the dirt, the river howling in my ears, my mother's red wool coat twisted up my hips. I can taste blood in my mouth, and can see a little bit of my yellow hair on the ground and my hand is like a dead bird, and I can see now that the gun is there and it is dead, too. The gun is a dead skunk. And my hand is just a white bird. And the skunk has made a bad smell. I wish my husband had tried harder, because then we would have had a chance. I wouldn't have done any of this. I just wanted to lead a good Christian life. But I was the Devil's wife, that's the truth of it. And even Jesus can't save you from that. For years I have tried to overcome my weaknesses. For years I have told myself that it didn't matter, what he did to me, all those years ago. That hot summer day when he knocked on my father's door. I was just this little girl, a black taste like tar in my mouth when I picture the real truth to that. And he was already a man, he had hair on his face, a well-defined Adam's apple, a deep voice. I was just a small skinny girl with cuts on my knees and burrs stuck to my dress. He took that from me. He stole it. And I want it back now, pathetic as it may sound to you. I want it back.

The detective's name is Bascombe, a windswept man in an old hunting coat, with a face unaccustomed to smiling. He takes off the coat and throws it onto the couch across the room. Now I see his shirt, a simple white button-down, and the worn blue jeans held up by suspenders. He is nearly fifty, a patient man, a hunter. I can tell by his face that he is alone, unmarried, and carries a deep sense of regret. It is his talisman, regret. It keeps him safe. He is a man, I realize, with little faith, and I tug on my cross to remind him of my own. Because even a jaded detective knows that a man without faith is lost.

A cop comes in with some coffee, places the paper cup in front of me, then leaves the room. The detective sits in his chair behind his cluttered desk. The rain batters the window behind him and it is almost dawn and I can tell they've gotten him out of bed and that the coffee is a necessary stimulant. Scattered across his desk with alarming clarity are the photographs of my father's house, large black-and-white prints that portray an aspect of the awful things I've done, but only an aspect. There is the body of the man I've shot. The bullet wound on the upper flesh of his thigh. The hole that has burst and ripped through the legs of his pants and the blood splattered like paint around it.

I don't realize that I'm shaking until I take the cigarette. The detective reaches across the desk and lights it and I meet his eyes and he smiles a little. It is an appealing gesture, and as we smoke together it is as though we are friends sharing the quiet emergence of morning, and not bitter enemies. His eyes, gray as wet slate, tinted with the history of all he has seen, watch me relentlessly, without even a glimmer of mercy. He seems immune to my beauty, which normally spreads like a viral rash across the skin of a man. "Are you comfortable?" he asks, pushing the ashtray across the desk. "Is the coffee all right?"

I haven't even tasted it. "Yes, it's fine, thank you."

"Do you understand why you're here?"

I drink to avoid answering. The coffee tastes like turpentine; I wonder if they've put something in it.

"Why don't you tell me about your relationship with Dr. Knowles," the detective says.

I try to think. I don't understand the word relationship. "He's my friend."

"And his wife?"

I look at the detective directly. "What do you want, Detective? What do you really want?"

"What do I want?" He looks surprised. "I'm interested in your side of things."

This makes me laugh, but then the tears run down my face. He takes a handkerchief out of his pocket and hands it to me and I wipe my eyes and smell the square of white cloth. It smells clean and fresh, like laundry detergent, and I am reminded for a moment of my mother. It makes me cry, it makes me cry and cry while the detective sits there and watches. He isn't in any hurry. He doesn't make me feel bad. "Take your time," he tells me and I stutter to catch my breath, spitting and gasping and stuttering, and I imagine it is a good performance for the detective, who is the type who cries secretly at movies, who is easily betrayed by women, and I think perhaps it will make him feel sorry for me, it will make him care. He gives me another cigarette and I smoke it gratefully and I remember my husband the day we met that hot afternoon on my father's porch. Simon Haas was a nothing then. A bumbling artist. He wanted to do my portrait. He'd been watching me all afternoon, hiding behind the brambles. But I saw him; I knew. I was *playing with the cats, one was orange, the other calico. He knocked on the door. Portraits for sale, he said with his lips trembling. I stood there. I could feel him wanting me. My father, who was on the couch, moldy with disease, hired him. Money's no object was what he said, a plan already festering inside his twisted mind. When Simon went out to get his paints, my father told me to fix my hair. I raced up to Mama's room, used her tortoiseshell comb, dabbed on her lipstick, which was ruby red and crumbled like an old crayon when I pressed it to my lips.*

That was the day I smoked my first cigarette.

"Have you ever been in love, Detective?"

He doesn't answer me.

"I was just a stupid kid. I didn't know anything." The words tumble out slowly, as if I am reciting a poem, a child's nursery rhyme. "He saved my life, you know."

The detective shifts, a confused expression on his face. "Who did, Mrs. Haas? Who saved your life?"

But I am crying too hard to answer.

The detective reaches across the table and takes my hand and for a moment I enjoy the warmth of his flesh, the rough care he shows me. But then I pull away, I have to. I don't want his pity. "No," I say, shaking my head, the tears rolling out. "I can't tell you, I won't."

But this isn't true. I'm bursting to tell. Bursting.

PART ONE
Bones

1

SOMETIME AFTER MIDNIGHT Michael Knowles wakes to the sound of his beeper and picks up the phone. "You want Finney," he tells the page operator. "I'm not on call tonight."

"You are now, Dr. Knowles," the operator says officiously, and puts him through to the ER. A nurse comes on and brings him up to speed in a voice shrill with hysteria. The patient, she explains, a thirteen-year-old girl from Arbor Hill, is in labor, four months premature. "Boyfriend dropped her off about an hour ago and split. No prenatal care, no insurance. Now she's bleeding all over the place and I can't get anyone to give me a consult. Your partner's puking his guts out in the men's room. I'm told it's food poisoning."

"Give me twenty minutes," Michael mutters, and like a man called to the service of war he grabs his coat. He had fallen asleep on the couch in the study. He climbs the stairs quietly, feeling strangely like a guest in his own home, wary of the light that burns on his wife's bedside table. He enters the room uneasily, dreading a strained encounter, but Annie is asleep and all the lines of discord have vanished from her face. For a moment he marvels at her beauty, her glorious brown hair, the fleshy protrusion of her upper lip, her T-shirt twisted appealingly across her breasts. His heart begins to pound. She has squandered her beauty, he thinks. He does not know what will happen between them now. But no matter how much he rationalizes what she did, and he *does* rationalize it, no matter how much he tries to talk himself into hating her, he finds himself loving her more. His love for her is ripe in his mouth. The fruit has rotted perhaps, but he refuses to spit it out. With routine compassion he picks up the book at her side and sets it on the nightstand. For a moment he stands there, half-expecting her to wake, almost hoping that she will. Not to fight anymore, but to find each other inside a single, wordless moment. To find each other and remember what brought them both there in the first place, and why neither has left. But it's too late for that, and she doesn't wake, and they're paging him again. He writes her a note, GOT PAGED, and leans it against the base of the lamp, where she will find it in the morning. Then he switches off the light and steps into the hall, listening to the yearning silence of the big house. It makes him think of his kids and he looks in on them now before he goes. First comes Henry, his ten-year-old son, sprawled across the mattress amid blankets and toys and forgotten stuffed animals. The boy's hamster, Harpo, spins obsessively in its cage and for a moment Michael just stands there, contemplating the creature's useless exertion. In the room next door, Rosie, who is six, sleeps with perfect stillness, maintaining the meticulous hierarchical positioning of her dolls at the end of her bed. Michael can't imagine loving anything more than his children and feels a pang of guilt because he rarely sees them. *Quality time,* that's what he's resorted to. All part of the failed equation, he thinks, heading down the crooked stairs of the old house and out into the cold night, where it has begun to snow again. The flakes are thick and white like the feathers of birds. He takes a moment to zipper his jacket, to pull on his hood. The night is quiet, the sound of snowfall a comfort somehow, and he pushes himself on, cursing himself for wasting time.

The Saab starts with a lusty roar that makes him grateful that he owns a good car, even though he does not consider himself a man of attachments or possessions. The car smells of leather and promise and his own pathetic gratitude and it comes to him that he's been a fool in his marriage, that what came between him and Annie is his own goddamn fault. It's about him, not her, he realizes. It's about everything he's not.

Angry now, he pulls out of the driveway and speeds down the road, blowing past the squad car parked on the corner. Ever since he delivered the sheriff's babies none of the cops pull him over for speeding. They know people are waiting for him, people in pain, and they respect that. One of the benefits of living in a small town like High Meadow, he thinks, gunning the engine, winding down the hill past Slattery's cow farm, the fields dark and dense and silent, veiled in a dusting of fresh snow. Too early in the season for snow, he thinks, just a couple of weeks shy of Thanksgiving, but the weather is always unpredictable in upstate New York, and after all these years he's no stranger to it. Ordinarily in weather like this he'd take Route 17 down to Bunker Hill, but he's worried about the girl in the ER and decides to take Valley Road instead to save time. Under ideal circumstances the shortcut is dangerous, complicated with tight, snakelike turns, but it takes fifteen minutes off the trip. Tonight Valley Road shimmers with ice. The naked trees seem to tremble in his headlights. The sleet comes out of the dark like millions of pins and he is forced to decelerate, taking the curves slowly, methodically. The suffering girl will have to wait, he tells himself; nothing he can do about it now. At the end of Valley Road he turns onto Route 20, streaming into a line of traffic behind a behemoth snowplow, then onto the interstate, the city of Albany like a white blur before him.

Downtown, the streets are deserted except for a few homeless stragglers. The green neon cross on St. Vincent's Hospital blinks and buzzes like some divine Morse code. Only now, as he pulls through the mammoth jaws of the doctors' parking garage and climbs the labyrinth of concrete to his spot on level four, does it occur to him that something may be amiss. That perhaps the phone call had been a hoax: the bleeding girl, Finney being sick. Now that he thinks about it, he hadn't recognized the nurse's voice and he knows all the nurses at St. Vincent's. The garage is deserted. The hanging fluorescent lights move in the wind, squealing slightly on their hinges. He knows he's paranoid—*Comes with the territory,* they'd told him when he'd first started at the clinic, and he'd been more than willing to accept that, but now, tonight, he senses danger and he hesitates getting out of the car at all. He looks up at the glass doors a hundred feet away, where a nurse passes by in her pink scrubs, and the sense of routine comforts him. His beeper sounds again—*I'm coming, hold your fucking horses*—and he grabs his bag and opens the door and they're on him, three or four or even five men, dragging him across the concrete into the dark. Cursing him, shoving him, laughing a little with their raised fists, taking turns splitting open his face, pushing him from one man's arms into another's. A greasy terror sloshes through his head. And then he's down on his knees, someone throttling him, wrapping a cord around his neck, and as the air leaves his body like a pierced balloon he wonders if they are finally going to kill him. The fat one speaks in a cold, even voice, sweat splashing off his lips: "We've had enough, Dr. Knowles, we've had enough of your bullshit," and then a shock of pain in his balls, excruciating and dense, and he doubles over and pukes—and he is glad for a moment, puking, because he thinks they will leave him alone, but they don't, they kick him again, and again, and he is down on all fours like a dog amid chewing-gum wrappers and cigarette butts and shattered glass and his own puke and he suddenly begins to cry. Where is the guard, he wonders now—why hasn't anyone seen them, some nurse, some technician, some doctor? Why isn't someone calling the police?

"Let's medicate the poor bastard." Someone yanks back his head and pries open his mouth, dropping in pills. He doesn't swallow, but then he gags and chokes and the bitter powder burns his throat. Water comes next, and more pills, and he can't breathe. *Surrender,* he tells himself, *you have no choice!* His body lax as butter, everything blurred and slow and jangling with silence. *I can't fucking hear you!* he thinks dully. Their big hands, quivering faces, mouths open in laughter. *I can't hear anything.*

They put him in the trunk. The road vibrates under his head like a jackhammer. For the moment he is relieved to be left alone; he is relieved to be alive. And then it comes to him, suddenly, vividly, that he is going to die.

For months he has waited for this moment, feared it, and now that it is here, finally, now that it is happening to him, *yes, to him,* it is all the terror he imagined and worse.

Snowflakes on his face. *The sky is kissing you, Daddy,* he hears his daughter whispering. The men are talking but he cannot make out a word of it. He feels the prick of a needle, the warm drug rushing through him, bringing a taste into his mouth, *cotton candy,* and a feeling throughout his limbs that is not entirely unpleasant. The men smell of whiskey and triumph as they grip his body and pull him out of the dark place. Staggering with his weight, they bring him in their arms to a car and they put him into it, behind the wheel. Even in his dementia he knows it's his own car, he recognizes the smell, Rosie's paddock boots in the back, Henry's chocolate bars for Cub Scouts, and they strap him in and turn the key and the engine screams. He wants to tell them that he can't see, he's in no shape to drive, but his mouth won't work, his tongue is too big, and now the car is moving, it floats for a moment in midair, then tumbles through the dark like a clumsy animal. Suddenly he understands what they have done and he doesn't care, really, it doesn't matter anymore, and he forgets it, he forgives them all their stupidity, and he can only remember her face, her beautiful mouth. *Annie!* He screams inside his head. He is screaming and screaming. *Annie!*

But it is too late. And his wife can't hear him.

2

THEY WAIT UNDER the marquee of the X-rated movie house. There are six or seven of them, mostly men. The women like wilted flowers. Some of them carry signs, emblems of their helplessness. She does not know if they have just come out, or if they have been waiting all night. It is almost five, the sky still dark. It could be day or night to these people, she thinks; it is all the same. Sleep is a luxury none of them can afford. Inadequately dressed, they shake and dance in the cold, waiting for an opportunity. You'll see cars driving up slow. Negotiating. Sometimes they get in, sometimes they don't. Depends on the job. Depends what it entails. Mostly sex favors, things of that nature. That's what happens when you're desperate, Lydia thinks. You'll do anything for money. Well, she knows about desperate. No one has to tell her. And she needs somebody desperate now.

She parks the rented Taurus across the street and watches for several minutes, trying to decide which one she wants. She's been down here plenty with her church. A part of the city where no woman feels safe, even in daylight. The street lamps are already decorated with Christmas ornaments, but there's no sign of merriment here. Just broken-down people with nothing to lose. Shaking in the cold. She considers the random poetry of their signs. She doesn't want the one with AIDS, with her luck she'll probably catch something, and *Hungry* just stands there, forlorn as a scarecrow. *Will Work for Food* smiles at her and gives a little wave. Looks like we have a winner, she thinks almost gleefully, and pulls out fast to the other side of the street. The man shuffles over, toking on his cigarette. He's wearing a flannel shirt, trousers, black boots. She leans across the seat and puts the window down. "I need somebody strong. You strong?"

"Depends what for?"

"I need something moved."

The man hesitates.

"It won't take long. And it pays."

"Pays what?"

"Fifty."

"Don't want no trouble."

"Won't have any."

"All right, then," he says, "I'll go along with it." He gets in and smiles, reaches out his big hand. "Name's Ooms. Walter Ooms."

"Hello, Mr. Ooms."

His clothes carry the smell of cheap rum, a tawdry medicinal smell. It puts her in mind of her father, when she was just a girl in the oppressive silence of their house.

"You from around here?" she asks him.

"Up north. My daddy had a cow farm. But that's all gone now. Anyway, he's dead."

The wind sweeps the snow along the street. Snowbanks, gray from exhaust, hunker like inert animals. It begins to sleet and the streets clear of people. Even the hookers disappear, their faces smeared by the hard wind. Cars twist and scatter on the ice.

Ooms adjusts the vent so the heat hits him in the face. "I got rolled last week; they took my coat. I got a sister down in Florida. I ought to just go down there, but we ain't spoke in years. Don't need no coat down there, don't need no heat." He snorts into a scrap of newspaper and coughs a few times.

"There's some whiskey down there if you want it."

"All right."

"In the bag down there. That'll warm you."

"Yes, ma'am."

He takes out the bottle, gulps it down. "That's good," he says. "That'll do the trick."

"Have as much as you like."

"All right, then. Don't mind if I do. Course I don't drink much as a habit. Don't have the taste for it."

She knows this is a lie. "Unlike my husband, who can't get enough of it. But he can't get enough of most things." She smiles. "It's a personality disorder. He's just a big spoiled baby."

"I got married once. Long time ago. She left me. That's when my life took a turn."

Walter Ooms coughs and wheezes, spits out the window. It is a distraction, she realizes. His way of changing the subject. Stopped at a traffic light she spots a squad car in the Stewart's lot. Two cops drinking coffee, laughing over some joke. *The circumstances were beyond my control,* she imagines telling them. The light changes and she turns onto the interstate ramp. The highway is dark, thick with snow.

"Cigarette?" she offers, and he takes it readily, lights it up, drags deep. Ooms is a man who takes what is offered him, no matter what. He is shorter than her husband, wiry and nimble, a man accustomed to being on his feet. His face is smooth, glossy. He has the lazy eyes of a crook.

"Won't be much longer now," she tells him.

He smokes and nods, watching the road, his face going light and dark under the drooping highway lights. Riding in the car through the darkness with the strange man, she begins to feel a deepening sense of dread. It hums in her ear like a ghost. It makes her weak, her belly taut with fear. There's no turning back now.

She gets off the interstate and heads down Valley Road, where they'd staged the accident. Now the car is dark and silent except for the distraction of the wipers, and her heart begins to pound with anticipation. The road runs parallel to the highway, an obscure shortcut with no posted speed limit, overlooked by police. Winding, heart-squealing curves and no guardrail, a thirty-foot drop on one side into a valley of trees so thick you can scarcely see the cars flying by on the interstate. One or two houses high on the hill, secluded in dense pockets of overgrowth. The houses are dark, and the road is empty. Three miles into it she pulls over and cuts the lights. Shadows swirl and scatter on the windshield. "Out," she says.

"What for?" He looks around blandly. "Hey, lady, what is this?"

"You want your money or not?"

"I already done said I did."

"I got five hundred dollars in my wallet, you interested in that?"

"Well, now, that depends." He looks around at the wild darkness. "I hadn't counted on working outside, out in the cold and whatnot." His eyes graze her breasts, her legs. "I think that's worth a little something extra, don't you?"

For the first time she notices tattoos up his forearms, barbed wire around both wrists. A keen whine begins to churn in her chest. She thinks of reaching under the seat for her pistol, but she does not want him to see it just now. "You'll get what you want, Ooms," she promises, putting her hand on his leg. They get out. The wind pants and churns. Freezing rain falls from the sky like slivers of glass. She starts to shake. She gets the blanket from the trunk and hands him the flashlight and together they start down the hill, sliding in the snow, fighting the onslaught of branches that attack like some medieval infantry. The doctor's car is nose down, obscured by the heavy trees and the opaque curtain of sleet.

"What in hell is that?" Ooms shouts.

"An accident. Hurry!"

Descending the hill, she slips on a sheet of ice and skids down on her back. Snow in her mouth, in her fists. Walter Ooms pulls her up and they move on, breathing hard, their bodies wet and brittle in the cold. The battered car ticks and shifts under the sighing trees, the smell of gasoline like a threat. "It's leaking out of the tank," Ooms warns.

She opens the driver's door and grapples for a pulse, feels the beat of life in the doctor's veins. Tears rush to her eyes. Prayers fall from her lips, soft as flower petals. *Our Father who art in heaven, Hallowed be thy name.* The doctor mutters for her help, his head lolling deliriously, his shirt saturated with vomit, a cumulus gust that makes her reel. She pushes him back against the seat, wincing at the gash on his forehead. "Please, mister, help me get him out."

Ooms gathers the man in his arms, pulls him from the wreck, and unfolds him on the blanket. The doctor whines in pain like a suffering animal and her heart winds up with remorse. *Please don't die on me now, Dr. Knowles.* They wrap him in the blanket like a mummy and start to drag him up. The hill is steep, the ground uneven and reckless, and they struggle with the burden, the wet wool of the blanket slipping in their hands. The plan in her head starts to dissipate. The plan was good, but now she doesn't know. It's so much harder in real life and it weakens her and she doesn't think she can go through with it to the end. "I can't," she says, letting go, the blunt sting of ice on her fingertips. Ooms groans with effort as he drags the doctor up and she scrambles after him, shouting until her lungs ache for him to wait, if he will just please wait she will help him. He turns irritably and she trains the flashlight on him, his face ablaze in the spotlight, and she can see him for who he is, and she knows that he will want something from her now, far more than she is willing to give, and he will not let her alone until he gets it.

3

ANNIE WAKES in a quandary at half past seven: the alarm didn't go off; the children will miss their bus and she will have to drive them to school, which will undoubtedly make her late for her morning class—she is *always* late for her morning class—and she still has a stack of midterms to correct. She finds Michael's note and crumples it up. She'd been awake when he came in last night but had feigned sleep, afraid to see his face. It had been cowardly of her, and it has left an ache in her heart like a thorn. She picks up the phone and tries to page him, picturing him rushing through the hospital corridors, or coaxing a swollen infant out of the womb, but she doubts that he will call her back and part of her hopes that he won't. She feels weak with ambivalence, unable to imagine what he will say to her when he finally comes home. Yet she refuses to take all the blame for what's happened. She'd warned him, after all. She'd given him plenty of time. At one point she'd even suggested a therapist, but Michael wouldn't have any of that—*he* was a doctor, he didn't need some stranger, *some fucking shrink* solving his goddamn problems.

After clever negotiation—expensive bribery—she succeeds in getting the children into the car in various stages of dress. Henry, in Michael's old Grateful Dead T-shirt and yesterday's jeans, bargains relentlessly for a new set of Kinex, while Rosie argues that she never gets anything new: "It's *my* turn to get a new toy, he always gets *everything!*" Her blond head resembles a flattened dandelion and her black high-top sneakers are on the wrong feet; nonetheless, they are presentable, their lunches are made, their homework is done, and they are in the car, going to school; the day has begun. They stare out at the dreary landscape with melancholy tenderness, the snow like powdered sugar over the dirty world.

St. Catherine's is a Catholic women's college just north of town, situated in a Gothic compound that was once a monastery and features ornate steeples and turrets and long drafty breezeways. Although Annie has been teaching at the school for less than a year, she already enjoys a fierce popularity. On the first day of registration, her class Images in Popular Culture had filled within ten minutes, due, in part, to the fact that she is the only female professor on the faculty who refuses to wear plaid. Unlike her female colleagues, who favor dowdy kilts or madras slacks, Annie prefers loose, gauzy skirts and sheer blouses that boldly announce her breasts. She wears long, dangling earrings and clunky turquoise rings and when her thick brown hair gets in her way she twists it into a precarious bun with a number two pencil. The students are attracted to Annie Knowles because she is young and clever and a little dangerous. She is a journalist by training, and like any good journalist she relies on her instincts, even in the classroom. It is oddly thrilling for her to be addressed as Professor; it suits her ego, sharpens her intellect. It has, in a small way, turned her into somebody else.

Her students are gathered around the long wood table on fussy, ladderback chairs. The room is warm, close, and smells of hair conditioner and perfume. The table is cluttered with pages torn from fashion magazines that have elicited a variety of heated responses. There is a photograph of a young model in a black bustier, writhing on the floor, her eyes glittering with something almost evil. There is a wan girl draped in gold lamé, wearing an expression of sour disinterest. Countless others promote a lifestyle of deviant abundance. The students seem both transfixed and disturbed by the images. Mary, a hefty redhead, holds up the photograph of the model in the gold lamé. "Look at her face," she tells the class. "She looks dead, you know. She looks like one of those police photographs."

"It's just fashion," Clarice defends. "Shock value. They're just trying to sell clothes. I think we're reading too much into it."

"But they make us look weak," Mary argues. "Look at this one. She's so thin she can't even get off the floor."

Anorexic Sara Downy clears her throat. "I happen to think they look very beautiful."

"You would," Mary says. "You're about to vanish into thin air."

Sara looks as if she may burst into tears. Annie decides to interrupt. "It's easy to sit here and make judgments, but out there in the world, where our behavior matters, it's tough." Then she poses a question: "Is it natural for women to want to be weaker, smaller? Do we want to be dominated or protected by men? Are these photographs encouraging us to behave in a certain way or are they confusing us?" Annie wanders the room, glancing thoughtfully out the windows. "Are these images a sort of propaganda, or are they simply interpretations of who we really are?"

A few hands go up. Annie shakes her head. "I want you to think about these questions and write an essay on the subject, due next Wednesday before the break. That's all for today."

The girls meander out, arguing among themselves, and Annie turns toward the windows, where the sun has suddenly made an appearance. The yellow light warms her face, the tops of her hands. Laughter rises up from the quad, where a group of girls play on a snowbank, making a fort, hurling snowballs at one another. And then she sees something strange. Charlotte Manning, the English Department secretary, is walking toward the building with a police officer. Annie hesitates at the window, trying to process what has brought an officer onto campus, and why, moments later, Charlotte and the man are standing in her classroom doorway, wearing the sort of guileless expressions one saves for inexplicable tragedies. Annie understands that something has happened, something terrible.

"It's Michael" is all Charlotte says.

The cop begins to explain, but Annie has trouble understanding him, as if he is speaking from a place high above her, a great distance away. "They found the car on Valley Road, down in the ravine. One of the neighbors saw the smoke. The car caught fire and was completely destroyed. Your husband was badly burned." The cop hesitates. "We need you to make a formal identification."

"Oh," she says softly, suddenly unable to stand. She drops into a chair.

He didn't return my page, she thinks. They stand there, watching her. "You mean he's . . . ?" She looks up at the cop, tears streaming down her face.

"Afraid so, ma'am," the cop says.

St. Vincent's is a bulky fortress that had been built in the forties out of pale yellow bricks. The hospital is renowned for its center courtyard, a sobering addition by the architect, which contains imposing marble statues of Christian saints. The cop parks haphazardly in the Emergency lot. Inside, the hospital is jammed. They wade through reckless corridors where doctors and nurses rush by, wearing the strain of their profession on their faces. Annie can almost feel Michael's presence among them and she searches in vain for his face. They take the elevator down to the basement level, where the heat is on full blast, wafting noisily out of the vents. Her heart thumps wildly in anticipation as they pass through the clouded glass doors of the morgue, the domain of the county medical examiner, Dr. Singh.

Dr. Singh is expecting them. She recognizes him from some of the hospital functions, a short, stocky man with skin the color of red pears and eyes that swim with longing. He takes her hand and tells her in his melodic accent that he is sorry for her loss. His assistant lurks in the corner, an amphibious young man with long sideburns and wet lips, stroking his chin with deep curiosity. Another man enters the room, stirring up their attention. "Ah, Detective Bascombe," Singh says. "This is Mrs. Knowles."

"Mrs. Knowles." The detective shakes her hand. He is middle-aged, wearing blue jeans and a flannel shirt, black clogs. A man who has lived hard and seen too much, she decides. His eyes are watery and suspicious. "I'm with the sheriff's office in High Meadow. We're all sorry about your husband. I'm told he was a good man." *You are not above suspicion,* his eyes say.

"Where is he?" she says. "I want to see him."

Bascombe and Singh exchange a look.

"I don't recommend it, Mrs. Knowles," Singh says. "You will not recognize him."

She swallows hard, her eyes brimming with tears. "I want to see my husband."

"All right. Mrs. Knowles, if you insist." Singh nods to the assistant, who pulls the body out. Michael is covered with an orange sheet and his feet stick out. They strike her as odd, their waxy yellow color. A white tag around his ankle says KNOWLES in big black letters. Annie grabs hold of a chair, afraid that she might fall down or throw up or both, and the detective takes her arm and holds her up. It is amazing to her, surreal, that her husband, the man she has loved for over a decade, is under that sheet. It feels like some bizarre elaborate magic trick, only it's no trick, it's real.

Michael, she whispers to him in her head. *Forgive me.*

"We will take a look, then?" Singh says, but it is not really a question and without waiting for her reply he jerks back the sheet. And then the shock: Michael's face burned beyond recognition, completely featureless, his limbs charred black, like a tree, she thinks, like a dead tree. She jumps back as if she too has been burned, her eyes tearing from the smell. Bascombe hands her a handkerchief as her tears flow out.

"I know this is difficult for you, Mrs. Knowles," Dr. Singh states. He takes her arm, leads her away from the body, because that is all it is, no longer her husband, and she sits down in one of the metal chairs. "It is a most unpleasant experience."

She nods her head, trying not to cry. Trying not to come apart.

"We believe your husband was on drugs at the time of the accident. In fact, it may be what killed him. We're waiting on the blood work to confirm our suspicion of a morphine overdose."

"Morphine?"

"When a person dies under these kinds of circumstances, we are required to do an autopsy."

"Of course," she whispers. "Of course I want an autopsy."

"Generally, in cases like these, suicide may prove to be the ultimate goal."

"No," she says. "No, he wouldn't do that." But the memory of their last night together floats up like something ghastly. The cold look on his face as he went into the study and shut the door. Still, she can't believe Michael would end his own life. "This was *not* a suicide," she says quietly.

The doctor shrugs. "We have seen cases where doctors indulge in drugs because they can, and it often gets the better of them."

"Not in this case," she spits. "My husband didn't do drugs. He was on his way to the hospital to save someone. There was an emergency and he got called in. He wasn't even on call but he went in anyway because that's who he was. Do you understand me? That's who he was."

Bascombe and Singh exchange a look. "There was no emergency, Mrs. Knowles," the detective tells her.

"We've looked at the log," Singh confirms. "There was no OB emergency last night."

The room begins to float. The bright lights. The vicious metal instruments. They are talking to her as if through a long tunnel, their voices muffled, undetectable. She shakes her head, gasping for air. "I'm sorry, I'm not feeling very well." The detective grips her under the arm and rushes her upstairs and out into the courtyard, where she sits on a cold stone bench among the looming statues. She brings the air into her lungs, tasting the new snow, the promise of winter.

"You all right, Mrs. Knowles? You want a cigarette?"

Annie shakes her head. "He didn't kill himself," she says. "And he didn't do drugs."

"Are you sure?" He looks at her so hard she has to look away. "Tell me, Mrs. Knowles. You and your husband. Were you close?"

"Excuse me?"

"Your marriage. Was it a good marriage?"

Was it a good marriage? She wants to ask the detective what her marriage has to do with her husband's death. She wants to scream that he has no business asking her personal questions. But she says none of these things because she isn't sure, she doesn't know. "I'm sorry, Detective, I can't answer that right now."

He studies her face. His eyes soften a little. She can tell he is trying to estimate the depth of her intelligence, the hues of her emotions. "I'll leave you alone," he says finally and hands her his card. "You want to talk, call."

Annie sits there for a long time in the company of the saints, who glance down at her with pity as she cries her heart out. The gray sky opens and the clouds separate, allowing the sun. Someone's hand drops onto her shoulder and she turns, startled, to see a man in silhouette. The sun is bright, and she squints up at his face. "Mrs. Knowles, let me help you." He offers her a Kleenex, and she takes it from him. It's not that she wants it, but he seems a kind man, she does not want to insult him.

"I'm all right," she manages.

"But you're not all right," he says, his eyes ornate with sympathy. "We both know that."

She looks at him dully; he is vaguely familiar. He pauses for a moment, thoughtfully, and sits down beside her on the small bench. "I'm Reverend Tim. I'm one of the chaplains here at St. Vincent's." He looks down at his hands, which are open in his lap like a book. "I know about loss, I've suffered with it all my life. If you need to talk to somebody, I'm a good listener." They sit there for a moment in silence, and then he stands up. He pats her on the shoulder and leaves her alone. He has a crooked gait. The good leg does most of the work while the shorter one shuffles to keep up, twisting awkwardly from the hip. Her heart swells with compassion for the man, and she feels an almost pitiable envy, for she is a woman in excellent physical condition who at the moment is utterly paralyzed.

4

THE DRIVE IS LONGER than she remembers it and there's snow on the Northway. Over the county line Lydia Haas stops at a vacant lookout and gets out of the car. For a moment, she feels a deep sense of peace, having accomplished a godly act. But it doesn't last. She studies the afternoon sky the way one studies a painting, the distant mountains like velvet, the branches of the trees tinkling with ice.

The doctor moans and twists on the backseat. She opens the door and lifts him up to a sitting position and loosens the blanket. She is relieved that his hands are tied, but this also terrifies her, the very idea of it, this bound man in the back of her car. As if sensing her alarm, his beeper goes off and she grasps it off his belt. The device hums in her cold hand like an insect. She studies the number: the hospital page operator. It makes her wonder if they've found the doctor's car. It's likely, she reasons, that somebody saw the smoke. She'd started quite a fire down there, after all. With a rush of anticipation, she closes the car door and walks to the edge of the lookout and hurls the little black box into the air.

The long road winds through the wastelands of upstate New York, the sky whipped bleak from the storm. She takes the Amsterdam exit and drives the back roads up to Vanderkill, the town where she was born. There are landmarks, reminders of her childhood. The desolate filling station that has always been desolate. A pumpkin field. The crumbling glove factory where her father worked. When she was little and he took her with him, she'd run through its wide corridors, the big windows bright with sunlight, the deep smell of leather and dye, the chatter of sewing machines, *Tosca* on the radio in the background. The women with their gold teeth and dark eyes. Her father bringing home boxes of gloves, gentlemen's gloves of fine black leather that he'd yank over his suffering hands. *But I will not think about that right now,* she tells herself, concentrating on the winding roads, like the worn verses of childhood songs. Like the prayers she sang in school over and over until her throat went raw.

She turns down the dirt lane that leads to her father's house. The house is set back, shrouded by trees, and when she sees it her heart slows and pounds. It's been ten years. All this time, Simon has paid the taxes without complaint. Once she begged him to sell it, but he refused. *To remind you,* he said. *So you don't forget who you are.*

The house looms and beckons under the black clouds. When she was little she tried to imagine that it was pretty, but now she sees that it was always just a poor man's house, with crooked shutters, a vicious slant to the front porch. She parks in the frozen grass and gets out and walks up to the house with her throat feeling tight and a weight in her chest like a dead squirrel. Looking up at the worn clapboards, the rusted gutters, she feels very small. The old house, like a forgotten relative, waits for an explanation. She wonders if the house is smiling. She does not know; she does not think it is smiling. She imagines her mama upstairs at the window, pulling aside the curtain. Her mama with her long silver hair, full of dead moths. *It's me, Mama,* she thinks. *I'm home.*

The car rocks and shimmies as she drives over the bumpy field to the back of the house. She parks alongside the metal doors of the cellar, gets out of the car, and sweeps the snow off with her bare hands. A long time ago, her father had painted the cellar doors red, but now the paint has chipped and there are weeds all around them, brittle stalks poking through the snow. She unlocks the padlock and opens the doors. A cold mist rises up as if out of a tomb. She hurries down the stairs and brings out two planks of wood and leans them against the steps, creating a ramp. With that done, she returns to the car and opens the door and notices for the first time the awful wounds on the doctor's face. The beating had been a hateful, awful ordeal and she is sorry, now, that she'd been part of it. She is sorry for so many things. But there is no time for regret. Now she must keep moving, she must get the doctor inside, where he will be safe. He won't see it that way, she realizes. He will want to escape, and he is smart, smarter than her, and she will have to be careful.

She sprints across the white field, takes the steps of the old porch two at a time. The key is around her neck, on an old shoelace, and she uses it now to open the door. A smell hits her as she enters the house, of dust and mold, and a draft swirls around her feet. She stands perfectly still for a moment, listening to the house—it was something she had done years before, when her father was sick, when she was waiting for him to die. With some trepidation she opens the hall closet, confronting dark wool coats like hanged men, a broken umbrella, various pairs of forgotten shoes, and the keen white handles of the wheelchair. They'd needed it at the end, her father so weak he could hardly get out of bed. She used to take him for long walks. She used to push him up the back hill to watch the sun rise over the cold field.

Pulling out the chair she feels a strange confidence. *I've done this before,* she thinks, pushing it across the scuffed floors, clumps of dust skittering like young mice. Outside, the sky has turned an ominous shade of yellow. A small fox slinks across her father's field, its red back rising and falling through the brown stalks that push up out of the snow. Her hands sweat on the cold metal, the plastic handles. She pushes the chair across the snow to the car. The field is empty, there's no one around. No one but Jesus.

Her father's ghost whispers over her shoulder. She can almost see him sitting there, the bony blades in his back. The car waits expectantly. High in the black branches of the trees the crows jeer savagely. The doctor stirs in the weak sunlight. "I have a gun," she warns him. "I will not hesitate to use it. I will bury you in this field and no one will ever know about any of this. Do you understand me, Dr. Knowles?"

He doesn't move.

"You're dead, Michael, they killed you. There's no going back." Gently pressing the barrel to his forehead, she cocks off the safety. "Now, I'll ask you again. Do you understand?"

He nods his head.

"Good. Now, will you please try to get into this chair?"

"I'll try." He grimaces, tears streaming down his cheeks, but she can tell he isn't really trying and he makes little progress. "I can't," he spits.

"You *can*," she says, pushing the gun into his skin. "You can and you will."

"My ribs," he gasps in pain.

"Don't be such a baby."

"They broke my ribs." Now he is crying. "My hand, too. I can't move."

"Why don't I shoot you and put you out of your misery." This shuts him up. She shoves the gun into her waistband and gets down real close to his ear. Even so close, she can see that he's millions of miles away from her. The rims of his contacts catch the light, floating discs over dilated pupils. She hadn't known about the contacts. They will have to come out. "Now, we're going to get you into that chair, understand? It may hurt for a moment, but then we'll be on our way."

He shakes his head again, fat tears falling out. "I can't. Please."

She wraps her arms around him. "Ready? One, two . . ."

An anguished howl curls out of him as she pulls him into the chair. He mutters obscenities, which she chooses to ignore. "There. See? That wasn't so bad." Pushing the wheelchair through the snow is hard work, all the way to the cellar doors. Her body runs with sweat yet she feels chilled to the bone. "You don't seem to realize the favor I've done you," she manages to tell him. "You don't seem to *get* that I saved your life."

He doesn't say anything now, but she can see that his face is all wet and a sound rises from his throat, more animal than human. At the cellar steps, she turns the chair around where he can see the bleak, snow-covered horizon, the watchful, indifferent trees. "Say good-bye to the outside world, Dr. Knowles—you won't be seeing it for a very long time." With the utmost care, she guides the chair backward down the makeshift ramp into the damp mystery of the cellar, a place where she would hide as a young girl, among the bulging sacks of potatoes and jars of canned peppers that her mama had made years before. They're still here, covered with dust like specimens in a laboratory.

"You'll be safe here," she reminds him. "No one will know, no one will suspect."

"They will," he mutters. "They will."

"Never!" she insists. "They'll never find you. You just do what I tell you and you'll be all right, because I may just lose my patience with you and if that happens it's not going to be pretty. You got that, huh? You got that?"

He shows her no response, just droops in the chair. She wheels him over to the mattress, then dumps out the contents of her bag. Canisters of pills fall out like hail. She opens the canisters and makes a little pile in the palm of her hand. "I want you to take these pills, an antibiotic and something to make you sleep. I have a friend in the ICU. I can get anything you need. You just tell me what you want. You just tell me what to get. Here, come on, take these. It's just some Keflex, and some painkillers—it's good stuff, I'm told, four bucks a pill on the street." He shakes his head wildly like a singing blind man, tears running down his face. "Here, Michael, look, I'm not trying to poison you." She directs his face to hers and for a moment their eyes lock and he lets her feed him the pills and she watches them sink down his throat. Next she maneuvers him out of the chair, onto the mattress. Again he whines in pain. "There." She fluffs his pillow. "Are you comfortable? Is the pillow all right?"

He doesn't answer her.

"I'll need your contacts now." Without waiting for his response, she pinches out the warm discs and feels his tears on her fingertips.

"I can't see very well without them."

"I'm sorry" is all she says.

"You're not," he whispers. "You're not sorry for any of this."

"You're wrong," she says. "And I'll find you some glasses, I promise." She covers him with several wool blankets. "I know it's damp. I'll turn the heat up a little, but you'll have to be strong. We can't take any chances. I don't want the oil company showing up unannounced. My husband pays the bills on this house; just enough heat so the pipes don't burst. If I turn up the heat, he'll know, see. He's smart, he'll figure it out. These blankets should do for now. Don't fight the drugs, Michael. You need them now. Promise me. In a few days you'll feel better, stronger. I know what I'm doing," she says, her voice gaining confidence. *I know what I'm doing.* "I worked in a nursing home once, they taught me certain skills. I took care of my father when he was sick. For months I did it, in this very house. I'm at St. Vincent's all the time; I'm a volunteer. I watch the nurses, I see what they do. I'm not stupid. I learn fast. I'm here to help you. You have to believe that. You have to trust me."

Soon the pills take hold of him and his eyelids flutter with sleep. Using scissors, she cuts him free of the wretched clothes. She fills a bucket with water and takes up the soap and a washcloth in her hands. Gliding the soap across his limbs reminds her of her father, in the very last days of his life, and she recalls with tenderness how very close they were at the end, when it was just the two of them. When you walk somebody up to the great white gates you are their angel and there is no one else. This was what she'd done for her father. And she is willing to do it now for the doctor, if that is necessary, but she hopes it isn't. The doctor is going to live, and they are going to get through this awful thing together, and she is going to help him, and he is going to help her.

Tending to him she feels a sweltering intimacy. The cloth wanders down his chest, onto the concave plain of his belly, lingers just above the waistband of his undershorts. Gently, she tends to his cuts with alcohol preps and ointment, then dresses him as best she can in some of her father's old clothes. An hour passes as she sits by his side, watching him sleep, whispering prayers. A calm falls over her, consumes her, as though she has swallowed a strange and wonderful pill, the effects of which she cannot predict.

Driving north, winding through humble rural towns, she finds a supermarket. The long yellow aisles are drafty, smirking with the stink of boiled ham. Music drones overhead, distracting her from her thoughts. Randomly, she tosses items into her cart: canned meat, tins of sardines, canned salmon, crackers, shortbread cookies, cashews, chocolate. The cashier hardly looks at her, preoccupied with bagging the items, and she finds herself discreetly touching her wig to make sure it's on all right.

Back in the car she drives behind the market to the Dumpster and tosses in the plastic bag that contains the doctor's clothes. Fifteen miles north, where the snow is deeper and the roads have not been plowed, she finds a hardware store with warped wood floors and scrawny hovering cats who eye her suspiciously. In the musty silence she purchases several cans of kerosene, a new kerosene lamp, a Coleman stove, a heavy chain, and an expensive padlock. The burly clerk helps her carry the items out to the car. He coils the heavy chain into her trunk and slams it shut, the wind crawling up her neck.

Driving back to her father's house she passes the graveyard where her mother lies, and the caretaker's stone cottage, its windows covered with boards. She feels a rush of terror as she pulls around to the back of her father's house and parks in a cluster of pines, hoping it will snow some more to cover her tracks. Scattered amid the glittering white powder she notices the splintered walls of a birdhouse, a dented beer can, a dead field mouse. She enters through the back door and puts the provisions in the kitchen. Stacking the canned food on the cupboard shelves, she reasons that there is no need for her to worry; the old Crofut house will seem exactly as it has been for the past ten years: vacant, neglected, aching with ghosts. Still, she can't help worrying that someone will find out.

The stairs to the second floor wait like the long zipper down a woman's back, a fancy woman like from the old movies, the way they always turn and wait: *Would you get this for me, darling?* Feeling drained now, impossibly weary, she climbs the stairs, half-expecting her mother to emerge from the lush pink folds of her past. On the landing she stands for a moment, hearing the windows rattle in the wind. The empty rooms wait blatantly, drenched in the red light of the setting sun. Her childhood room beckons her. Something stirs in her heart, and she lies down on the bed and weeps, she weeps and howls in the silent house, and she does not know if she will ever stop.

5

OUT IN THE COURTYARD the hours fade away, and Annie begins to feel cold. People come and go, smoking in small groups. The nurses. The orderlies. "Come on, Annie, I'm taking you home." She turns toward the voice of Hannah Bingham, one of the labor nurses Michael worked with; his favorite. Hannah stands there like an angel in her pink scrubs, with the murmuring sun at her back. "It's getting cold out here, isn't it?"

Annie stands up and lets Hannah put her arm around her. Together, they enter the bright corridor, the large lobby with its maroon chairs. The detective nods at her, a notebook in his hands. "I'll be in touch," he says, and she nods back. She doesn't know how she feels about the detective, and she doesn't want to think about it right now. Hannah leads her to the elevator and they ride up to the doctors' parking garage. With her long silver hair and a crystal hanging around her neck, Hannah reminds Annie of a wizard and she is glad for her help now. The fourth floor of the parking garage is empty, quiet. Annie steels herself past Michael's old space, searching the concrete for some scrap of evidence, but the floor looks swept clean.

"Come." Hannah puts her hands on Annie's shoulders and guides her to the car. "We need to get you home now. Your kids are waiting for you."

The mention of her kids makes her heart prickle. She doesn't know what she will say to them. They are home with Christina, her loyal babysitter, a student at the college. They will all be wondering where she is by now, waiting for an explanation. She will tell them the truth, she decides, because at this point that is all she has. They get into Hannah's silver Pontiac, two baby shoes hanging from the mirror, a plastic Virgin Mary wobbling up on the dash. Annie stares at it, feeling contemptuous. There is no God, she thinks. Not for her. Not now.

"My kids put that there," Hannah says. "They think she keeps me safe."

"Maybe she does."

"It makes them feel better, that's all. Just knowing she's with me."

Annie nods, thinking about Rosie and Henry, what she will be able to offer them to ease their pain. Even she can't soften this for them. She does not mind having the long drive to think, to gather more strength to face them. She is grateful that Hannah Bingham is taking her home, out to the country to their beautiful house. Only it's no longer beautiful, she thinks. Without Michael nothing is beautiful.

Hannah pulls out of the parking garage and winds down through short, one-way streets toward the interstate. "What did the detective say?" Hannah asks her. "What do they think?"

"Suicide," Annie blurts. "A morphine overdose."

Hannah scoffs. "Michael? Morphine?"

"It happens, they said. Sometimes. It happens to doctors."

"It may happen, but not to Michael. I can't imagine that."

It's my fault, Annie thinks. "Did he seem depressed, Hannah? Did he seem depressed at work?"

"No, honey, he did not seem depressed. He loved his work. He always had, you know, a real good attitude. Unlike some of the other doctors. They get moody, you know, 'cause they're so tired all the time. But not Michael. You never saw that in him. And his patients loved him, Annie, you should know that. They looked up to him. Especially in the birthing suite. They'd come in and they'd be all nervous and right away he'd get them calm. They'd be cursing and throwing things and he'd walk in and the whole climate would change and everybody would relax. He meant a lot to people. You could just see it, the way they'd look at him. Like he was their hero, you know?"

"It's my fault," Annie whispers. "We were having . . . problems."

Hannah gives her a knowing look. "It's not what it's cracked up to be, is it?"

"What?"

"The doctor's wife thing."

Annie shakes her head. She hates to admit it, but it's the truth.

"Look, honey, whatever happened, nobody's perfect."

"He wasn't home very much."

"Didn't even take a day off, did he? Good ole Finney plays golf every Wednesday, but not your husband. Oh, no. Not Michael."

"You knew about the clinic?"

"They don't call it Smallbany for nothing." Hannah smiles. "And between you and me? What Michael did on his afternoons off is none of the pope's business."

Annie nods, grateful for Hannah's admission. "We were getting threats," she says. "They were giving Michael a hard time. Remember that doctor who got killed up in Buffalo? It's the same group. And these people mean business."

"I can't imagine they got too far with Michael. As I recall, he wasn't exactly open to other people's opinions, especially when it came to medicine. Some people thought he was arrogant, but he didn't care. He liked his power. He'd fucking earned it."

"Well, it didn't get him very far, did it?"

"I suppose not."

They don't talk for the rest of the way. Annie looks out the window at the red sky, the black trees. They drive through dreary towns where the people on the streets hunker under hats and scarves, hiding from the wind. A gray despair wanders in their eyes, the landscape sketched in gritty haste across the sky. At the Stewart's in Nassau, they turn onto High Meadow Road, leaving the rest of the world behind. They pass the Hubbles' dairy farm, winding down into the hamlet and past the post office, where Warren Hicks, postmaster, is closing up for the night. His buddy, Rudy Caper, waits loyally in his sheepskin coat, a boy in a man's body, slow as winter sun, his feeble yellow dog sniffing at his heels. The same things every day, she thinks, like landmarks. Only today is not the same. Nothing will ever be the same.

They cross the old metal bridge into High Meadow, the wide creek purple with frost. The trees stand in solemn witness to the rushing cold. Annie directs Hannah down slippery unmarked roads, nothing but fields and trees and sprawling horse farms. "It's the next one," Annie tells her. "Turn here." Halfway down the road their house appears, a strapping white Federal with black shutters. Over the wide black door, wrought-iron numbers declare its age: 1812. Their dream house, Annie thinks.

"I believe there was a war that year," she remembers Michael saying.

"A war *and* an overture," she'd replied.

They'd come upon the house that first afternoon by mistake, having gotten lost in a labyrinth of dirt roads. When they finally pulled over to consult a map, which did them absolutely no good at all, they saw a For Sale sign hanging in a bramble of raspberry bushes. "A little spit and polish" is what the real estate agent, a woman in a fake leopard coat and gum boots, had said when they saw the house that afternoon. "Spit and polish and a pile of dough," Michael had whispered to Annie, but they'd made an offer right away, and the owner, who was in a nursing home upstate, had accepted it immediately, which, of course, had made them curious— happy, but curious. When all the pipes started leaking, and all the lights started blinking, they were not the least bit surprised.

Michael didn't seem to mind. A true optimist, he always saw the bright side, the cup half full, and she was always the one to pour it out.

Where she tended to be doubtful and suspicious, Michael had faith, he could wait things out. When they fought, he would avoid her for hours afterward, sometimes days, and the time would soften the harsh corners of their argument and suddenly there would be no more fighting and neither of them could even remember what had gotten them started in the first place. Thinking about it now, Annie starts to cry, and she wipes the tears hard and fast, not wanting the children to see. "Honey, you okay?" Hannah asks.

Annie nods, but she is anything but okay. "Do you want to come in?"

"Only if you want me to."

Annie shakes her head. "No, it's okay, you've done enough already. Thanks for bringing me home." She leans through the window and hugs Hannah good-bye.

For a moment Annie stands in the driveway, watching Hannah pull away. She can hear the birds in the trees and a dog barking somewhere far away. It's hard to even imagine walking through the door. It makes her body ache. But there is nowhere else to go, and she takes a deep breath and steps inside.

It's warm in the kitchen and smells of cookies the children have baked. Annie grabs hold of the counter, feeling like the victim of a hurricane, her life strewn to pieces. Everything seems to be floating. "Are you okay, Mrs. Knowles?" Christina asks. Before Annie can even think about what to say, the children have run into the room and are standing right before her, noticing at once her distorted expression, her skin bleached white. Without words, they seem to understand, they seem to know, that something has happened, something too awful to utter. Words only make it worse, she thinks, pulling them close, her arms going round them, thinking, *ashes, ashes, all fall down.*

6

IT ISN'T EASY leaving the doctor behind, when she has to go back to her life. She thought it would be easier, but now she's trembling, praying he will survive. His face didn't look right when she left, his skin like dull pewter and his blackened eye oozing pus. Without her, Knowles will die a desperate, tedious death, and she will have that on her hands. The responsibility of his care weighs heavy on her. It frightens her to death.

She calculates that it has been just over eight hours since she'd left the scene of the accident. It had been sunrise when the sky rolled up its tawdry yellow shade. She hadn't planned on killing Walter Ooms, but he'd left her no choice, and when it was over a new plan had come to her, one that would only help her situation.

It is important to keep busy, she tells herself, to continue as if nothing has happened, nothing out of the ordinary. She doesn't know what to do about her husband. He will ask questions; he will know something. Like a blind man, he knows things about her. He can smell her fear when they are together. The muscles in her belly grow tight. The reality of her marriage makes her weak.

At three P.M. Reverend Tim pages her. Lydia stops at a truck stop and uses the pay phone, her fingers shaking as she punches the numbers. When she hears his voice, she bursts into tears. Reverend Tim is patient and kind and understanding. He suggests she meet him in the hospital cafeteria. He wants to look at her, he says. He wants to see her face.

For a moment she considers getting into the car and driving away forever. Sifting through locations like a game of solitaire, she can't imagine which to pick, where she'd go. It doesn't matter, she realizes, because Reverend Tim could find her anywhere. He's got people all over the country who are willing to help him. *Just name a state,* he'd told her once, *and I can find somebody who's ready to demonstrate his commitment to Jesus.*

The cafeteria is empty at this hour. There is a table with three nurses drinking coffee, another where a couple of orderlies are sitting. She buys a cup of tea and sits by the picture window. Reverend Tim appears at her side as if out of thin air, and she tries to hide the fact that he has startled her. He joins her at the table with his glass of tomato juice. The juice spills a little on account of his limp. They sit for a moment.

"You all right?" he asks. He reaches across the table and takes her hand. "You're cold."

"I'm scared."

"You don't have to be scared, beauty."

She has always liked him calling her that, just the sound of it, plush and exotic as a kumquat. *Beauty.* Like horses dancing. Like the sudden miraculous flash of a deer. But now it makes her stomach flip. The first time she met him she felt it: a jolt, like a cattle prod. The whisper in his eyes that said *trust me.* A kind of power; otherworldly. Like a saint. She'd seen an open door in Reverend Tim and walked right through it.

"When I start questioning my life," he tells her, "all I have to do is picture all those innocent babies. That's all I do. And I feel justified." He drinks the juice in one gulp and sets the glass soundlessly on the table. "I suggest you stay home for a while. Be a good wife."

Lydia drives home on empty back roads, speeding. The snow has stopped and the roads are clear. She warms to the thrill of speed, the rushing wind, the shadows of heavy trees whispering across the glass. It is almost unbearably beautiful to see the heavy longing of the wet brown hills. Longing to be green and swollen and fragrant with wildflowers. Longing to be trampled by children. Oh, to be a child. To run breathlessly up a great hill with the sweat spilling down your back and the smell of raw black earth and dirty sunlight. To be a child at the top of the hill where the sky spreads itself out behind you like a great blue banner.

Someone pounding on the window. A black leather fist. A cop. *I'm caught,* she thinks, dreamily, not without relief. Like a wriggling fish. *Caught.*

"You all right, ma'am?"

Lydia rolls down her window, sits back. She feels as if she's suffocating. *I can't breathe,* she thinks, but she smiles and tells the cop she's fine.

"Looks to me you drove off the road for some reason."

"I must have fallen asleep."

He glances around inside the car. Her black wig sits beside her on the seat, curled up like a sleeping cat. "I'm gonna have to ask you to get out."

She wonders if her shoes are still on, she can't remember, and has suddenly lost all feeling in her legs. Wondering if she will fall, she gets out and steps on the hard ground, her toes spreading out inside her black boots. She is wearing galoshes she has owned since high school, there is a hole in the bottom of one of them and she can feel the wet ground seeping into her sock. I am dressed for the weather, she reminds herself, even though the snow is gone and the sun hisses down. The cop holds up a finger, making her follow it with her eyes. It gives her a headache, but she has no trouble impressing him with her abilities. She can walk the straight line, too.

"What happened, ma'am? Any idea?"

"The sun got in my eyes. There's a glare."

"Let me take a look at your license."

She picks up her purse and hands him her wallet, noticing for the first time her trembling filthy hands, her fingernails caked with mud or blood, she can't tell which. "I'm sorry, but I'm feeling somewhat dizzy now. Would you be kind enough to drive me home?" The cop hesitates. "You can handcuff me if you're afraid," she says with a smile, and he just looks confused.

"That won't be necessary," he says, forgetting about her license, handing her back her wallet. He grins generously and helps her into the backseat. She turns, watching her car fall away in the distance. It is nice in the cop car. Blue seats. The smell of horses. He drives and asks her where she lives and when she tells him she sees it register in his eyes. Now he eyes her through the cage like she's an exotic animal. The road is long and evening spreads its cruel blue paint across the sky. Soon it will be winter. She thinks of the doctor in the dark cellar and her stomach churns; she should be back there with him, she should be tending him. The cop is almost handsome, with blue eyes and dark black hair. He scratches the back of his head and she sees a wedding band. He is a cop. And she is just somebody who lost track of things on the road. And he will tell his wife about her later, shoveling the woman's warm food into his mouth. He didn't even give her a ticket and this makes her think that he is a good man, with a good heart. He is impressed, the cop, pulling up to the house, and doesn't seem to notice that it's falling apart. That there are pieces of this house scattered and strewn in the dead leaves but now he doesn't see, he doesn't *choose* to see because it would depress him. She catches her husband at the window, pulling aside the curtain, already in a rage over whatever it is she's done. Then the front door opens and he's out on the porch, wearing an unruly grin of distaste. "What is it this time?" he shouts over the clanging chimes.

"Your w-wife." The cop stutters a little. "She seems to have passed out at the wheel. Dizzy spell or something to that effect. She's all right. The car's all right. It's over on 66, near the post office. You won't have any trouble getting it out."

"Thank you, Officer, I appreciate your bringing her home." But he won't look at her.

"Take care now." The cop waves and gets into his cruiser. Lydia feels Simon's arm going around her tight. He is smiling after the cop as if to say *Thank the Lord my wife has come home safe and sound.* Behind them the dogs whimper and scratch at the door. They watch the cop's car pull slowly down the long driveway. The moment he turns out of sight, Lydia frees herself and runs into the house, ignoring the panting, restless Danes, and up the stairs into the bedroom, where she shuts the door. The bed is rumpled, an empty whiskey bottle on the nightstand, cigarette butts in the ashtray. The TV blinks silently. All the curtains are drawn except for one, where he'd looked out to see the cop coming up the hill. Lydia takes off her clothes and shoves them into her drawer, she will deal with them later, and gets into the shower and scrubs herself hard, turning the skin on her body a bitter pink. Surveying the cuts and scrapes, the bruises up her arms, around her neck, up inside her womb, she feels a fierce darkness envelop her. She sits on the floor of the shower, feeling the hard water rain on her back. *What have you done, what have you done, what have you done?*

She hears Simon's feet climbing the stairs, ice tinkling in his glass. Out of the shower and into her robe, yanking open her drawers, searching for clean underwear and finding none. *When was the last time you did any laundry?* She can't remember now.

He comes in and sits down heavily in the chair, staring into his glass. She can tell he's a little drunk. "I'd like to know where you've been."

"A party," she mutters, "with people from church." She is almost too tired to lie. "Look, *look*"—her hair in her face—"I don't want to get into it right now." Searching for her brush. Tossing things off the bureau. Him standing there watching her with distaste.

"I'm getting tired of this, Lydia. This group you're in. This fundamentalist crap."

"I believe in what we do," she says. "You can't understand that because you don't believe in anything."

"I used to believe in you."

"You don't even know me, Simon. You made me up in a painting once."

His eyes widen and he smirks at her, but he says nothing.

She does not want him to see her body, and she fumbles hurriedly with her clothes, pulling on an old T-shirt, a pair of sweats. He sits there, a disgruntled lump, and finishes his drink, sighs. "I think I've finally had enough."

She shakes her head, the room a blur.

"Enough," he repeats, the word rolling off his tongue like an obscenity.

She stumbles to the bed, climbs in, pulls the covers up over her. *I will not cry,* her brain screams. *I will not! I will not!*

"I thought, perhaps, that you'd grow up."

"Please, Simon, I'm sick, I have to sleep now."

He grabs her, shakes her hard. "You will not sleep. You will not sleep until you tell me the truth."

"I told you." Tears dripping. "I swear."

Her husband tilts his head, his eyes cold with doubt. "I don't believe you for a fucking minute." He grabs her arms, examining her scratches. "What happened here? What's this?"

"There was a party. A crowd. I got pushed down."

"You have an answer for everything, don't you?"

"Please, Simon, let me alone. I'm sick."

He stands up and watches her for a moment, then leaves her alone, his footsteps echoing dully on the staircase. A moment later she can hear him on the phone. She does not know who he is talking to and she does not care. Sleep comes on hard and fast, trampling her like a thief, and she gives herself up to it, and it takes and takes until there is nothing left.

7

THE CHILDREN EAT very little at dinner. Annie leaves the dishes on the table and brings them upstairs. She ushers them into her room and all three of them climb onto the bed and for a long time, nearly an hour, they just lie there in silence. Wondering, Annie supposes, what will happen next. Rosie puts her face up close to Annie and whispers into her neck, "I miss Daddy."

"Me, too, sweetie."

"What are we going to do now, Mom?" Henry asks.

"I don't know yet, Henry, but I promise you I'll figure it out."

"What about Thanksgiving?"

"We'll go to Grandma's just like always."

"When?"

"Soon. Next week. I promise you we're going to be okay." She says it, hoping it will make them feel better, knowing it won't.

"Yeah, right," Henry says, angry, and he turns away from her. Annie rubs his back and he shrugs her off. "Just leave me alone."

"Henry," she says. "I'm sorry, honey. I know it's hard. I know it's awful."

Henry doesn't move, and then he starts to cry. "It's not fair," he says.

"I know."

Rosie squints and swallows hard. "Mommy? Are you scared?"

The truth is she's scared out of her mind, but she won't tell them this. "I'm sad, Rosie, and I know you and Henry are, too. We're all sad without Daddy."

"Do you think he's up in heaven?" Rosie says.

Annie nods, tears roaming down her cheeks. "Yes," she whispers. "He's up in heaven. He's with the angels."

The children fall asleep in her bed and she lies there trying not to move, not wanting to disrupt them, knowing that sleep is a necessary drug. She listens to their breathing, taking comfort in it, and tries to fathom the reality that her husband is dead, but her brain refuses to accept it. *He's dead*, she tells herself. *He's dead*.

Images of Michael flash through her head. His beautiful shoulders, his long beautiful arms, the way he'd squint with approval when the kids made him proud, the way he looked when he slept, his big hands pressed together, as if in prayer, under his cheek. The things she loved most about him but never let on because she was too uptight, too angry all the time—

too selfish. Always seeing things from her side. In her mind, she was always the one getting the short end, not him. Her head always stuck on the disappointment. *Stupid,* she reproaches herself. He worked his butt off for her, for the family; he worked like a fucking dog and look how she repaid him. And now he's gone.

Gone.

The morning edition of the *Times-Union* runs a story on Michael's crash without notifying her. The headline reads: "PROMINENT PHYSICIAN DIES IN ACCIDENT: Driving While Intoxicated, Morphine Overdose Suspected." The paper has printed other articles about the pervasive incidence of doctors becoming addicted to drugs. Furious, Annie calls Gavin Riley, the editor in chief, and screams at him over the phone. "After all the years we've worked together," she says. "How could you do this to me?"

"Only doing my job, Annie" is his reply.

"You bastard." She throws the phone across the floor and drops to her knees, beating the rug with her fists. *"Fucking animal!"*

For endless hours she lies around the house, wrapped up in one of Michael's old coats, her brain like a big knot of twine. Too frightened to go anywhere. She is sick, weak. Can't eat. Can't sleep. The children are dull and edgeless, going through the motions. They lie in the big bed with her, watching cartoons. It seems impossible that Michael won't come back. All those hours when he was away from them, taking care of *strangers.* All those wasted hours, she thinks, and for what. *For this?*

Eating marshmallows, drinking sugary tea. The bare branches at the window. The sunlight falling all over her like a drunk. Her parents are flying home from their Elderhostel program in Napa; her sister, Margaret, is driving up from the city. All day long family and friends wander her big house, dazed, spilling their drinks. Looking after the children. Everything coming apart at once. Strings in her hands. Threads.

I'm lost, she thinks. *I'm lost without him.*

Late in the afternoon Celina James comes to the door. She stands there in her black dress in the pouring rain, her hair twisted in tiny braids, her toffee eyes wrecked with pain. But Annie has no sympathy for her. *I don't want you here,* Annie tells her silently, but Celina grabs her and pulls her close. "I loved him, too," she says.

They drink coffee together in the kitchen. All around them the house bustles with people. Nervous relatives. The children. Celina holds her hand. "It wasn't an accident, Annie," she whispers finally. "That's what they want you to think. It was *them*. It was that group." New tears fill her eyes. "And I'm next."

8

IT IS LIKE FLOATING in water, the way his body feels, floating on a black sea. Remote. He drifts and floats, thinking of Annie. There is a sound he cannot place. He is dreaming, shivering. His mother, dead five years, appears at his side. She stands over him, shaking her head. *What have you done now, Michael?* She smells of mushrooms and is a little green with death, but no, the sun is out, it is wickedly bright, and they are on the beach. There she is in her checkered bathing suit, in her fluffy pink bathing cap, holding something in her hands. An animal. What kind of animal? It is a rat. She holds it up, swings it by its tail. And he can hear it, like a clock. *Tick, tock, tick, tock.* His mother stands on the shore, growing smaller, waving to him, waving her arms. He is out too far. The raft has drifted. Maybe he has fallen asleep. *Come back, Michael!* He doesn't care. It doesn't matter. *I am laughing now. I am laughing and laughing.* The more he laughs, the harder it is to breathe. The water is black and deep, thick as tar. It pulls him down, grips his feet. *It isn't fair! I'm caught.* Hands smash through the surface, trying to pull him out. He twists and reaches, but cannot grab hold. *I can't breathe!*

Later. Hours later. No, seconds. Something crawling on his head. Warm fur, sharp feet, a long wet tail. He tries to catch it, but it is too quick. And he is afraid of it. He would not know what to do with it if he caught it. *Kill it with my bare hands.* He does not like the idea of catching the rat.

Now the woman is near. He can smell her: tea rose, lemongrass. It is a familiar scent, yet he cannot place its origin and it confuses him because it reeks of springtime, the citron ache of grass before rain, and he knows that it is autumn now. She is washing him, humming a tune he has heard innumerable times but still cannot name. He does not know for certain if he is dreaming, because the woman is beautiful, as if in a dream, and her voice is sweet and the sound of her singing comforts him. The way she moves, like the lines of a poem, making him see things in his head. *I know you,* he thinks, yet he cannot place her. *I've seen you before.*

Her hands wringing out the cloth, the sound of water like rain in a storm, a single drop running down his ear, all the way down inside of him. Her breathing, like wind, a warm wind that smells of bread. The cloth glides down his chin, his neck, down the length of his arms. She feeds him more pills and he swallows them willingly. Anything to escape, if only in his mind. He wants to tell her about the rat, he wants to tell her that he is terrified of it, but he cannot move his mouth and he knows that it will return. The lines of her body mingle with the shadows as she moves to do her work, singing, always singing. Whispering her prayers. Once he thinks she is crying. *Who are you?* his brain screams. *What have you done?*

Much later, she whispers his name. He does not want to open his eyes. He hears her strike a match, smells the tiny, sulfurous explosion. The flame hisses as it melts the wick of a candle. She is a blur, her hair the color of ripe corn. He breathes in her wet-wool smell. In the half-dark of what he imagines is late afternoon, he discerns the shapes that make her whole. A red sweater. A green scarf. *You had black hair before,* he implores her with his eyes. She wears the smell of snow like a child. The smell of freedom, like too much perfume. It makes him want to throttle her. She shakes off the cold, rubs her hands. "Michael," she says again in the warm voice of a lover.

Yes, what? What do you want?

He cannot dream of speaking.

"Are you feeling better? You look much better today, really, much much better."

He doesn't feel better. In fact, he feels worse.

She moves away and for a few horrible moments there is nothing but space and silence and it terrifies him. He listens to the silence and discerns the sound of her breathing and imagines that she is just sitting there, watching him, the way one observes an animal in the zoo.

"I wasn't always like this," she whispers, and he smells her cigarette. Wanting to see her face, he twists slightly, prompting a spasm of pain up his spine. "I won't hurt you if you're good."

He doesn't say anything, his throat jammed up with anger. Then she's gone again and he hears something rattling on the cement, snaking across the floor. Moments later he feels something cold and tight coiling around his ankle. A chain, he realizes, hearing the snap and click and spinning of a lock.

"There's a rat," he mutters at length, unable to address the chain just now.

"No," she answers matter-of-factly. "There are no rats. There are no rats in this house."

"Why are you doing this?" he hears himself say.

"Why am I doing this?" She laughs a little.

"What do you want?"

"I want you to rest. You've been badly hurt." Her tone is curt, void of emotion.

"Is that—is it a chain?"

"Yes, it's a chain. But it's long. You'll be able to get to the toilet. There's a sink, too."

"No." He struggles to speak, overwhelmed suddenly. "Please! Let me out of here."

"Rest now." She starts up the steps. "You're hurt, Michael. You need to rest."

"You won't get away with this," he blurts. "I have friends. My wife."

"Your wife. I'd forget about your wife if I were you."

"They'll be looking for me."

"They'll never find you here."

They'll never find you here.

"What is this place?"

"This is my childhood home," she says dryly. "This is where it all began."

"What? What are you talking about?"

"This is Papa's house."

"How long have I been here?"

"Two days. No more questions, Michael." But she stands there waiting. "I have to go now. I'll be back in the morning."

Her footsteps echo dully as she climbs the stairs. Overhead, the squeaking floors. Then the distant sound of a car door, an engine turning over. And then nothing. Nothing at all.

Two days.

He lies very still, listening feverishly, attempting to identify the sounds around him. There are the rats, scampering across the floors overhead. Although he sees no windows, he can hear the wind wafting against the windowpanes and it is an empty sound that depresses him. A shutter slams against the side of the house, reminding him of the beating he took from those people, their relentless cruelty. He can hardly breathe, his broken ribs sharp as knives. Wind rumbles over the metal cellar doors like the feet of children, a small boy, perhaps, the age of his own son. It comes to him that his face is drenched with tears. He cannot remember the last time he cried.

9

THINKING BACK on it now, Annie understands that there is no escape. They had tried and failed. Like people running from a blazing circus tent, they had left the suburbs of Albany behind, the manicured cul-de-sacs, the trim, paved driveways, the benign, redundant perfection, hoping to find a new kind of freedom in the country, where they would be left alone, removed from the scrutiny and judgment of well-meaning neighbors. "Land of the free and the brave" Michael used to call it, but it was true in a way, and everyone who lived there knew it. In High Meadow, they'd met people like themselves who lived in crumbling old houses full of eclectic antiques purchased at local auctions and displayed like props on a stage. Cracked plaster walls were adorned with paintings of strangers from earlier centuries who gazed out from their crooked gold frames during dinner parties as the guests dined on roast lamb and potatoes and conversed about books and movies and the awful state of politics and the next school function, for which they would all doubtlessly volunteer. High Meadow was a strange little town, known for its abundance of pristine homes and horse farms. Just twenty miles from the city of Albany, it had miraculously staved off developers. The village consisted of a single paved road, Main Street, which was flanked with charming little shops that appealed to the weekenders from Manhattan and Annie's students from St. Catherine's. There was a bank, a post office, and the famous Black Sheep Café, with its cast of droll regulars who met each morning over coffee to discuss the morning paper while half a dozen stray dogs dozed at their feet. The Knowles' neighbors were horse people, both rich and poor. They drove pickup trucks or Land Rovers. They walked the long roads in great hulking sweaters. Annie and Michael knew nearly everyone by sight, and everyone knew them back, and there were town gatherings where they'd meet newcomers, who were rare—the annual Fourth of July parade, the Halloween party at the fire station, and the spring pig roast, where everybody drank too much homemade wine and fell asleep under the stars on the town green. The children attended the public school, after which they spent long afternoons running through fields, up to their hips in yellow grass, or biking down dirt paths strewn with rubble, or skipping rocks in the creek, or lying on their backs in an open field, watching the sweeping drama of the sky. At night the front lawns were littered with skateboards and toppled bikes, the twisted heads of abandoned Barbie dolls. Doors were left unlocked and it was not unusual to glance at a woman's purse left on the seat of her car, always there the next morning. In fact, there were few crimes to speak of. A group of teenagers were once caught getting drunk in an abandoned house. Three members of the Women's Art League were fined for making tombstone rubbings in the graveyard after hours. Occasionally, a patrol car would turn down their road, easing past the scattered houses like a parade float, but it wasn't routine. Because everybody knew that nothing ever happened in High Meadow.

Until now.

She doesn't know why she drives out Valley Road. Perhaps a morbid curiosity is all. To try to understand what happened, to see the car, to put it all together in her mind.

The road is slippery and she has to drive slowly. A fire truck rambles past her, heading back to its firehouse. Coming upon the scene, she sees orange cones lining the road. Patrol cars are parked in hasty diagonals. Several cops in high black boots, watching the tow truck pull up the burned-out Saab. Annie pulls over to the side of the road and parks. She gets out of the car and surveys the scene. Smoke haunts the air, and there's the stink of burning rubber. Immediately, a cop comes up to her. "Sorry, ma'am, you can't stop here."

"I'm Annie Knowles," she says, her chest heaving. "That's my husband's car."

The young cop looks sorry for her. "You sure you want to see this?"

She nods, and he takes her arm and leads her over to the other side of the road, where together they watch the car come up out of the dense ravine.

10

MICHAEL WAKES in a cold sweat, a black shape swooping over his head. He thinks wildly that it is a bird of some sort, a bat perhaps, and he can feel the wind of its flapping wings. But it is not a bat, he sees now, it is a gun. It is a gun in the woman's hand.

The cellar is dark and cold. It stinks of mildew. His body quakes and shivers and somewhere inside his head he understands that he needs to drink, he needs to get warm, but he cannot tell her. She lights a match, the wick of an oil lamp, and shadows swarm the room. *I'm cold,* his eyes rush at her, but she is not even looking at him. Her face is intensely familiar to him and he wonders if perhaps she is one of his patients; he cannot possibly remember now. His brain is too weary to make such connections. But still, her face. The way she has her hair pulled back, her gray eyes, the high Slavic cheekbones. The smoke billows and spreads across the ceiling and he watches it, like a net, enveloping him. For an instant he catches her profile, the way she concentrates on the cigarette, the orange glow brightening with each drag she takes.

"You were dreaming," she says. "Was it a nightmare?"

He doesn't answer her.

"You had a dream about Annie, didn't you?"

The sound of his wife's name in this woman's mouth frightens him. "Do you know my wife?"

"Of course."

She sits down and continues to smoke. He does not want her sitting there. He does not want her anywhere near him. He watches her, all the colors smearing together. The drugs she gives him, making him sick. He wants to ask her how she knows Annie, but he is too tired now. He does not have enough energy to make words out of air. It is better if he lies perfectly still. It is better if he pretends he is dead. *I'm dead, can't you see?* "I'm sick," he mutters.

"It's just the drugs." She lights a cigarette off the first and gets up, roams the room like a restless animal. "You don't remember me, do you?" He doesn't move, concentrating on focusing. His heart twisting. His mouth like he's swallowed warm sand. "Jack's party. We had a conversation in his kitchen."

Jack?

"I cut myself. My husband was so embarrassed. He nearly knocked my teeth out when he got me home." She laughs and then it slams into him: Lydia Haas, the painter's wife.

Yes. "I remember," he manages. "In the kitchen."

He'd gotten paged and went to use the phone. She was at the table, doodling on a pad of paper the way a child draws, her mouth tight, making flowers, hearts, rainbows, gripping the pencil awkwardly.

"I was drinking vodka," she reminds him. "There was a great big knife and I went *oops* with the big knife, didn't I? I went *oops*," she says in a baby voice.

He hadn't done much, he recalls. Wrapped her up with a napkin, then went and found her a Band-Aid.

"I liked you right away," she says. "You listened to me. You put your ego in your pocket. You weren't a big show-off like your wife."

"It was a fun party," he says just to keep her talking.

"No, it was not fun."

"Why not?"

She goes quiet suddenly and shakes her head, then stands up and begins to gather her things. Their visit is over. A slow deep agony flourishes in his ribs. His breathing is shallow, labored. Just the turn of his head sends the pain down his spine.

"Why?" he says, his voice a ragged whisper. "Why are you doing this?"

"He told me to," she says in a singsong voice. "For the ghost in my womb."

"Ghost?" he spits uselessly.

This makes her quiet. She stands up, weaving slightly. "I don't want to talk about my ghost right now. Anyway, you wouldn't understand."

"I will," he says. "I'm a doctor. I understand about ghosts."

She turns, her face in the shadows.

"There was somebody else, wasn't there? You had help getting me here."

"No."

"I remember someone. A man's voice."

"You don't have to worry about him."

"He may tell someone. The police." He cannot disguise the hope in his voice.

"No. Not even a remote possibility. I'm very thorough, Michael, that's something you need to realize about me. When I set my mind to something. No loose ends." She drops the cigarette to the floor and puts it out with her shoe. "The car wasn't supposed to catch fire. That was my little bonus." She smiles. "See what I mean? No loose ends. No tattletales."

It comes to him that he is completely at her mercy.

"You need to rest now." She climbs the stairs.

"Please, don't leave me here."

"You'll be *fine*, Michael. Don't be a scaredy-cat."

He remembers his hands, bound together at the wrists. "Untie my hands at least."

"Not yet. You need to sleep and you won't do that if you have your hands. Try to remember that I know you, Michael, I know the way you think."

"You don't know me."

"In a strange way, we're almost like family." She laughs. "Now, get some sleep." The door slams and locks.

I will not sleep, he tells himself. But he can't hold on. Shivering, he feels himself sinking into the smothering darkness.

11

ANNIE SEARCHES Michael's drawers, the pockets of his trousers, looking for something she may have missed, some courier of fate that may have predicted his death, but finds nothing. She topples over the basket of laundry and searches the pockets of Michael's dirty pants. A slip of paper comes out in her hand. There's a name on it: *Theresa Sawyer.*

She hears a car crunching up the driveway and glances out the window. It's Bascombe's blue cop car. She hurries downstairs and opens the door.

"They've completed the autopsy," he tells her. "Dr. Singh wants to see you."

"I'll get my bag."

She leaves the children with Christina and they ride into Albany in Bascombe's car. The weather is treacherous, all sleet and freezing rain. "Not exactly four-wheel drive," he says, trying to make a joke. She attempts a smile, but her heart pounds and she's afraid she is going to cry. Sleet pierces the windshield, and it begins to hail. The bare branches of the trees are clawlike, monstrous. The sky is unusually dark, tinged with a watery fluorescence. Bascombe turns off the expressway and weaves up to the hospital. People hurry down the sidewalks under umbrellas as the hail pummels them with menace. It is a strange scene, the yellow hail like an alien presence. Bascombe glances at her. "Hail fucking Mary."

Singh is expecting them. A yellow folder sits before him on the desk. Bascombe pulls out a chair for her, and Annie sits down. "I'll come directly to the point, Mrs. Knowles. We have determined that the man they found near the car is not your husband."

As if someone has pulled a white shroud over her head, the room goes hazy and white. Her body spins. *Did I hear him right?* Singh's obeisant assistant gets her some water.

"The first indication was in his mouth. The deceased's teeth are either completely decayed or missing. After consulting your husband's dental records, we found that he was quite meticulous about his teeth." Annie pictures Michael's mouth, his white teeth and easy grin. "Once we got into the chest, we discovered a pacemaker."

"My husband didn't have one," she says softly, nearly disbelieving.

"We traced the registration number on the cardiac device. The man who was burned in your husband's car was a drifter from Utica. His name was Walter Ooms."

"Does that name mean anything to you, Mrs. Knowles?" Bascombe asks.

"No, it doesn't."

"I made a copy of the report for you, Detective."

Bascombe takes the file. He puts on his bifocals and reads over the report. "Thank you, Doctor."

"You're quite welcome," Singh says.

"Come on, let's get out of here." Bascombe takes Annie's arm, but she pulls away.

"I need to see him one more time," she says. "I need to make sure."

Without hesitation, Singh's assistant pulls the body out and swiftly lowers the sheet. Annie stares at the burned body for a long time. Her eyes roam the outlines of his shape. "Did he steal the car?" she asks no one in particular.

"Possibly," Bascombe says.

She turns toward him, shaking. "Do you think he's alive?"

Bascombe sighs, says nothing.

She grabs hold of his arms. "Please, Detective, you've got to find him."

"We'll do everything we can, Mrs. Knowles."

"No, that's not good enough. Please. *Please!* You've got to find him!"

Bascombe raises his eyes slowly, with pity, and pulls her toward him and holds her in his arms. This display of emotion overwhelms her and she starts to cry. "I will find him, Mrs. Knowles," the detective promises. "I will find him."

PART TWO
Flesh

12

ALBANY WAS A CITY that wept bitterly and did not apologize for its weeping, a city of pale brick buildings, faces like spoiled potatoes pulled from the dirt, acres of row houses, churches, firehouses, pale stricken faces, and faces yellowed like the pages of old books. Michael Knowles was the youngest of three partners in a small private obstetrics and gynecology group adjacent to the hospital, in the Medical Arts Building on Hackett Boulevard. St. Vincent's Hospital was a sprawling edifice with overcrowded floors, overscheduled doctors, and discontented nurses. Dour nuns roamed the narrow corridors, which were painted a sallow shade of mustard yellow and reeked of paint whenever they ran the heat, which was almost always, no matter the temperature or season. The windows had been painted shut that summer, and the air-conditioning, which hissed and chortled in earnest, wafted sticky malodorous air all throughout the building. Michael had been born there, as had his own children, and it was the oldest teaching hospital in the city, one in which many of the attending physicians, including himself, engaged in bedside teaching. He worked tirelessly, and when he left the office at the end of the day it was never without a heady sense of relief. Over the years, he had grown accustomed to the routines of private practice, the growing bonds he felt with the nurses and residents, the patients who looked to him for guidance. The satisfaction he felt in healing them. His patients were various and wore the scars of a complicated age. Some came with bruises, strange torturous marks. One patient had severe burns on her ankles; she was three months pregnant at the time. When he questioned her she shrugged dumbly, her apathy obvious as her cologne. She gave birth in the fifth month to a mangled creature the size of his fist. Abuse of one form or another was common, even routine. There were days when he questioned his whole existence. There were days when he wondered why he'd become a doctor and even regretted it. The work was often grueling and continually exhausted and frustrated him. But then there were good days, when a patient would confide in him, when she would share her deepest admissions and seek his advice. Or when he treated a difficult problem, either with drugs or surgery, returning the health that the illness would have devoured, watching pain vanish from a face that has been distorted by suffering, that made all the rest of it worthwhile. It was what kept him going.

It was why he agreed to help Celina James.

She paged him one morning in early August, just after he'd finished his rounds. He called the number and a woman answered the phone in a chipper voice. "Free Women's."

"It's Dr. Knowles," he said. "Somebody paged me."

"Oh, yes, please hold for Dr. James."

A moment later she came on the phone. "Hello, Michael." Her voice brought on a swarm of memories.

"Celina. I can't believe it. What's it been, ten years?"

"Twelve, darling. Time flies when you're having fun."

"How've you been?"

"Dandy. And you?"

"Working like a dog," he said.

"I'm intensely curious to see how you've aged."

"Badly," he said.

"I doubt that."

"All work and no play."

"Poor baby."

"What can I do for you?"

"Actually, I have a proposition for you," she said softly. She hesitated, then asked if he would meet her for lunch.

He didn't usually take lunch, but he supposed, for her, he could make an exception and told her so.

"Oh, goody." Her voice warmed with enthusiasm. "How about Lombardo's, one o'clock?"

"All right." When he hung up he realized he'd broken a sweat. What could she possibly want from him? Standing there in the hospital corridor, he felt her presence return like a fast, alarming storm. They'd been lovers, briefly, during their residency and although it had been a long time ago he had not forgotten her.

Their relationship had started at a party one of the residents had thrown: *postcall intoxication fest*—a lot of people drinking enormous quantities of gin out of stolen beakers. Celina was there with some girlfriends; he noticed her immediately. She had, he recalled, the lithe build of a dancer, an angular elegance. It wasn't the first time he'd seen her. They'd worked together in the ER a few times. Once or twice they'd shared a table in the cafeteria, shoveling their food down in the welcome silence. He had known she was from Albany, but unlike him she had not gone to the academy, and their paths had never crossed. Michael was two years ahead of her; she was a wide-eyed intern when they met, eager to please, a beautiful black face in a crowd of dreary, overworked white students. He'd heard she was the smartest in her class.

Although he denied it in those days, Michael was a lightweight when it came to alcohol, but the liquor was a lousy excuse because he wanted her, there was no doubt about it. And much later, in the wee hours, they stumbled down the hall together and made love, rather savagely, in a stranger's bed. The affair continued for a few months after that. They shared impassioned interludes in the call rooms between shifts, ripping off their scrubs for what they joyfully called stat satisfaction. And it was satisfying, deeply satisfying, until he met Annie. Convinced that Annie was the woman he wanted to marry, he broke off his relationship with Celina, explaining that he was returning home to Albany for his infertility fellowship and it would be too difficult to maintain a long-distance relationship. Several months later, after his and Annie's engagement, he ran into Celina at a medical conference in Philadelphia. He didn't like to think about it now, but they'd gone up to her room after a few drinks and taken a shower together, among other things. They had what he liked to think of as a sexual connection, nothing more, which was not to diminish his feelings for her; he admired her greatly, and considered her to be one of the best clinicians in their field.

But Celina had a reputation that often got her into trouble. She flaunted her intelligence; in some circles she shoved it down people's throats. Her arrogance offended people. The fact that she was African

American and had clawed her way out of the slums of Arbor Hill to attend Harvard on a full scholarship meant little to her. She'd never liked Boston. He remembered her saying it was a city for white people. When she'd finished her training, she'd come back to Albany and, with the help of a handful of wealthy libertarians, started a small family-planning clinic, *an abortion clinic,* on South Pearl Street, in her old neighborhood, taking over an old dilapidated bowling alley. Upon its completion, the clinic inspired a prickly controversy among the city's politicians.

Lombardo's was an Albany institution, a bustling Italian restaurant with a dwindling old-world elegance. Michael stepped into the narrow dining room with its black-and-white mosaic floors and red leather booths, murals of Italy on the walls. He spotted Celina immediately, sitting at a small table in the back and reviewing a stack of files. She was still beautiful, he thought, maybe even more so now. The only evidence that she'd aged was the pair of bifocals she wore on her nose, but she promptly removed them when she saw him. She'd acquired a woman's sophistication, he thought, a penetrating gaze of wisdom.

"Celina James."

"In the flesh." She flashed her famous grin, and stood up and shook his hand. "You can do better than that, can't you?"

She clutched his arm and pulled him toward her for a kiss, and he lingered there at her cheek a moment longer than he should have. She smiled. "That's much better."

"It's good to see you, Dr. James."

"Been a long time. You look"—she paused—"married."

He laughed. "Do I?"

"She looks good on you."

He slid into the booth and for a moment they sat there appraising each other.

"I never thought you'd come back here." *I never thought I'd see you again.*

"Well, I have. Back with a vengeance," she said almost adamantly. "My grandmother died and left me her house. I came back for her funeral and never left. I've got people here, you know?"

"I'm sorry about your grandmother."

"She was a lovely woman. I miss her terribly."

A waiter appeared and asked Michael what he wanted to drink. He ordered a Coke, and then they both ordered lunch.

"I've been hearing all sorts of nice things about you, Dr. Knowles," she said flirtatiously. "You're very famous with the nurses."

"Oh, yeah, especially the ones in habits."

"How's the lucky woman?"

He couldn't help detecting her sarcasm. "Annie? She's well. Busy with the kids. The usual stuff."

"The usual stuff?"

"Her work, her writing." He stumbled in meek defense of his wife. "She started teaching over at St. Catherine's."

"Now, there's an exciting place. The cutting edge of academia, I'm sure."

"Actually, she likes it. She likes her students."

"Insipid white girls in Fair Isle sweaters."

"Something like that."

"Well, good for her. Doctor's wife that she is." Celina smiled. "Unlike our dear Mrs. Finney. Now, there's what I call a full schedule. Eighteen holes of golf and lunch at the club—oh, and let's not forget the pedicure. No wonder he drinks so fucking much. Talk about insipid."

"Finney's all right."

"I hear Tony B's giving up the deliveries." She was referring to his other partner, Bianco, who had just turned sixty. "More work for you, you lucky boy."

"Lots of women out there having babies, it's good for business." The waiter appeared with their order and they began to eat. "What about you? I thought I heard somewhere you got married." He hadn't, but he was curious.

"Me, married?" She said it like a dirty word. "I don't think so." She grinned apologetically. "I do, however, happen to be madly in love."

He chewed his lettuce. Suddenly it didn't taste so good. "Lucky you."

"I've never been so happy."

"That's great. That's great news."

"Look at you, you're jealous! Aha!"

He laughed, embarrassed. "I suppose you caught me."

She touched her heart. "I'm immensely flattered."

"Amazing, isn't it, after all these years," he said. "But you started it. You've been flirting with me ever since I sat down."

"You're right. I can't resist flirting with you, Michael—you're so delicious."

"Now *I'm* immensely flattered."

"Anyway, it's harmless, isn't it?"

"Thoroughly harmless."

"And it was fun, wasn't it? What we had."

"Yes, it was."

"And now we're old."

"Not so old."

"And you've got all those kids."

"Just two."

"And your incredibly capable wife."

"That's my Annie."

"Your Annie," she repeated, gazing at him with her big eyes. "Are you happy, Michael? Have things worked out the way you'd hoped? You were such a starry-eyed resident after all, weren't you?"

He thought for a moment. "I guess I was, wasn't I." He smiled. "You'll have to come out and visit us. We bought this great house in the country."

"Ah, you escaped."

"We got the fuck out of Loudonville, all those women in their Suburbans."

"Those women are your patients, Michael. I wouldn't disparage them if I were you."

"It got too intense here. We just wanted a different life. We wanted space."

"Space." She smiled. "Well, I hope you've found it." She finished off her iced tea and glanced at her watch. "I've got to go. Don't worry about the check, I took care of it."

"I thought you were going to proposition me."

"I was. But I've changed my mind."

"I don't get it."

"You're too damn happy. I don't want to spoil that." She shoved her files into a briefcase and pulled on her blazer. "But it was a very nice lunch."

"You hardly ate anything." He reached out and caught her hand and she stopped, suddenly flustered. Her hand was cool and delicate. "What can I do for you, Celina? Just tell me."

She settled back into the booth and hesitated, as if she were trying to make up her mind. "I need help, Michael. I wouldn't ask you if it wasn't completely necessary." She took a card out of her pocketbook and gave it to him. It said FREE WOMEN'S HEALTH AND WELLNESS CENTER and listed the address. "You may have heard that I started a clinic. On South Pearl Street. It's been an enormous challenge, an overwhelming challenge at times, but also an amazing part of my life. A lot of our patients live up the road, in city housing. Most of them don't have insurance. We offer family counseling, pregnancy-crises counseling, and intervention. We've got a hotline—the works."

When Celina talked about her work, her eyes seemed lit from within. He found her passion inspiring. But Celina had always been different. As a resident, she'd been out every night on the streets treating homeless people, venturing into crack houses, tenements. That was her world; she'd grown up inside it and had at last returned to it. Money didn't seem to be an issue. She'd never had it; he imagined she could go on living without it. Whereas he'd grown accustomed to having money in his pocket. He had kids; she didn't. He doubted, for some reason, that she ever would, and kids made a difference in the way you thought about money. Still, it took a lot of courage to do what Celina was doing; he didn't know if he could do it. "You always wanted that," he said. "Remember that bum we met?"

"That *homeless* man," she corrected him.

They'd found him outside the hospital, middle of winter, without shoes. She'd taken him to the store and had bought him a pair of sneakers.

"You bought him orange juice," he remembered.

"Ah, yes. But I don't think he was that kind of thirsty," she said with a laugh, but then her smile faded and she looked almost frightened. He sensed her uneasiness, her uncertainty.

"When I heard you were at St. Vincent's I thought you might be our last hope." Her eyes glimmered with tears that she irritably swatted away. "I'm sorry," she said, regaining her composure. "It's been a hard time for me."

He took her hand. "Tell me what you need, Celina."

She leaned toward him and spoke softly. "It's an ugly subject these days, but we do abortions. We're the only place in town. We've had other doctors, but they've dropped out. They couldn't take it."

"Couldn't take what?"

"The threats. I'm not going to lie to you. This is a fairly conservative town when it comes to this subject. It gets pretty intense sometimes."

"What kind of threats?"

Her forehead tightened and he knew that things were worse than she would say. "Crank calls, mostly. There's an anti-choice group, Life Force. They're big around here and they're very tenacious. With the election and stuff they're trying to make a lasting impression."

"I've heard," he told her. "I've seen pictures in the paper."

She met his eyes head-on. "Most of the new guys getting out of residency don't even know how to do the procedure. They're shunned if they show any interest. It's unbelievable. It's frightening. It's a war out there, Michael. I really mean it, you're our last hope."

He realized they were still holding hands. "Talk about a little pressure," he said, trying to make a joke. She took her hand back and folded her arms across her chest, waiting for him to decide.

They didn't do abortions in his group unless the woman's life was at risk, and even then it required a bit of red tape. Michael's two partners, Finney and Bianco, were staunch Republicans; he didn't imagine they would appreciate his volunteering at an abortion clinic, especially for Celina James. It also meant more time away from his family, something he and Annie didn't need right now. They had little time together as it was, not to mention the rare occasions he spent with his kids. On the other hand, his wife was adamantly pro-choice; she'd respect him for doing it. Annie admired people with churning political fervor, people who put themselves on the line, and he knew she thought they'd gotten complacent over the years. "A compost pile is not my idea of a political statement," he recalled her complaining. Although he sensed that it was not a good idea to get involved with Celina James for a variety of obvious reasons, he didn't like the idea of not helping her clinic, which embodied his own political ideology. He supposed he could try it for a while and see how things went. He could keep it from his partners. They didn't have to know what he did on his days off.

"Obviously, I can't work when I'm on call," he told her.

"Of course you can't," she said, and then she grinned. "How about tomorrow?"

He smiled. "I don't believe I'm on call tomorrow."

"Well, come on by. I'm sure we can find something for you to do." She leaned across the table and kissed him lightly on the cheek. "I knew I could count on you, Michael. Thanks." And then she was gone.

He sat there for a moment, reflecting on her beauty. Who had succeeded in capturing her heart, he wondered, amazed that he was actually feeling jealous. His pager sounded, but he didn't bother to answer it, and he sat at the table for a few minutes more, remembering their intimate times together. The way she had smelled when her body went damp—like wet hay, he thought, like mist. The outrageous underwear she wore under her scrubs.

"Can I get you anything else?" The waiter's voice startled him.

"No, no," he stuttered, like a man who'd been caught stealing. He stood up, grateful for the interruption. He had no business thinking about Celina James, not like that.

Michael would have to discuss his plans to work at the clinic with Annie. The idea of him working on Saturdays would not sit well with her, he knew. And although they had what he considered to be a strong marriage, Annie was always on his case about needing more time with him. She'd complain that he wasn't home enough, that he wasn't *there* for her. Sometimes she even seemed suspicious that he might be seeing someone on the side. She'd playfully question him about the nurses at the hospital— did they flirt with him often, did they hit on him—but there was always an edge to her voice that made him think she worried about these things more than she should. He was, in fact, enormously faithful to his wife. There had been occasions when he'd gotten a certain feeling from one of the nurses, a kind of warm interest, but he'd never encouraged or pursued it. But Celina was different; she'd been in his life before Annie, and although their affair had lasted only a few months, it had been powerful.

That night, Michael drove home faster than usual, feeling rather pleased with himself. Of course he would help Celina. Why shouldn't he? After all, they were doctors in the same community, they had to stick together—and he believed in what she was doing. An expansive mood rushed through him. He could hardly wait to see her again.

He put the windows down and accelerated, inviting the smell of plowed fields into the car. It was the wild smell of freedom, and he breathed it deeply into his lungs. The sky was dark and clear and smelled of wood smoke. Millions of stars glittered overhead. He couldn't imagine a more beautiful night.

The house was all lit up when he pulled up the gravel driveway, and he could see Henry in the living room practicing his violin. Then Rosie's towhead flew into the room, bobbing this way and that like a sunflower. Michael sat there for a moment, pondering their good fortune, admiring the large windows casting their yellow light onto the grass. He had to admit, it was an impressive old place. Suddenly the front door opened and Annie came out, wrapped up in her ratty brown cardigan, followed by the children and the dog, all of whom raced across the lawn to his waiting arms.

The kitchen was in its usual state of chaos. Spaghetti boiling over on the stove, a salad in progress on the counter, wet watercolors rippling on the table, peanut shells scattered across the scuffed wood planks. Backpacks tossed haphazardly, lunch boxes, muddy shoes. Annie handed him a glass of wine. "Hey, nice to see you for a change."

They kissed. "Nice to see you, too."

Henry leaned in the doorway, considerably less enthusiastic. "Hi, Dad."

"Hey. High five." Michael held his hand up and their hands met in midair. "What's up?"

"Finished my project."

"Cool, Hen. Can I see it?"

"After dinner, guys," Annie said, holding a bowl of steaming spaghetti. "Everything's hot and ready."

"Just the way I like it." Michael squeezed her from behind and she smiled at him, flushed, maneuvering her way to the table. Unwittingly, he found himself comparing Annie's breasts to Celina's. Annie's were wondrously abundant, whereas Celina's were modest. He remembered Celina's skimpy bras like slithery vertebrate animals. Annie's bras were huge, maternal contraptions. Annie was staring at him. "I'm sorry," he said. "Did you say something?"

"I was wondering where they went."

"Who?"

"The *kids*." Annie frowned and then screamed, *"Dinner!"*

Henry and Rosie charged in and noisily pulled out their chairs while Annie prepared their plates. Molly rambled after them, panting, wagging her feathery tail. "Molly, you're out. Can you put her out, Michael?"

"Come on, Molly. Out you go." He grabbed one of her treats and tossed it into the dark. Molly ran out after it.

"Try not to eat like animals," Annie said to the kids, to which Henry promptly snorted like a pig, which delighted Rosie, who followed suit.

Annie shook her head. "I just don't know what we're going to do with these little animals." Rosie squealed with laughter and Michael laughed, too, and snorted for good measure. "You're as bad as they are." Annie smiled at him. She poured herself more wine and drank some of it, then resumed the wild routine of getting the rest of the meal on the table. His wife was not industrious when it came to cooking. A week's menu, generally speaking, included any of an assortment of variously shaped pastas and a salad of some sort. Tonight it looked like spinach.

He drank off the whole of his wine and poured himself another glass, letting his mind drift for a moment around the room, over the heads of his wife and children, through the window, where the warm air smelled sweet like buttered toast. He saw the white picket fence that they had painted laboriously as a family, and the lilies that Annie had planted along the edge of it. He saw the barn in the distance with its rooster weather vane, and the apple trees beyond, twisted and black. People thought they were crazy for moving out here. "How are you going to survive without a Blockbuster?" he remembered Finney asking him. But the land, the space, was extraordinary. It changed the way you thought about things; it had changed him.

"I only got to play for ten minutes," Henry was complaining about the afternoon's soccer game. "I had to sit on the bench."

"Why, honey?" Annie looked concerned.

"I'm no good," the boy answered glumly. "I'm too slow."

"You can't get better if you don't play," Michael said. "I don't like that he makes you sit out."

"Only the good people get to play."

"Maybe you and Daddy can practice together this weekend," Annie said.

"Okay, Dad?" Henry squinted up at him hopefully.

"Sure, Hen," he said, but it was a lie. He knew he wouldn't have any time with his son this weekend.

"You're not hungry?" Annie noticed his full plate.

"Had a big lunch." This was as good a time as any, he thought. "Lombardo's."

"One of the drug reps?"

"Someone from Harvard." He explained how he'd gotten the call from Celina James.

Annie grimaced. "I remember her. She's the one who had the hots for you."

To his knowledge, Annie knew nothing of his relationship with Celina before their marriage. "What are you talking about?" he said casually, but he was intensely curious.

"She was always flirting with you."

"I don't remember that."

"Yes, right in front of me. We were engaged, for Christ's sake, and she'd come over and flirt with you. It was humiliating."

"What's humiliating?" Rosie said.

"I don't know what you're talking about," he said. "I hardly even knew her."

"Well," Annie said ruefully, "she knew you."

"Mommy?" Rosie pulled on Annie's sleeve, her face the spitting image of her mother's. "What's humiliating?"

Annie looked at him, her eyes spoonfuls of regret. "It's when somebody makes you feel like shit." She waited a moment, then added, "Excuse the language."

"Oh," Rosie said, trying to decide how she felt about it. "That's not very nice."

"No it isn't, sweetie." Annie narrowed her eyes on him. "Well, how is she after all these years? She's an OB?"

"She started a clinic down on South Pearl Street. I hear it's a pretty controversial spot."

"Oh, yes, I read about that place. That's her?"

"Yup."

Henry looked confused. "What's a clinic?"

Annie shot Michael a look and he shot it right back. *Take it,* his eyes told her. "It's like a small hospital. For women, honey," Annie answered softly. "Family planning, stuff like that."

"Family what?" That wasn't going to do it.

"When women get pregnant and they need help," Michael said.

"Why can't they just go to the hospital?" Henry asked.

"Sometimes women get pregnant," Annie explained, "and they're not able to go through with the pregnancy."

"Why not?" Rosie frowned.

Annie met Michael's eyes. "How did we get onto this subject, anyway?"

"Celina James. I should have known better."

"You should have. You see that? She's already causing trouble."

Michael cleared his throat and wished he hadn't mentioned seeing Celina at all. He should have waited till the kids went to bed. The children were staring at him, waiting for more information. "Sometimes women have a baby growing inside them at the wrong time in their lives."

Rosie shook her head. "Why?"

"Well, they might not have enough money," Annie said. "Or maybe they're not married. Maybe they're very young. Maybe they don't feel ready to be a mommy."

"I'm only six," Rosie argued, "but if I had a baby in my tummy I'd be its mommy."

"When you get older you'll understand better," Michael said.

"No I won't," Rosie insisted. "It's mean not to take care of your baby."

"You're right, Rosie," Annie said gently. "It is mean. But people can be mean to their children, too. Not everybody should become a mommy. And sometimes those women decide not to and they have what's called an abortion."

Henry made a face like he was grossed out. "Well, what is it?"

"It's a procedure we do to remove the fetus."

"What's a fetus?" Rosie said.

"It's a baby, stupid," Henry said.

"Technically, no, Henry," Michael said. "It takes several months for a fetus to become a baby. That's a medical perspective, anyway." Michael glanced at his wife. "Other people argue that life begins at conception."

"Well, does it or doesn't it?" Henry asked, suddenly impatient.

"Life is present in the womb, cells are multiplying just like mold on a sandwich. It's not like you can put Pampers on a six-week-old fetus."

"So, then, it's okay to kill it?"

Michael shook his head. "I don't know, Henry. I don't know if it's okay."

Henry shrugged and shook his head and brought his plate over to the sink, humming the famous tune to *The Twilight Zone*. "Well," Annie said, getting up to clear the table, "I guess we covered *that* subject. Who wants dessert?"

Over ice cream, Henry described his science fair project. "It's a windmill. I rigged up a fan to make it spin."

"It's really cool," Rosie said importantly.

"It's an amazing windmill, Henry," Annie said. "I'm really proud of you."

"You're coming tomorrow, right, Dad?" Henry's face froze expectantly.

Michael detected a change in Henry, a chiseled solemnity in his jaw. He'd never noticed it before. Or had it just happened, as if overnight? It came to him that the distance between them was widening and he had no one to blame but himself.

"Tomorrow?" Michael searched Annie's face.

Annie scowled at him. "Don't tell me you forgot."

"Yeah, Dad, it's tomorrow. And let me guess, you're not coming." Henry backed out of his chair and tramped down the stairs.

"Henry, wait!" Rosie went after him, loyal soldier, but stopped first to let in the dog. Then she skipped after her brother, down to the cellar, with Molly right beside her.

Annie got up and started to clear the table. "So, what is it this time?"

"Actually, this happens to be important." It came out sounding like a confession. He told her about his conversation with Celina. "They've got appointments scheduled and nobody to do the procedure. I told her I'd show up on Wednesday afternoons and Saturdays." He hesitated and tried to look apologetic. "Starting tomorrow."

"Saturdays, Michael? You're never home as it is and now we have to lose you on Saturdays?"

"I'm all they've got, Annie. There isn't anyone else."

She turned away from him at the counter, scraping the plates into the sink, then setting them noisily onto the counter. "I don't know what to say. I know it's an important cause. You know how I feel about the issue. And I do think you should do it. It's just hard for me, sometimes."

"I know."

"When it comes to the rest of the world you're right there. When it comes to us, it's take a number and get in line."

Michael put his arms around her. "I'm sorry you feel that way."

"It's true," she whispered. "I do."

"I'll call her and tell her I can't make it," he said, knowing that Annie would never make him do it. Annie had a fundamentally magnanimous nature. She wasn't the type to deny anyone who needed help.

"No. That's not the right thing either. She needs your help. I understand that." She turned and looked at him. "Give it a try and see how it goes. Maybe it won't be so bad. But you'd better go explain it to Henry."

Michael had given Henry a science kit for his tenth birthday, and since that day the cellar had been renamed the laboratory. Henry had already decided that he was going to be a scientist and not, as he often reminded his father, a doctor. Doctors were never home, he would lecture Michael, whereas scientists needed to look no farther than straight down their noses into a microscope. Henry spent most of his afternoons down here, immersed in some new experiment, and Rosie, who was just a first grader, was often his loyal assistant. Rosie, too, had an interest in science, it seemed, and had concocted a few experiments of her own. Her latest, she excitedly informed Michael, was a new dog-hair dye for Molly made from crushed-up watercolor paints and condensed milk, mixed together and set on the radiator for an hour or two to "cook." Molly languished away the hours on the cellar floor like a proud mother, and hadn't seemed terribly concerned when Rosie painted the awful brown mixture onto her fur.

Tonight his kids were sitting side by side on stools, fine-tuning Henry's extraordinary windmill. Michael went over and toyed with the contraption—the tower had been constructed out of Popsicle sticks, the wheel out of tongue depressors and a wire hanger. Henry had set up a small fan to keep the wheel spinning. "Wind-generated energy," Henry explained, launching into a lengthy description of the project. "When I grow up I'm going to change things," he said seriously.

"I believe you will, Henry," Michael said. "I wish you were running for president."

Henry looked up at Michael cautiously. "You're not coming tomorrow, are you?"

"Well, actually, Hen—"

Henry cut him off. "Actually what?"

"Remember I told you about Dr. James and her clinic? She needs my help tomorrow. It's important. I told her I'd help her out."

"Doing what?"

Michael considered lying to him, but then admitted, "Doing what we were talking about before, at dinner."

"I don't think it's right," Henry said directly.

This information astonished Michael. "You don't?"

"No, I don't." Henry went to the stairs and for a moment Michael grappled for a rationalization to offer him, a way of making abortion seem okay. But then Henry said, "I don't think it's right for a father to miss his son's science fair."

"I know, Henry," Michael said, relieved. "But sometimes it's difficult."

"You never come to my school. You never do anything for me."

"That's not true and you know it."

"Forget it. I don't want you to come anyway." He charged upstairs to the second floor and slammed the door to his room.

"That's not nice, Daddy," Rosie admonished. She crossed her arms over her chest and marched upstairs. "Come on, Molly."

Molly cocked her head and stared at him, then slowly, with her tail between her legs, climbed the stairs.

—

Henry lectured Michael for twenty minutes about parental responsibility. Michael promised his son that he'd try harder to be home more, but it was such a lie that he had trouble saying the words out loud. His work kept him away from the people he loved most, and there seemed a bitter irony in that. It was like an elaborate knot, and he could not seem to yank it out, no matter how much he believed that he wanted to.

When the children were quiet, he found his wife at the sink, her hands full of suds. His heart felt heavy in his chest. He regretted the thoughts he'd had earlier about Celina. It was Annie he loved, from the moment he'd first seen her, and he would never betray her. He went up behind her and kissed her neck, her back, sliding the soapy water over her arms, her hands, her fingers. "Annie," he whispered. She turned in his arms and they kissed some more, giggling in the now silent kitchen, their lips meeting and breaking apart with their laughter, and then they started upstairs, giggling even more, tiptoeing mischievously past the doors of their sleeping children, the sound of the wind rushing through the attic eaves. Even the way she looked now, all wet from the dishes, her hair tangled down her back, she was the most beautiful woman he'd ever seen and, although he had enjoyed other women in the past, women like Celina, he knew that Annie was his true mate.

They stumbled down the hall, into their room at the end of it, and found their way to the bed and made love across the old crazy quilt her mother had given them on their wedding day. He could hear the windows trembling, rattling in their cold frames like the applause of ghosts, and he wondered distantly about the weather, the cool air of autumn, the change it would bring.

13

THE FREE WOMEN'S HEALTH and Wellness Center inhabited a nondescript brick building with a glass double door. To Michael's surprise, a small crowd of protestors, maybe twenty in all, had already convened out front, picketing behind police barricades. They held up signs: STOP THE MURDER, and GENOCIDE, and IT'S A CHILD NOT A CHOICE. A sense of dread filled his heart as he pulled into the parking lot and took the space next to Celina's old red Blazer, the back of which was affixed with pro-choice bumper stickers. As he parked, two of the protestors came out of nowhere holding large wooden crosses and tried to swarm his car, but a police officer grabbed them and held them back. They were chanting at him, "Murderer! Murderer!" It was the first time he regretted having MD plates. He got out of the car, shielding his head with his canvas bag as if, any minute, something heavy would fall out of the sky and hit him. Once inside the building, it was business as usual. "Well, now, that was a festive welcome," he said to the receptionist.

"You'll get used to it," she answered in broken Russian. "I'm Anya. You need something you just ask, okay?"

"Thanks, Anya."

"We have pastry here." She nudged him with a plate of cheese Danish. "You want?"

"Maybe later."

"You'll feel better if you eat," she told him with certainty.

"Maybe you're right." He took a bite and smiled his thanks.

"Good morning, Michael." Celina appeared in her pink scrubs, happy to see him. "We are so grateful that you're here. Come on, I'll give you the fifty-cent tour." She took his hand and led him down the hall, introducing him to various members of staff they encountered on their way. They were an earthy bunch of women in scrubs and white clogs and long silver earrings. The demonstration outside the windows didn't seem to faze them. Celina showed him her office, a tiny room crammed with plants. The walls had been painted yellow and were covered with photographs of women: her grandmother, several patients and friends, and a host of women she admired, some of whom he recognized—Emma Goldman, Rosa Parks, Bella Abzug, Simone de Beauvoir, Ella Fitzgerald—and many more that he did not. A large Calderesque mobile hung from the ceiling. She sat him down and gave him a cup of coffee. "You'll need to sign that W2 form. You get paid once a month. It's not a lot; it's the best we can do."

"It's not like I'm doing it for the money." The truth was, he'd do it for free.

"I know." She handed him the form and he filled it out. "I want to show you something." She turned on the VCR. The video had been distributed by the group outside the windows, Life Force, and supplied inaccurate pictures and descriptions of the abortion procedure. First, there were images of motherhood under the very best of circumstances. Pretty pregnant women contemplating their bellies, pretty women holding newborn infants. Little black and white children in parochial school outfits, frolicking in the autumn leaves. The narrator was an older man with a kind, caring voice. "Believe in yourself," he said at the end. "Choose life."

"I'd like to reshoot that film in my old neighborhood. All those ruined little thirteen-year-old girls with big bellies, living in rooms with torn-up ceilings and stuffed-up toilets and their mamas getting raped in the stairwells. You know sometimes these little girls come in here with their eyes full of pride. Like being pregnant is this big accomplishment. Something they've done on their own, you know? They don't even have the sense to *think* they got better things to do. 'Cause life isn't this beautiful miracle in there, it's more like an affliction. A deep dark hole and you can't climb out."

Celina had grown up in one of those tenements; she'd been lucky to get out. Michael thought of Annie, who'd grown up on an estate in Bedford and had gone to a fancy boarding school. She'd spent her summers at home at the country club, where she became an avid tennis player. She'd told him once that she used to screw the club's tennis coach in the clubhouse basement after her lessons; didn't even bother to take off her skirt. The idea of it filled him with dismay, because if Annie had done that, so might Rosie one day. "How about all those pretty Loudonville girls getting laid on their canopy beds," he said.

"Oh, yes," Celina sighed. "We had a ninth grader in here last week. From Sacred Heart. Guess her mother wasn't ready to be a grandma yet."

A nurse poked her head into Celina's office. "Your first patient is here, Dr. Knowles."

"Okay. I'll be right there."

"Michael." Celina touched his shoulder. "Thanks again for doing this."

"You're welcome," he said, and his heart turned with emotion. He was glad to be here, glad to be part of this place, this refuge. He didn't know if it was right or wrong. He only knew it was necessary.

He would never forget the first time he'd caressed the radiant mound of a pregnant woman's belly, the extraordinary heat of life under his hands. And the elation he felt with each delivery. There was nothing like it, nothing at all. No matter how many times he did it. Encountering the warm skull of the infant as it twisted into his hands often filled him with a momentary rush of madness.

But today he was here to end life, not help it begin, and it made him feel strange and weak, even though, intellectually, he could easily justify it. Annie had been pregnant once before they were married and they'd agreed to terminate the pregnancy; he was a resident, she was in graduate school. They simply weren't ready for the demands of a family. He didn't know if that was a viable excuse, and at the time he hadn't cared.

It was a difficult subject, he thought. And difficult subjects had no definitive answers. They were the stuff of controversy. He thought of the protestors outside and could sympathize with their side of things. It all depended on how you looked at it.

He didn't know how the world had gotten so big and ugly. Maybe it had always been big and ugly. He didn't know *the meaning of life*—if there was one. He had been raised to make the best of his situation; he tried to do that. If he could do something to help others, then he would do it. He'd spent ten years of his life becoming a doctor because he wanted to help people, to make them better. It was a simple motive, and not very glamorous, but it was the truth.

The nurse showed him into one of the rooms and introduced him to Dana, the assisting nurse, a woman besieged with freckles. The patient was a woman in her forties; she already had three children. To Michael it was a procedure that he would perform to the best of his ability. But for his patient, regardless of her decision, it was an emotional upheaval. He noticed the tears running down her cheeks. "We can't afford another child," she whispered, trying to justify what she was doing.

"You don't owe me an explanation."

She looked at him gratefully.

He pulled on his gloves and eased her back onto the table. "Let's get this over with."

Dana placed the woman's feet on the stirrups. Within minutes the procedure would be over with and the woman would return home to her husband and children and get on with her life.

It was dusk when he stepped into the empty parking lot with Celina James. He walked her to her car. "You okay?"

"Yeah." She nodded. "I'm good." They stood there together under the buzzing street lamp. "Thanks for coming today, Michael."

"You're welcome."

She got into her car and started the engine.

"Where do you live?"

"Near here. Couple of blocks."

What was he waiting for? Did he want her to ask him over? The quiet suddenly felt awkward and he couldn't seem to get beyond their past, the fact that he'd known her flesh as well as his own wife's, yet now she was a stranger to him. It left him cold.

"Well, you take care."

"You too, Michael."

He watched her drive off. It was nearly dark now and the street was empty. A police cruiser was parked in front of the clinic. All the protestors had gone home long ago. The cop was just sitting there, with his lights on. Michael waved, but the cop, who seemed to be looking right at him, did not wave back.

He got into his car and put on his lights. That's when he saw her. She was only a girl, maybe fourteen or fifteen, and she was standing in the shadows across the street, watching him. His headlights had startled her, and she began to run down the sidewalk. He pulled out of the parking lot and drove slowly past her. She was running at a good clip, her two black braids like the reins of a runaway horse. Her red windbreaker had two white wings on the back, over which her name was printed in large white letters: SAWYER. A high school student, he ascertained, a girl on the track team. He supposed she'd been running and had stopped to rest. He didn't approve of girls running alone at night, especially in this neighborhood. It was a stupid thing to do.

The girl turned down a side street and he lost sight of her. He hoped she was near her home. At the corner he stopped at the light. It began to rain. Still thinking about the girl, he switched on his wipers and turned onto Delaware Avenue, suddenly anxious to get home. A car came up behind him with its high beams on. Michael squinted in his rearview mirror. The car behind him was a black sedan and the light from its own beams illuminated the driver's face, which, despite the weather and the hour, hid behind a pair of mirrored sunglasses. *What the fuck do you want?* Michael thought. He sped up and took a right turn toward the expressway, hoping the man wouldn't follow, but the black car pursued him aggressively and bore down on his tail. This was no typical case of road rage, he thought. The man in the black car seemed to know who he was, and had every intention of scaring the shit out of him. The rain fell harder as he came to the bottom of the hill, where just a few yards away stood the entrance to the expressway. Michael blew past the stop sign and sped onto the entrance ramp, blaring his horn at the sluggish station wagon in front of him. He looped around the wagon and accelerated rapidly, hoping to lose the black sedan in the thickening traffic. But the driver of the sedan had no trouble catching up, and before long they were driving bumper to bumper at over ninety miles an hour. Other cars cleared the fast lane, desperate to get out of the way. Michael cut off a Mack truck, hoping to evade the Cutlass, but just at the moment he was certain he'd succeeded, the Cutlass cut over and was behind him once again. The Mack truck cranked its horn and pulled into the middle lane, sending a van zigzagging off the road. The Cutlass shoved his bumper, causing Michael to swerve. Again he felt the bumper's kiss, and again he swerved and nearly ran off into the median. Sweat poured off him, the wheel slippery in his hands, and he cut across two lanes of traffic to the slow lane. He was breathing audibly, sucking the air in terror. He searched his rearview mirror for the Cutlass, but it was completely dark now and he could not be certain where it was. Several yards behind him came the flashing lights of a police cruiser. Michael braced himself for what would come next, imagining that he would be pulled over and given a stiff ticket, but the cop ignored him completely and sped right by.

Breathless, Michael got off at the next exit, praying he would not be followed. After a few miles, when he was sure that he was alone, he pulled over and vomited in the grass.

14

LYDIA'S HUSBAND was not a religious man. "Worker bees, that's what those people are," he had told her once. Lydia had been raised a strict Catholic and still longed for its sacred rituals, but there was no Catholic church in High Meadow. The new church on Mill Road interested her. People said its minister, Reverend Tim, had jumped out of heaven's palm. Women thought him wildly handsome, his eyes like the clear blue water of the creek. They liked his crisp oxford shirts and corduroy blazers, his renegade country club look. Men liked his straight-shooter style. He had a way of talking to people, of getting them to think things through. He spoke their language.

One Sunday, when her husband was still asleep, Lydia drove down Mill Road to attend the morning service. Even from outside the small clapboard building she could hear everyone singing. There was a piano and a guitar, too. Lydia slipped inside and sat down on the old pew. The church smelled like coffee and cinnamon doughnuts and there were people from town in casual clothes, with their children on their laps or on the floor at their feet, coloring in pages from coloring books. Coloring in Jesus.

Nobody seemed to notice her, which was a relief. Her husband's paintings had made her notorious, and people would stare at her with rude fascination, as if she were grotesque, when in fact she was nearly flawlessly beautiful. Her beauty, which so many had envied since her childhood, had become an evil thing in her life, and now, as an adult, she did her best to ignore it. She tried to pretend that hers was a common face, with features that didn't quite fit. But it wasn't the truth, and, especially in church, under the gaze of Jesus, her beauty radiated. Many of her fellow congregants had seen her in Simon's paintings. Many had studied her naked form, lingering obsequiously before a canvas in a gallery or museum. But here, now, in this quiet place, as she sat alone in the pew, she felt an unerring sense of peace, the sense that Jesus was sitting right next to her.

"I, too, have developed a mistrust of organized religion as we know it," the minister told the group. "And now it's time to find our own way.

Will you help me do that?" Everybody shouted yes, yes they would, and she shouted too, *yes!* A chill of inspiration went through her body like the breath of Christ. She did not think she would ever be the same.

Lydia told her husband that she would be going to the new church every Sunday, whether he went with her or not, and she asked him to make a donation to it. "For me," she said. "Because it's important to me." Simon seemed stunned. Without a word, he wrote her a check for five hundred dollars. It was the only time over the rigorous course of their marriage that she had ever asked him for anything.

Several weeks later, on a sweltering August Sunday, Lydia stopped by the community bulletin board to read the flyers. She liked looking at the bulletin board, with all its different colored papers and announcements of good things to do. She had been dreaming about getting a job, and Reverend Tim had gone throughout the community gathering listings for people and putting them up on the board. He said work was good for people; it made them useful. Well, she thought, maybe there was something here that she could do. A yellow flyer caught her eye: *Operator needed for growing company. Fair pay, good benefits. No college degree required.* Reverend Tim came up behind her, startling her, and tore off the little yellow tag with the phone number on it. "Don't let an opportunity like that pass you by, Mrs. Haas."

The little yellow notice sat in her pocketbook for a week before she mustered the courage to make the call. Her husband didn't want her to work. Church was one thing, but other than that he didn't like her going out of the house. He told her people wouldn't understand her. How could she stand their scrutiny? They would try to take advantage of her. It wasn't safe, he insisted.

Lydia took out a stack of bills that he hadn't bothered to pay, shoving them under his nose. "How do you expect us to pay these, Simon? Tell me that." Drinking up all his money, his modest salary at the college. The drugs he took on occasion, *to feel inspired,* not that they worked. He hadn't painted anything good in years. "We have no choice," she told him. "We need the money." She went up to him and kissed him. "You can't keep me cooped up in here forever."

The company was situated in a sprawling warehouse chopped up with cubicles that represented workstations. It sold clothing and accessories through a glossy mail-order catalog called McMillan & Taft. Her supervisor, Martin Banner, a studious-looking bald man, hired her on the spot. He explained to her, at length, the kind of consumers the company appealed to, using words that made Lydia feel exotic and important: *upwardly mobile, aggressive, status-conscious*. The catalog, he explained, with its photographs of attractive people in captivating settings, allowed the consumers the fantasy of a privileged life and gave them the stirring feeling that they were part of a larger destiny. Mr. Banner tugged on his little beard when he spoke, his eyes wandering in the dreamy fashion of a poet reciting a verse. "It's all there," he told her, handing her a copy of the catalog, "like a contract. All they have to do is buy." He gave her a serious look and shook her hand. "You make them feel good about what they're buying. Not like any ordinary purchase. Like they've done something wonderful. Like it's a significant accomplishment."

The work was easy, and she took to it well. She enjoyed getting phone calls, a new experience for her since the phone rarely rang in her own home. It made her feel needed. Each morning, she took her time getting dressed for work, carefully pinning up her hair and applying her makeup, copying the instructions in the fashion magazines. Lydia recognized many of her coworkers from church, but they seemed distant. Lydia knew it was because of Simon. The art world was foreign to them. Their husbands were carpenters and electricians, or worked at the factory down the road that made plumbing parts. Most people thought they were rich from Simon's art, but they'd gone through that money, *he'd* gone through it, long ago. Simon had a reputation for being wild and dangerous. In the old days, when his work was popular, they'd find photographers peeking through the windows of his studio, stealing shots. Once Simon had discovered a photographer in the toolshed and beaten him with a shovel. He didn't work at home anymore; he'd rented a studio downtown. Nobody knew the real truth about her and Simon, and Simon wanted to keep it that way.

Lydia had hoped, in vain, that Simon would notice the changes in her once she started working, that he'd be proud of her. After all, this was her first real job. But his reaction was quite the opposite. He seemed to resent her independence. He'd drink, and accuse her of being disloyal. He'd throw the past in her face. "After all I've done for you," he'd scream. "I should never have gone back to that fucking house. I should have put you in the orphanage, good fucking riddance!"

She turned her computer on, logged in, and answered her first call. The woman's voice was hoarse from too much smoking. Perhaps she'd been up all night with her lover, Lydia fantasized. Lydia's customer spoke softly, with some urgency. She ordered the satin tap pants and camisole set on page 24 of their Intimates catalog. "Going on holiday?" Lydia asked, waiting for the woman's card to clear.

"You could say that," the woman blurted. "I'm spending the weekend with my boss."

Lydia watched Martin Banner circulate the room.

"Oh, that sounds like fun," Lydia encouraged, but they were rehearsed lines. In truth she found the woman's affair with her boss disgusting.

"I never thought I'd be doing something like this," the woman admitted. "He's older. He's got kids, for Christ's sake, like he could be my father."

Lydia waited, thinking of her own father. Then the woman said, "Let me ask you something. Is that teddy on page fourteen really as nice as it looks?"

"The black lace one? That may be sold out." She asked the woman her size. "Hold on a sec, I'll check." Even though she knew there was no shortage of merchandise, Lydia paused, retrieved a Life Saver from her roll on the desk, then went back to the customer. It was a trick one of the other girls had taught her, and it always worked. "You're in luck, we've still got two left."

Her customer sounded relieved and ordered both. Lydia completed the sale and hung up.

Patty Tuttle, a coworker of Lydia's, leaned over the wall of the adjacent cubicle to say hi. She had on her sky-blue pantsuit and her matching eye shadow. She fanned out a handful of snapshots taken at the birthday party of a little girl. "Take a look," she said. "My little jewel."

Lydia examined the photographs. The child, who was three, didn't look right.

"She's got Down's syndrome," Patty explained. "I guess that's just the way the Lord wanted her. But we still think she's beautiful."

"She is beautiful, Patty."

"I've got three others. All girls, can you believe that? Oldest one's in college. You have any children yet?"

Lydia shook her head. Unexpectedly, something kicked over in her belly and her throat went tight. Then, from somewhere deep, she heard herself admit, "We lost a baby, once." It was something she'd never told anyone. "My husband didn't want it," she said.

"Oh, you poor thing," Patty said.

Lydia felt tears streaming down her cheeks. "I don't know why I just told you."

"I'm so sorry, honey."

"I was fourteen."

Patty shook her head and took Lydia's hand. "Sometimes we go through things, Lord knows why."

"It's been ten years but I still think about it."

"You never forget a loss like that, honey." Patty squeezed her hand. "And I'm so sorry you had to go through that."

Lydia and Patty became good friends after that. They ate lunch together in the employee lunchroom. They smoked together outside. Lydia never seemed to have cigarettes and Patty always gave her one. Patty smoked Salem Menthols and Lydia liked the taste of them. Patty was almost like a mother to her. Several weeks went by and one afternoon on one of their cigarette breaks Patty glanced around covertly and lowered her voice to a raspy hush. "We've been wanting to ask you to join our group," she said. "A couple of us from church."

"What kind of group?" Lydia said.

"From church. Let's don't talk about it here. Can you come to a meeting tonight?"

"I'm not sure. Maybe."

"Well, let me give you some of our literature. You can read up on our cause and let us know." Patty's eyes were a blazing shade of blue, and the expression on her face made Lydia think the woman was capable of anything. "I thought, well, when you told me—" She stopped suddenly.

"Here, it's pretty self-explanatory." She handed Lydia a pamphlet on pink paper. "I know you're committed to leading a good Christian life." Lydia glanced at the pamphlet. The cover had a picture of a pregnant woman on it with a crucifix drawn across her belly. The cross turned into a dagger at the bottom, heading for the woman's womb. The woman's head had the special tilt of the Virgin Mother, only there were tears falling from her eyes.

"We've got a lot of interesting people involved. Educated people. People from the college. I think you'll be impressed. You know Reverend Tim. Well, he's our leader. He's just a wonderful man. I've been involved for a few months now. It's changed my life." Patty paused, trying to put the intensity of her feelings into words. "Suddenly everything made sense. It was like I woke up one day and I didn't question anything, I just knew what I had to do."

After work, Lydia drove over to the church and found Patty in the big room they used for recreation. "Good for you for coming, Lydia. Come over here and have a seat."

"Thank you."

A few other people were already there, people she recognized from Sunday service. Somebody took her hand and showed her where to sit. It was the woman from the beauty parlor in town. Lydia had always been afraid of the woman and had never gone into the shop because of it. But now she was sitting right next to her, and it felt all right. Some of the people had brought their kids and they were off to the side on the floor, coloring or doing homework or playing with toys. The walls of the room were pistachio green, and the chairs were uncomfortable metal and made fart noises whenever you moved. People would look at you with scandal in their eyes. Lydia noticed Reverend Tim standing in the corner, talking quietly to a man in a postal uniform. He had his hand on the man's shoulder in what seemed to Lydia as a gesture of comfort. Patty came over and sat down next to Lydia and squeezed her hand. Reverend Tim walked over wearing an easy smile. He had a boyish face under his yellow baseball cap. He had on a crisp white oxford shirt, khaki pants, and penny loafers. "I see we've got a newcomer," he said, smiling at Lydia. "Well, that's just great. Welcome, Mrs. Haas."

Reverend Tim sat down at the front of the room and began to talk. She could see he had on argyle socks. "I just hoped we could share our perspectives on things," he said, "in an informal manner." He cocked his head and smiled as if he were somewhere far away for a moment. "Life is full of chaos, I know you all feel that from time to time. The complexities we face drive us to make certain choices. One man chooses order, another chooses *disorder*. Now, I don't know about you, but I don't see too many happy people around. You think the system works? Well, then, explain the confusion I see on your faces. Explain to me the bitterness and dissatisfaction. How can a person be content if they can't trust their government to do the right thing? How can an individual be content living in a society that condones the murdering of innocent children?" People had given up, he said. They didn't have anything to believe in. There was no real trust, no real devotion, no purity of expression. "What this world needs is for us to get down to basics. If you're a man, go out and work. Support your families. Provide for the people you love. And if you're a woman, well, then use your blessed gifts and raise your children. Raise up your children like flowers under the sun. Be fruitful and multiply and you will be blessed and Jesus will reward you."

They were all there for the same reason, and that comforted Lydia. They all had problems in their lives, and they wanted to fix them. They wanted to make a better world. It made them feel good about one another, and it encouraged them to move forward, without judgment, to a higher place, where they were closer to God, where they could feel His concentration, His warm, brilliant light.

They went around in a circle, each one sharing a problem or concern in turn: an alcoholic wife, a drug-addicted child, a mother who'd gone senile. When they came to Lydia she began to stutter. She wasn't comfortable sharing her problems with strangers. "My husband," she began haltingly. "We don't have the same religious views. He doesn't understand my commitment to Jesus."

They nodded sympathetically, and to her relief nobody had any comments.

After the meeting Reverend Tim came up to Lydia and took her arm. She felt a little nervous with him. He looked at her closely, examining the details of her face, and touched her shoulder. "I'm grateful that you're with us, Lydia."

"Thank you."

"Forgive my candor, but you look like you could use a friend."

She felt her face going gray and hazy, like a TV screen full of snow.

"Come down to the study, we'll have a little talk." He took her arm and looped it through his and they walked down the corridor like a newly married couple tingling with future plans. He had a crooked rhythm to his walk and she found herself adapting to it, slowing her body down, and she wondered how he had acquired the disability. She didn't dare ask. They went into the study and sat down together on the couch. The upholstery was the color of applesauce and the Oriental rug spiraled in hues of green and blue. He touched her hand. "Mrs. Haas? May I call you Lydia?"

She nodded.

"I'd like to be able to help you if I can. If there's something I can do, anything, please just let me know." His was an ordinary face, boyish and sincere, the sort of face she may have seen before, at the supermarket, at the post office, at the five-and-dime. A scar the size of a fingernail hung over his left eye like an apostrophe, lending his overall appearance a sense of astonishment. Looking into his blue eyes, she felt peaceful, calm. "I'm sorry about your husband, that you're not communicating."

"It's hard sometimes, that's all."

Reverend Tim smiled thoughtfully. "I'm proud of you, Lydia. Coming over here on your own. It's not easy stepping outside your marriage for a larger cause, and I admire you for doing it."

"Thank you," she said softly.

He put his hand on her shoulder. "Marriage is a challenge for us all. You're not alone. Try not to forget that."

"We've grown apart." Her eyes blurred over with tears. "He doesn't love me anymore."

She began to cry openly and he pulled her close, holding her like a father. Not *her* father, no, he'd never held her like that, but the way she'd seen fathers on TV hold their daughters, with sympathy and compassion. Lydia cried for several minutes feeling his strong hands on her back. It came to her, during those moments, that she could trust Reverend Tim, and she opened up to him. In a torrent of words she revealed things about her past, private things. Her childhood had been difficult without her mother, she told him. Her father scarcely let her out of his sight. He'd put cornstarch in her hair to dull the shine and dressed her in itchy wool clothes in the somber colors of the earth. He clipped stories from the newspapers and taped them on the walls of her room. One story was more awful than the next: murders, suicides, rapes, hurricanes, massive floods. Her father wanted to warn her, to frighten her, but those people, those victims, were like relatives to her. She knew their stories by heart. Reverend Tim listened carefully, showing little reaction. Suddenly, his beeper went off. "I'm needed at the hospital."

When she gave him a confused look, he explained that he was one of the chaplains.

"It shouldn't take long. Why don't you come along?"

She glanced at her watch; Simon would be expecting her at home. Reverend Tim squeezed her hand. "It may do you some good, you know. And it'll give us more time together to talk. I'd really like to get to know you, Lydia." He sat back and watched her for a moment. "You know, sometimes you've got to cross over to the other side. It's hard, I know, but once you get there you realize that it was well worth the effort, the risk. I think we fear change the most in life, yet sometimes it's just what we need to make us better people."

She didn't know what to say to him. She nodded her head and followed him outside to his car. Like the gentleman he was, he opened the door for her and she got in. "We will do good work together, Lydia," he said when he got into the car. "I had that sense about you when I first saw you, and I have that sense about you now. God bless you."

They left the church in Reverend Tim's black Cutlass and drove together into Albany, down streets that seemed foreign to her, and strange. She did not often go to the city—Simon did not permit it—and for the first time Lydia felt that she was on her own, independent from Simon and his complicated life. Reverend Tim opened a bottle of water and drank from it thirstily, holding the bottle in his hand as he pointed things out to her. She felt as though she were seeing the world for the first time. "Jesus walks these streets," he told her. "You look in the windows, you learn about this good country. Families sitting down together, saying prayers over plates of supper. Where does the chaos start?" He looked at her, waiting for an answer. She didn't have one. "Right here." He tapped his chest. "In your heart."

He turned down New Scotland and went over to the hospital, winding up through the parking garage to the very top. Out on the roof, he took her to the edge to look down on the city. The sky was purple with dusk. It was almost like a painting, she thought, with all the colors of the row houses: yellow, mint green, muddy brown. She suddenly thought of her husband, and it was as if someone were pinching her heart.

Lydia followed Reverend Tim into the soupy warmth of the bright corridor. The receptionist nodded a greeting to him and he smiled importantly. Reverend Tim took Lydia's arm and pulled her into the crowded elevator. She could feel Jesus peering down at them like an overgrown boy. *If we are not careful, we will all break in Your clumsy fingers,* she told Him in her head.

They got off on nine, the critical care unit, and she followed him down the corridor to one of the rooms. "You'd better wait out here," he said softly. He pulled several coins out of his pocket. "There's a waiting room down the hall with a candy machine."

He went into the room, leaving the door slightly ajar. A woman lay in the bed, surrounded by her family; she was dead. Reverend Tim embraced an older man—the woman's husband, Lydia imagined—while the two sons stood in their overcoats with their hands at their sides. Lydia wandered down the hall into the waiting room and found the candy machine. She fed the coins into the machine and purchased a PayDay bar, even though she had no appetite. The candy tasted like plastic, lumpy down her throat. She sat for a few minutes on one of the orange chairs. It was strange to be here with Reverend Tim. It was strange to be away from Simon for so long and she knew, when she returned home, there'd be a scene.

She felt someone's hand on her shoulder. Reverend Tim smiled down at her. "Come on, I want to show you something."

They took the stairs down to another floor and she followed him over to a window that looked in on brand-new babies, all pink and bundled in little flannel blankets. Images of her own brief pregnancy flurried through her mind: her sickness, how Simon in the night had carried her to the car, how she'd woken up to see the sun glimmering on the skyscrapers, the countless silver windows, the countless rooms filled with strangers.

"Now, this is what we're all about," Reverend Tim said gently. "They're really something, aren't they?"

Lydia nodded, her eyes going moist.

"I don't care what anybody says, it's a miracle every time one of these babies is born. A blessed miracle. I've dedicated my life to these children."

Looking at his face, bright with excitement, she had a queer feeling inside, a sense of deep purpose, as if she were in the presence of a saint. It made her want to sing and shout. She thought she might do anything for this man.

He took her arm again and led her down the hall and around the corner to the neonatal intensive care unit. These windows had curtains, but they weren't closed all the way. A baby lay in an incubator, its tiny body complicated with so many intravenous lines it resembled a marionette. "You see that child? Even in his compromised state he's made a choice. Life over death. He's begging Jesus for his life this very minute. That child's life is in God's hands, nobody else's. Not the doctor's. Not the parents'. If he dies, which may very well be for the best, it'll be God's decision. Nobody else's."

Back in the car they drove for a while in silence. She was not uncomfortable with the silence. In this case it seemed appropriate, even meaningful. He rolled down his window, allowing the cool air into the car. They drove around Washington Park, working their way down narrow one-way streets, then twisted around to Muldeen Avenue. He cut the lights, pulled along the curb, and stopped in front of a small house with a screened front porch. A single lamp was lit on the second floor.

He punched a number into his cellular phone, and when the person picked up he spoke in a calm, even voice. "Hello, Dr. James, it's me again. Take a look outside your window."

Lydia could see a woman pulling aside the curtain. The lamp went off. "What do you want?" the woman shouted into the phone, loud enough for Lydia to hear.

"Now, now, just settle down. We're not going to get anywhere if we fight. I just wanted you to know that I'm out here for you, any time you want to talk. You know what we want you to do, Celina. You know it's the right thing. Even your grandmother, if she were alive today, would tell you the same thing, wouldn't she? She was the one who raised you. Not your mama. Your mama didn't want you, did she? If it hadn't been for your grandmother and her respect for Jesus Christ, you'd have been sucked out and flushed down the toilet. Now I heard you got yourself some help over there. But he won't last long. I can promise you that."

"You stay away from him!" the woman shouted.

Reverend Tim shook his head. "We just want you to stop, that's all, ma'am. Stop killing those poor innocent children. And then we'll leave you alone. It's as simple as that. All you have to do is stop."

The woman on the other end was cursing now, and then she hung up. Reverend Tim gave Lydia a satisfied look. He leaned over and kissed her forehead. "Thank you for tonight. Thank you for showing me that I can trust you."

Lydia felt the wet outline of his kiss on her forehead. It tingled, like a snowflake. She wanted to wipe it off, but she didn't want to insult him. It was strangely exciting, sitting in the car outside the woman's house. But she wasn't sure she deserved the privilege. She'd been on the other side, once, and she felt she had to tell him.

"There's something I have to tell you, Reverend," she said quietly.

He just smiled at her. "I don't believe I need any further personal information from you, Mrs. Haas," he said, starting the engine. "You've already told me everything I need to know."

15

ON SEPTEMBER 5 Annie turned thirty-five. She spent the day solemnly working at her computer on an article for the *Times-Union*, listening to Sarah Vaughan and wallowing, a bit indulgently, in discontent. Thirty-five seemed conspicuously adult to her. She was planning a quiet, unceremonious evening at home when Michael burst into the room with two dozen irises and announced that he was taking her out. Christina appeared behind him, grinning. "At your service, madame," she said, giving a little curtsey.

"I see you've thought of everything."

Michael handed Annie the flowers and kissed her on the mouth. It was a kiss that a man gives to the woman he loves after many years of knowing her, a kiss intended to remind her of all she means to him—a kiss that whirled her back to their past and all they had shared together. "Happy birthday, Annie."

She hadn't thought he'd remember her birthday—he'd been at the hospital all night delivering twins—and the fact that he'd gone to the trouble to make a reservation made her incredibly happy and she kissed him again and went upstairs to change. She chose her reliable black dress and her grandmother's crystal beads and the earrings Michael had bought for her on their honeymoon in Paris, all of which, when assembled together, produced what she liked to imagine was a beguiling sensuality. Downstairs the children were running through the house, screaming wildly as Michael tackled them on the floor, tickling them mercilessly. After supplying Christina with a list of instructions (no eating in front of the TV, lights off at nine o'clock), none of which would be followed, they walked out, leaving behind the jubilant chaos of their life together—*their life together*—and suddenly it was just the two of them, opening the doors to Michael's car with terrific nonchalance as if they did this sort of thing all the time, when in fact they rarely went out together. He took her to Etoire, a swishy French restaurant on the lake, where they indulged in two bottles of expensive wine, behaving like strangers on a first date. As they eyed each other over the flickering candle with the black water out the window, he looked good to her again and she loved him after all, of course she did, and he loved her. They had changed over the years—children did that to you—and she was no longer the college girl Michael had fallen in love with, in a black leotard and print skirt, arguing with feverish eloquence some obscure topic of importance. Now she wore turtlenecks and itchy wool sweaters, wool clogs and baggy jeans, and refused, for political reasons, to wear sexy undergarments. She made cookies and bread and planted bulbs in the garden and had chapped hands that smelled of onions, and she succumbed readily to sentimentality; even the Pledge of Allegiance could move her to tears.

At thirty-five she was his, and she would be his at seventy—of this she had no doubt.

—

Fall semester began at St. Catherine's and soon the narrow black paths were covered with yellow leaves. Annie put aside her writing and focused assiduously on teaching, happy to discover that she was something of a celebrity on campus, even though her fierce, incendiary articles were usually relegated to the pages of obscure and progressive quarterlies that her students had never seen. As a journalist she had a reputation for tracking down misery and deceit, she had a nose for it, and a few of her articles had gained her notoriety. But her minimal success gave her a sordid feeling of worthiness. As a writer Annie had maintained a safe distance from the problems of the world. Although she had a deep sense of compassion, she'd never really put herself on the line for anybody, and she saw this aspect of herself as her most significant flaw. While her early stories might have inspired her readers from time to time, they didn't really change anything, and on some nights, after a glass or two of chardonnay in the sweet warmth of her kitchen, her own hypocrisy was enough to make her choke. The truth was, she no longer had the courage to invite the lives of desperate strangers into her heart, and this explained her diminished passion for her work. But to the dean, Jack Spaull, a scrupulous administrator and the man responsible for hiring her, she was a great success, an exciting addition to the faculty, and certainly *not* an imposter.

They gave her an office in the South Cottage, a little room crammed with books and an array of dust-covered trinkets that the other visiting professors had left behind. The office overlooked a sculpture garden and the path that led to the art building, the domain of the painter Simon Haas. For a period of time, Haas had been at the very top of the modern art world. He'd fled to High Meadow and lived in a house on Crooked Lake, guarded by six vicious Great Danes, who lurked in the unfenced woodlands around the property and had once chewed off the hand of a photographer who'd snuck in one night to get some shots. Years ago, when Annie was a graduate student in Manhattan, she'd attended the artist's first gallery opening, an exhibition of paintings that had caused quite a stir. The art dealer, Norma Fisk, an elegant vulture of a woman who was famous for exhibiting work by new artists, had discovered him on the street, selling his paintings out of a battered station wagon. *Home-*

less was the word she'd used, tsk-tsking with relish as she described the young artist as being so hungry he could barely stand up. But the talent— her beady eyes watering, her mouth savoring the bloody gravy of success—the talent could not be denied. Annie had been disturbed by the paintings, which focused rather obsessively on a girl at the height of puberty, no more than thirteen or fourteen, a beauty so aching and suffering you almost couldn't bare to look at her or, perhaps, you felt it was wrong to look. Her dark eyes, the raw flesh of her lips, the hesitant, disparaging smile. Haas had painted his subject immersed in various routines of hygiene, but unlike the works of the Impressionists he'd studied obsessively as a boy, his results were vastly different. The girl had been displayed in every conceivable position, the paint applied with a kind of feral contempt, vigorous strokes of color that only repressed her beauty and slaughtered her youth. There was a certain palpable nastiness, dare she say misogyny, that could not be overlooked and seemed to encourage aggression in the viewers, suggesting that the girl deserved whatever she got. The show was a great success. Most of the reviewers had chosen to overlook the obvious exploitation of the girl, emphasizing, instead, the vigor of the artist's brushstrokes, the thrilling evocation of sexuality. Both Fisk and the artist contended that the girl was merely an invention, but shortly after the opening, the *Enquirer* published photographs of Haas in a motel parking lot, kissing a teenager who resembled the girl in his paintings, generating a host of unpleasant accusations. Shortly thereafter, Haas disappeared. He became a recluse, moving from place to place like a fugitive, leaving nothing behind. People would spot him here and there; a few were even lucky enough to get snapshots that would turn up in the supermarket rags, portraying the artist as a mythical iconoclast, brandishing a bottle of Colt 45, his long hair the color of tarnished bronze. His collectors had no quarrel with his disappearance; it only enhanced the value of his paintings. It was not until Annie had begun teaching at St. Catherine's, where Haas was chairman of the Art Department, that she realized that the girl in the paintings was the artist's wife, Lydia Haas.

Annie had spied on him now and again through the windows of his studio. Even from outside, she could smell the tart odors of oil paint and linseed oil, and could hear the Doors on his crappy stereo system. His students stood at their easels, sketching a nude woman who was lounging on a platform that had been draped with a velvet tapestry. The woman wore an expression of resolute impassivity, putting Annie in mind of the nudes by Matisse. Haas appeared, closing the door to his office, a cigarette in his mouth—the fact that smoking was forbidden in campus buildings seemed of no concern to him. He roamed the room like a prowling lion, as if the very air annoyed him, snarling with disapproval, inspiring in his students nothing more than loathing and self-doubt. They slouched with defeat. A few students emerged from the building and caught her spying; their conversation halted and they pretended, with grand finesse, to ignore her. Annie conjured a look of terrible importance and walked away, managing to conceal her embarrassment. The art students possessed a certain insouciance that intimidated her. Their dreary thrift-shop clothes and indiscriminate body piercings seemed to declare them as members of an exclusive tribe. Her journalism students were far more predictable. They were not fearless participants, keen to alternative points of view; rather, they preferred to observe events from a safe distance. She wasn't sure where she fit in anymore.

On numerous occasions she had passed Simon Haas on the stone path. He'd be walking with students, immersed in heated discussion. Or sometimes he'd be alone, his head to the ground like a man consumed with his own genius. He had very blue eyes that teared in the cold and he was seldom dressed properly for the weather. He walked briskly with his arms hugging his chest as if to protect himself from the wind, a wool scarf the color of violets around his neck. She'd see him from time to time on campus, riding a wobbly black bicycle with a transistor radio in the basket, blaring out the Spanish station—he did not, to her knowledge, speak the language. Rumors clung to him like flies to butter, and the entire staff of the college indulged in speculation. There were reports that he retreated to his office between classes to drink. He had a reputation for mistreating the students and, once or twice, had been reprimanded for making sexual overtures. It was known that he had a violent rapport with his wife, and that the wife had been briefly institutionalized at Blackwell, the tony private hospital in Saratoga, but to the trustees these were discourteous details. The artist's controversial presence attracted students, making his nasty discrepancies more than tolerable.

Their first real meeting was in the pool. Annie had been swimming on teams all her life and had a swimmer's body, tall and leggy with broad shoulders and big hands. She still worked out like an athlete, without compromise, but the truth was that she'd never liked competing. Now she just swam to stay in shape, *to maintain her sanity,* and that morning her sanity had been somewhat compromised. Just trying to get the children ready for school had demanded an inordinate amount of effort. The alarm had failed to ring, and the children were groggy and disinterested, in no particular hurry. They'd inevitably missed the bus and she'd raced them to school, hoping to beat the morning bell, driving well over the posted speed limit, *risking their lives* simply to avoid the grim consternation of the teachers, only to get stuck behind a logging truck and arrive late anyway. Her forlorn children had had to go to the office for late slips—*oh, the shame, the shame*—while other mothers stood idly chatting in the parking lot in their riding chaps and boots, pretending not to notice, *their* children having been there on time. When she'd finally entered her small classroom with its stained glass windows and pigeons cooing on the rafters, her students had eyed her with casual suspicion, a hint of contempt. Her excuses were pedestrian, the travails of maintaining a civilized existence: wife, mother, professor, can't even find her lipstick, her hairbrush, socks that match. Bumbling through the hours, trying to sound coherent. Just wait! she thought hotly, accosting them with her sweet gaze, you with your jaded minds, your impaired curiosity. She pressed on, lecturing vaguely, feeling as though her mouth were full of peanut butter, watching their eyes drift and waver, lulled to drowsy distraction by the somnolent wheezing of the radiators.

After class she crossed the muddy brown field to the athletic center, where she planned to swim out her frustrations, even though the idea of removing her clothes and immersing herself in cold water held little appeal. The pool was nearly empty: two women in the slow lane and a man in a gold cap cranking down the fast lane. In no mood for competition, she chose the empty middle lane, where she could lose herself in her thoughts. She slipped into the cold water, adjusted her goggles, and began her laps. The man in the gold cap stopped at the wall, briefly, and eyed her through the foggy lenses of his goggles. Even behind the goggles she could see that it was Haas.

They swam side by side in adjacent lanes. Throughout the half hour, she was conscious of his stroke, the way he moved, his rushing wake. Once he even brushed her thigh by accident, sending a fluid quiver up her side. She kept swimming, flustered, pretending she hadn't noticed. When she had finished her mile she saw that he was sitting on the wall in the shallow end, watching her with interest. "You're a hell of a swimmer," he told her.

"Hello, I don't believe we've ever met." You touched my thigh, but we've never met. You stroked my flesh—*inadvertently*. She reached out her hand for a shake. "I'm Annie Knowles."

"Yes." He paused. "I know." He eyed her steadily, then slipped back into the water, sidling closer to her in his skimpy black trunks, the kind that Michael wouldn't be caught dead in. For a man in his late forties, Haas was in excellent shape. He had a wide, muscular chest and developed arms that suggested he'd been athletic for most of his life. His goggles were pulled up on his forehead, making indentations in his skin. "How's it going for you here? Everything all right? It's been years since they hired anyone new—a stagnant pond till you came along."

"I hope I'm not making too many waves."

"On the contrary. I hope you are." His smile sliced through her. "I trust people are treating you well?"

"Yes."

"And your students?"

"Very nice. Hardworking."

"Well, good. Glad to hear it. I happened to read something of yours the other day. I was at my therapist's."

"Really?" *A therapist, huh?*

"He's a very erudite fellow."

"Your therapist?"

"*Massage* therapist, actually—very erudite indeed. He's got *Playboy* and the *Christian Science Monitor* cohabitating on the table—I couldn't live without the man. Anyway, I started flipping through a journal of some sort and saw your name."

The journal was an esoteric little magazine published by a couple of aging hippies in Colorado. They'd printed an article she'd written on late-term abortion. "You mean you weren't reading *Playboy*? I'm impressed."

He smiled at her. "Truth is, I'd already seen that particular issue. Never seen so many fake tits in my life. Disappointing, actually, but then perfect women bore me."

He had succeeded in completely flustering her. She stood there and said nothing and waited for him to go on.

"Anyway, I read the entire article, which for me is quite a feat. I'm not much of a reader—I don't ever finish anything, truthfully, I have the attention span of a mosquito—but, really, I was quite enthralled, even though, as I said, I know nothing about medical ethics and the issue, for me, is somewhat"—he paused—"difficult." He glanced at her again. "The abortion stuff. I'm not"—he coughed—"really sure how I feel about it." He smiled meekly. "But you. I can see you're somebody with strong feelings."

"Well, yes, about certain things it's true, I have strong feelings." She paused for a moment. "I have strong feelings about magazines like *Playboy*, for example."

He looked at her carefully. "You're very interesting, aren't you, Annie Knowles?"

"I don't know what gave you that impression." She smiled. "You're the one with the interesting life, Mr. Haas."

His face flushed crimson. "You of all people shouldn't believe what you read in the papers."

"It's all true, I presume?"

"You know those journalists, they love to make up stories. But that's your department, isn't it?"

"It always helps to have a couple of interesting characters. You know, people with passion and substance." She smiled at him and his eyes danced around her face.

"What do you say we have a race, a little friendly competition among colleagues?"

"A race? You're kidding?"

"Just for fun."

"Okay." Racing Simon Haas was the *last* thing she felt like doing, but she didn't want to seem like a poor sport. It was important that he liked her, that they became friends. "All right, what stroke?"

"Freestyle, up and back." He slid down into the water and pulled on his goggles. Even though he was wet, she could smell his aftershave, a murky sandalwood. "Hey, Claudia," he called out to the lifeguard, "come over here a minute."

Claudia took her time walking over, giving them the opportunity to scrutinize her incredible body. Annie had overheard two of the male professors talking about her in less than professional terms. "Pool's closed in three minutes, Professor Haas," the girl said. "Team practice."

"We'll only be a minute. Come over here, we need a referee." He grabbed her ankles with authority, making the girl stand near the edge of the pool. If it had been her, Annie would have been annoyed, but Claudia seemed unruffled.

"Okay, okay, get ready," Claudia said, yawning.

Simon smiled at Annie. "Go ahead, Claudia, put your lips together and blow."

Claudia tugged on her whistle awkwardly. "On your mark."

Simon turned, his mouth wet and serious. Annie tried to concentrate, but her head was jumbled now with girlish thoughts, and then the whistle blew, and she was already behind. She hadn't raced anyone since college, and it came to her that she didn't miss it. Even in college she'd hated it. It had been her father who'd insisted she stay with it, and she had because she was that kind of daughter, she did what her father told her.

Simon's feet slipped out of sight and she knew she had already lost. She turned, shot back after him, but it was too late. She suddenly felt enervated, flailing through the water like a blind whale.

"You weren't concentrating," he said when she'd reached the wall.

It took her a moment to catch her breath. She looked at his face, unable to mold hers into an amiable expression. "I've never been very competitive," she told him.

"You're feverishly competitive, Ms. Knowles." He smiled, moving closer. "You could have won, we both know that." He climbed out of the pool. "See you around, Professor."

He walked across the tiles, slapping five with Claudia before entering the men's locker room. Annie shivered in the water. Maybe he was right: maybe she hadn't been concentrating, maybe she'd psyched herself out. Even worse, maybe she hadn't wanted to win. If she had won, she thought perversely, it might have turned him off.

Disgusted with herself, she swam five furious laps, ignoring Claudia's obnoxious whistle, then got out, apologizing profusely.

"Hey, Professor Knowles," Claudia said with a knowing smirk. "Better luck next time."

The locker room was crowded now with the girls from the crew team changing into their suits. They moved swiftly in their borrowed spaces, their manufactured cubicles of privacy, trying not to look at one another but looking just the same, always turning away with some mock gesture of humility. Annie walked to the showers naked, trying not to feel self-conscious. It was hard not to feel exposed under the harsh fluorescent lights, and every time she passed a mirror all she saw were flaws. Compared to the girls in the locker room she looked old. Frustrated with herself, she dressed quickly and hurried out to the parking lot. It had begun to rain. She spotted Simon Haas across the lot, closing the trunk of a vintage black Porsche. He nodded to her, his face ruddy with good health. She smiled and waved, then hurried into her wagon and started the engine, tuning in NPR. A moment later he was knocking on her window.

"I'm sorry to bother you again."

"You're not bothering me."

"Do you think you could give me a jump?"

"What a thrilling proposition." She smiled a little wickedly. "Unfortunately, my husband keeps the cables in his car."

"You wouldn't know what to do with a pair of jumper cables, would you?"

"I'm very resourceful under pressure."

"I'll bet you are." He squinted around the parking lot, looking for somebody else.

"I could drive you home if you want."

"I don't want to put you out. I'm out on Crooked Lake."

"It's no trouble." She gave him a reassuring smile. "Get in."

She shoved a stack of library books off the passenger seat and onto the floor, into the ever-present pile of trash: old napkins, fast-food receptacles, gum wrappers, Popsicle sticks, wrecked and twisted toys. "I'm sorry about this mess," she said. *It's only my life.*

"Oh, I'm used to a good pile of shit. I feel right at home, actually." He grinned, climbing in and making himself comfortable. His boots, she noticed, were untied, caked with mud, reminding her of Henry. The children's schedule rushed through her head: Christina would be meeting them at the bus; Henry had his violin lesson at five o'clock with Mrs. Keller, his saturnine teacher, who came to the house.

"That's quite a car you drive," she said.

"It's a hell of a car."

"What's wrong with it?"

"A rather sensitive disposition," he said. "Moody is a better word. Very pretty but not very practical. Most pretty things aren't, as it turns out. I take it you're of the practical sort, hence the Volvo?"

"You mean very practical but not very pretty?"

"No, that's not what I mean."

"It's true, actually."

"I mean the car. You drive safe. You're a careful person."

She smiled. "Boring, isn't it?"

"There are worse dilemmas."

"It happened when I had kids," she told him, biting into an apple. "Like this bolt of lightning and suddenly I'm my mother." She backed out of her spot onto the driveway and drove down to the main road. The rain fell hard on the windshield and she switched her wipers on.

"At least you're not wearing galoshes like my mother. Remember those? Galoshes," he repeated. "What a delicious word."

"You're thinking goulash. Maybe you're hungry."

"I'm always hungry." He smiled at her. "But not for goulash."

"Does your wife make you goulash?"

"No, my wife does not make me goulash. She makes substantial wholesome meals for people I don't know. Things like roast pork and sweet potatoes."

"People you don't know?"

"She's active in her church."

"That's nice."

"She's incredibly devout, my wife. Her father was religious. Catholic. Very intense. I thought she'd grow out of it, but it's gotten worse. Much worse. She's gotten involved with one of those New Age churches out in High Meadow. You know, they all sit around grooving about Jesus."

"People don't generally grow out of their devotion."

"I've come to that conclusion."

"That must be hard, being someone like you." Her voice trailed off awkwardly. She felt herself blushing.

"Married to someone like her," he finished her sentence. "It's a fucking pain in the ass. Take the next left, I'll show you a shortcut."

Annie turned down a dirt road that ran along the lake. The rain had made it muddy, and the trees hung down heavily, brushing the roof of the car.

"I looked you up in the handbook," he said. "I didn't know you went to Smith."

"A predictable choice after Miss Porter's." She saw that the name didn't register. "A boarding school for girls. In Connecticut."

"Oh, well."

"My parents were very into that sort of thing while they were off gallivanting."

"Gallivanting, what a concept."

"I was a bit of a rebel, actually."

"Ah yes, little Annie, baking hash brownies and reading Marx."

She laughed because it was true. "Well, I have to admit I didn't really get Marx. I hail from a long line of guileless capitalists. I can remember throwing that little red book out the window."

"Maybe you were eating too many of those brownies."

"Now you're getting personal."

"You're somebody I'd like to get personal with."

"I don't know how to respond to that comment."

"You don't have to respond to it," he said softly. "Not right away, anyway."

She watched his face, the rain shadows dripping down it like tears. "Where did you grow up?"

"You don't want to know about my measly past."

"Maybe you don't want to tell me."

"Maybe I don't. The mystery is infinitely more interesting."

"Oh, yes, you have quite the reputation."

He smiled a little bashfully. "It's a very small pond here at St. Catherine's, Ms. Knowles."

"And you're a very big fish. And a very good swimmer I might add. You owe me a rematch."

"I thought you weren't competitive."

"I'm not. Not really."

"Just slightly aggressive."

"Just slightly."

"A dangerous woman."

"No," she said softly. "Not dangerous. *Hardly.*" There was an awkward pause; she didn't want it to be awkward. "I sure do miss those brownies, though."

"I'm sure you can dig up the recipe. In fact, now that we're on the subject . . ." He started digging through his pockets and produced a joint. "Ah, yes." He lit it, took a drag, and passed it to her.

"Oh, no, I couldn't."

"Why not?"

"I haven't smoked pot in years. Years!"

"What better excuse?"

"I have kids!"

"All the more reason." He took another drag. "A gift from one of my students. Lovely girl. Here, take a hit. It's not going to kill you."

She watched him sucking on the joint and reconsidered. Maybe one hit wouldn't hurt. "All right." He gave it to her and she dragged on the cigarette. It crackled and sent little sparks down to her thighs. Within seconds she felt her body vibrating, humming. I'm humming, she thought. Like the strings of a harp. "My husband would kill me."

"I wouldn't tell him, then," he said a bit deviously. "I imagine he'd be somewhat suspicious."

She laughed suddenly, a little excited by the idea. "And your wife. What would she think?"

"My wife is always suspicious."

The rain fell harder now and she suddenly became conscious of the wheel in her hands, the sound of the road, the tires, the movement of the trees. The trees seemed to be crying out. The branches groped the sky like blind zealots. Simon's directions became elaborate, sending them down a labyrinth of dirt roads. I'm stoned, she thought. I'm totally wasted. She hoped she wouldn't get lost on her way out.

"We're just down there," he said. "That house there, through the trees."

The house sat up on a hill overlooking the lake. You had to take a narrow dirt road to get up to it. The road was rutted and muddy, and the Volvo bucked and rocked over the bumps. At last the house appeared, looming over the sprawling trees. It was a rambling old place, in surprising disrepair. The paint had chipped and several of the shutters had come off their bottom hinges and hung crookedly, giving the house a haphazard gloom. A light shone in a window on the second floor. Annie parked near the steps to the porch. The roof had been strung with a collection of chimes of all shapes and sizes and colors, all of which were twisting in the wind, producing, in Annie's state of mind, an eerie cacophony. Annie could see the lake, which looked black and ominous in the growing dark. Within seconds a pack of Great Danes had surrounded the car and were barking savagely. "My goodness," Annie said.

"Don't mind them, it's all bark. They're actually very gentle animals, but most people don't know it. They've seen too many James Bond movies."

"They don't look gentle."

"That's the whole point, of course." He gathered his things together, a canvas rucksack stuffed with papers. "There was a time, a few years ago, when we needed the protection. My wife, you see, on account of the paintings. We were hounded, no pun intended." He smiled at the memory. "We've actually grown attached to the beasts. But that will happen, I suppose. In time, we all get attached."

"It's a beautiful house."

"Was a beautiful house, a century ago. Come in for a minute, meet my wife."

"I should use your phone. My cell phone's dead."

Annie followed him up the steps onto the porch, the dogs sniffing at her heels. She noticed that the paint on the porch floor had been scratched to shreds. To her surprise, she felt anxious about meeting Lydia Haas, as if something had already been established between her and Simon that his wife would no doubt discover. When they entered the house, it was quiet. His wife was not at home.

"Lydia's not here," he told her, as though reading her thoughts.

"Come, we'll go in here." Simon led her into the sparsely decorated living room, where a fire smoldered in the fireplace. There was a Chippendale sofa, covered in a faded salmon-colored velvet, and a leather wing chair, and an impressive antique secretary cluttered with sheets of stationery, letters in the process of being written. The worn Oriental carpet looked dirty, covered with dog hair and ash from the fireplace, and the cold room smelled of smoke and ash. Simon brought in some wood and dumped it on the fire and the flames sprang up at once, casting an orange glow about the room.

"It's a lovely room," she said. "The fire feels good."

"It's damp out. I see it's raining again. You may as well wait till it lets up. Have a drink with me."

"All right. I'll just call home." She followed him back into the foyer, then through another door to the kitchen. It was a bright, sprawling space, cluttered with the disarray of cooking. She smelled something baking in the oven and watched as he opened it and peered inside.

"Smells good," Annie said, looking for the phone.

"Apple pie. We must be having company—she doesn't cook like this for me."

"You don't sound terribly excited."

"No. In fact, I dread these dinners of hers. People from her church. They sit around discussing psalms, for Christ's sake. I can't think of anything more depressing."

"And what do you do while they're discussing psalms?"

"What else? Drink. Telephone's over here."

Annie went to the phone and dialed her number. Rosie picked up. "Hello?" Annie could hear Henry practicing his violin in the background, the screeching sound of the strings.

"Hi, honey."

"Mommy! When are you coming home?"

"Soon. Can I talk to Christina?"

A moment later, Christina came on. Annie explained how she'd driven Haas home. "I'm leaving in ten minutes."

"Did you say Haas?" Christina blurted. "The art professor?"

"Yes, that's right."

"Watch out, Mrs. Knowles. He's a *letch*!"

Annie put the phone down and found Simon in the living room, stoking the fire. He handed her a glass of bourbon, which she readily accepted even though she rarely drank hard liquor, especially in the afternoon, and the two of them sat down together on the couch. She felt surprisingly good. Outside it was getting dark and the rain was falling hard and she liked the sound of it coming down on the roof. Through the windows she observed the loping hides of the dogs pacing on the porch, their wet snouts pressing against the glass.

"Here's to your dinner party," she said.

"Yes, yes, another evening of folksy chat around the kitchen table. It's my penance, I suppose, for all the years I exploited her. Payback time."

"Is that what you did? Exploited her?"

"Isn't it?" He looked at her and smiled and held up his glass. "Cheers."

They drank their drinks and a moment passed where they said nothing to each other.

Just then a blue Mercedes appeared in the driveway and pulled into the unattached garage. "My wife is home," he said without emotion. Silently they watched Lydia Haas run through the rain to the house. She was carrying a brown paper grocery bag.

"We're in here, Lydia," he called. When there was no reply, he sang out her name childishly: "Lydia! We're in the living room!"

Lydia Haas came to the doorway wearing an old coat with wood toggles and brown corduroy trousers and muddy black boots. She was perhaps the most beautiful woman Annie had ever seen. She stood shyly in the doorway and said nothing.

"You're all wet, silly girl," Simon said.

"I got caught," she answered, shrugging awkwardly.

"Well, for God's sake, go and dry off."

"You have a visitor," she said, waiting to be introduced.

"Hello." Annie stood up, reaching out her hand. "I'm Annie Knowles."

"Remember, I told you. The new professor," Simon explained. "Ms. Knowles was kind enough to drive me home."

"Not your car again?" She tossed Annie a dark look. "I come home every night to find another stranger in the house."

"But look at all the nice friends I'm making," Simon said lightly, winking at Annie.

"I was actually on my way out," Annie said, starting toward the door. "I've got kids waiting for me. The pie smells wonderful."

"We're having some people from church," Simon's wife said haltingly, shrugging off her coat. "Or else I'd ask you to stay."

"I've got to get home," Annie gently dismissed her. "I'm sure my son has stacks of homework, none of which he's done."

"Another time, perhaps," Simon said. "I'll walk you out. There's an umbrella on the porch." Annie could see Lydia at the oven, a flowered apron around her waist, her face flushed in the heat. Simon hurried in front of her and ushered her outside.

"Well, good-bye, Lydia."

"Bye." Lydia Haas raised her hand in a solemn wave.

Annie could feel Lydia's gaze like heat on her back as she followed Simon onto the porch. He had the umbrella open and escorted her through the pouring rain to her car. The dogs surrounded them again, sniffing and yapping at her thighs, their wet fur dampening the legs of her pants. Simon dug in his pocket, producing a handful of dog biscuits, and tossed them into the woods. "Ah, the old dog-biscuit trick," she said.

"Works like a charm." He hesitated, watching her. "Like all angry creatures they can be appeased. The trick is finding out what they want." He smiled at her meaningfully, then pulled her toward him and kissed her on the mouth. She broke away from him immediately.

"Please, Simon, your wife is right inside."

"Yes, I know. I couldn't help myself."

"It's inappropriate, don't you think?" She said it more out of obligation than distaste. The truth was, she hadn't minded his kiss at all.

"Yes, it is inappropriate." He looked at her deeply. "I'm sorry. I'm sorry if I seem awkward."

"You don't."

"It's just that I . . . my wife and I . . ."

"You don't have to explain." Now she just wanted to go home; she should have left a long time ago. It was her own damn fault. She got into the car and started the engine, her heart beating hard and fast. A guilty pressure roiled her belly. She'd been kissed by Simon Haas! He gave a lit-

tle wave and went to the door. Annie's eyes went after him, an unconscious reflex, and she caught the flutter of the curtain in the window. Lydia Haas was standing there; she was looking right at her.

16

SIMON HAD HIS CAR TOWED to the service station and the next morning
his wife drove him to the college. His wife didn't seem right; he wondered
if she'd taken her medication. The way her face looked, raw and beady-
eyed, as if she hadn't slept. Often she would not sleep and he would find
her next morning on the couch, the floor below scattered with the pages
of torn-up magazines. Ever since he'd known her, she'd vacillated between states of extreme contentment and vicious depression. This morning she'd combed her yellow hair and put on makeup. She was dressed
for work in gray slacks and a black turtleneck. She was concentrating terribly hard on the road, gnawing on her bottom lip. He shuffled his students' papers on his lap and began correcting them.

"I gather those are for your morning class?"

He squinted at her. "Yes."

"You really amaze me," she said. "And they actually worship you,
don't they?"

"Yes, Lydia, they think I'm a genius."

"One of these days somebody's going to figure you out."

"And you already have, haven't you?"

She winced and looked as if she might start crying, which he hated.
He hated it when she cried because it often became difficult to get her to
stop.

"You don't love me anymore," she said.

"Let's not start that again, Lydia. You know it's not productive." He
tugged a handkerchief out of his pocket and gave it to her. "I will always
love you, you know that."

Gulping, swatting at her face, she pulled up the campus driveway to
the art complex. He hoped nobody he knew would see them.

The truth was, he had never really loved her and by now she knew it.

He got out and slammed the door—a bit ungenerous of him, he admitted, but it would give her something to stew about all day long when she sat at the telephone at work. He hurried across the black path to the art studios and dumped his belongings in his office. He got the coffee going, then glanced at himself in the little cracked mirror over the sink. He saw his father staring back, old and ugly. Lighting his first cigarette, he surveyed the room for items that would make an interesting still life: a slender blue apothecary bottle, a squat green dish, a jar of buttons, and a hunting knife with a keen silver blade.

Later that afternoon, with the low sun glimmering in the windows of the cathedral, Simon crossed the quad to the South Cottage. He had thought of little else but Annie Knowles all day. The door to her office was ajar and he glimpsed the young professor talking with a student. The student was an overweight girl with a punk haircut, and Annie was listening to her intently. She had her feet up on her desk, contemplatively fondling her crystal beads. Her eyes were dark and shining, her lips painted a deep persimmon. Had she thought about him even once? he wondered. Something told him she had not. He rapped on the door and poked his head in, catching a whiff of her perfume. "Can I talk to you a second?"

She got up without smiling and walked toward him. "You'll have to wait." She closed the door in his face.

He waited over an hour, feeling like a fool. Finally, the student wandered out, looking elated. "She said you can go in now, Professor Haas."

Simon met Annie's eyes across the worn Moroccan rug. A bright glare poured in through the window. "Sit down," she said.

He fixated on his hands for a few minutes, then looked at her. "I just wanted you to know I'm sorry about that kiss. It was, as you said, inappropriate. I don't know what came over me."

"Apology accepted."

"You're not mad?"

She shook her head. "No, I'm not mad. But I don't think we should do it again."

"I agree. Absolutely."

"For one thing, it's completely unprofessional."

"Yes, you're right."

"And for another, I'm a married woman—we're both married, for God's sake. It's not that I don't find you attractive," she told him softly. "But I couldn't live with myself. My children. I wouldn't be able to look at them."

"I understand completely," he said wryly, and he went out. He had planned to ask her for a ride to his mechanic, but now he thought better of it and decided to walk. It was only three or so miles; the air would do him good. He walked down to the road in the high wind with his hands in his pockets and the leaves spinning down like origami birds. He went over their conversation in his mind, the way her face looked, the way her hands flew about when she spoke. He wanted her so badly his stomach ached, but he could do nothing about it. Nothing except wait. Wait for her to change her mind. And unlike his other conquests, he was not at all certain that she would.

Mal, his mechanic, brought his car around from behind the garage and handed Simon the keys. "She's starting to show her age, Mr. Haas."

"We'll just have to hope for the best," Haas told him. "Thanks, Mal."

He took the keys and got into the car and started the engine. The Porsche responded with a lusty roar that filled Simon with hope. Although he'd never admitted it to anyone, he loved the damn car. He loved everything about it. The shiny black exterior, the red leather seats. The wood steering wheel. And he was glad he had it, even though it had been his father's. Driving home he thought about his wife, how beautiful she'd been when they'd first met and how different she was now. The beauty had never sustained him, he realized. Sometimes, when he watched her sleep, when it didn't matter who she was during the day, he could still believe he loved her. Her dedication to the church, her passion for it, bewildered him. After her father's death she'd fallen into God's arms and never looked back. It was her guilt, he realized, that kept her there.

He didn't feel like going home to her now.

He stopped at Flo's, ordered a glass of whiskey at the bar, and slid a few coins into the jukebox. He wanted to hear a woman's voice, a raunchy expression of love. He wished he could paint his way out of his marriage. But he was in too deep for that. Lydia would never let him go. And his paintings weren't selling anymore. Oh, one or two here and there, but in general people looked on with cool appraisal, having been told by the "experts" that he was no longer the painter he used to be. Facing all that was hard enough. Simon had gotten to the point where he could look at his work with the callous hands of a butcher. He could take a painting and hack it to shreds, soak his hands in the blood of his failure. He could study his work, which over the years had grown ugly and weak and bitter with promise, and he could stomach the rejection, the reality that he'd been ruthlessly abandoned by the people in art who mattered.

He had no one to blame but himself.

He ordered another drink and wandered back into the smoke, where everybody was shooting pool. He shot a rack with a Vietnam vet, then they split a pitcher of beer. The vet called himself Marrow, "as in Bone," he said, and wore camouflage pants and a leather coat. He invited Simon back to his apartment to get stoned. Simon took him up on it and they walked together through the empty town with the dark storefronts, the wind blowing in their faces. Marrow rented an apartment over the post office, sparsely furnished. Just being there with the stranger getting stoned made Simon feel better. He felt inexplicably free and wished he could stay indefinitely. But then the vet's wife came home and the mood changed. She had on a maroon waitressing uniform from Friendly's. She had a snarl on her face, like an angry cat. Marrow said, "Hey, baby." He was stretched out on the couch, staring at the TV. "Light us another joint."

"Who's that?"

"That's the professor. Be nice to him."

She stood in front of the TV, the colored light flashing across her ass, and stared at Simon. "Where'd you pick him up?"

This is the way I will paint you, Simon thought. *In front of the TV, with your big ass full of the eleven o'clock news. I will paint the stains on your teeth, the worry in your face, the music that runs down your tits to your cunt.*

"Get out," she said. "It's too late for company." She stood in the doorway, watching him with a kind of intense sexual hatred as he went down the stairs to the street.

Entering the keen silence of his own home he sensed his wife waiting up for him. He imagined her in their bed, stiff, alert, poised for attack. It made him feel like a prowler. He glanced around the kitchen, taking in the white bowls left to dry on the counter, luminous with moonlight, his wife's red sweater curled on the chair like an extravagant animal. The soft plums scattered on the table. The wicked shadows that the tall pines had crosshatched across the walls. It came to him that he was thinking like a painter again, and it had been a long time, and it felt good. He knew it had something to do with Annie Knowles, and he found himself daydreaming about her now.

He did not want to see his wife, nor did he have anything to say to her, but he found himself climbing the stairs to their room. She was sitting up in bed in her nightgown. Her face looked clean, glossy. He wondered if she'd been crying.

"What took you so long?"

"I had to get my car. I had to wait."

She tossed her magazine off the bed and pushed her head onto the pillow. "I was worried," she said. "You should have called me."

"Yes," he said. "I should have."

"You stink of cigarettes."

He began to get undressed. He went into the bathroom and washed his hands and face. He confronted his presence in the mirror. What had Annie felt when he'd kissed her, he wondered, imagining her blue lips in the rainy light. He wished he could call her, hear her voice. But he knew that was impossible. And the next time they saw each other it would be awkward; it would always be awkward.

"Are you coming to bed or not?" Lydia called.

"I'm coming," he answered, "ready or not."

17

FROM HER FIRST GLIMPSE of Annie Knowles, Lydia Haas knew that her husband would fall in love with her. Lydia had been waiting for someone like her to come along for years, and now here she was. Annie Knowles was just the type to unglue her husband. It wasn't her looks that had Simon in such a horny pickle. After all, Lydia herself was the great beauty. It was the fact that Annie Knowles had a college-girl mind, what her husband so fondly described as an evolved sensibility. The fact that she wrote newspaper articles and walked around in sheer blouses—flopped around was more like it—and gazed at Simon like a rock-star groupie.

That's why, when the invitation to Jack's party came in the mail, Lydia insisted on going.

"You'll be bored," he told her. "The faculty parties are always boring."

"I'll be lonely here by myself."

Simon cast her a dark look and she knew he was remembering the last time he'd taken her to a faculty party. She had gotten bored and stolen some Valium out of the upstairs medicine chest. She'd taken a bit too much of it and had ended up in the hospital. Her husband didn't think she was ready for parties. She knew he didn't trust her around his friends, around all their precious things. "We'll see, Lydia," he told her.

On the afternoon before the party, Lydia had the whiskey out when he came home from work. She'd left the catalog early, telling Banner she had a dentist's appointment, and when she got home she sat in the old wing chair by the window, waiting for her husband like a faithful dog, watching the changing light, her thoughts roaming and wandering with the heady tension of their past. It was a beautiful day, the trees lush with early autumn, yellow leaves spinning and floating through the air. The sight of his car coming over the hill always filled her with a feeling of anticipation, at once exciting and frightening, and she handed him the drink when he walked in the door and his eyes danced lightly across her face as if he were pleased. Her husband rarely refused a drink, and he swallowed it up instantly, and then she refilled the glass and snuck some for herself and he started playing with her feet, tugging off her socks, stroking her calves. He wanted more, of course, the selfish bastard always wanted more, and she allowed him to handle her like a valuable object, she did not refuse him as she normally would, and they ended up on the floor in the kitchen with the chairs toppled over and the ice spilling out across the linoleum and him thrusting away inside her, hurting her, always hurting her. She knew that Jesus made it painful for her because of the awful things she'd done in the past, but it was a pain she had learned to tolerate, a pain she could make her husband interpret as ecstasy. Afterward, she simply said, "I'm going with you." He glanced at her deferentially, as though he were seeing her in a new way. "All right, Lydia," he said, "but don't embarrass me."

They took his old Porsche. Lydia liked the car, content to just sit there beside her husband the way other women did when they rode in nice cars, looking out the window at the crooked old houses and leaning barns, her thighs still damp and tingling, the wild taste of freedom rushing through her. She felt a sudden impulse to open the door and bolt and never look back, but then the fear of doing that, the terror of it, overtook her completely. Where would she go? Without Simon, she'd be lost. He'd taught her everything and nothing. He was all she had.

Although they'd lived in High Meadow for nearly six years, Lydia had visited the Spaulls' home only once. Simon had known Jack as a boy. They'd grown up in the city together. Jack was older, and Simon had looked up to him. It had been Jack who'd arranged Simon's position at the college, a gift they were both grateful for. Times had been hard in their young marriage. They'd been driving around the country for months, living on canned beans and whiskey. They'd pull into one town or another and Simon would try to paint something. The backseat was full of unfinished canvases. Simon drank throughout the day; he was lost, he told her, kneeling before her in a motel room, his face wet with tears. They were driving up the Taconic into the deep countryside when he came up with the idea to find Jack, to ask him for help. Jack was like a brother to him, Simon told her. They'd played stickball in the street together and kissed the same girls. Jack was the only person who really knew him. Jack was a man who could be trusted. Simon had grown a beard and his hair was long and he had a wild look in his eyes, of seething determination. They'd been driving in hard rain for hours and his whiskey had run out. He'd gotten disoriented on the long dark roads. He pulled over into a field and wept with the engine running and the rain pounding down while Lydia just sat there, doing nothing. After a while she got tired of listening to him and shoved him over and got in behind the wheel. He'd never taught her to drive, and it was raining miserably, and he was drunk and yelling at her, telling her she was stupid. "You're the one," he kept saying, "you're the one who brought me down." Well, she'd learned to drive that night anyway, around and around in a lumpy wet field, little frogs jumping up in her headlights. She'd pulled into a shopping center and Simon had staggered into a phone booth, flipping dizzily through the pages of the phone book to find the number. Like thieves, they'd tracked Jack down, banging on his door at three o'clock in the morning, with the rain pounding down and Olivia, Jack's nervous wife, coming through the dark in her long nightclothes, like a ghost. They'd been invited inside, dripping on the Oriental rugs, and Simon kept mumbling over and over like a chant, "I've hit bottom, old man, I've finally done it. I've finally gone and done it."

Two weeks later Simon was teaching at the college. He'd given Jack and Olivia a painting in return for their help, and Simon had told Lydia it was worth a lot of money. Lydia hoped they hadn't hung it because the painting was of her.

18

ANNIE LIKED TO THINK of herself as an honorable person. She'd been raised that way, to do the right thing, and she was highly critical of herself and, yes, of others, too. Her mother often accused her of being judgmental, and thinking about it now she supposed she was. Not that she was sanctimonious, no, *God forbid*. Yet with all her introspection, she could still find reasonable ways to rationalize her behavior on the rare occasion when she acted disreputably. Simon Haas, for example. When he'd kissed her that night in the rain, they'd been stoned. Why, then, she wondered, had she thought of little else since?

Several hours before Jack's party, Annie paged Michael at the hospital. It was Hannah Bingham who called her back. "He's in the middle of something, Annie," she said with a shopworn cheerfulness.

"I'm just calling to remind him about tonight. We have a party. It's just a faculty party, but we shouldn't be late."

"Didn't he tell you? He's on call tonight."

"I guess it slipped his mind."

"Naughty boy," Hannah chirped. "Needless to say, with the way things have been going around here, I don't imagine he'll be joining you."

Annie hung up, annoyed. Weeks before, when she'd told Michael about the party, he'd promised to arrange for coverage. The fact that he hadn't was insulting. She was always going to his things, hospital fund-raisers, the annual Red Cross Ball, various cocktail parties where she stood around making idle conversation with the wives of other doctors, the names of whom she could never seem to remember. Annie's cup of tea sat on the table, cold now, next to a stack of papers she had yet to correct. The kitchen had been massacred by the children and their friends that afternoon—divide and conquer, that was their motto—and still smelled of burnt oatmeal cookies, a disastrous event, the spoils of which were now in Molly's stomach. Christina had taken them outside, and for the moment the house was quiet. She sat down and got to work, marking papers with caustic abandon, scribbling indecipherable comments in the margins simply because she could. Two hours later, when the sun had dropped like a peach into the basket of trees, Annie heard Michael's car pulling in, and she felt a tingle of excitement thinking that perhaps he could come with her after all. But the moment she saw his glum expression, she knew he'd be spending his evening at the hospital.

"I have three women in labor," he explained sheepishly, avoiding her punitive stare.

"Sounds like a party."

His beeper went off. "I'm getting killed."

"Poor baby."

"Look, I'm sorry."

"No you're not."

He shrugged. "I'm going up. I need a shower."

And he left her standing there.

Annie stood at the window, watching the children playing out in the yard, throwing a Frisbee for Molly. Their faces were flushed in the crisp air, their eyes shining with happiness. At least she and Michael had given them this much, she thought, this open space, this good life in the country.

Organizing the kitchen, Annie noticed a book Christina had left on the table. It was a children's picture book called *The Path of Our Lord.* Annie wondered if the girl planned on reading it to her kids. She knew Christina's parents were born-again. They had four daughters; the youngest child had Down's syndrome, and they were all homeschooled.

Christina was the first of the children to go to college. Annie knew they struggled financially, and Christina put all her babysitting money toward school. Annie flipped through the book. It looked harmless. So what if she did read it to the kids.

She climbed the worn wood planks of the staircase. Sunlight quivered in the panes of the transom window. She could hear Michael on the telephone in the bedroom. He was sitting on the bed speaking in a tone of plodding arrogance. One of the residents, she surmised. He could be nasty when it came to the house staff; the residents lived in fear of him. She had to admit, he'd gone through the same thing when he was a resident. "I'll forgive you this time, Bernstein, but you'd better get your shit together before I show up." He hung up.

"Ooh, you're tough."

"Those lazy fucks. They don't know what work is." He glanced up at her wearily. He looked worn out, his face a blur of exhaustion. She didn't know how he kept going. She didn't know how he held it together. It was hard to be mad at him when he worked so hard.

"They must hate you."

"I don't give a shit if they hate me."

The shower had been running full blast for several minutes—he was marvelously good at wasting water—and the bathroom had filled with enough steam for a small tropical country. Michael took off his scrubs, splattered with something dubious, and left them on the floor, where they would remain until she decided to pick them up. His beeper went off again. "Fuck." Naked, he went to the phone and called in.

Annie undressed in the open doorway, hoping to inspire a bit of carnal interest in her husband, but he was too involved now in the telephone, joking around with the person on the other end and ignoring her completely. She stepped into the shower and a moment later he joined her, sheepishly dealing out excuses like a cardsharp. He always seemed to be apologizing for the choices he made; apparently there was nothing he could do about them.

Out of the shower, they went about their business, aloof as statues in a park. Standing naked at the mirror, she found herself thinking about Simon Haas. She wondered if he would be at the party.

Annie opened her closet and tried to decide what to wear. She didn't want to look too stylish. Some of the stodgier females on the faculty actually wore kilts and cable-knit sweaters with patched elbows; she hadn't owned a kilt since high school, when she'd played field hockey. She chose a black skirt and a black cotton sweater, and draped a strand of pearls around her neck. The outfit, a predictable choice in her case, projected a serious, unadorned beauty. It was an image she'd been cultivating for years.

"You look nice," Michael offered, pulling on fresh scrubs.

"Too bad you're not coming."

"If I get finished, I'll come by, okay?" He kissed her cheek and hurried out—the daring hero off to the battlefield. A moment later she heard his car roaring down the driveway. She knew he liked driving fast and having a reason to do so. And she also knew, no matter how much he complained, that he loved the casualties of the ER, being in the trenches with the people who came in off the street. He loved being the one they all needed most.

Annie felt a little sad just then, remembering the way she'd been in her twenties, the saucy journalist, back in the days when they were crazy with love, when the world seemed wild with possibilities. When his wanting to become a doctor had turned her on, his fascination with the body and all that went on inside of it, his tireless determination to help people. What had once been shared now divided them. Like a lover, his work had stolen his heart. Now their lives were *complicated* like some elaborate jigsaw puzzle, and it was hard to sort out all the pieces. There was work, the mortgage, the children, the rigorous monitoring of the day's routine, and a mood of indifference that had drifted into their marriage like a noxious gas.

The Spaulls lived on the outskirts of town in a sprawling Federal painted a murky shade of apricot, with muddy brown shutters and window boxes full of strangled pansies. Pots of mums lined the stone path, and fat pumpkins sat on the front steps. Annie felt a bit anxious, wishing Michael had come with her, angry with him all over again because he hadn't. The front door was ajar and an enticing odor of the evening meal encouraged her inside. She stepped into the empty foyer, hearing scales of laughter coming from the terrace. Through the large French doors at the end of the hall, she could see some of the guests, a string of multicolored Japanese lanterns bobbing over their heads. She took a moment to admire the house, peering down narrow meandering hallways that led into oddly shaped little rooms. There was a great deal of art all over the place, lovely old canvases in gold frames and primitive antiques and wonderful quilts. An enormous painting by Haas hung in the living room, covering nearly the entire wall. It was a strange, absorbing work, dense with mystery, that portrayed a bare-chested man in brown trousers, hunched in stature and solemn in expression, standing in the midst of a gray background that resembled the smoke of a dream. A young girl, naked but for a pair of underpants dappled with little rosebuds, sat on a chair, intently playing cat's cradle. On the floor at her feet was a white box full of leather gloves, a pair of which the man struggled to pull over his enormous hands. The two figures shared the space but remained detached. The colors were muted, the faces drawn and withered. It was really a fabulous painting, Annie thought, but, still, it made her sad and a little angry because the girl in the painting, who might have been twelve or thirteen when he'd painted it, was now the painter's wife, Lydia Haas.

Her host backed out of the swinging kitchen door holding a tray of hors d'oeuvres, the perennial cigarette balanced between his lips. Although he suffered from emphysema, Jack smoked Dorals with tireless enthusiasm and spoke in a breathless, ruined voice that gave him a kind of swarthy eloquence. "Well, hello there, Annie." He removed the cigarette and kissed her cheek. "Where's the hubby?"

"I'm sorry to say he's on call tonight. Couldn't switch his schedule."

"Poor fellow—the last of the noble professions. Come on outside, I'll get you a drink. We're all out here. Olivia's made mint juleps. Have you ever had one?"

"No, actually."

"Come. It's a beautiful evening to be out of doors."

Spaull, at sixty, had a certain old-world elegance that Annie had come to know as a child, observing her parents' friends during dinner parties through the posts in the banister on the second-floor landing. He was not a handsome man, yet he had a disarming presence. His yellow hair sprang from his scalp like the bleached grass of summer, and prominent cheekbones set off his rather small, dark eyes. He had on a rumpled seersucker suit that undulated around his gaunt frame, and scuffed penny loafers without socks, flattened at the heels like mules.

She followed him out through the French doors onto a stone terrace that overlooked several acres of lawn and the state forest beyond. It was a cool evening for late September and the air smelled of wood smoke and burning leaves. Several of the guests had convened around an old pine table laden with large platters of food and assorted bottles of alcohol. A pretty white pitcher sat in the center, full of tiger lilies. Most of the guests were from the English Department, but there were a few outsiders she recognized from Math and History. Miss Rose, the eccentric Latin professor, sat off by herself with her little white terrier on her lap, drinking her vodka contentedly and smoking a cigarette out of a swishy black holder. Across the field, the sun glowed behind the tall evergreens. Annie joined the group at the table, exchanging greetings and handshakes, accepting a glass of wine from a passing hand, everyone asking for Michael and frowning with pity when she admitted that he was still at work. There was a festive mood in the air, the exhilarating splendor of autumn, and they toasted Annie, the brilliant journalist, and she smiled and raised her glass and saluted them. Her colleagues were academic lifers and all shared the yellowed, malnourished pallor of the condemned: Joe Rank, professor of rhetoric, given to incomprehensible babbling about the mysteries of the written word, a man with bushy eyebrows and a spitball that consumed one's attention and was the joke of the school (Joe was probably the most boring person Annie had ever encountered); Joe's sour wife, Edna, boldly pregnant with their fifth or sixth child—Annie wasn't sure—who suffered from a slew of mysterious allergies that left her overwhelmed with oozing tissues; Felice Wendell, one of the few professors of color at the school, a renowned expert on twentieth-century African American literature; Dana Roach, a bustling authority on Virginia Woolf, rolling her cigarettes with fiendish alacrity; and Charlotte, the doomed department secretary, who sat at the end of the table with her pack of Pall Malls and a tidy roll of breath mints, observing the gathering with shrewd owl eyes and speaking to no one.

As it turned out, Simon Haas had been invited and predictably arrived late, but nobody had anticipated seeing his wife. "My, my," Felice Wendell whispered when the notorious couple stepped out onto the terrace. "Look what the cat dragged in."

The group went silent as they devoured Lydia Haas, her eyes skittish with embarrassment as she fumbled childishly with her pocketbook, looking for a place to put out her cigarette. She was dressed like a schoolgirl in a green plaid skirt and white blouse, a gold cross at her throat, her pale skin without even a hint of makeup, her blond hair pulled back severely in a bun. One could not overlook the protruding cheekbones, the full lips, the deep gray eyes. Few of the guests had ever spoken to her, but they had witnessed her every private act on his canvases. They knew her intimately, like a lover, and she drew their eyes with the voracity of a goddess. It was not beneath any of them to crave seeing more. Annie's curiosity gnawed at her, a churning mixture of admiration and jealousy that both compelled and sickened her.

Olivia handed Lydia a drink, and the two women went back into the house. Annie could see them through the French doors, looking at the painting. They sat on the couch. Olivia was doing all the talking while Simon's wife just sat there, poised as a Siamese cat. It put Annie in mind of Simon's work and she imagined one of his cryptic titles: *Woman Sitting. Woman with Drink.* Or simply *Wife.*

Simon made himself comfortable at the table and poured himself a drink. Looking at him under the soft colored lanterns, she saw a big, lumbering man with powerful limbs, a man who could still rely on his physical strength if he needed cash. He wore worn khakis and a Mostly Mozart T-shirt and his tennis shoes were splattered ominously with red paint. His hay-colored hair was pulled back in a ponytail; she found it highly appealing. His eyes were tinted with gloom, and suggested a lifetime of inner struggle. His students, she imagined, admired this quality. To them, he was the incarnation of a true artist.

"Hello there, Annie," Haas said to her now, extending his hand for a shake. When their hands collided, his was warm and big. He held on. "I was sort of hoping I'd see you."

They smiled at each other.

"And your husband? Is he here, too? I was hoping to—"

"On call." She supplied the answer rather quickly.

"Off saving lives, is he?"

"Delivering them, anyway. He's an obstetrician."

Simon Haas considered this. "He must be a busy man, your husband the baby doctor."

"That he is. We're in the midst of another baby boom. Do you have children?"

"God, no."

Except for your little wife, Annie thought.

"I'm too much of a selfish bastard," Simon added.

"That's a good reason then."

They didn't say anything for a moment, and he lit a cigarette.

"I saw your painting inside," she said, "the one in the living room. It's very good."

"It's an old painting."

"Who's the man in the gloves?"

"You're not going to make me talk about this, are you?"

"I'm guessing it's her father."

"Like I said, it's an old painting," he said dismissively. "He was a glove man."

"A what?"

"Her father. He worked at the factory up there. In Gloversville."

"Oh, I see. That explains it."

"That explains nothing." The moment wavered and she thought the subject was closed, but then he continued. "I was painting the factories. I liked the buildings. The windows. In the evening when the sun is low they turn copper. I was interested in the workers, too. Many of them had stained hands, you know, from the ink. I started to explore the area around the factory, where most of them lived. Trailer parks. Small houses. A gloomy town. I happened to turn down this dirt road and there was this old house, set way back. There were so many trees I almost drove right past it. I wish I had. But there was something about the house that interested me."

"What was it?"

"I don't know, exactly. I sketched·the house several times. It seemed like such a sad place. And then I saw her, this young girl. And I think the

fact that she was there, in the midst of all this gloom—it intrigued me."
He went quiet suddenly. "She was," he said, "astoundingly beautiful."

"Love at first sight," Annie said a bit dryly, incredulous that she was actually feeling jealous.

"I'm not sure it had anything to do with love. I'm sorry to disappoint you. I can see you're a romantic."

She swallowed more wine, feeling her face growing hot. "I'm not sure what I am."

"Meaning what?"

"Remember how you apologized for being awkward? You probably don't remember."

"I remember," he said readily.

"I feel awkward now."

He nodded at her and poured more wine. "Awkward interests me," he said. "At least when you are feeling awkward you are always thinking. When you are feeling fabulous, for example, rare occurrence that it may be, you stop thinking altogether. Which gets you into all kinds of trouble. Hence, you are far better off feeling awkward. Just the sound of it on your tongue. Like chewing on screws."

She laughed. "Very tough to swallow."

"Most awkward things are," he said.

"Not for the weakhearted."

"Nor the weak-stomached."

They laughed and drank some more.

"What are you working on these days?" she asked. "Are you still painting pictures of your wife?"

"My wife is an intriguing subject," he said. "I'm still trying to figure her out."

"Mystery can be useful in a relationship," she said, eager to pry him open like the lid on a tightly sealed Mason jar. "It keeps you guessing."

"It can also be very tedious. I'm a painter, Ms. Knowles. I'm interested in the truth."

"The truth is a dubious pursuit," she said darkly. "An abstract ideal. You never really know the whole truth about a person. You have to trust, that's all. You have to have faith."

He lit another cigarette. "Tell me, Ms. Knowles, do you trust your husband?"

"Implicitly."

He leaned toward her and whispered, "Liar."

She forced a smile, suddenly insecure. "I do."

"Liar, liar, pants on fire." He sang it softly into her ear.

"I don't know what got us onto this conversation." Embarrassed suddenly, hoping no one had overheard them, she glanced around at the other guests, who were huddled in small groups on the creaky patio chairs. Felice Wendell noticed her and gave a little wave.

"I'm coming over to interrupt," Felice said. "What's the subject?"

"We were talking about my wife," Simon said. "The truth is, to answer your question, Annie, I haven't painted my wife in years."

"He hasn't painted *anything* in years," Felice Wendell said, pouring them each a fresh glass of merlot. She stood behind Simon, rubbing his shoulders playfully. "He's in a slump."

"While his public waits in vain," Joe said sourly, joining them, pouring his wine into a tall glass and drinking it down like milk. "I should be so lucky."

"We're all in a slump around here," Felice said. "It's the St. Catherine's curse."

"We do a lot of landscape painting," Simon offered as an explanation. "The board of trustees has an aversion to self-expression. I'm convinced it's been the very thing that squelched my work."

"Squelched?" Annie said.

Simon slammed his big hand down on the table. "Squelched," his voice boomed. All the guests looked at him with alarm.

"Ooh, that hurts!" Felice said.

"Speaking of the board of trustees," Joe Rank interrupted. "I've been meaning to discuss something with you, Ms. Knowles."

"Here we go," Felice said, rolling her eyes. "Big Daddy isn't happy. Remember, Annie, I warned you about him."

"Everyone is entitled to their opinion, Ms. Wendell," Rank said.

"Thank *God*," Felice said.

Rank gave Felice a sharp look, then narrowed his eyes on Annie. "I was on the committee that considered your application, Ms. Knowles, and I've read all the work you submitted, including a disturbing article in a rather unimpressive publication that you carefully omitted. I think you should know that people don't appreciate that kind of sentiment around here."

Annie knew he was referring to the late-term-abortion article. She met Simon's eyes across the table.

"What was it about?" Felice Wendell asked.

"The legislation regarding late-term abortion." Annie supplied the answer matter-of-factly. "It was just an informative piece. It wasn't biased in any way."

"Well, that's *your* opinion," Joe said.

"Oh, that's a tough subject for Joe," Simon said. "Just look at poor Edna. Barefoot and pregnant is an understatement in his case. He doesn't even bother taking off her shoes."

Annie could see Edna through the window, sitting on the couch next to Lydia. Edna took Lydia's hand suddenly and placed it on her belly to feel the baby kick. Lydia's face brightened for a moment but then returned to its sullen stare.

"I don't have to listen to this." Joe stood up.

"I'm just joking around, Rank," Simon said. "You're taking it too seriously."

Dana Roach patted Joe's hand in an obvious attempt to appease him. "You can rest assured, Joe, that unlike the rest of us sots you'll never lose your job, and when you die you'll have your glorious spot in heaven."

Simon and Felice snickered.

"Laugh all you want, but there are people in this town who don't support her line of thinking. Prominent people. Our trustees, for one."

"I didn't mean to offend anyone," Annie said. "That was certainly not my motivation."

"Let me put it this way, Ms. Knowles. At St. Catherine's, we try to encourage basic family values."

Like what, she wondered. *How to do hospital corners? How to assume the missionary position?* "Basic family values?" she repeated.

"Uh, forgive me, Joe," Simon said, "but what are those?"

Joe ignored him. "You can do what you want, Ms. Knowles." He gave her a savage look. "But I'd be careful if I were you."

"Careful of what?" Now she was getting mad.

He stood, holding up his hands as if he were under arrest. "I wanted to say it, and I said it."

"I have no intention of stirring things up, Mr. Rank. I'm not interested in making anyone uncomfortable, I have more important things to do with my time. But I won't compromise what I believe in. And I certainly won't keep information from my students."

Simon Haas raised his glass. "Hear, hear!"

"If you'll excuse me," Rank said, "I think this conversation has gone far enough." He left the table gruffly and went inside. Annie could see his wife standing up, Joe pulling on his coat; they were going home.

"He's an old-timer here at St. Catherine's," Felice tried to explain. "It's an ownership thing. We all just ignore him."

"Yes," Simon reassured her, squeezing her hand. "Ignoring Joe Rank is a very good idea."

19

EDNA RANK HAD LEFT HER stranded on the couch. Lydia cringed at the thought of going outside on her own. She'd been sitting there entertaining the garish fantasy of her father jumping down off the canvas and strangling her. Lydia had never liked the painting, and she didn't like being in the same room with it now. Yet she was too afraid to talk to anyone, and perhaps Olivia, who was coming toward her, could see this on her face. "You're much prettier in person," she said, nodding at the painting. Lydia smiled gratefully as Olivia poured her a fresh drink. "Come," Olivia said, the magnanimous hostess taking her hand, "let's go outside."

They went through the French doors out onto the terrace. Simon was busy talking to the new professor, Annie Knowles. With her dark eyes and gushing brown hair, Knowles exuded a confidence that Lydia had only witnessed in the pages of the fashion magazines. The way she moved, looking off in distraction at the yellow Labs romping in the grass, then returning to Simon's eyes with a casual shrug of her shoulders, as if she wasn't impressed with whatever he was saying to her, which he, of course, assumed was brilliant, but to her, well, she couldn't care less. Lydia sat down with her drink, sipping it quickly, relishing the warm release it gave her, and watched her husband and Annie Knowles laughing and talking, completely absorbed in each other. Watching them made her feel sad and she drank the whiskey quickly, like her father always had because he was always sad, and suddenly she was back in her tight little room hearing the knob slowly turning, rolling over to see her father sitting at the foot of her bed, stinking of bourbon and sobbing like a child.

A hand on her shoulder, Simon's mouth at her ear. "I told you you'd be bored."

"I'm not bored. I'm watching you. You're very entertaining."

"There's a TV in there, if you're interested."

"I'm fine, Simon. Go back to your friends."

He looked uncomfortable, as if he'd just swallowed a pit. "Why don't you come over and I'll introduce you to everyone." He pulled her up, squeezing her wrist, a threat. *Don't speak, just stand there and be quiet.* He brought her over to the group. They studied her; they feasted their eyes. "This is my wife," he told the group. "The famous Lydia Haas."

Later, after she'd had three or four drinks, she felt much better, and took it upon herself to wander about the house. She found various interesting things. Upstairs, in the Spaulls' master bathroom, the medicine chest was abundant with lovely pills, some of which she decided to swallow with the rest of her drink, *Forgive me, Father, for I have sinned,* and others that she slipped into her pockets for later use. The Spaulls had an inviting home, with books all over the place, and lovely little paintings by undiscovered artists, and clay pots—*ceramics,* Simon would correct her—that they'd purchased in other countries and carefully toted back to place on their shelves and windowsills and nightstands. There were photographs, too, all over the place, black-and-white pictures of their children, two boys, the twins, who were at college (*They're at Brown,* she'd heard Jack say), and a daughter, who was a speech pathologist in Boston. Feeling the pills now, she watched her husband through the window on the second-floor landing, out in the grass with Annie Knowles. They were laughing raucously, enjoying themselves enormously. They brought their glasses together in a toast, laughing and laughing with their eyes stuck on each other, and it came to her rather sharply that the woman outside would bring about a force of change in her life, and the change would be ugly, and it would be soon.

20

OLIVIA SPAULL SERVED dinner outside: curried potato soup and Moroccan chicken over couscous with grilled vegetables. The food was delicious and they ate by candlelight in the growing dark. Simon and Lydia Haas sat together and ate without speaking. Lydia picked at the food warily, as though the piece of chicken on her plate were a live bird. Simon ate hungrily, like a peasant, licking his fingers, helping himself to seconds. Watching him eat made Annie feel anxious, as though the food tasted even better in his mouth. He looked her in the eye as he ate, as if he were reading her thoughts, and smiled as if to say, *I want you, too.* There was something between them; she sensed it the way an animal senses a brewing storm. What either of them would do about it remained to be seen.

After the meal, Olivia turned the television in the living room on. "I don't usually do this at dinner parties, but I thought you'd all like to watch the debates. They won't take too long, and we can have our dessert afterward." Several of the guests, including Lydia Haas, immediately went inside and stood in front of the TV. But Annie and Simon didn't move.

"I can't think of anything more boring," Simon said. "It's like a fucking sporting match."

"You're right," Annie said, wondering whose side he was on.

"I'm for Nash, of course," Simon said. "He's got my vote."

Annie shot him a look: *You can't be serious?*

Jack Spaull sat down and handed Simon a cigar. "He's the only man for the job, as far as I'm concerned."

Hearing this, Annie had to control the urge to walk out. Now that dinner was over, she could say she needed to get home to relieve Christina. Spending time with people who supported Nash, whose right-wing agenda made her stomach turn, was like waltzing with the enemy. Still, she couldn't take her eyes off Simon Haas, who was now relishing his cigar. Was it possible that he actually supported Nash? she fretted incredulously. Nash was adamantly opposed to abortion and gun control. He had limited legislative experience and had aligned himself with the Christian Right. Annie hoped in vain that Simon was lying for Jack Spaull's benefit, but she couldn't be sure of that; she couldn't be sure of anything when it came to Simon Haas, and if he *was* lying for Jack's benefit that, too, would disgust her.

"Hell of a cigar, Jack," Simon said.

"Nothing like a good cigar after a fine meal," Jack said. "All I need is a smoking jacket and a pair of satin slippers."

"Where's the girl in the cake, that's what I want to know," Simon said. "You see, Annie, he's corrupting me."

"I don't think that's possible, Simon," Jack said. "In fact, I know it's not."

"Fill me in," Annie said. "It all sounds awfully interesting."

"He's referring to my indulgent past," Simon said. "Far from interesting."

"Come now, Mr. Haas. Don't underestimate your shortcomings, they may be all you have left." Jack stood up and patted Simon on the back. "I'll leave you two alone now. But behave yourself, Simon."

"I intend to do just that," Simon said, finishing his drink and smiling a little devilishly as Jack walked back toward the bright lights of the house. "We were close once. As kids. He's like a brother, he likes to torture me about stuff."

Annie felt herself falling into his grasp. She couldn't seem to help it. *Catch me*, she thought. *I'm falling.* "What kind of stuff?"

"He helped me out when I first got here. I was kind of broke. He likes to remind me from time to time. He saved my life, basically."

"Well, that's a hell of a good excuse to celebrate," she said, pouring them each another shot. "To saving lives."

A burst of applause sounded from the group in the living room, followed by uproarious laughter at the TV.

"Saving lives," he repeated.

They sat there for a moment in silence.

"It's a good bourbon," he said. "But that's like Jack. He's got good taste. He's a man you can count on."

"Yes," she agreed, although she hardly knew Jack Spaull. "I have that feeling about him. I have that feeling about him, too."

"I can count on old Jack. Because he's seen me at my worst. And it didn't matter. He's been good to me. He's helped me out. I was down. I was an asshole. And he was there."

"What happened?"

"I've made mistakes," he said. "I've done things. Awful things. But not you, right? You're not the type to make mistakes."

"I've made my share," she said. She wanted to ask him what kind of awful things, but she didn't have the nerve.

"It's a rare thing," Simon said, sounding very drunk all of a sudden. "It's a rare thing to be able to trust someone. I don't trust anyone, really. I know we were attempting to discuss it earlier and we didn't quite crack the nut, did we? The truth is, the *truth* is, I have never really been able to let go." His eyes came at her. "Do you know what I mean? To let go, just the sound of it. Like falling through the air." He reached out and took her hand. "I would jump off a cliff with you."

"You're crazy."

"Forgive me for being a drunken fool, but I would."

In her head she saw a wide blue sky, fluffy pink clouds. She imagined falling through the air with Simon Haas and smiled. "You hardly know me."

"I *sense* you."

"Ah."

"As in *sensual*."

"You're drunk."

"As in animal, you know, as in *instinct*."

Her heart began to pound.

"As in natural selection." He smiled at her. He seemed to be enormously pleased with himself.

"I don't usually drink this much," she said, feeling a little afraid of him. "Do you?"

"Always. It can be very entertaining."

"I'm actually sort of enjoying it."

"Let's have another, for God's sake." He poured her some more and lit a cigarette. "Don't take this the wrong way, but I think you should know that I find you incredibly attractive."

"What?" Had she heard him right?

"Your face. I think it's extraordinary."

"Now I *know* you're drunk."

"Truly."

"Your wife is the one who's extraordinary, Mr. Haas. I've never seen anyone like her."

"I wish you wouldn't do that."

"Do what?"

"Undermine my compliment. It's meant for you. I don't want to talk about my wife."

"I'm sorry," she said softly. "It's just that I've never thought of myself as particularly attractive."

"Oh, but you are. Right here"—he touched her cheek—"this hollow. The way it grabs the light."

"You can't be serious."

"I'd like to paint your face sometime if you'd let me. At the risk of sounding piggish, I'd like to stare at you for a very long while."

"I thought you were finished with painting. All washed up."

"I'm beginning to feel inspired."

Much later, when they were both quite drunk, they found themselves sitting in a pair of Adirondack chairs way back in the deep shadows on the lawn, far from the house. The other guests, including his wife, were all on the terrace, having dessert around the table under the colored lanterns. Annie was feeling quite loose and did not mind indulging in the bottle of whiskey that they had surreptitiously removed from Jack Spaull's liquor closet. The clouds were thick and yellow, brewing a storm, and the air smelled of rain and honeysuckle. Distantly, she wondered if Michael would show up; now that she was having so much fun on her own she hoped he wouldn't.

"We should go over there," Annie said. "They're having dessert."

"We should."

"But we're not getting up."

"We're drunk."

"They'll think we're antisocial."

"Let them. I'm a painter, for Christ's sake. I'm supposed to be antisocial."

"Do you hear something?" They listened. "What *is* that noise?"

"Deer," he said. "Look, over there." Five or six deer had appeared several yards away. "They come out of the woods. Look at them, they're frolicking, for God's sake."

"They're eating the apples."

"Getting drunk on them, they're rotten. Drunk deer, can you imagine! Look at them stumbling around." He laughed and started traipsing around after them with his arms spread out like a monster. It was something Henry would do, she thought wistfully. "Shoo, deer," he shouted. "Shoo!" Annie sat there alone under the thick clouds. She wasn't sorry that Michael hadn't come. She'd had a better time without him.

Simon came back to her, breathing hard, pulling her to her feet. "They're going into the woods."

"Good for you," she said. "You're an excellent deer chaser."

"Not the deer, *them!*" He pointed to some of the guests, who were walking into the woods with lanterns. "They're going up the trails."

"How fun," she said. "Let's go."

"All right," he said with some hesitation, his eyes flashing back to the house.

"Maybe you should take your wife, Simon."

"I don't want to take my wife." He looked at her.

"Do we need to get one of those lamps?"

"It's much more exciting in the dark, don't you think? Anyway, I know these woods backwards and forwards. You'll have to hold on to me, that's all. You'll have to *trust* me. Aha, there's that word again, keeps cropping up." He swept his hand under her chin. The gesture surprised her, and she was moved by it. "Will you trust me, Annie?"

"That depends," she said. "How's your sense of direction?"

"Strategic."

"In that case." Annie held out her arm and he took it, and they went together into the woods, lured by the sounds of the others, who were some distance ahead. It was a narrow trail, very dark, and she could hardly see. She looked up through the trees and saw the black sky churning with clouds. It would rain soon, she was certain of that, and this was probably not a good idea, but somehow she could not turn away. As if they were leaving their lives behind, for a few splendid moments, as if nothing really mattered except for the two of them, walking into obscu-

rity together, and yes, having to trust each other because there was nobody else. They didn't talk, just walked side by side, and she could feel a
strange intimacy embracing them. It began to rain, lightly at first, patter-
ing on the leaves, and she could hear the others turning back, growing
closer, and then she could see their lamps, large circles of light coming
through the dark.

"We should turn back, too," she said. "It's getting worse."

"But you haven't seen the best part," he said, his breath ragged.
"There's a place up ahead I want to show you."

The group was upon them, and they were all laughing, surprised to
find Annie and Simon Haas there without a lamp, and Dana Roach
wanted them to take one of theirs but Simon refused. "We don't need it,"
he said, "we're right behind you," which seemed to satisfy Dana, and the
group ran down the trail as the rain fell harder. Simon pulled Annie in the
opposite direction, up the incline, and she began to protest. "No, Simon,
we have to go back. We can't stay out here in this rain."

"You said you trusted me," he said, continuing on, refusing to let go.

They were drenched now, and she felt a little frightened. There was
something almost mad in the way he charged through the dark, unhindered by the assault of branches and leaves, long twigs scratching up her
calves. She clung to him fiercely, like a blind woman, and he was nearly
dragging her now, her feet stumbling over the reckless array of rocks and
underbrush. They reached a clearing, and he pulled her closer with the
rain falling wildly, and she could hear him wrestling with the branches,
thrusting his hand into a thick tangle of vines. She felt something cool
against her lips, a small round shape pressing into her mouth—it was a
thrilling sensation—and then he whispered, "Eat it." She bit down, feeling the plump grape squirt in her mouth, and then there was another, and
still another, and he kept feeding her grapes, and she felt his lips upon
hers, the hungry swell of his tongue, and he was kissing her madly, deeply,
recklessly, and she pushed him back, saying, "We have to go! We're lost!"

Twisting loose, she started back down the trail. The rain fell in sheets,
making it impossible to see. She could hear him calling her, "Wait, for
God's sake. *Annie!*"

But she did not wait, wanting to be free of him, running blindly
through the maze of trails until she tripped and felt herself stumbling to

the ground. She gasped, amazed by her own clumsiness, embarrassed by it, spitting dirt out of her mouth, winded, confused. She was suddenly very frightened. "Simon!" Her voice rose desperately over the rain. "Simon!" And then he was there, taking her hand, pulling her up, embracing her, apologizing. "I'm sorry, Annie, forgive me, will you please forgive me?" And not waiting for her answer, not really wanting it, he led her back to the world.

They returned to the house to find the others waiting for them with some degree of consternation, including Michael, who had shown up in scrubs and a sports jacket. Annie imagined that she and Simon were quite a sight, both of them dripping like stray dogs while everyone looked on, grave with suspicion. "We were about to send out a search party," Jack Spaull said.

Annie went over to Michael and kissed him awkwardly, as if she were trying to establish something, to disprove the obvious mistrust in the air. "Nice of you to show up."

"I've been here for nearly an hour," he said, displeased.

"I'm afraid we got lost," Simon apologized. "Hello, Michael, I'm Simon Haas."

Michael nodded coldly.

"Here." Olivia handed them each a towel. "You're drenched. What a night. I haven't seen rain like this in months."

"It was completely my mistake," Simon said. "I thought I knew the trails better. Then the rain started." He looked around, his eyes wide as a choirboy's. "We were completely lost."

"Well, the important thing is that you're back safely," Olivia said.

Simon's face darkened suddenly. "Has anyone seen my wife?"

"She's had a small accident," Michael said.

"Where is she?" Simon was growing more agitated by the minute.

"In my room," Olivia said, trying to calm him. "She's fine. She's resting."

"She cut herself," Michael explained. "She's had quite a bit to drink."

"Cut herself where?" Simon asked, giving Annie the impression that his wife had done it before.

"Her hand," Michael answered. "Slicing lemons. I bandaged her up, but she could use a few stitches if you're worried about a scar."

"I don't give a damn about any scar." Simon charged up the stairs. The guests glanced at Annie warily. Annie felt dizzy, faint. The floor overhead began to tremble, and they could hear Lydia crying the way that a teenager cries, an urgency in her voice as she tried to explain herself. The group stood there, a silent vigil, uncertain what to do next. Then the door upstairs opened and a moment later Haas was pulling his wife down the stairs and she was crying and hiding her head like one of those cheesy actresses trying to escape the paparazzi. Olivia ran to get the girl's coat, her voice a gentle tumble of excuses: *You're just tired, my dear, you need a good rest is all, go home and get into bed with a nice cup of tea,* as if that was a suitable remedy. Simon ushered her out the door, muttering his apologies. They all watched through the windows, relishing the scandal, as the tormented couple got into the car and drove away, swerving into a trash can, leaving a trail of litter in their wake.

Soon after, Annie and Michael went home in separate cars. When Christina left they cleaned up the kitchen in silence. Annie put the leftover dishes in the dishwasher while Michael took Molly out. Later, in bed in the dark, he asked her, "What happened back there, Annie?"

"We got lost," she said, without turning toward him.

"I was worried about you."

Now she looked at him. "I'm sorry."

"I was thinking we could take a trip together. Sort things out."

"What things?"

"Us. You and me."

"I didn't know we needed sorting out."

"What's with you lately," he said, angry. "You seem . . ." He hesitated.

"Seem what?"

"I don't know. Distracted."

"I wish I *were* distracted." She turned on the light and looked at his face, an older version of their son's. "I don't know if you noticed, Michael, but you're never home. We hardly see you anymore."

"I'm sorry. I can't help that."

"Celina sees more of you than I do," she complained, sounding like a jealous wife.

They lay very still in the silence of the room.

"We're drifting," he said finally.

"I know."

"I don't want to drift. I want to be still." He brought his face to hers, whispering. "I want to be right here."

Annie lay awake for a long time. Her mind reeled back to the party and her strained conversation with Joe Rank. She was embarrassed, now, that she had drunk so much. She remembered her journey with Simon into the woods, how he'd pushed the cold grape into her mouth and then kissed her.

A whirling desire went through her.

She felt tense, guilty. Twisted up in knots. It wasn't right, she thought. It wasn't something she should be doing.

The next morning she stayed in her office, correcting papers and drinking coffee. At noon she discreetly entered the cafeteria, grateful that it was crowded. She hurried through the line and chose a salad. Just as she was filling her cup with coffee, Simon came up behind her and placed his hand on the small of her back. It made her jump and spill. "God, you scared me, Simon."

"I'm sitting with Felice. Come join us."

It was more of a command than a request. *I'll go over and say hello, just to be polite,* she decided, but when she arrived at the table and began exchanging pleasantries with Felice, she felt him tugging on the back of her sweater. "Sit," he said. And she did.

"How goes it in the South Cottage?" Felice said brightly. "Any rumblings from Joe Rank this morning?"

"He's been keeping his distance. He's not so bad."

"Yes he is," Felice said, sipping her coffee. "But I admire your diplomacy."

"A man of passion and substance?" Simon teased.

"No comment," Annie said, amazed that he'd remembered their conversation in the pool.

Felice glanced at her watch and stood up. "Oops, I've got a one o'clock. Ta ta." She picked up her tray and hurried off.

Simon smiled at Annie. "You okay?"

"Fine."

"You don't look it." He touched her hand and she quickly pulled away.

"Please don't do that."

"Do what?"

Touch me. "Your hand. There are people around."

"What's wrong?"

"Look, about last night. I can't do this."

"Do what?"

"This. Us."

He gazed intently into her eyes. "I *want* you, Annie."

"It's not that simple."

"You're making it complicated."

"I'm married," she hissed under her breath. "I thought we agreed."

"I'm not asking you to change anything about your marriage."

"It *will* change. It already has." She got up. "I have to go."

He hastily gathered his things. "I'll walk you."

Outside it was cold, the wind rushing through the bare trees. They walked quickly, wrapped in their coats.

"It's not like I've ever done this, Annie."

"Bull*shit!* You're notorious for it."

He stopped where he was on the path, the wind in his face, his eyes tearing. "Never."

He'd unraveled her, and now he was winding her toward him like wool. She stood in front of him with the wind in her ears. "I'm sorry."

"I have something I'd like to give you," he said.

"What?" she said a bit impatiently, angry with herself for being curious. "What is it?"

"It's in my office. Won't take a minute."

"We'd better hurry, then," she said, "because that's all you've got."

He grunted at her, disbelieving, and she knew he could see right through her.

The building smelled like sawdust, linseed oil, turpentine. They went through the large studio, where students had displayed their work on the walls. Simon unlocked the door to his office with a skeleton key. The small bulletin board on the door was covered with notes from his students, some of which seemed boldly flirtatious: *Let me show you my etchings, Professor Haas* and *I need an anatomy tutorial ASAP.* He caught her reading the notes and offered, sheepishly, "I don't know what Joe Rank is talking about. These Catholic girls are witches. *Witches*, I tell you."

She laughed in spite of herself.

His office was small, cluttered with papers and canvases and his students' portfolios. He offered her an old chair, the sort of chair you pull off the curb, ripped and bursting. She dropped down into it, gasping with surprise—the springs were busted.

"Keeps my students in their place. They're all so damned cocky if you ask me."

"I see your office is impeccably organized." His desk was piled with an array of junk: stacks of papers and books. A dying plant. An old leopard-print toilet seat, suspended from the wall, served as a basketball hoop. He picked up a rubber handball and tossed it in. "It's quite a good system, actually. Once you get the knack of it."

Annie noticed a canvas leaning against the wall. It was a strange painting; it didn't look finished. "That's Lydia, isn't it?"

"Oh, that? It's awful. Don't look at that."

"It's not awful, Simon. Nothing you paint is awful. And your wife is too beautiful." He gazed at the painting with a glimmer of longing.

"I wish I'd never stopped at that house. I wish I'd never seen her." A blizzard of leaves fell outside, distracting them. He looked at her then and she could feel something between them, a kind of heat that made her almost desperate for air. "People think I exploited her. She exploited me. She's ruined my life."

"What happened at the party?"

"Look, Annie, my wife has an emotional disorder. She tends to get violent. Sometimes I have to use force to restrain her. I don't expect you to understand. We've been together for a long time. It's something I've grown accustomed to."

"Which part? Her behavior, or your so-called force?"

He didn't answer her for a moment. Finally, he said, "Both."

She looked at his face. His eyes were red; he looked exhausted. "Help me up," she said. "I've got a class in five minutes."

He pulled her up but didn't let go. "I have something for you," he told her.

"What is it?"

He kissed her then, deeply, and she kissed him back, she couldn't help it. "I have to go," she said, in no particular hurry. "I have a class."

"I'm sorry." But then he kissed her again, slow and deep.

"I have to go. I'm going. Right now." But she did not go anywhere.

PART THREE
Need

21

SOME PEOPLE called him a workaholic, some called him an arrogant son of a bitch. He didn't care. Get the job done right was his philosophy. It wasn't always pretty. Go in and clean up the mess. As the weeks passed, Michael found himself growing more and more involved in the world of the clinic. Working with Celina had sharpened his view. He realized that he'd grown complacent over the years, passive to the system. She had challenged him to do more, to be proactive, and he'd responded.

At home, they'd begun to get prank phone calls. The calls would come late at night and emit the sound of a crying baby. They were upsetting to Annie. She called the phone company and had their number changed to an unlisted one, but within a week the calls returned. When he made his rounds at the hospital, he'd begun to get nasty looks from some of the other doctors. A few of the nurses refused to help him. One nurse anesthetist, a devout Catholic, had herself removed from all of Michael's cases. On his rounds one morning Michael saw a young woman who had shown up in the emergency room with an obstructed bowel, a result of a mangled abortion at another clinic. She now suffered with a host of other complications. That morning he found her in terrible pain.

"Didn't you get your pain medication?" he asked.

"The nurse wouldn't give it to me," she told him. "She said I deserved to be in pain. She said God was punishing me for what I'd done."

Michael had the nurse removed from the service and asked the head nurse to consider having her fired, but he knew the hospital wouldn't let her go. There was a nursing shortage for one thing, and the nurse had been employed at St. Vincent's for nearly thirty years. "I know I don't have to remind you that we *are* a Catholic hospital, Dr. Knowles," the head nurse stated, peering up at him over her bifocals.

His patient's case prompted him to research the other abortion providers around Albany, of which there were few, including the office that had so severely damaged his patient. He was shocked to discover that these clinics offered patients only a local anesthesia during the procedure, instead of the preferred intravenous drugs, like Versed and fentanyl, which not only obliterated pain but also quelled the emotional stress of the event. It seemed to him a decisively punitive omission, and he likened it to having root canal without novocaine. When he raised the issue at a gynecology conference on medical ethics, a doctor from one of the big hospitals upstate snorted and said, "I have no sympathy for women who get themselves into this situation."

On any given Wednesday afternoon, Michael performed sixteen abortions in four hours. The way he saw it, he had thirty seconds to make a connection with the patient, to make her feel like she wasn't just a hunk of flesh. Most of the cases were routine, but there were also stories that made his hair stand on end. Once, after examining a thirteen-year-old girl who'd been raped by both her brother and her father, on separate occasions, *and* was twenty-five weeks pregnant at the time, he'd excused himself and gone into the men's room to vomit.

How to process these acts he could not say. He stored them up like mementos of a nightmare. The most pathetic aspect of his work was the reality that the majority of his patients who came in to terminate a pregnancy were hardly able to take care of themselves, let alone an infant. A doctor's role was to decipher the cause of an illness. But there was no easy remedy for sexual misconduct or apathy. It was an enormous ugly mess and it oozed into every corner of society. It was easy to practice war from the high tower, he realized. But when you were down on the ground, getting blood on your hands, you saw things differently.

One night, before leaving the Medical Arts Building, Michael found a strange pamphlet in his mailbox. Cheaply produced, it looked like a comic book, its characters rendered in blue and black ink. The main character, the Abortionist, was a short, disorderly man with a five o'clock shadow and a nose that resembled a dill pickle. They'd dressed him in undershorts and a T-shirt with his beer belly sticking out. His dirty white coat had pockets crammed with whiskey bottles and cigarettes. A fat cigar protruded from his huge, salivating lips. *The Abortionist is unclean. The Abortionist is a whore chaser, a bumbling alcoholic, a filthy embarrassment to the medical profession.* He put on his coat and stuck the pamphlet in his pocket.

He noted the time; it was six o'clock. Anxious to get home, to spend some time with the kids, he grabbed his coat, but Finney stopped him on his way out the door. "Michael! Got a minute?"

Here we go, he thought. "Of course."

They went into Bianco's office, the walls of which were covered with pictures of the infants he'd delivered over his thirty-year career. Bianco was sitting behind his desk with his bifocals on, dictating charts into a microphone. He turned off the tape when they walked in and stood up, extending his hand to Michael for a shake. Bianco had a stout build and long sideburns framing his bald head. The nurses joked that he had no fashion sense. Everyone gave him ties for his birthday, one more outrageous than the next. Today's tie had Bugs Bunny on it. "From my kid," he explained. His "kid" was thirty-two. Finney, on the other hand, projected a good-old-boy image in his khaki pants and striped shirts and little bow ties. His freckled skin and red hair gave him a wholesome innocence, but the man was no pushover. The younger married women gravitated toward him, Michael had noticed. Bianco's patients were on the older side, women he knew from the club.

When Michael had joined the group, his partners had made it clear to him that they were both Republicans. "Vote for Nash or your job is hash," Finney had said to him once, jokingly, but Michael knew he wasn't really kidding. Earlier in the year, they'd asked Michael to contribute $10,000 to the Republican Party. "They're looking out for the docs, Mike," Bianco had pressed. "Do us a favor and throw some money their way."

Michael had done no such thing.

"Take a seat, Mike," Finney said, and Michael sat down.

"What's up?"

"Just wanted to catch up." Bianco shrugged, hypercasual. "How are things going?"

"Things are going great." Already Michael felt defensive.

Bianco squinted at him. "You seem just a wee bit unfocused of late."

"What gives you that impression?"

Bianco patted the stack of charts. "I believe these are your charts I'm dictating. I have to admit, it's a bit tricky reading your handwriting."

Michael began to apologize, but Bianco cut him off. "No need to apologize. We've all been under stress from time to time. And I don't mind helping you out if that's what's necessary."

"I guess I am under stress," Michael admitted. "My wife and I . . ."

"No need to go there," Finney said. "Been there, done that."

"You know, Michael, we were hoping to get you over to the club this weekend, join us for a round of golf before winter kicks in?"

This weekend he would be helping Celina at the clinic, but he didn't dare tell them that. "I'm not much of a golfer."

"We've got a terrific pro over there. This guy is just incredible. Let him give you a couple of lessons. You know, it's good for a young doc like you to get out on the course once in a while."

"All right. I'm sure I can find the time," he offered, knowing it was a lie.

"You just tell us what you need, Mike. We're here to help you out. I know it's a bitch and a half doing so much call. We've been talking about hiring another man, putting an ad in the *Journal*. But, hey, until then don't let it beat you down. You need something, you just ask, *capisce?*"

Michael nodded and waited for a signal that the meeting was over, but nobody stood up. Then Finney said, "About that friend of yours."

"Sorry?"

"Celina James?" Finney tossed him a newspaper. "She's hit the big time, front-page news."

Michael glanced at the paper. The photograph showed Celina standing in front of the clinic among a throng of protestors. Bianco and Finney were waiting for his reaction; they may as well have been holding a spotlight at an interrogation. "I hear she's doing well," Michael said plainly.

"Has she approached you?" Bianco asked.

"What?"

Finney cleared his throat and changed the tact. "She may approach you, Michael. I hear they need doctors. She usually gets the rejects." Finney looked at him meaningfully. "Nobody with any class would do that."

Michael understood that they suspected him, but Finney didn't need to know for sure. The point of the meeting was to let Michael know they didn't approve and that, if he was involved with Celina James, they expected him to end the arrangement immediately.

Michael shrugged in denial. "We never got along," he said. "She hates my guts."

"Really?" Bianco said, noticeably relieved.

"We used to give her a hard time when she was an intern. I remember this four-hundred-and-fifty-pound woman came into the ER. I made her do the rectal. Her first time. She never forgave me."

Bianco chuckled. "We don't support what she's doing, Michael. I hope you understand that. We have our reputation to think of. I know I don't have to remind you that this is a very small town."

"Of course."

"Good." Finney flashed a smile. "It's like my grandfather used to say: you lie down with dogs, you get fleas."

The meeting broke up and Michael said good night and walked outside. He felt queasy suddenly, and couldn't imagine getting into his car. A walk would do him good, he thought, and he started up the sidewalk in the direction of Washington Park. The meeting with his partners had troubled him. He knew, eventually, that they'd find out. It wouldn't be long now.

He reached the park, where huge forsythia bushes scrawled their branches along the sidewalk. The sun had begun to set and the light glimmered like fire off the windows of the brownstones. They were lovely old buildings, all lined up next to one another. Regardless of gentrification, Washington Park was still a marginal area, but there was history here, and grace. It was easy to imagine women in long dresses, and horses with carriages, and lamplighters lighting the old gaslights.

Exhausted suddenly, he found his way to a bench. Obviously he was stressed, he thought. Christ, he could hardly breathe. He waited, taking deep breaths, squinting at the sun's gold reflection in the windows of the buildings. A young woman appeared suddenly, unfolding out of the city landscape, and joined him on the bench. He recognized her immediately, the girl he'd seen outside the clinic that first night. He remembered her long black hair, which again was twisted into braids. She had on her track team jacket. "Hey, there," he said, but she did not return the greeting, and it left him cold. She began to adjust the laces on her sneakers, tying and retying them, and mumbled quietly, without looking at him, "You should know you're being watched. They know everything about you." She glanced at him for a split second. "Be careful."

With that, she got up and resumed her run, her braids swinging to and fro against her back. Again, he read her name on the back of the jacket: SAWYER. He looked around stealthily, but it was impossible to judge if he was being watched in such a large place. Skateboarders circled the monument in the center of the park. There were young couples with children near the playground. Another young couple was kissing on an adjacent bench. If the girl had gone to the trouble of warning him, he had to assume that there *was* someone out there watching him, someone he couldn't see. He stood up and started walking down Willet Street. A bar on the corner caught his eye and he retreated into it and ordered a glass of beer, glad for the noisy distraction of the place. He felt weak, suddenly. *They know everything about you:* the girl's words echoed in his head like a foreboding refrain. He thought of calling Annie but made no effort to do so. He drank the glass of beer and left the money on the bar and went back outside. He made his way along the street, walking quickly, brushing the shoulders of strangers. The clinic on South Pearl Street was five blocks away and he found himself walking toward it. He desperately wanted to see Celina.

The McDonald's on the corner was crowded with teenagers hanging out under the yellow lights. Someone's boom box was blasting a rap tune and Michael could feel its pulsing beat under his feet. He was the only white person around. The clinic looked dark, but when he pushed the buzzer Celina's voice immediately responded. "Yes?"

"It's Michael."

She unlocked the door and let him in. They stood there for a moment in the dark foyer. She still had on her white coat, but her hair was down and full on her shoulders. He handed her the pamphlet he'd gotten in the mail.

"I got a whole stack of those in the back. Terribly sophisticated stuff, isn't it? Here, I'll put it in the paper shredder, where it belongs."

They walked back toward the offices. They stood there watching the paper glide through the shredder. He told her about the girl in the park. "She's got wings on her jacket."

"Albany Track. I was on that team, too, once."

"Her name's Sawyer."

"Seems to me," she said, frowning, scanning the wall of charts, "seems to me I had a patient by that name. Ah, yes, here she is." She pulled out a file and flipped through it, then handed it to him. "Here's your guardian angel. Theresa Sawyer. I did a D & C on her last year. She was thirteen."

He opened the file and read it.

"What were you doing in the park?"

"I needed some air," he said, and told her about the meeting with his partners. "They warned me about you."

"Oh, they did, did they?" She seemed almost pleased.

"I hear you only hire the rejects."

"Yeah, right. Remind me now—you were what, fourth in your class at Harvard?"

"Third, actually."

"Some reject. I guess I know how to pick 'em." She smiled at him. "Your partners aren't too fond of me."

"It won't be long before they find out."

"Do you even care? They're assholes."

"They're my partners, Celina." The comment pissed him off. "I have to care what they think. It's not like I can afford to lose my job right now. I've got kids, you know. I've got expenses. We're different people, you and me."

"You got that right." Now she was offended.

"I just meant we have different priorities."

She spun around. "What do you know about my priorities?"

"I know this place is one of them."

"Don't do me any favors, Michael." She opened a closet and pulled out her coat.

"I didn't come here to fight," he said. But she was a bundle of tension, buttoning the coat, pulling a crumpled tissue out of the pocket and blowing her nose. "Hey." He put his hand on her shoulder. "I'm not going anywhere. You don't have to worry about that."

She glanced up at him apologetically. "What if they ask you to stop working here?"

"I tell them to go fuck themselves."

She shook her head. "Now I feel stupid."

"Don't."

"You know me, hot under the collar."

"Oh, yes," he said. "I remember that. That temper of yours has gotten you far."

"Sometimes I wonder how far," she said. "The truth is, I don't know what I'd do without you."

At that moment, those were the words he needed to hear. "Are you worried, Celina? Are you frightened?"

She looked at him. "All the time."

In the spirit of solidarity, they went out for a few beers together, reminiscing about their residency days, carefully avoiding the subject of their past intimacy. Still, it seemed to haunt their conversation, and he was grateful that she didn't bring it up.

It was after eleven when he finally made it home. The house was quiet. He hoped Annie was asleep because it was late and he hadn't called her and he knew she'd be angry. He didn't know why he hadn't called. It wasn't something he'd ever done before. He went to the kitchen and poured himself a glass of Coke and realized that he hadn't eaten dinner. For a moment the house was silent, forgiving, but then he heard her on the stairs.

"Where've you been?" she said, entering the kitchen in her robe, her expression disorganized, ambivalent. Her eyes looked red and glassy. "I've been worried sick."

"I should have called. I apologize." He finished his drink and put the glass in the sink.

"What were you doing?"

Without looking at her, he moved into the hallway. Laboriously, he began to climb the stairs. He hadn't realized how tired he was. Annie followed him up and into the bedroom, where he began to undress.

"Michael?" she asked.

"I was at the office," he lied. "I was at the office, dictating charts."

"Why didn't you call me? I've been paging you for hours."

He took his pager out to show her. "I turned it off." A sinking feeling of dread came over him. *What was happening to them?* "The work has to get done, Annie," he said reproachfully. "I lost track of the time."

She said nothing, just sat there on the bed scrutinizing him.

"Look, I'm sorry," he said.

"I just don't understand."

"For God's sake, Annie! I fucked up, all right?"

Annoyed, he left her alone and went into the bathroom to shower. Standing under the steaming rain, he closed his eyes, letting the water onto his face. A growing tension had curled around their lives like the restricting tendrils of a vine. Neither of them seemed able to control it. And then it came to him: maybe he didn't *want* to.

When he opened his eyes he saw that Annie had entered the bathroom. Her shape, beyond the shaded glass, looked opaque and distorted. She leaned over the sink in her baggy boxers and T-shirt, washing her face. The image was so familiar to him that it made him want to get out and hold her. More than anything, he wanted to make her understand how much he loved her, but the words would not come and she was in no mood to listen.

"Kids okay?" He asked from the doorway, drying himself off.

"They miss their father."

She climbed into bed wearily and grappled in her nightstand drawer for a sleeping pill. "I can't sleep, you've gotten me so upset." She swallowed the pill and dropped down into her pillow. "I thought something happened to you tonight."

"Nothing happened."

"I was about to call the police."

Michael sat down heavily on the bed and rubbed his face and he kept his face there in his hands, without looking at her.

"Who comes first for you, Michael?" she asked. "Who comes first in your life?"

"You do," he said softly, sheepishly. "Of course you do. And the kids. You know that, Annie."

"I don't know it. Not anymore."

"I don't believe that."

"I'm too upset now to sleep next to you." She grabbed her pillow and walked out of the room and went downstairs to the study. He heard the door shut. He didn't know why he had lied to her. He suspected it had something to do with his guilt, but of what he was guilty he could not say for certain. He felt vulnerable, frightened; yet he could not discuss these feelings with his wife. Overcome, he curled up on the bed and shook. He shook and shuddered and the whole world went dim.

Confusion had burrowed in Michael's brain like a small, helpless animal, and his only escape from it was on his bike. When he rode he could think things through. He woke early the next morning and dressed, avoiding the cold reproach of the study door. Outside it was cool and windy and the air carried the heady scent of fallen apples. He pulled on his helmet and opened the barn and wheeled out the bike. It was an agile piece of equipment and he loved having it. He looked up at the white clapboards of the old house, imagining his sleeping family inside it, and was struck with a momentary sense of calm.

If they are going to kill me, so be it, he thought. He would not live in fear. He would not hide from the world.

His route was twenty-two miles long, through the town of High Meadow and then due north on 66, around Crooked Lake and back, passing the sheep farm down Shaker Road. The roads were winding, with little traffic, and he concentrated on working his body, pushing himself slightly harder than he had before. The black road spilled away beneath him as he tunneled the wind. There was the yellow line luring him, the wind in his ears like a song.

After his fifth mile he allowed himself to relax and retreated into his riding head, an intense, abeyant place without sound. On the stretch of road outside the village, it began to drizzle. He thought of turning back, but a mile later the sun was out again. Miraculously, he saw a rainbow. Suddenly, out of nowhere, he heard someone approaching on another bike. He glanced back over his shoulder and saw a man dressed in high-tech biking attire, wearing a black helmet. The man had a surgical mask over his nose and mouth and dark sunglasses. What surprised Michael most was the man's speed; he had caught up in a matter of seconds. They were shoulder to shoulder when the biker withdrew a pump like a sword from his backpack and thrust it out toward Michael's rear tire. Michael pedaled harder, but the man was determined and shoved the pump through Michael's spokes. Michael went down. He rolled off the bike into a ravine. The bike had crumpled, the rear wheel bent beyond repair. He could feel a sprain swell up in his ankle, as he climbed back up to the road. *Son of a bitch.* He searched the distance, but the road was vacant, just an eerie mist rising off of it.

Michael didn't want to leave the bike, but he knew he could not carry it all the way. The isolated road presented few options. No telephones. Cars passed infrequently. There wasn't much else to do but walk, and he put his thumb out when a car went past. Before too long a green pickup truck pulled up. TUTTLE'S MOBIL was printed on the door. The driver leaned across the seat to open the door. He had on orange coveralls, a safety match in his mouth. Mirrored sunglasses reflected Michael's own face back to him in duplicate.

"What happened to you?" the man wanted to know.

"Someone knocked me off my bike," he exclaimed. "Look what they did to my bike!"

"Now, why would a person do that?" the man asked, uninterested in hearing an answer.

"Are you going to town?"

"You're in luck. Throw the bike in the back."

Michael loaded the bike and got in the truck.

"I guess somebody up there's looking out for you," the man smirked.

The truck smelled sweet, like pipe tobacco. They drove without saying much of anything and Michael was glad when they got into town. The man pulled into the Mobil station and they both got out. "Appreciate it," Michael said. The man grunted, then pulled the truck around to the side of the garage and went into the little office. Michael noticed a bumper sticker on the rear fender. BELIEVE IN YOURSELF: CHOOSE LIFE.

22

THE NEXT AFTERNOON, Annie discovered a small package at her office door. It was wrapped in postal paper and tied up with twine. Annie took it into her office and eagerly unwrapped it, thrilled to discover a painting by Simon Haas. The canvas was no larger than a postcard and depicted purple grapes on a plate. Not just ordinary grapes. These grapes bulged and sprawled indecently across the canvas. Annie gasped, bringing her hand to her mouth. She laughed abruptly, spraying the painting's surface with spit. The phone rang. She was almost too frightened to answer it. "Hello?"

"Are you hungry yet?" It was Haas.

Starved, she thought. "It's a lovely painting," she said. "Thank you. It was very nice of you."

"There was nothing nice about it, I assure you."

"I'm glad to see that you're painting again."

"You inspired me."

"I refuse to take responsibility for that."

"You can refuse all you want, but it's the truth."

"I'm glad. That's a good thing." She didn't know what else to say to him. This famous painter. This enigmatic icon of modern art.

"Yes, it's a good thing. It's a very good thing. I'd like to return the favor. I'd like to inspire every inch of you."

The very idea of it terrified her. "Well," she said. "I don't know what to say. The truth is, I haven't been properly inspired in a very long time."

"Well, then, I suggest we get started right away."

"I have to go," she told him.

"Will you think about it?"

"Yes, I'll think about it."

They hung up, and for the next hour and a half she did absolutely nothing but sit there and think about him. When she had finally had enough of it, she got her things and went out. *I have no time for this,* she thought. *I'm a* mother, *for God's sake. I'm a married woman.* What he wanted with *her* eluded her.

She had a few minutes to spare before getting the kids and decided to stop at Brewster's to pick up some groceries. She had an uncanny desire for grapes. Rushing toward the produce section, Annie felt delirious with excitement. She ran her fingers over the tender, swollen fruit in the same way one caressed the keys of a piano, then chose an ample bunch and set them gently in her cart.

Heading toward the cashier, she turned down the cereal aisle; to her complete astonishment, Lydia Haas was standing at the end of it. She didn't see Annie, her back half-turned away from her, and she was wearing her shabby toggle coat and muddy boots. Annie stopped where she was, hoping to back away before being seen, but Lydia's odd behavior compelled her to stay a moment and observe. Lydia had taken down a box of Froot Loops, the contents of which she began to vigorously consume, shoving handfuls of cereal into her mouth. With each thrust of her hand, cereal spilled out onto the floor, but the woman seemed determined and when she finally found the prize at the bottom of the box, an expression of delight lit her face up like neon.

Time to go, Annie thought.

The store manager appeared at Lydia's side with a broom and dustpan. Annie took advantage of the disruption and turned around, paid for the groceries, and got out of there. In the car, more than a little surprised at herself, she plucked a grape and ate it, savoring the sweet thrill of its pulp.

Arriving at High Meadow Elementary, she found the kids waiting out front, looking forlorn and bedraggled. Henry was pouting. "What's the matter, Henry?" she asked when they got into the car.

"The kids ran away from me at recess," he said. "No one wants to play with me. It's because of Daddy."

"What do you mean?" she asked, incredulous.

"Daddy kills babies," Rosie piped in.

Annie's heart churned. "Daddy is doing something very important. And some people don't understand it. Some people think it's wrong, but others don't. It's a very hard subject and people have strong feelings about it. I know it's a lot to ask, but you're going to have to be very brave now. You're going to need a very thick skin. People are mean. They'll say things that hurt. And you've got to be strong." She turned down their street, relieved to be home. "Let's get the mail."

When they'd first moved in, Henry had painted the mailbox green and put yellow flowers all over it. He had written their name in wobbly black letters and turned the o in KNOWLES into a smiley face. Ever since, it had been his job to retrieve the mail. Annie pulled the car up to the box and with routine importance he put his window down. He leaned out and opened the metal door, but instead of getting the mail, his arm retracted like a snake had bitten him. "Gross!" he yelped.

"What's the matter, Henry?"

"There's a baby in there!"

"What?" Annie hurried out of the car and walked around to the mailbox, feeling as though she were being watched. There were a million places to hide out there. Taking a deep breath, she opened the mailbox and looked inside. Henry wasn't kidding. There *was* a baby inside it.

Not a real one, but it *looked* real. Its arms reached out from the darkness within as if from a womb. Its skull was dented and had been dipped in bloody paint. Gingerly, Annie pulled it out slightly, just enough to see that someone had written DON'T KILL ME, MAMA! across its chest.

"It's hurt, Mommy." Rosie put her head out the car window. "It's bleeding!" she cried. "Can we bring it inside and fix it?"

"It's not real, Rosie. No. We can't." Annie pushed the doll back in and slammed the box shut. Back in the car, the children were strangely quiet, heady with judgment. She couldn't help wondering what they were thinking. She pulled the car into the garage and ushered the kids into the house. Once inside, she dead-bolted the door and closed the curtains. She put the TV on for the kids, then paged her husband at the hospital. He called back at once. "You need to come home."

At the first sound of Michael's car, Annie instructed the children to stay put and grabbed her coat and ran outside. Michael was stiff, angry. "What is it? What happened?"

"Look in the mailbox."

He opened the box and peered inside. For a moment he just stood there, staring at it. "What the . . . ?"

"It's weird, isn't it?"

"This is fucked." He grabbed the doll and pulled it out. Upon closer examination, the doll looked incredibly lifelike, wearing Pampers, its face pinched and pink like a newborn infant's. Michael shoved it back in the box and slammed the door shut.

"Let's call the police."

"I already did. They're sending someone," Annie said, and, as if on cue, a patrol car pulled up the driveway. To Annie's relief, Sheriff Baylor stepped out. He was an imposing man in a brown leather jacket and regulation brown trousers. Annie knew his wife from the PTA, and Michael had delivered his children.

"Sheriff." Michael shook the cop's hand. "Thanks for coming."

"What's going on here, Doc?"

"Somebody put a doll in our mailbox," Annie said.

"A doll?"

"A bunch of fanatics. I consider it a threat," Michael added.

"A threat, huh? I don't like the sound of that."

Baylor opened the box. "Now what in heck?" Squinting inside with apparent distaste, he turned on his flashlight to get a better look. "A doll?"

"We know who did it," Michael said. "We want to file a report."

The sheriff pulled the doll out and read the words that had been scrawled across its chest. "I don't get it," Baylor said. "What's it supposed to mean?"

"It's a threat," Michael said. "There's a group of people who don't like doctors like me."

"Oh?" Baylor scratched his head. His expression changed slightly, revealing his discomfort with the subject. He shook his head. "What do you suppose they want?"

Annie and Michael exchanged a look.

"They want me to stop doing abortions," Michael said.

"Well, now." Baylor scratched his head again. "We've never had a problem like this before. We've never had anything like this here in High Meadow."

"We want to file a report," Michael repeated. "We want something on file just in case."

"In case what?"

"In case things get worse."

"Well, the truth of the matter is, Dr. Knowles, there's no real danger here. A little neighborly harassment is all, seems to me."

"There's nothing neighborly about it." Michael raised his voice. Annie could hear a faint echo coming back with every word he spoke. "I pay taxes on this land and I consider it a violation of my rights. I don't give a goddamn what you call it, call it *trespassing* if you want, but I want a report and I want it filed." Michael took Annie's hand and led her back into the house. Baylor stood there for a moment, staring at the doll in the mailbox, then took out his pad.

When they were finally in bed Michael said, "The cops around here aren't used to dealing with this sort of thing. Raccoons in attics, foxes in chicken coops, but not this."

"I'm not used to dealing with it either." She looked at him. "You know

I believe in what you're doing, Michael, you know where I stand on the issue. But what if things *do* get worse? I've read about these people. Doctors have been killed. Remember the doctors in Florida? That guy in Buffalo was shot in his own home."

"What do you want me to do, Annie? Quit? And then what? They threaten somebody else? And what about in ten years, when Rosie's in high school and, God forbid, gets pregnant? What then? How can you, in good conscience, suggest that I quit? What happened to the feminist I married? Where's my journalist wife?"

"She became your children's mother." Her eyes were burning. "I don't want to lose you over this."

"Look, I know you're scared. But think of all those women out there. They come to me in desperation. I'm their last resort. And they expect nothing. They're so grateful. I just can't justify giving up the clinic when I see such a need. I can't. Not for those creeps."

"What about for us?"

He didn't answer her. He turned away from her and went to sleep. She felt like they were standing on opposite sides of a great abyss. How to build a bridge across? she wondered. How to cross without falling into the deep black hole?

Henry woke her out of a deep sleep. "Mommy!"

Annie blinked at the clock: seven-fifteen. Michael had left for the clinic hours ago. He was probably already into his second case by now. "Henry, it's *Saturday*. Why aren't you sleeping?"

"Rosie locked her door. She won't let me in."

Annie got out of bed and pulled on her robe. She went to Rosie's door and knocked. "Rosie?" Annie tried the door. "Rosie Knowles, you open this door this minute."

"I don't want to," Rosie answered, wobbly voiced.

"Why not?"

"Because I'm mad."

"What about?"

The door opened. Rosie was holding the doll from the mailbox. She'd wrapped it up in one of her baby blankets. A chill went through Annie; a lump rose in her throat.

"Gross, Rosie," Henry said.

Rosie's eyes welled up with tears and she began to close the door again. Annie caught it in her hand. "Let me see, lovey."

Rosie held out the doll. She'd washed off the blood and had wrapped its deformed plastic head with every conceivable kind of Band-Aid. Annie crouched down and spoke quietly. "Is she feeling better?"

"I saved her. She didn't like it in the mailbox. It was scary and cold."

"You've done a very nice job, Rosie." Annie took Rosie into her arms and held her close.

"I just want to play with her, okay, Mommy?"

Annie nodded. "But no locking doors."

"I'm going to introduce her to all my dolls."

"That's a good idea." Annie swallowed hard, but the lump in her throat was still there.

Michael had the day off on Sunday. They avoided each other, drifting through the hours and accomplishing very little. Every time she tried to talk to him about the clinic he changed the subject. On Monday, after her morning class, she went for a swim. The pool was empty and cold and she swam hard, trying to sort out her feelings. Michael's obstinacy made her angry. She could give him an ultimatum, she thought: Quit the clinic or quit the marriage. But she didn't feel right about that either. Although she hated to admit it, the Life Force propaganda was getting to her. Images of twisted fetuses and nearly full-term infants with bashed-in skulls. She found them incredibly troubling. On the other hand, no matter how many times they called Michael a murderer, they couldn't be further from the truth. The issue seemed to be more about control than anything else. They wanted it; they knew how to get it.

Another swimmer had entered her lane and was coming up behind her. Undeterred, she swam harder and flip-turned at the wall, only to glimpse Simon's gold cap swiftly approaching. He was the last person she wanted to see just now. Striving to keep her lead on him, she cranked down the lane, feeling the whirl of his turn behind her. But he caught up easily and passed her, running his hand, like a fish, along her thigh, sending a wicked rush through her loins. The desire quickly turned to anger, *how dare he,* and she pushed herself to compete, her body pumping with adrenaline until she passed the cocky bastard and took the lead back. When she reached the wall, she climbed out and disappeared into the dressing room with her heart pounding. *Touché,* she thought.

Stepping into her clothes, she realized she was shaking. She didn't know what to do about Simon Haas and it terrified her.

Gathering her things, she rushed into the corridor, heading toward the double doors that led to the parking lot, praying she wouldn't run into him again. The hall was empty and a smile played on her lips as she pushed open the heavy door and stepped out into the rain. But there he was, waiting for her under an umbrella.

"Surprise, surprise," he said.

"I would have thought you'd be the type to primp," she said.

"I didn't want you to get wet."

"It's only rain."

"You're right." He closed the umbrella. "Getting wet is much more exciting."

She stood there looking at him in the rain. If only he wasn't so goddamn appealing.

"You wouldn't want to get a drink or anything? There's a nice little bar across the street."

"What for?"

"Maybe I shouldn't answer that."

She frowned, bustling toward her car.

"Look, Annie, I'm sorry if I've distracted you."

She turned to face him. "Distracted me?"

"Your cozy little life."

The comment hurt; that was hardly the life she was leading these days. "You have no idea about my life. You have no idea what we're going through right now. You want to know about my life? There's nothing cozy about it."

"I'm sorry, Annie. Truly. I shouldn't make assumptions about your life."

"It's not that I don't want—"

"People have been making assumptions about me for years and, frankly, I'm sick and fucking tired of it. And that's why I wanted to ask you a favor."

"A favor?"

"I want you to write something about me." He looked at her. "I know you want to."

She stood there; he had her now.

"Maybe you haven't admitted it to yourself," he went on. "But that's who you are. You can't help it, and I wouldn't expect you to be any different. And it's a good story. People have been trying to get it out of me for years. Well, guess what, I'm ready to spill the beans."

She swallowed hard. She felt a little sick. "I wonder what's so interesting about a middle-aged artist on the verge of extinction?" She was testing him now.

"That's just it," he said. "That's the part they like most—the scent of failure. It's quite intoxicating, actually."

"You don't believe that. And anyway, you're not a failure."

"Thank you, Annie. It means a lot to me. But as we've already established, you're a romantic. You always see the best in people. It's liable to get you into trouble." They looked at each other and he sighed. "Assuming you would agree, I took the liberty of arranging an editor. I hope you don't mind. She's a friend of mine." He handed her a slip of paper with a name and phone number on it. "She's at *Vanity Fair*." He glanced at her for a reaction, which she would not supply, and he frowned with obvious disappointment. Annie could tell he had expected more from her, but with calculating measure, she showed him nothing, not even the slightest glimmer of pleasure, and it clearly agitated him. His voice soured. "I said they could have the interview on one condition, that you be the one to write it. I have to warn you, it took some convincing. Your name didn't ring a bell. She had to look you up on the computer. Said she wasn't sure you had the experience, didn't know if you could handle it. I gather you're not quite in the loop." He smiled coldly. "She's waiting for your call."

"She was right," Annie said. "You're out of my league. You are one tough subject, Mr. Haas."

He shook his head. "You don't understand."

"Understand what?"

"You're the only one I trust." He seemed utterly pleased with his tactics of manipulation.

"Don't kid yourself. I'm as cutthroat and heartless as all the rest of them. In fact, I'm worse."

"I have feelings for you, Annie." He reached out and cupped her chin in his hand. "I've been dreaming about you."

"Please stop dreaming," she said softly. "It's time to wake up."

Leave it alone, she told herself. *Stay away from him.* But that afternoon, she found herself dialing *Vanity Fair* from her office telephone. She asked for Tina Chase and was connected with her secretary, who asked Annie to identify herself. To Annie's surprise, the secretary put her through right away. "I've been reading over some of your work." Chase spoke with a British accent and had a deep smoker's voice. "Strong stuff. If you can pull this off before the retrospective, I imagine you'll be fairly desirable to have around in the future."

Retrospective? "Forgive me, but I'm not aware of a retrospective."

"At the Whitney. The first week in April, I believe. They're doing a whole thing on the body painters. They're doing Haas, Lucian Freud, Fischl, Pearlstein, a whole bunch of fabulous people. Lots and lots of naked bodies. It should be very exciting." She hesitated, inhaling a fresh cigarette. "We'd like to print your piece right before the show. That gives you about three months to finish it. It's not much, but I'm sure you can handle it."

"Sure. No problem," Annie said, trying to sound confident when in fact she was trembling.

"I hear he's quite the animal." Chase waited for a reply.

"Well, yes," she said, "he has that reputation."

"Makes for good storytelling," the editor said. "Don't be shy, Ms. Knowles."

"No, of course not."

"Righto, then. Keep in touch. Best of luck."

The woman hung up. It came to Annie that this was the break she'd been waiting for. She hadn't earned it, not really, but she'd grabbed it just the same. She'd been waiting for something like this for a long time. Now that it had finally come, it was impossible to resist. But it wasn't something to celebrate, not like this.

Rain began to fall outside the South Cottage. When she stepped into the courtyard Simon Haas was waiting for her. "You didn't mention a retrospective."

"I wanted it to be a surprise."

"That's very exciting."

"So you'll do it? You'll write the article?"

"Yes, but don't expect anything more from me. And don't expect me to thank you, either."

He smiled, watching her closely.

"I mean it."

"No you don't. Why can't you just admit it to yourself."

"Simon. Please."

"Please what?" He came toward her, backed her up against the building, the old brown stones, and moved his enormous hands under her coat. "Please what?" he repeated, urging her back into the vestibule, into the small hallway where the bathrooms were. Now they were kissing, consuming each other, and he pulled her into the men's room and locked the door. She didn't look at him; she couldn't and he seemed to know this, and kept his eyes on her body, which shook in his hands. It was quiet, and nearly dark, just a rectangle of light in the small window, and all the faucets were dripping, *gossiping,* and he kissed her violently, working her body into a funnel of pleasure that begged to spin apart. *I will* not *do this,* she thought.

"I can't." Annie pushed him away, roughly, but then her voice crawled out weakly. "I can't, Simon. I really can't."

"You can."

"No."

She left him there and ran out into the cold, across the quad to her car, hoping he wouldn't follow, knowing, somehow, that he would not. The quad was empty, silent. A thin layer of mist hovered over the grass. She got into the car and locked the doors and sat there for a moment, trying to collect herself. Her body rushed with anticipation. The awful thing was that she *did* want him. Her body would not let her deny that.

Annie started the engine and turned on the heat. She felt as though she were caught between her two selves: a wife and mother versus the woman underneath. Was it so wrong to want to be with another man? she wondered. Was it so wrong to desire someone other than her husband, and to be desired? Was it so unnatural? It didn't *feel* unnatural, but it went against everything she'd been taught.

What are you doing, Annie? she asked herself, and for the first time in her life she didn't have a clue.

———

"I have some news," she told Michael when he got home from work. She handed him a beer.

"Are we celebrating?"

"Yes, as a matter of fact." She clinked her bottle against his. "I've been asked to write an article about Simon Haas."

"You mean the dead artist?"

"He's not *dead*, Michael—don't be mean. It's for *Vanity Fair*."

"Wow. Hot shit. How'd you swing that?"

"He asked me to write it. He chose me."

"Really?" he said. "That old fart's trying to get into your pants."

"You may be right," she said seriously.

"He's not exactly your type, is he?"

"Not exactly. So, do you think I should do it?"

"What? Let him into your pants, or write the article?" He smiled and she found herself smiling back.

"Both."

"Hell, yes. Go for it." He rolled his eyes. "You're not *that* desperate, are you?"

"I just may be," she said.

23

SIMON HAD LEARNED early in the game that it was always best to be honest with Lydia, lest her imagination get the better of her, so that morning over coffee in the kitchen, he told her about the article Annie was going to write.

"I've consented to give an interview to *Vanity Fair* magazine" was how he put it. "It's about us."

"What?"

"Well, it's not about us, really. It's about me, my work."

"Your *work*?" She stood up and went to the window, watching the finches in the bird feeder. "I *am* your work."

Summoned by her small, indifferent back, he went to her and put his hands on her shoulders. "It's important for me. It's important for the new paintings."

"I don't give a damn about the new paintings."

A dark mood circled over his wife's head like a vulture. He put his lips to her neck and kissed her gently. "Please, Lydia. Please don't be sad."

"How can I help it," she said desperately, and twisted around in his arms. She looked like a little girl again with the soft sunlight on her face, and it brought him straight back to the awful day they'd met. "It's because of her, isn't it?"

"Because of who?" he said, feigning confusion, but he knew exactly who she meant.

"That woman. That new professor you like."

She knew him well, he gave her that. He also knew that each word he spoke was for her a jagged little knife opening a wound. "Well, yes, actually. She's a journalist. She's the one who's going to write it. Frankly, I think that's the real reason she's teaching at the college. Not that she'd ever admit to it."

Lydia's face went dull and she spoke so softly he could barely hear. "You got *her*?"

"I had nothing to do with that," he said defensively. "That was the magazine, not me."

She sniffled uncertainly. "She's going to interview you?"

"Just a bit. Nothing to worry about, though." It was time to go, he thought. He pulled on his coat and filled his cup with coffee.

"Nothing to *worry* about?"

"I don't plan on discussing anything personal, if that's what's worrying you. I don't plan on going into any detail."

Lydia stole a look at him.

"I'm sorry, but I have to go. I'm late." He kissed her and her hand flew up to her cheek as if to catch it, as if to keep the small token of love from flying away. He drank the coffee in one gulp, swallowing the burning liquid willingly, a punishment for the sins he would soon commit. Then he set down his cup and walked out, feeling her eyes on the back of his head, a sniper aimed and ready. One day she would finally pull the trigger, he thought, and it would not surprise him if it were soon.

24

A WEEK AFTER the mailbox incident, the phone rang at quarter to six in the morning. When Michael answered it, he heard Celina crying on the other end. "You'd better come down here," she told him.

Even from two blocks away Michael could see the confusion in front of the clinic. There were cop cars and television trucks, and a helicopter hovered overhead. The place was swarming with reporters. A cop stopped him at the parking lot and asked to see his ID. Through the windshield Michael could see that someone had spray-painted across the front of the building: AS SURELY AS I LIVE, I WILL GIVE YOU OVER TO BLOODSHED AND IT WILL PURSUE YOU. SINCE YOU DID NOT HATE BLOODSHED, BLOODSHED WILL PURSUE YOU.—EZEKIEL 35:6. The paint was red and dripped down the cement like blood.

He found Celina in her office, sitting behind her desk, a wreck. "Do you think we should cancel appointments?"

"We're not canceling anything," he said. "You've got a waiting room full of people out there."

She looked at him, her face ashen with fear. "I'm scared."

"We need more security here. We need a guard out there full-time. I found a Web site that sells bulletproof vests."

"Where's the money coming from for all this protection?"

"I'll pay for it."

"No, Michael," she said. "I never should have dragged you into this. I don't feel right about it. You've got kids. I never should have asked you for help. It was selfish of me. I regret it."

"Celina, you know I can't let you do this alone."

"I have this guilt." She made a fist against her heart. "I have this guilt in here, over you."

"Don't."

"I feel like I'm messing with your life, and I don't like it. I don't want you to feel like I took advantage of our past."

"I'm helping you because I think it's important. Not because of what we had. I'm not doing you any favors. My time's too valuable for that." He stood up. "Speaking of which, we've got people waiting out there. Let's get to work."

25

IN PREPARATION for the article on Simon Haas, Annie spent hours in the campus library trying to dig up information about him. Very little had been written; his entire youth remained a mystery. She found a few scant pieces in *The New York Times, Art Monthly, Art in America.* The few pictures of him, taken years before in his studio, showed Haas as a gangly young man with leonine hair and brooding eyes, wearing a white T-shirt and trousers, his bare feet splattered with paint. There was the ever-present cigarette, the demeanor of gloom. One of the featured paintings, *Disposable Love,* portrayed a man with silver loins in a motel room with a young girl—it was Lydia—who sat on the floor, naked, Indian style, eating French fries out of a cardboard container while watching the *Road Runner* cartoon on TV. The relationship between the two figures was left ambiguous. One did not know if they were lovers or not. One did not know if the girl was a prostitute, or a runaway, or even, perhaps, the daughter of the naked man. The suggestion of impropriety left the viewer hanging. Simon did not judge his subjects, nor did he judge his viewers for wanting to look.

Sifting through the photographs, she felt herself wanting to be the one person who could know him better than anyone else. His asking her to write the article had been a calculated method of seduction—she was certain of that now—and it provided each of them with a perfect excuse to spend time together. And she wanted that. Oh, yes, she wanted it. She had not chosen him, yet curiously he had come into her life. He seemed to know her in some significant way; he seemed *to know her,* voraciously, fundamentally, better than Michael did. How strange, she thought, remembering his hands on her body, urgently taking ownership.

She returned to her office and began to write an outline. There were gaps, of course, things she needed to find out. His life with Lydia was a mystery. Why had he dropped out of the art world so suddenly?

The phone shook her alert. A woman's voice came on the line. "This is Susannah calling for Simon Haas." The woman had a deep, velvety voice. "He'd like to know if you'd be willing to have lunch with him."

Momentarily disarmed, Annie said, "What?" *Who in God's name was Susannah?* And then she added uncertainly, "Lunch? Sure, what time?"

The woman muffled the phone with her hand and Annie could hear some giggling in the background. "One o'clock. He'll meet you on the path halfway."

Annie hung up, annoyed. Why hadn't he just called her himself? She went into the bathroom and looked at herself in the mirror. She hadn't planned on seeing him today and now regretted the old black turtleneck, the jean skirt that had seen better days. On her feet were a pair of clunky Bean boots and indecently holey wool socks. Her lipstick, which might have salvaged her appearance, was somewhere in her car, having rolled into the sticky abyss beneath her seat.

At ten of one she threw on her coat and went downstairs. The truth was, it felt good to be writing again. She remembered her days in the city during graduate school when, with the help of her father's connections, she'd gotten an internship at the *Times*. She had fond memories of her tiny studio apartment, living on coffee and cigarettes and the happy hour chicken wings they served at her neighborhood bar. Thirsty like a vampire when it came to her work, hunting down victims, winning their trust, then biting them in the throat. She'd given it up when Henry was born and they'd moved to Albany for Michael's fellowship. Motherhood had changed her; she had lost her fangs and had never thought she'd want them back. Until now.

The black path was thick with yellow leaves. Some of the students had gathered an enormous pile of them and were jumping in them like children. They called out to someone—it was Simon—and he said something and they all laughed. Everybody liked him, she realized. They all looked up to him even though he was enigmatic as a Hollywood icon. People liked the mystery, she thought, and he liked it, too. He did little to enlighten them.

Now he was coming toward her in his lumberman's coat, a black watch cap pulled over his ears, his violet scarf around his neck. Whenever she saw him her heart began to thump. "Who's the girl with the voice?"

"That would be Susannah. My secretary. Used to do phone sex. Amazing what a voice can do. Conjures up all sorts of exciting images. You're thinking tight sweater, short skirt, right? Couldn't be further from the truth. Stop by sometime and take a look. I don't think the scale goes up that high."

"You have your very own secretary? How'd you pull that off?"

"Lots of red tape. Stopped handing in grades, evaluations, et cetera. The following Monday Susannah was there." He smiled, thoroughly pleased with himself. They crossed the yard and headed toward the parking lot in the direction of his car. "She's my, how do you say, my conservator."

"Is your car actually running?"

"Yes, but be careful, she's very sensitive."

An old VW Bug, the pale orange color of acorn squash, pulled out of a spot and came toward them. The driver was Jack Spaull, smoking a pipe. He rolled his window down. "Afternoon, Simon. Annie."

"We're getting some lunch together," Annie offered. "Want to join us?"

"She's lying, Jack. I'm going to ravage her body as soon as I get the chance."

"That's marvelous. Couldn't think of a better way to spend the afternoon."

They all laughed.

"I've encouraged you to get to know each other better," Jack said. "Who knows, you may inspire each other."

"No doubt," Simon said.

Jack frowned playfully. "Drive safely, Simon."

"Always."

They watched him drive away.

"Shall we?" Simon opened the door dramatically, bowing as she entered, and closed it with the finesse of a valet. The car grumbled to a start and the radio came on, Aerosmith smashing the silence. Simon shut it off, grinning sheepishly. "Sorry."

"I didn't know you were into heavy metal."

"I'm into heavy, basically. Heavy is good. Heavy is really good."

"I bet you sing when you're alone."

"I do a lot of interesting things when I'm alone." He raised his eyebrows mysteriously.

"Let's hear a little melody."

"No, I couldn't. I'm very shy about my singing."

"Do you sing in the shower, too?"

"I sing opera in the shower, of course."

"Now, that I'd like to hear. I'm an opera enthusiast."

"An opera *enthusiast*? Well, now, I'm impressed."

"My mother loved opera. You'd hear it all through our house growing up."

"How sweet. How positively *cultured*."

"When I was home, that is."

"Oh yes, I nearly forgot. *Little Annie's away at school.* Miss Porker's, was it?"

"Very funny, Simon. *Porter's.* Of course *La Bohème* is my favorite."

"I expected that. Romantic that you are."

"I could cry when I listen to it." She looked out the window. Her heart felt tight suddenly. She didn't want to be talking about this right now. Not with him. "This is a wonderful car."

"It was my father's car. He won it in a game of cards. Only thing he ever gave me. One day he goes down into the cellar and hangs himself on a water pipe. Leaves me a note and the keys to his car."

"That's horrible, Simon. What did the note say?"

"*'So long, sucker.'*"

"My God, that's awful."

"Yeah, well. He wasn't Mr. Sensitive."

"And that's it?"

"He wrote a postscript with instructions about the car. Told me to change the oil every three thousand miles and check the brake fluid from time to time."

Her heart broke for him. "That must have been very difficult for you."

"Difficult? No. I hated the son of a bitch."

They were on the interstate, heading north toward Albany. He put the top down and it became too loud to talk. They drove side by side with the wind in their faces. The wet sun stretched over the rising city, its row houses, government buildings, and The Egg, where on several occasions she and Michael had gone to the theater. Simon got off the interstate at Arbor Hill and made his way through traffic to South Pearl Street. He parked outside of a tavern where a group of men had convened in a circle of ripped vinyl chairs to play pinochle. Simon took her hand and led her toward the adjoining walk-up, an orange brick row house, late nineteenth century, where they climbed up the stoop and went inside. "I have a studio here. On the third floor. I thought you'd like to see it."

The building was silent, desolate. Light poured in like milk from the old window in the roof. Pigeons were cooing, loud as rain. They went up, their footsteps echoing on the worn marble steps. His door was at the end. He took out a ring of keys. "I haven't been back here for a long time," he told her. "The truth is, I didn't want to come here alone."

Surprising herself, she touched his back, wanting him to know that she was happy to be there with him, even though she wasn't able to tell him this just now.

It was a large empty space with tall windows and scuffed wood floors. Several blank canvases leaned against the wall. He went to a cabinet and found a bottle of wine and two glasses. "I'll show you the terrace," he said, presenting the fire escape. They sat out in the sun and drank the wine, looking out on the Hudson, the port of Albany. "It's not such a bad town," he said. "I've been worse places."

"Where did you grow up?"

"The Bowery. My father was a crook."

"Where's your mother now?"

He shook his head. "I don't know." He looked out at the landscape. "Out there somewhere."

She sensed he wasn't telling her the whole truth. "Here in Albany?"

"We lost track of each other."

"What was she like?"

"My mother? She was pathetic."

"How so?" she pressed.

He looked at her fiercely. "She walked into one of those traps. Like a squirrel, bleeding all over herself, but couldn't do a damn thing about it."

Annie went quiet. She didn't want to ask him too many questions at once. The fact that he had arranged for her to write the article meant that he wanted her to know about certain aspects of his life, perhaps he was willing to tell her, but it would be on his terms, she was well aware of that. "When did you start painting?"

"I don't remember starting. It was just something I always did. I was good at it. My father hated that. He wasn't good at anything. He wasn't even a good thief."

"What did he steal?"

"Things. All kinds of useless things." He looked at her. "My mother."

The sun was lowering itself behind the dark buildings. Less than a half mile away, her husband was racing through the corridors of St. Vincent's. "I need to go soon," Annie said.

"Yes, I know."

"Why don't you paint this?" She gestured to the cityscape before them.

He smiled. "I suppose I could, couldn't I? But anyone could paint this. Even you."

She laughed. "No. I could not paint this."

He stood up, pulled her to her feet. The wine had made her light-headed. "It's not about rendering it. Just that word, *rendering.* Like something dead in the road. It's about much more than that. It's not what's there that matters. It's what you don't see. It's what the mind creates behind the closed door."

"What do you see when you look out there?"

He squinted out at the buildings, crammed together like crooked teeth. To Annie it was a downtrodden city, blighted by poverty and bureaucratic complacency. To Simon, she supposed, it was myriad shapes and colors. "I see dark rooms with yellow shades. Dirty windows that poor, snot-nosed children scratch their names into. Fat ladies with swollen feet. Fake teeth. Smoke." He took her hand and turned her toward him. "I see a woman standing on a fire escape with the sun in her eyes."

"Why did you stop painting?" she asked softly, and he didn't answer her. "Was it because of your wife?"

He shook his head, as though he didn't want to get into it. And then he said, "My wife is a dangerous woman. Like one of those bullets. She gets under your skin and rips you up in places you never knew existed."

"How can that be, Simon? She's young, she's practically a teenager."

"Oh, no." He grinned bitterly, shaking his head. "She was never that."

26

"I WAS A STUDENT when I met her," he told Annie. "At the Art Students League. I was living in Manhattan." They were sharing a booth in a small restaurant in south Troy. He'd brought her there because the place was far away from the college and it was unlikely that they would see anybody they knew. She'd ordered a bacon, lettuce, and tomato sandwich and he was having beer and onion rings. A couple of cops sat on stools at the counter, and another table was occupied by a group of women who might have been employees of the bank next door. Their table was in the back, where they had the smoking section all to themselves.

"Truthfully, I was an arrogant son of a bitch." Simon finished off his beer and ordered another one, and then he lit a cigarette. "Do you want the long version or the short one?"

"Unabridged," she said.

"Promise me you won't hate me."

"Why would I hate you?"

"It's a nasty story."

She reached out and took his hand. "I could never hate you."

Although he did not believe her, he began. "People called it a gift, my art, but I saw it as an affliction, a kind of tedious deformity." Even during the years of his youth, his extreme sensitivity had been a burden that often embarrassed him. As a young man, he had few friends, and so he focused on his work. At first, the canvas provided him with the ultimate escape, and like many of the notable painters before him, he painted pastoral landscapes and scenes of the hunt. For months he explored the small rural enclaves in upstate New York, flawlessly rendering cows and horses, stone walls, wide fields stippled with shadows and slender black trees. And then, on one of his journeys, something changed. He felt inexplicably drawn to the mystery of the back roads, the rusty trailers and flimsy shacks, the acres of grubby brown land. The lost yellow fields strewn with busted car parts. He saw the poverty he had known as a boy, the loss it caused, the emotional blight.

It's where she came from, his wife.

He first saw her in cutoff shorts and a man's work shirt, hanging sheets on the line behind her father's house. He hadn't been sure of her age; he had little experience with girls. He parked on the road and walked through the woods behind the house, where he could watch her without being seen. In the shade of the pine trees, he sketched her all afternoon. When she had finished the laundry she mowed the lawn, then sat on the back steps and drank a bottle of orange soda, a black cat twisting through her legs. It was almost dusk when he knocked on the front door. She opened it, looking at him curiously. She stood there, behind the screen, waiting. Up close, she was younger, and there were pimples on her cheeks.

"Portraits for sale," he said.

"Who is it?" a voice bellowed from inside the house.

The girl looked at him. "He wants to know who you are."

Simon walked in, toward the sound of the voice, and entered a small parlor where an old man lay on a couch under a wool blanket. The room smelled of sickness and stale cigarettes, and there were several medicines on the table at his side. The old man looked him over. "Whatever you're selling, we're not interested."

"How about a portrait of your daughter?" Simon said.

The girl's father was thin as a skeleton, wearing a worn green cardigan with holes in the sleeves. His hands were huge and yellow, like the claws of a buzzard. "Turn that damn thing off," he said, wagging his finger at the TV. The girl turned it off at once and stood by her father's side. The old man pulled himself up, and she propped the pillows behind him. "What is it you're selling?"

"Portraits, sir. I'm an artist."

The old man squinted at him with a sour smile. "Well, tickle me pink. An artist. Let me see something you've painted."

He could have shown the man the sketches he'd done that afternoon, but he said, "I don't have anything to show you. You're my first client of the day."

"First client of the day! Well, isn't that lush. It's nearly four o'clock."

"I've been roaming the countryside," he told him.

Her father scoffed. "Looking for a sucker like me?"

"Daddy, please," the girl said softly.

"How am I supposed to know if you're any good?"

"You'll have to take my word for it. You'll have to trust me."

The old man laughed. "Now, look, boy. I may be poor, but I ain't stupid."

"He has an honest face," the girl offered.

"An honest face," her father repeated with a grunt. "They're the worst kind. But you're too stupid to know that yet." He took a noisy drink of water and wiped his mouth. "If it's money you want, you won't find any here. We're factory people around here. You go down south, that's where you'll find your suckers."

"It's not the money, sir."

The old man laughed. "Can't take your eyes off her, can you?"

"Sir?"

"Looks just like her mama, only better. Cursed with it, is what I always said. I don't let her out much, see? 'Cause I know what they'll do to her. Give 'em a minute with her and that'll be it, a slut and a whore, lickety-split. Just like her mama was." The old man started to cough, a cascading hack that turned his face crimson. The girl got his water glass and helped him to a sip. When he had recovered, he leaned back against the pillows and lit another cigarette. "I'll tell you what, son. I got a feeling about you, understand? You've got ambition and I admire that in a man." He pulled a piece of tobacco off his tongue and nodded at his daughter. "I'm gonna let you paint the girl, but I ain't payin' for crap. It's got to be good, real good, understand?"

Simon went out to the car to get his paints and canvas and the wobbly easel he had stolen from the art school. The sun was low in the sky and the air smelled of wet earth and rain. When he went back inside he saw that the girl had put on lipstick and pinned her hair back in a barrette. He established himself in a corner of the living room, away from the scrutiny of the old man, who had turned the television back on, the volume up full blast. He sat the girl in a wooden chair and allowed his eyes to study her the way a scientist might observe a rare species of animal.

"Lydia, is it?"

She nodded shyly.

"I'm Simon Haas." He began to paint, then frowned, putting down his brush. He tilted his head this way and that. It was her hair, he realized. He went and took out the barrette and her long blond hair swung down over one eye. "There we go," he said. "That's much better." Then he tossed her a cloth. "Get that stuff off your lips."

She blinked as if he'd insulted her. "You don't need it," he said. "You look better without it." Her eyes returned to his and he smiled and he was relieved when she smiled back. He wet his brush. "How old are you?"

"Fifteen," she said, but he suspected she was lying.

He told her she looked older, which seemed to flatter her enormously. Girls like her were easy, he realized. He knew he could probably get her to do almost anything.

"Does your father know a lot about art?"

"My father knows a lot about everything. He didn't even graduate high school but he's the smartest person I know."

"What's the matter with him? Is he sick?"

"Cancer. In his lungs."

"Where's your mother?"

"Dead."

He looked at her strangely. "I'm sorry." He put down his brush and fiddled in his pocket for a cigarette. "Let's go out on the porch for a minute."

"All right."

They sat on the porch and he smoked. He dragged on his cigarette, looking at her face. He'd never seen such a beautiful creature; it made him tremble. "Do you go to school?"

"With the nuns," she said.

"I wanted to be a priest," he told her, "before I started painting."

This made an impression on her. "You'd have to hear confessions. You'd have to absolve people of their sins."

"Yes," he said quietly. "That's what I do with paint. I absolve people."

She looked at him curiously. "Can you do that for me?"

"You're just a girl," he told her. "You don't have any sins."

Her eyes were huge and sad, reminding him of those pictures of starving children in magazines. "But I do," she said.

He painted her all afternoon. The girl sat patiently, like a cat, and didn't complain once. She was like something under the earth, he thought. Would she bloom like a magnificent flower or be consumed like an ordinary turnip? He could feel a strange tension between them, as though the afternoon had been predestined, as though the turn he'd made down her father's road hadn't been arbitrary. Still, he didn't want to be there. There was something wrong in that house, a bizarre tension that at once compelled and frightened him. He stopped painting suddenly and threw a sheet over the canvas. He told the girl he'd be back tomorrow, knowing in his heart that he had no such intention.

He returned to the city with her face fixed in his memory. Her haunting eyes, expressing some inexhaustible sorrow. Her long, gangly frame, the pale skin mottled with cuts and bruises, mosquito bites, dirt and bicycle grease and tiny blades of grass. The little mounds of flesh that were her breasts. Her nipples, like sweet raisins waiting to be devoured. He reasoned that his was a painterly fascination, not a sexual one, but he doubted his own excuses. His attraction to her embarrassed him; he was nearly thirty-six.

In the city that night he avoided the other squatters and hurried up the back stairs to the fourth floor. Even though the building had been condemned, it still provided good shelter. There were fifteen of them living there together. Artists mostly. One musician who played guitar all day and night. It was hard to have any privacy. They tried. They made places for themselves. His mattress was in a room that had once been the pantry. There were shelves, where he kept his few belongings. The linoleum had curled, but most of the subflooring was intact. At night, when he lay on his mattress, he'd hear the rats tumbling behind the walls. He climbed onto his mattress and arranged the cardboard around himself, creating a room of his own. Privacy. He took out the sketches he had done of the girl pinning her father's laundry to the line. Her hands perched on the rope like small white birds. He had watched her mowing the lawn, the intensity in her face in the bright sunlight, the way her lean thighs exerted themselves under the pressure of the machine. The deep green color of the grass. Her glittering sweat. The wild yellow hair. The mystery in her eyes. He felt the alarming rush of an erection; it embarrassed him, it sickened him, but he could not ignore it, and he toiled, feverishly, with melancholy, until his ugly need went away.

The morning brought him peace, and he felt newly inspired. He gathered his materials and rushed uptown to his class at the Art Students League. The studio was already crowded and he admonished himself for being late. It seemed no matter how organized he could be, he was always the last to arrive, sneered at by his fellow students. He had to settle for an easel in the rear of the room, near the heater, pulling the heavy contraption across the floor to achieve the best possible view under the circumstances.

The model entered in her robe, a tattered kimono that she'd picked up at one of the secondhand shops in the Village, clutching the fabric at her bosom with flagrant modesty, and climbed onto the platform. She possessed a restrained anguish that intrigued him, the narrow intensity of her eyes, the hollows of her cheeks. The students busied themselves with preparations, allowing the model the illusion of privacy as she removed her robe and assumed a pose. It was during those fleeting moments that Simon Haas found his focus: the gentle lift of her shoulders as the robe dropped to the floor, the thrilling display of her nudity, her allowance of it, her delectable vulnerability. She wore her deep red hair pulled up in a loose chignon and he could smell her cologne, like vanilla. How easily they accepted each other, he thought. How willing she was to expose herself in the lofty name of art. They warmed up with several two-minute sketches, then settled into a twenty-minute pose with the model seated on a metal stool that scarcely accommodated her generous hips and squealed with her slightest movement. How easily she opened her legs! Her arms akimbo on her knees, her breasts plunging down like lavish ornaments. He noticed a bruise on her inner thigh, a curious place for a wound indeed, and, unlike his fellow students, he did not omit it.

In the lounge on their break he attempted a conversation with the model, but she frowned with impatience and wandered away to have a cigarette. He had never had much luck with women, and romance, in general, seemed a remote abstraction. The room, with its mint green walls and long windows, was full of smoke and the busy rush of conversation. He stood in the corner, watching. He detested most of them. He kept to himself, mostly, but they knew him for his work, which was among the best in the class. He preferred to keep his distance; he didn't trust any of them. There were few of them in that room who would last, he realized.

He spent the afternoon painting on the roof of the condemned building. He liked painting out in the open, up in the sky with the birds. There was plenty of room up there for his canvases, which were large. He liked the feeling of working big, of using his body to make a painting, of putting his whole self into it. The length of his arms and legs. The bold insistence of the light. The frank brutality of the light on the streets. And when evening came, like a beggar, dragging its dirty rags, he'd use his binoculars, insinuating himself into the homes of strangers. The filthy kitchens where women sweated and cried and stuffed themselves with their own cooking. Where men took their wives by force, their faces foul with desire. Where children screamed or simply sat alone in the chaos of neglect. A child like that captured his interest and he would watch for a long time with a burning in his throat. He'd been that child. Sitting on the chair in his mother's kitchen. His father coming in, the chair going over and his father's hand wrapped around his neck. The alarming weightlessness of his little body flying across the room. His father standing over him, *Get up, boy, get up!*, his mother pushing her body between them, trying to divert him, *Leave him alone!* Then taking his father into her room, the door closing, his father's slow drunken groan easing through the cracks. Simon would sit on the kitchen floor for a long time, unable to move, his little body pulsing with terror. Humiliated by the smell of his urine. He'd wash the floor quickly, so they wouldn't see, they wouldn't know, and hurry into his room, hearing his mother's voice through the thin walls, the way she'd whisper to his father, quiet and soothing as a nun. He lay there for a long time, waiting for her to come in. To tuck in the sheets, caress his forehead, whisper apologies, like mothers were supposed to do, but she never did.

He knew a woman like her, like his mother, shackled with compromise. He had found her window; he knew the cherry walls of her room, the brass bars of her headboard. And the various men she'd entertain there. Their raging buttocks as they fucked her. The blue neon of the flashing sign, NUDE DANCERS! illuminating her common face.

Later that afternoon, when the sun was low and the windows of the buildings glowed orange, he decided to pay the woman a visit. He found the building without trouble and rang all of the buzzers at once and continued to ring until the lock on the door released. He climbed the stairs to the fourth floor, smelling the rife odors of tenement life, burnt grease and fried bananas, the piquant draft of curry and saffron. He had counted the floors to her apartment from the outside, watching her clients arrive at the fourth-floor landing through the small window in the hallway, how they'd straighten their ties and slick back their hair before knocking, and now that he was inside it was easy to estimate the location of her door. It was four o'clock in the afternoon, the time of day, he had observed, that she kept to herself. When she would wash her stockings, perhaps, and hang them over the shower railing to dry. Or when she would shave her calves, or the sensitive area around her pubis. Sometimes she would paint her nails by the window, listening to the radio, the Cuban station, her body rocking gently with the music. It made him a little sick, visiting her now; still, he knocked on her door. "I just want to talk," he told her when she opened it.

She frowned. "What about? You a cop?"

"I'm a painter."

"A what?"

"An artist. I was wondering . . ." He cleared his throat. "Would you be willing to sit for me?"

"To sit?"

"For a painting. A sketch or two. I'll pay you, of course."

"What are you, a pervert or something?"

He smiled and raised his hands. "I refuse to answer on the grounds I may be incriminated."

This made her laugh. "You want to pay me just to sit there."

"That's right."

She shook her head like she still wasn't sure. She studied his face. "It's your money," she said finally, and invited him in with an extravagant wave of her hand.

"Splendid."

She lit a cigarette and began to remove her clothes.

"Leave them on," he said. He wanted the red kimono. He wanted the black ribbon around her neck.

"Suit yourself, da Vinci." She dropped into an old wing chair with torn upholstery, bulging guts of yellow foam.

"Long day?" he asked, just making conversation, getting out his pad, his pastels.

"You kidding? I'm bright-eyed and fucking bushy-tailed." She blew the smoke right at him. "How'd you find me, anyway?"

"You're not easy to miss."

She smiled slowly, flattered. She let him draw her for half an hour, then poured them each a glass of whiskey. The whiskey tasted good, and since he hadn't eaten it warmed his belly.

"I'm just curious," she said, wiping her mouth on her wrist. "Why me? Why aren't you out there painting buildings and the fucking East River? Why waste your time on some old whore like me?"

He reached out and took her hand. He held it, the yellow skin, the chipped and bitten fingernails. Her thin, elegant wrists. "You interest me," he said simply.

She looked at him strangely and tears came to her eyes. "You must be pretty hard up."

"What's your name?"

"Grace."

"Grace," he repeated. "That's a beautiful name."

The room was nearly dark now, the streets outside fluid with rush-hour traffic. She came to him quietly, kneeling between his legs, and kissed him. Her mouth tasted of whiskey and nicotine and he drank from it willingly. She went to the dresser and took out a small tin box that had once contained tea. She opened it and retrieved a tiny bag of white powder. She put out the lines on the shiny tin top and offered it to him and he accepted it. He'd been secretly hoping for this and he indulged in the ritual feverishly, desperately. They went to the bed. He was suddenly afraid of her. The pungent odor in the sheets and the soiled pillow smelling of hair tonic and cologne. She began to kiss him as her fingers wandered inside his pants.

"No," he whispered, "that's not necessary."

But she did not stop. She wrapped her hand around him and worked him hard and harder and it hurt. He grabbed her wrists and held them down and she struggled and he took her brutally, watching her face twist in a kind of rapturous melancholy.

"You're all the same," she said bitterly. "Every last one of you."

When he woke it was dark, and she was gone. He dressed in the strange blue light, imagining himself on the roof across the street, looking into this life, his own past, the whore, like his own mother, a willing victim of circumstance.

———

A month later, in the violent heat of August, Simon drove to Amsterdam, New York. His intentions were not entirely despicable. He hoped to finish the portrait of the girl and receive his payment, trusting, of course, that the girl's father would be satisfied with the finished product. It was something he should have done long ago. He felt his stomach churning although there was nothing in it but the flat beer he'd drunk that morning from an open can somebody had left behind. He had a cigarette butt left, he'd smoked half of it the night before, and he lit it now, a tiny scrap of flaming tobacco singeing his hand. He looked at his reflection in the rearview mirror, wondering how he would appear to the girl and her father. He wondered if they would be able to see his condition for what it was and he hoped, of course, that they wouldn't. At least he had the car, which was worth plenty under the circumstances.

He found the girl's house with little trouble and turned down the long dirt lane. The house was dark, the shades pulled. It seemed neglected. The grass had become overgrown with weeds. He did not see anyone around. Two black crows sat on the porch railing and cawed at him when he got out of the car. Frightened, he charged toward them, waving his arms madly about, and they flew off shrieking. He had a strange feeling, then, like he should turn away. As if returning there had been a mistake. But he didn't. He climbed the steps and knocked on the door. There was no answer. He peered through the dark dirty glass and saw the hallway and part of the dining room with all the shades and curtains drawn. He tried the knob, and the door opened. He had a peculiar sensation that he was being watched, but the house appeared to be empty and was nearly silent save for the buzzing of flies. There seemed to be a lot of them flying about and the air was close and smelled of spoiled food. Simon walked toward the back room, where the girl's father had been on the day he'd started the portrait. The buzzing of the flies grew curiously louder and an odor permeated the walls, an awful rotten smell that he could not place but knew was the result of something repugnant. And when he entered the room, he nearly vomited from the ghastly sight.

The man had been dead for several days, his rigid corpse swarming with flies. Standing there over the body Simon felt the flies attacking his own skin and he could do little to get them off. He reeled out of the room, gasping, his eyes tearing, and ran to the sink in the kitchen to wash his face, which he did not bother drying. He climbed the stairs slowly, murmuring her name over and over, but he heard no reply and he wondered if he'd even spoken it.

He found the girl in her bed, nearly unconscious and apparently hallucinating. The room was stifling with the windows shut tight and he flung them open, angrily, using his body, sensing the power of it. The walls of the room had been papered with old news clippings, certain details of which had been circled with pen. "THREE DIE IN EXPLOSION," "GIRL LEAPS TO HER DEATH," "LOCAL GIRL FOUND IN RAVINE." A furious rain fell from the sky and he lifted the girl and carried her downstairs and out into it. The rain fell hard, and he washed her with it, and she began to come around.

"I didn't know what to do," she said.

"It's all right," he told her. "I'm here now."

"Don't leave me," she begged him, clutching his shoulders.

The house didn't have a phone, so he drove up to the graveyard and found the caretaker's cottage. The caretaker was a reasonable man and helped him at once. They put a pine casket in the back of the man's truck and drove together to the old man's house. The caretaker gave him a cigarette.

"She'll have to go into the orphanage now," he said. "Ain't but fourteen."

Simon Haas remained quiet.

"The world won't be any sorrier without the old bastard, I can tell you that. I don't imagine she'll miss him much." The caretaker passed him a knowing look. "She never forgave him for what he done to her mama."

"What did he do?"

"She got around with men. Came down sick with something, something bad, and her husband wouldn't let her see a doctor. Like a punishment, see. For betraying him. He kept her locked up inside that house till she died. The girl was just four or five, I don't know which."

The story affected Simon; he felt sorry for the girl.

"She don't got no relations in town," the caretaker went on. "Far as I can tell, she ain't got no relations period."

Simon got to thinking.

"You ain't no relation, are you?" The caretaker squinted at him, waiting for an answer that Simon readily supplied.

"I am, in fact, a distant relation. There will be no need for any outside help." He rolled down the window, tossing the cigarette out into the rain. "She'll be in good hands with me."

It had been a mistake, he realized that now. He'd been thinking only of himself, his art. That's how he'd been taught. To be thoroughly consumed. To think of nothing else. Painting, the paint itself, the intoxicating odors, the colors, the light rushing through the windows—it was all part of the indulgence, for it was an indulgence, and he controlled every aspect of it. He did not know if it was Lydia who'd made him famous, or if it would have happened anyway, if he'd been painting landscapes, for example, like some of his classmates. He couldn't help thinking it was her, the strange mystery of her face, her slim child's body. He liked to think he had saved her, but, he supposed, that was indulgent as well. In truth, he was frightened of her. She'd been his muse, the embodiment of his perversions, but apart from that, apart from how he'd used her, she was a complete enigma to him.

Several months after he'd moved into her father's house, he woke one night to find her down on the floor in a puddle of moonlight, crying hysterically and beating her fists into the wood. He would later paint her that way, in greasy black lines, a muddled green background save for the splash of ocher, like urine, all around her—it was one of the paintings that had made him famous. "Lydia," he whispered, moving toward her, not wanting to frighten her. "Lydia, what is it?"

She wouldn't speak and he went beside her and held her, rocked her, and she cried. "My father," she said finally. "I killed him."

She clung to him. Shaking, wet, she held him; she begged him not to tell.

"I couldn't stand it anymore. I just put the TV on and closed the door. And then you came."

Her fingertips were full of splinters. It took hours to remove them all. He wondered, to this day, if he had managed to get every last one.

27

"BASICALLY HE DIED of dehydration," Simon explained. "She'd stopped feeding him. He would have died anyway; she just sped up the process."

Annie sat there, overwhelmed by the story. She finished her coffee, which by now was cold. "What a terrible story."

The waitress came over. "You folks all done here?"

Annie pushed her plate away. "Yes, thanks."

Simon looked at her, his eyes watering. "I warned you."

"Was it really her fault?"

He wiped his eyes, nodding. "I believe it was."

"What was it like, after that? When you knew?"

"She was just a kid. A fucking teenager. What could I do? Put her out in the street? Turn her in to the cops? I had no choice but to let her stay."

"You were, what, twenty years older?"

"Twenty-two years. I was thirty-six and she was fourteen."

Annie shook her head. "You're right, it is a nasty story."

"And I can see you've begun to hate me."

"No. It's just . . ."

"I never touched her, if that's what you're thinking. That's something you have to understand. I waited."

"How long did you wait?"

"Five years. I waited until she was nineteen. And then I married her."

28

THE HUM DRUM MOTEL was fifteen miles west of the college. Simon had left a note on Annie's office door that morning, asking her to meet him there. The motel had been built in the fifties, a white clapboard structure with window boxes full of plastic geraniums. The man who ran the place had lost an eye and did not wear a patch where the socket had been sewn. "He's in there already," the man told her. "Room 11. Been here almost an hour." He shoved the key across the counter like a dare.

She took the key and walked down a cement path to the room. She knocked lightly and the door swiftly opened. Simon stood there, smiling at her. "Hello, Annie."

"This is an interesting place to meet."

"I thought you'd like it. Actually, I didn't think you'd come."

"I almost didn't."

"And are you besieged with guilt?"

She stood there awkwardly. "I'm cold."

"I have a remedy for that. Come." The room was damp and smelled of tangerines. He pulled off the garish bedspread and they got into bed with their clothes on. "Are you as nervous as I am?"

"Yes," she admitted gratefully. "More."

Their hands mingled.

"Your hands are cold," he said.

"Freezing."

He put his hands under her shirt. "Ah, that's better. Warm. And what beautiful breasts you have." Their mouths found each other and they began to kiss and the kissing was good and for several fleeting dreamlike moments she was somewhere else. Yes, it was good kissing him, it was divine, and she didn't care about his wife, or his life outside of the little room, or her husband, or her children, or even the article. She ran her hands through his hair as he moved down her body, kissing her with both longing and fulfillment, wandering under her skirt, the wicked stockings, his tongue grazing her belly, her ripe sweet grass, and the dark space between her legs. She pulled him back up and kissed his mouth and tasted herself inside it, and their hands grappled with clothing, pulling and pushing and opening and tearing as though to save each other from this urgent anguish. And there was recognition in their discovery, as if they had been lovers in another life and this was their joyous reunion. He *knew* her body; he knew her cold.

Now tears ran down her cheeks. "What is it?" he said, his hands around her face. "What's wrong?"

"I'm sorry. It's stupid to be crying. It's just, I don't know, I'm overwhelmed."

"I'm grateful you're here. I know it's hard. It's hard for me, too."

She nodded and let him kiss her wet face and her breasts and her nipples, budding with desire. And then he went into her and she knew, instantly, that everything had changed.

Besieged with guilt, she thought as she was getting dressed in the anonymous room. She did not mind that it was anonymous. She did not mind the smell of this man in her life. The smell of him on her body under her clothes. He was someone she needed now, and she did not know how long it would last and she did not care. It didn't change how she felt about her husband, she reasoned; she still loved him, but they'd come to a place in their marriage where they were blind to each other, and it was mutual.

Annie opened the dusty curtains, allowing in the loud busy light of afternoon. Simon sat on the worn chair near the window and pulled on his socks. The gray light fell on his face. She put on her coat and went over to him and kissed him on the mouth. "Are you okay?" he asked.

She nodded. He touched her face.

And then she left.

As the weeks passed, the warm hues of September gave way to early darkness, and October arrived with bleak overstatement. To Annie's revelation, her desire for Simon Haas took on an almost perverse urgency, with all the characteristics of an obsession. This unruly lust brought about the highest form of joy, and she did not make any attempt to suppress it. Simon seemed to know her deeply, profoundly, in ways that Michael had never dared to imagine. Simon revealed her; he opened her like a gift. Her flaws seemed only to fascinate him—her evolving imperfections—and his admiration allowed her a sumptuous freedom. Often, during lovemaking, she found herself willing to experiment, allowing him to dominate her, to choreograph their primal dance, behavior that she would adamantly denounce in the company of her women friends—but here, with him, it seemed an inexplicable thrill. When he touched her, she was someone else, someone without the fancy trimmings, pure flesh. No language, no discussions or debates. No ambiguity. Only pleasure, his scent on her skin, the shimmering light beyond the window. She thought about him constantly, waiting for him to call or hoping to catch sight of him someplace on campus. She'd find irony in ordinary pockets of her day. The love songs that came on the radio seemed to be playing just for her. At night, lying next to her husband, it was Haas she was thinking of. It was

Haas who filled her dreams now. And though she knew it was wrong, horribly wrong, she could not bring herself to stop.

29

IT DID NOT TAKE her husband long to conjure an obsession for Annie Knowles. It was fairly obvious to Lydia that he had fallen in love with the woman. Obvious in the way he moved about the house like a cautious guest, preoccupied with a gloomy longing that she, his *wife*, could not hope to fulfill. He ate his meals in silence, reading over his magazines or reviewing his students' papers. He had acquired a sudden sobriety when it came to his teaching. Lydia found this almost laughable: he was no longer the lazy, self-absorbed madman strutting about the art studio; now he was expansive and generous and haplessly dedicated, a total *bore*. She imagined that his students missed the old Simon Haas.

The memory of the Spaulls' party littered her head; her brain was a Dumpster full of ugly thoughts. How embarrassed she'd been when Simon had dragged her out of there, threatening to take her back to Blackwell for a spell of treatment, the idea of which had instantly sobered her. She'd cried softly on the way home while he drove wildly. They'd hit a raccoon, its blood splashing across the windshield; he hadn't stopped to clean it off. "You left me alone," she'd told him. "It's your fault."

"I'm sorry. I made a mistake."

"What were you doing? Where did you go?"

"We took a walk. It rained. I don't have to explain myself to you."

"You don't love me!" Her voice was shrill as a child's. "How can we go on? You don't love me, anymore. You're not in love with me."

"Stop, Lydia. Stop!"

"Where will I go? What will I do? I don't have anybody, Simon. You're all I have. You're all I have!"

He pulled over, jammed on the brakes. Took her into his arms and held her, rocked her, and she cried into his chest, and he was gentle with her, the way he used to be when she was younger. "It's all right now," he muttered with his whiskey breath. "We're going home. We're going home."

It had been two weeks since that night and she hadn't left the house. Like a sick person she wandered the rooms, almost afraid of the air outside. Patty Tuttle sent over homemade cookies, all of which she ate in one sitting. A wild hunger consumed her that no food would satisfy. There was an unpleasant swirling in her belly, an ensanguined pressure, a bloating of wretchedness. She hated Annie Knowles with every inch of her being. Hate had caught in her throat like a small bone. She went to bed with hate and she woke up with hate. It sat on her tongue, black as licorice, insidious as arsenic.

When she finally returned to work, her mind was preoccupied with other things and her supervisor called her into his office. "I heard you were ill," Martin Banner inquired.

She told him that she'd been sick with the flu. She was feeling better now. In time, she promised him, she'd be back to her old self, which was a lie. Martin Banner studied her carefully and asked if she'd ever seen a therapist. Lydia shrugged, mortified by the question. Banner scrawled a name on a piece of paper and handed it to her. The piece of paper went into her pocket, but the moment she got back to her desk, she put it into her mouth and swallowed it.

It was a slow day at work. There were only ten calls altogether, and nobody ordered anything interesting—*salacious* was the word Reverend Tim liked to use. Lydia spent the long hours thinking about Annie Knowles, imagining the various ways in which Simon touched her, imagining his body laid out next to hers, the shocking insolence of their nakedness, what he would do to her and how much she would enjoy it. Had she begged him for more? Had she screamed with pleasure? Lydia pictured Annie's thick hair on the pillow, her ordinary face, a certain nasty mischief in her eyes, the rude substance of her flesh. Lydia imagined the two lovers in vivid detail until she felt sick, and on some occasions would rush to the toilet in the ladies' room and vomit. And what would his lover think, Lydia wondered, if she should discover that he was still sleeping with his wife, his hands fumbling drunkenly in the dark like blind fish, the wicked rambling of his hands under her nightgown and the hopeless rot of his breath as he forced himself upon her night after night, greedy as a starving man. They were sharing him now, and in some strange way Lydia could almost taste the woman.

Her husband's betrayal became the focus of her attention; it never quite left her mind and it embarrassed her, it shamed her. Desperate for advice, she read countless women's magazines, but none offered any solutions. Suffering with her frustration, she decided to talk it over with Reverend Tim. It would be embarrassing, she knew, to admit that there were these awful problems in her marriage, but she felt she had no other choice.

After work, Lydia drove over to the new Life Force headquarters, out at the truck stop on the interstate.

Reverend Tim was just finishing up one of his healing workshops. The people looked content and serene as they stood around a table, drinking lemonade and eating cookies. Reverend Tim gave her a big smile and said, "Hello there, Lydia," but she could hardly even speak, and he could read her pain like Braille across her face. "What is it, what's wrong?"

She started to cry, she couldn't help it. Embarrassed, she covered her face with her hands. He led her outside, into the parking lot. She could see the trucks roaring past on the highway. "Lydia? You all right?"

But she could not find her voice.

"It's all right, now," he said. "You just take your time. I'm not going anywhere."

She looked at him and wiped her eyes. He wanted to know why she was crying. He was waiting for an explanation. "It's Simon," she said.

"Well, I gathered that." He waited.

"He's seeing someone. He's having an affair."

She could see that the information disappointed him, and he looked away from her. "Deception is the evil of our times," he said. His eyes found hers again. "Do you know who the woman is?"

She nodded. "That doctor's wife. Annie Knowles."

PART FOUR
Heart

30

SIMON HAD NOT SEEN Marrow since the night they'd gotten stoned, but he could not seem to shake the image of the man's wife, whose gritty rancor dripped through his mind like grease from the diner's griddle. She worked the dinner shift, behind the counter. He sketched her pouring syrup onto a man's plate as the man grinned at her, grateful as an orphan. Simon drank coffee all night, painting her inside his head. Collecting her tips, her chipped pink nails scooping up change, a dime rolling just out of reach. She spoke to someone on the pay phone, blowing smoke all the way down to her dirty white shoes. He watched her wipe down the counters, shine and replenish the napkin dispensers, and snatch the skinny forlorn flowers out of the little green vases. When she put on her coat, something fake that looked like rabbit, he followed her outside. She was hovering over a cigarette, trying to light it in the wind.

"Remember me?"

She cocked her head, scowling for his benefit. "Oh, the professor."

"You want to make some money?"

"Doing what?"

"Modeling. I'm a painter."

She smiled, flattered. They always smiled. "How much?"

"Fifty bucks an hour. You're not shy, are you?"

She shifted in the cold, smoking her cigarette. He worried that she'd slap him across the face and walk away. But she didn't. She shrugged her shoulders. "That all depends on you, doesn't it?"

He drove her in his car, the jazz station a raspy whisper. She smelled like French fries, a trace of honeysuckle. "You teach over at the college?"

He told her he did and she brayed with mockery.

"That must be a major pain in the butt. Fuckin' bitches. Fussy types. I know; they come into the restaurant. This one don't want no butter on her bread, she wants it on the side. This one don't want no mayonnaise. This one don't like American cheese, just the Swiss."

He parked under a streetlight. It was after eleven, the streets were empty. They went into the building and up the service elevator to his studio. He unlocked the door and they went inside. He looked around at the bare walls, the large white canvas leaning there, waiting for paint. He closed the drapes and opened a bottle of Jim Beam.

"I should call the Bone, but it'll just piss him off. Fuck it."

"Here, have a drink. I'll light us a joint."

"What do you want me to do?"

"Sit over here."

She sat like a woman who had been on her feet all night, her legs falling open, her back curved into the chair. He dipped his fingers into a puddle of raw sienna and smeared it on the canvas.

"My uniform's kind of dirty," she said.

"What's your name?"

"Gina."

"You have a beautiful neck."

He could tell she didn't believe him but wanted to. Desperately wanted to.

"How would you feel about taking the uniform off? I'd like to paint you in your bra and underwear," he said matter-of-factly.

"Ain't wearing nothing fancy."

"I don't like fancy."

She looked as if she were trying to decide. This posturing was a charade, he knew, and when more money was suggested it seemed to quell any moral misgivings. "I'll pay you seventy-five an hour."

She came over to him and turned around. "Well, unzip me, baby, the clock is ticking."

She seemed more vulnerable in her underwear. "Crawl onto that mattress over there," he told her. Her body had a fierce geometry that intrigued him. Her skin was chalky, mottled with freckles. She sat there on the mattress with the long window behind her and the yellow shade pulled halfway down. Even in the frayed underwear, she wore an expression of regal expectation, her posture defiantly dignified. It was an interesting contrast to the surroundings, her uniform crumpled on the bed, her name tag glowing.

After the session he took her home. He counted out the money in her shaking hand. He watched her through the dirty windows of the vestibule, unlocking the door and disappearing into her life. He wondered how she felt.

Back in the studio, he drank ice-cold vodka out of his lunch thermos and examined his work. She was still there, in a manner of speaking, her body, her flat little tits. He'd paint her all night if he could stand to. He'd paint her until he couldn't see anymore. And in a few months, she'd be on a wall in the museum and people would look at her, discreetly imagining the fleeting thrill of touching her, and they'd take her image home with them, savoring her sooty flavor like the memory of any ordinary meal.

"I want to draw you," he told Annie the following afternoon at the motel.

"Impossible," she said. She was naked under the sheets, her hair wildly matted after lovemaking. The room smelled gloriously of her sweat.

"Do it for me," he said, snapping off the sheet.

"Why should I?" she said, snapping it back on.

"You're afraid."

"Afraid of what?"

"I'll make you look pretty, if that's what you're worried about." The minute he said it he regretted it.

"Now, there's a challenge." She ripped off the sheet and got out of bed and began to get dressed.

"Annie." He used his placating voice.

Angrier still. "What?"

"You're beautiful, don't you know that?"

"Fuck you."

He grabbed the sweater out of her hand. She stood there before him with her magnificent breasts. "Fuck you," he whispered, and reached out for them, feeling their marvelous weight in his hands. He grasped her nipples and twisted a little and she came toward him and he knew he had her. He kissed her and she kissed him back, and then they were fucking again and he told her again that she was beautiful.

And now softly, she said, "What difference does it make?"

"In this world it makes all the difference."

"It bugs the shit out of me that I even care."

"Please, just sit over there in that chair so I can draw you."

After a moment's deliberation, she got up and went to the chair and sat down and crossed her arms over her chest like an impatient teenager, then crossed one knee over the other and wiggled her foot. He sighed, looking at her. "You're incredible."

"What's so incredible? It's just another body, isn't it?"

"No, Annie, it's you."

He opened the curtains and the gray light fell in on top of her. He studied her gently. He sketched her quickly, freeing himself in the lines of her body. Satisfied with the drawing, he held up the paper and mused, "I'll call this one *Just Fucked.*"

31

IN THE MIDDLE of the night Annie woke to find Michael's hands on her body, wanting to make love. "I can't," she told him, turning away, but he persisted. *"Please, Michael, I need to sleep!"* The awful truth was she no longer desired her husband. Unlike her lover's seductive wizardry, Michael's touch was clumsy and ineffectual. She felt contemptuous of him. Simon Haas possessed her now. Like an addiction, her need for him had become a torturous preoccupation. She was a ravenous beggar, yet it was not food she craved.

"What's wrong with you?" Michael said.

"Nothing. I'm tired."

He kissed her hard, determined, and she kissed him back and succumbed to him and when it was over she was relieved. Distantly, it occurred to her that she hadn't put in her diaphragm.

When the alarm went off at six-forty-five, Michael was already gone. Whipping off the covers, she climbed out of bed and went and roused the children. "Up! Everyone up! Rise and Shine! Start moving or I'm going to *tickle* you." Henry groaned and turned away. But Rosie giggled. Rosie always giggled at even the slightest notion of being tickled. "Up, my little bunny." She tickled squirming Rosie. "My little lemon drop." As predicted, scales of laughter. Into Henry's room, her cynical boy of ten. "Up my grumpy boy." She kissed her son's soft cheek. "Rise and shine, my little man."

"I don't want to go," he said. "I *hate* school."

"Up! No complaining! Hating school is not allowed."

"The kids are mean. Nobody likes me."

"That's not true and you know it."

"You don't *know*, Mommy. You don't know what it's like. You don't *understand*!"

She sat down on the edge of the bed and ruffled his hair. "I *do* understand and I know it's hard. But you have to go to school. You've got to *try*."

"It's Daddy's fault," he said.

"Henry. Don't say that."

"It is. Everybody knows what he does." He muttered under his breath, "I hate him."

Annie took her son's hand. "Henry, I know that isn't true. And you know Daddy loves you very much. He's doing the best he can right now."

Henry got up. "It's not good enough." He went into the bathroom. He was his father's son, she thought, wrangling the wild beast of life with his bare hands. What would Michael say if he knew how Henry felt? It would hurt him deeply, yet she had to wonder if he'd do anything about it.

Annie got dressed and went downstairs to start breakfast. Entering the kitchen, she couldn't help feeling like she was being watched. She was sure their phone was being tapped; every time she used it she heard a loud click. When she thought over the past few months, she remembered things that had happened that, at the time, hadn't seemed unusual but now gave her pause. Once, a man had pulled up to the house in a shiny red pickup truck and told her he was a photographer. Their house was so beautiful he wanted to take a picture of it, he'd said, and she'd smiled, flattered, and told him he could. One afternoon she'd come home to find dog shit on her Welcome mat. Just the other night, reading Rosie a bedtime story, she'd smelled cigarette smoke coming from somewhere outside. When she'd taken Molly out the next morning she'd found an empty Marlboro package on the driveway. Sometimes there were tire tracks in the mud of the front lawn. Strange as it was, they were getting used to it.

At breakfast, Annie reviewed her checklist of precautions. The children sat and listened, alert with expectation, of what she was not entirely sure. What pictures did they form in their heads, she wondered, based on her list of warnings? "No talking to anyone you don't know. Even people you do know. Be careful. Even your teachers. If, for example, they ask you to help them with something outside of school. If a teacher comes up to you on the playground and asks you questions about Daddy and me. You don't have to answer anything. Do you understand? Or if one of your friends' parents comes up to you and questions you or wants something from you. It could be someone you know, or it could be a stranger. You need to watch out for each other. Henry? Do you understand? You need to watch out for Rosie on the bus."

"Yes, Mom," Henry droned, bored with the subject.

"Rosie?"

"We understand, right, Rosie?" Henry urged.

Rosie said nothing and stared with bewildered concentration at the cereal box.

Rosie did not understand.

32

PATHETIC AS IT WAS to admit, Michael preferred the hospital to his own home. The hospital was predictable, familiar, and these days he took comfort in familiarity, no matter how fucked up it was. The balmy climate of the corridors. The lingering smell of food from the cafeteria. The benign faces of the nursing staff. The diagonal swish of the janitor's mop on the blue linoleum. But at home, he had no idea where he stood. Lately, Annie seemed habitually forlorn, and more than once he'd caught her staring vaguely into space, the slightest hint of a smile on her lips. On the rare occasion when they had dinner together, she hardly touched her food and their conversation was strained, limited to the activities of the children. After the kids were in bed, she would vanish into the bedroom to read. He would find her hours later, fast asleep, the book lying across her chest, the nightstand light shining in her face.

The stress was beginning to get to him.

When he entered the office that morning, Miranda, the receptionist, cornered him in the hallway. "Celina James is in your office."

"What?"

"I wouldn't let Finney see her. He'll probably call security or something."

"Maybe she wants to discuss a case. Bring in the first patient, I'll only be a minute."

For safety reasons, Michael and Celina had agreed that seeing each other outside of the clinic was, for the most part, not a good idea. He hurried down the hall to his office. Celina was sitting in the swivel chair behind his desk.

"Nice place," she told him. "Swank. You guys must have a hell of an overhead."

"Celina, we've been over this. You shouldn't be here."

"I was in the neighborhood, I couldn't resist."

"I've got a waiting room full of patients."

"I needed to see you." She hesitated a moment, as if she were going to say something, but changed her mind. Then she added, "I wanted to see your office, where you work."

"It's not terribly exciting."

"On the contrary." In no particular hurry, she walked around the room, studying the photographs he'd taken when he and Annie had traveled overseas after medical school. They were large, framed prints and he was immeasurably proud of them. "Where's this?" she asked, pointing to one of his favorite photographs of a group of young Guatemalan girls.

"Guatemala. They're some orphans we met." When he had taken the picture, he'd been considering pediatrics and the children on the streets had enchanted him with their uncanny strength and mystery. Another photograph showed a boy wearing a Mickey Mouse T-shirt. The boy had no shoes, and his feet were riddled with cuts. Michael had been pleased with the picture's inherent irony. "An interesting place," he said.

"I'll show you interesting," she scoffed at him. "I got kids like this right down the street. You don't need to take an airplane to get shots like these."

"No, I'm sure I don't. Now, if you're through patronizing me, I'd like to get back to my patients."

She looked at him and he saw that her lips were trembling.

"What's the matter? What is it?"

"These came just in time." She opened a large canvas duffel bag and took out a bulletproof vest. "Here, you'd better put it on. You're going to need it."

"What?"

"We're on their list."

"What list?"

"Their hit list. I checked out their Web site. They've got a hit list and we're on it."

"What, are you kidding?"

"No joke. Here, I printed it out." She took a piece of paper out of her bag and unfolded it. "I wanted you to see it."

Holding the paper in his hands he began to shake. It was an involuntary response, and there was nothing he could do to control it. There were two photographs positioned next to each other, one of him and one of her. Each had a caption underneath that gave their names and home addresses. Under his name were the names of his wife and children. At the bottom of the page, in big bold letters, were the words SHOOT TO KILL.

His legs felt weak suddenly and he sat down. "You'd better go, Celina."

"I know." She buttoned her coat.

"Be careful." He could feel himself shutting her out. He picked up the phone.

"Who are you calling?" she asked.

"I'm calling my wife," he said with surprising animosity. "Her name is on that list, too."

First he dialed Annie's office, but he got her machine. He tried her cell phone, but she hadn't turned it on. Infuriated, he called the house, but for some inexplicable reason it just kept on ringing and he sat there like that for several minutes listening to the repetitive sound, wondering why he never seemed to be able to get through.

33

PULLING ONTO CAMPUS, winding up the circular driveway toward the South Cottage, Simon began to feel a familiar mixture of fear and excitement. The acerbic tonic of love, he thought, that he could no longer do without. Annie was waiting for him on the curb, wrapped up in her long camel coat with the wind like a child's scribble across her face. One day he would paint her this way, he thought. He would paint the wind in a fury of brushstrokes, her face blurred and apprehensive. He parked and got out to open the door for her. She conceded to these old-fashioned gestures, he knew, because it gave a certain formality to their meetings, as if their courtship could lead to something other than misery. It would not be long, he knew, before this smart woman came to her senses.

He was taking her to the Whitney to see his painting, one of his earliest works. The Taconic was empty, and he tried to focus on the beauty of the scenery and the fact that his lover was sitting beside him, but in truth the excursion made him nervous. They spoke little on the drive, and when they arrived at the museum it was raining. He dropped her off in front, then circled the block numerous times before he found a space. He sat in the car for a moment with the rain beating down and wept.

He found Annie on the third floor, standing in front of the painting, which he had titled *Her Father's House*. In the painting, Lydia stood in the doorway of her father's crummy house in Vanderkill with the old man in the shadows behind her. He remembered trying to paint the word *lurk*, because that's how she'd described her father, that he was always *lurking* over her shoulder, even though the man couldn't get out of bed. Looking at it now, he was critical of some of his brushwork, the colors he'd used. The dirty white clapboards, the gray windows, the torn yellow shades, the mangled brown grass in the foreground. In the lower right corner, entering the canvas with prurient insinuation, was a rusty red mailbox.

The gallery was not crowded, and the space glowed nicely and hummed with the circulating heat. He observed Annie, who stood at the painting, tilting her head this way and that way, her shoulders slightly raised with emotion or ambiguity, he knew not which. He could not imagine what she was thinking. Regretting their visit now, embarrassed by it, he sat down on the bench behind her. Somehow, he felt lost. Melancholy whirled up inside him and he was struck with the distant memory of his father taking him to a museum, the Met. It had been one of their few outings together, their first visit to a museum. He remembered his father yanking him by the sleeve up the steps. Once inside all the sounds of the world faded. It was like being inside a cloud. The galleries with their glorious paintings. Massive canvases exploding with colors. His father rushed him through all the galleries, his face glowing with feverish sweat, until he found the painting he was searching for, a small Corot. His father sat him down hard on the wooden bench in front of it and handed him a sketchbook and pencil. "Draw that."

Simon was happy to be allowed to draw again, and thought, perhaps, that his father had decided to approve of him. When they got home he was given a small canvas, the exact dimension of the Corot they'd seen at the museum, and a box of oil paints and brushes. His father put out the drawing he'd done at the museum. "See if you can paint that. Do it perfect. You want to be in this family, you earn your fucking keep."

A week later, his father sold the painting to a man who peddled reproductions at a flea market in Brooklyn. His mother cooked pork chops and his father drank whiskey. Simon was nine years old.

"You okay?" Annie joined him on the bench. "You look gloomy all of a sudden."

"I'm fine," he lied.

"Is it hard? The painting, I mean. Seeing your wife."

"I stole her," he whispered. "You know how those people in tribes don't want their pictures taken because they claim it steals their soul? Well, that's what I did to her. I put her up on the canvas. I stole her soul."

Annie said nothing. Her eyes looked watery and sad.

"She was this kid and I showed up and I fucking stole her. And nobody tried to stop me. I just walked in and took her life and I never gave it back. I never gave her anything."

"I can't believe that's true," she said softly.

"I'm a despicable man. I'm going to hell for it."

They toured the museum together, then went down to the café for lunch. Annie picked at her food, glanced at her watch. She shifted on her chair as if she were sitting on a thumbtack. "I need to get home. I'm worried about the kids."

"Worried? Why, Annie?"

"We're being harassed," she told him, and went on to explain how an anti-abortion group had been threatening her family. "It's starting to really get to me."

"I didn't know your husband did abortions."

"At a clinic in Albany," she said. She seemed to be searching his face, attempting to discern a moral hue, which he did not supply.

Simon knew the group she was speaking of and suspected that his wife was a member of it. He'd seen their literature around the house. He knew Lydia participated in those rallies. She had mentioned them to him once. He had discovered her down in the basement, making signs. The floor had been cluttered with pictures of dead babies. When he'd questioned her, her face had glowed with excitement, like a teenager proud of a school project.

"I didn't know," he said again, wondering with horror if Lydia was at all involved in the threats.

"It's one of the things he does," she said cautiously. "You're not against it, are you?"

"I suppose it's a necessity in a society like ours."

She scowled at him impatiently. "It has always been a necessity. It's not like it's some revolutionary new procedure."

"You get mean when you're angry, I *like* that."

"Fuck you, Simon."

"I was kidding, okay? What kind of threats?"

"Phone calls, pranks. We're being watched. Michael skulks around like a thief." She shot him a look. "Don't tell me you're voting for Nash."

"All right, I won't tell you."

Her eyes watered. "You *are* despicable. Take me home."

"I'm sorry, Annie. I'm not very political. It's all the same bullshit if you ask me."

"That's a lame excuse."

They walked to the car and moments later were stuck in traffic. She sighed and said, as if to punish him, "I can see that it would never work out between us. I find your apathy insulting. Especially with what's been going on with Michael. You're totally absorbed in yourself." She rolled her window down, letting in the sound of the traffic. "Sometimes I feel like I hardly know you. Sometimes I feel like you're somebody else in my head. Somebody better."

"I'm not sure I like the sound of that," he said, feeling spurned.

"It never would work out," she said again. "We're different people."

"You know what they say: opposites attract."

"I still love Michael," she said softly, looking away.

"Although I am sick with jealousy, I never expected that to change."

"I wish you hadn't met Lydia," she said. "Because you might have had a different life. You might have been happier."

He didn't know why, but the comment offended him. "It's not in my disposition to be happy, Annie."

"You know what I mean." She gave him a dirty look.

"You're overlooking something. It's that naughty romantic in you again."

She crossed her arms over her breasts. "What?"

"You're overlooking the fact that, at my core, I'm inherently nasty. It's a survival skill I've learned to perfect."

"You know I don't believe that."

"If I had found you, Annie, I would have married you," he said, because he knew she needed to hear it. "You would have been a poor painter's wife. Mommy would not have been pleased."

"But you didn't find me, and I didn't find you." She frowned. "We can't regret the past."

"No," he said.

"And I don't regret that we've done this."

"Nor I."

"Everything happens for a reason. Don't you think?"

"If you hadn't married Michael, you wouldn't have Henry and Rosie," he said generously, even though he sometimes wished he'd been the one to father her children.

"And if you hadn't married Lydia, you wouldn't have any of those incredible paintings. You might not have become a famous painter. You might have become a used-car salesman."

"And I would have sold you a minivan."

This made her smile.

"I would have taken you for a test drive and stuck my hand down your underpants."

She laughed. "And I would have taken your sticky hand and bitten it."

"Ooh la la."

They drove for a while in silence, and then she asked, "Do you love her?"

He hesitated, then told her the truth. "No."

"If you're so unhappy with her, why don't you leave her?"

"I couldn't do that."

"Why not?"

"Because it would kill her."

34

THE MACHINE WAS BLINKING when she got home from the city. Michael had called. She rang him at the office. "Where the hell have you been?" he said, angry. "I've been trying to call you all day."

"I went to the city." She'd decided not to lie. "To the museum to see a painting by Haas. For the article. I'm sure I told you."

"Look, Annie, you need to be careful now, okay? Wherever you go. You need to understand that. It's for your own good."

"What's wrong, Michael? Is everything all right?"

"Everything's fine," he said levelly. "But I want you to be extra cautious. Pick up the kids right after school and don't be late. I don't want them riding the bus."

Her heart tumbled. "Michael, what's going on?"

"I got another threat, that's all. I just want you to be careful."

She could hear him breathing on the other end. "Are you coming home tonight?"

He sighed heavily. "I've got two women ready to pop. I'm on call tonight. We've got a lot of patients down here to see. I'm getting creamed. I'll be late. That's why I want you home. Pull the drapes, lock the doors. Don't answer the phone."

Tears ran down her face. "Please just come home, Michael."

"You know I can't do that."

"Why can't you switch with Finney?"

"Look, I'll get home as soon as I can."

"You're so fucking dedicated," she said contemptuously.

"Annie. Don't make this any harder than it already is."

"They fucking brainwashed you and I hate them for it." She hung up on him and burst into tears.

For the next hour Annie felt unhinged with doubt. It seemed impossible to do anything. Even cleaning the house was a complicated task. Molly wanted to go out, scratching at the door. Annie put on her Bean boots and took her for a walk in the woods behind the house. She felt keen to the sounds around her. The rush of dry leaves under her feet. As they ventured deeper into the woods, Molly grew agitated and then Annie heard a gunshot. It made her hair stand up on the back of her neck. She scanned the trees and saw a group of men, maybe five in all, in camouflage attire, carrying rifles. Tremulous, she broke a sweat and small gasping breaths escaped her mouth. For a fleeting moment she imagined in vivid detail these men storming her home—a mental barrage of carnal images stolen from television movies. Again she scanned the trees and saw that the men were laughing, sharing a joke. They all had hunting permits in laminated tags on the arms of their coats. *Of course!* she remembered, feeling a bit foolish; it was hunting season. The men had every right to be there.

"Come on, Molly, come on, girl." She tugged at the dog's collar, but the dog wouldn't budge. "Molly! *Come!*" But Molly had other plans, and twisted free of her, baring her fangs. She took off into the woods after the men, barking savagely. It wasn't like Molly to bark like that. Annie felt torn, afraid to go after her. She did not want to get near those men, hunting permits or not. She did not want to have to talk to them. Abruptly, Molly's barking stopped. It suddenly became quiet. Annie scanned the woods, but she didn't see the men now, and she didn't see Molly either. She stood for a moment, listening. A branch cracked in the distance. She had the feeling she was being watched. There was no way she was going in after Molly. She turned and ran back across the field to the house.

At three o'clock, she drove to the school and waited for the children. Everything appeared to be normal in the parking lot. She recognized some of the other mothers' cars, but when she made eye contact with them and smiled, they went stone-faced and turned away.

You're being paranoid, she thought.

At quarter past three, the doors opened and a throng of kids came out. She didn't see Henry and Rosie at first, and she could feel the back of her neck going damp—but there they were, Henry in his down jacket, lugging his pack, wearing his usual disgruntled scowl, and Rosie, neatly assembled in her little red coat, pink jumper, blueberry tights, and black high-tops, skipping toward the car. Rosie was holding something. It looked like a Barbie doll.

"Hi, Mom," Henry said, climbing into the front seat.

"Look what I got, Mommy," Rosie said, holding up the doll, climbing into the back.

Annie waited until the children were safely inside the car with the doors locked before asking to see the doll. Rosie proudly showed it off, and Annie saw that it was no ordinary Barbie. The clothes it had on looked familiar, and it swiftly came to her that the doll was wearing the outfit she herself had worn on her last visit to the motel. The doll's red sweater was an exact rendition of hers. Even the snow boots were identical.

"Isn't she pretty, Mommy?"

"Who gave this to you, honey?"

"It was in my cubby. It's a present."

"Yes, Rosie, but from *who*?"

Rosie shrugged. "It's a secret, Mommy, *okay*?"

A horn beeped behind them and Annie realized she was holding up the car line. "Put it back in your pack so she gets home safe," Annie said, and they drove home in silence. Once inside, she closed all the blinds and drapes and locked the doors.

"Where's Molly?" Henry asked.

"She ran into the woods." Annie tried to sound lighthearted. "She's off on a jaunt."

"Probably chasing foxes," Henry said.

Annie nodded her agreement, but in her heart she had a sinking feeling about Molly.

Henry went into the family room and turned on the TV. Rosie opened her pack and took out the doll. "Oh, no you don't. You've got homework," Annie reminded her. "No playing until it's done." Rosie frowned and dropped the mysterious doll into her pack. She took out her math sheet and sat down at the kitchen table, her forehead scrunched with utter boredom in the heel of her hand. She tapped her pencil irritably. The doorbell rang. Annie went to the door and peered out the side window, relieved to see Mrs. Keller with her violin case. Annie had forgotten that Henry had a lesson today. "Henry," she called, "Mrs. Keller's here." Henry groaned. Annie opened the door and smiled at the woman. "Mrs. Keller."

Mrs. Keller didn't seem to notice that the house was all closed up. While Henry sawed away at his violin, producing a high-pitched melody that Annie had learned to construe as progress, Annie returned to the kitchen to help Rosie with her homework. "Need some help?"

"No, Mommy, I can do it myself."

Annie puttered around for a moment, putting dishes into the dishwasher, wiping down the counter, and for a few precious moments everything seemed pleasantly ordinary, the way it used to be. With Rosie immersed in her math, Annie snuck the Barbie into the bathroom to examine it. She removed the doll's clothes, discovering white cotton underpants and a bra just like her own. Shaking, she removed the underwear only to discover the word SLUT written across its naked buttocks with a black marker. She turned on the water and attempted to scrub the awful word off, but whoever had done this had used a permanent marker. The word could not be removed.

She considered calling Michael, but then thought better of it. Unlike the other threats, this one was meant for *her.*

35

IN THE MEN'S ROOM at work, Michael took off his shirt and put on the bulletproof vest, surprised to discover that it fit comfortably. The literature boasted, *"Flexible Trauma Plate included, complete coverage with side protection Level IIIA."* He looked at himself in the mirror; you couldn't even tell he had it on. The strange thing was, he didn't feel any safer wearing it, as if it was an invitation to shoot him. As if wearing it acknowledged the fact that they would do it, and they would do it soon.

The fastest way to get these people off his back was to resign from the clinic, to leave Celina in the lurch, because that's what it was, that's what he would be doing. But he couldn't seem to do that. In some strange way, he felt as though he had no control over what happened next, only that he had to go forward, he had to confront whatever thing came his way, no matter how horrible.

Miranda knocked on the door. "I'm ordering out. You want anything?"

"Yeah, all right," he said, even though he had no appetite. "I'll take a turkey—"

"On white with extra mayo," Miranda finished. He ordered the same thing every day.

"I guess I'm pretty predictable."

"Oh, yeah." She smiled, and another face appeared behind her. It was Finney in his little round glasses and bow tie. He looked more like an accountant than a doctor, Michael thought. "Michael, come and take a look at this ultrasound, would you?"

"Sure." Michael followed Finney into the examining room. The patient's full-term baby was breech. The mother wanted a cesarean.

"I want a second opinion," the patient snapped. "I can't take this anymore."

Michael checked out the ultrasound. "Your baby's doing fine," he concurred. "There's no reason to do a cesarean. I agree that we should wait another week."

"Another *week*?" the patient screeched. "You're *both* crazy."

Michael smiled at the woman. "She's got it good in there, believe me. She knows exactly what she's doing."

The woman scowled at him. "I can tell you're one of those pushover types. You probably let your kids walk all over you."

"You're right," he said. "They walk all over me and I'm proud of it."

He went back to his office, feeling anything but proud. A weight sat in his chest, a longing for Henry and Rosie. He would have to find a way to make it up to them, he thought. One day he would.

A white Styrofoam container sat on his desk, *Turkey on White, Xtra Mayo* written across the top. He was suddenly hungry, eager for the distraction of eating more than anything else, and he opened the container expectantly. But he did not find a sandwich. What he found, instead, was a gun.

Astonished, he took the weapon into his hands. It was a small black pistol. Michael had never held a gun in his life and discovered that it fit perfectly in the palm of his hand. He examined it cautiously and with a surprising amount of ease figured out how to open the chamber. The gun, he discovered, was loaded. He shook out the bullets into his hand and studied them. How strange to think that a bullet no larger than a pistachio nut could end someone's life.

He went to his office door and peered into the empty hallway. He glanced at Miranda, who was eating a sandwich out of a container from the same deli. Everything appeared to be normal. Who would have done this? Who would have sent him a gun?

He shut the door. He took the gun and opened the chamber and reloaded the bullets into it, marveling at its compact sincerity, and then he carefully placed the gun in his coat and hung the coat on the hook on the back of his door.

The afternoon passed quickly with routine examinations.

At five-thirty he put on his coat. He could feel the gun in his pocket, jutting into his hip like a wound of the flesh.

Miranda looked up and smiled. "Good night, Dr. Knowles."

At the door, he stopped and turned back toward the receptionist. "By the way, that sandwich you ordered me. Was it from the same place?"

"Yeah, Harry's Deli. Was everything all right?"

"Yeah, sure, everything was fine." Michael left the office and walked around the corner to Harry's Deli. The deli did a big takeout business, but there were a couple of tables inside. He went in and sat down at one of them. A moment later a young woman came over to take his order. "I'll have some coffee," he said.

"We're making a fresh pot. You in a rush?"

"No, actually, I'm not."

"What else can I get you?"

"You got any pie? Something sweet?"

"Lemon meringue."

"A piece of that, and the coffee."

"Sure."

"Got a men's room?"

"In the back."

Michael got up and walked past the deli counter toward the back. The pink-and-black tiled floor dazzled him. The details in these old buildings continually amazed him. He passed the window where the orders came up and glanced through it into the kitchen. A gangly short-order cook stood at the grill, frying onions. Two Mexican boys were washing dishes. And then something caught his eye: a red jacket, with wings on the back of it, hanging on a hook.

His waitress came out of the kitchen. "Your coffee's ready," she said, rushing by.

"Yeah, I'll be right there."

He ducked into the bathroom and washed his hands. When he came out, the jacket was gone.

Michael put a ten-dollar bill on the counter and ran out onto the street. He saw the red jacket up ahead, turning down Delaware Avenue. At the corner, she stopped at the curb to wait for the light. It was Theresa Sawyer. "Theresa!" he called out to her. She turned slightly and saw him but did not return the greeting. Instead, she jaywalked across the busy street, and kept going. He did the same, jogging to keep up with her. He followed her for several blocks, into a modest neighborhood of houses crammed up against one another. Small yards with chain-link fences. Dogs chained out front. Virgin Mary statues. The girl went into a house and shut the door. How had she gotten the gun? he wondered. And what did she know that he didn't?

He stood there for a few minutes, looking at the house with its chipped black shutters. The air had cooled. Chilled, he shoved his hands in his pockets, feeling the outline of the gun. He felt a strange mixture of fear and comfort. Just having the gun in his pocket seemed to change everything. Something was coming, something bad, that much he knew, but instead of feeling protected, now that he had the weapon, he felt more vulnerable than ever.

He didn't mention the gun to Annie when he got home that night. He found her in the family room. She looked shaken, upset. He could hear the kids upstairs, watching TV. She hadn't even made dinner. "What's wrong?"

"Molly. She ran into the woods this afternoon and never came back. There were some men out there, hunting."

"I'll go out and look."

"No. I don't want you to. I'm frightened, Michael."

"I'll take the Gator."

Henry appeared in the doorway. "I'm going with you."

Annie looked at Michael and he nodded. "Get your coat."

They'd bought the Gator, a hardy farm vehicle, to traverse the fields quickly and to explore the neighboring pastures all around their land. The kids loved riding on it, and Michael let Henry drive it now and again. Michael took the wheel and Henry climbed in beside him, holding a flashlight. They drove out of the barn and Michael was glad Henry had come along. His chest felt tight with emotion, and he could not look at the boy. Instead, he focused on the journey, and the Gator roared over the rugged ground, pushing through a thick white mist that clung to everything in sight. They searched for over an hour, but there was no sign of poor Molly, and Michael knew they would not find her. "It's your fault," Henry muttered when they got back to the barn. He met Michael's eyes head-on. It was a look Michael would never forget, simmering with hate. Henry climbed out of the Gator and went into the house. Michael sat there alone for a long time, hearing the bats overhead squealing in the rafters with judgment.

36

THE FIRST TIME she went faint a little, even before they went in. Just the look of the building, the idea of what she'd do inside it, made her feel like she was drunk. The way it felt walking through the door with Reverend Tim, the way he smelled like limes, the way everybody looked at her and at him and stepped back just a little, and the way he stood up straighter and tugged on his belt, his chin jutting out like a challenge.

The warm, clean smell inside. New carpeting. Glue. *Safety.* Everybody smiling at Reverend Tim. Not just a greeting but a proud smile. *Family.* Everybody smiling at her because she knew him, because she was with him and that meant she was someone important. *Special.* And the long walk beside him down the hall, her chest full of hope as she held herself like a queen—no, *not* a queen, a *princess.* He led her into the glass box and she could see all the other shooters down the line, in their own private lanes, their faces serene and floating. Nothing to worry about. They had everything they needed right there. No complications. Nobody else.

Peace.

Reverend Tim looked at her like he wanted to tell her something, something deep. Like he wanted to reveal a quiet feeling. But he didn't say anything. He took out his gun and grinned, shaking his head. "This is a nine-millimeter, a Beretta. Open your hand."

She offered her hand, and her body went limp and white like a flower. Simon's face floated in her brain like mist. *I'm gonna shut down, I'm gonna black out.*

"Now, that's what I call a nice fit." He wrapped her fingers around the gun, molding them against the cold metal. He was right, it was an easy grip. Too easy, she thought, shuddering. The cold metal stayed cold, no matter how hard she held it. "It's all right to like it," he told her, his voice hoarse and quiet. "It's all right. I want you to." He looked at her again, deep, as if he could see her life, her past. And she knew, then, that she could do it and maybe he did, too. The way he was looking at her, like he knew. Like he could see that she liked it, the pleasure of holding it, the strength it gave her. *I want this,* she thought. *This is mine.*

Her heart wound up and up, almost like singing.

"Now, look at your target. Concentrate. Deep breath. It's about controlling yourself, that's all. That's what people don't get. Like any other sport. Controlling your body. Your reflexes. The way you react. Your own sense of timing." He moved away, behind her, watching her closely, and it was just her now, her and her body, the simple logic of the trigger, its reliable promise. Her whole life shot through the barrel over and over and over until the chamber emptied. Her life, her past. Her mother's dying arms. The smell of death in that house. Like swallowing something thick and warm, relishing the drink only to find out after it's gone down that it's poison. *You're already dead*, she thought wildly. Her mama whispering. Beckoning her. "Let it go, girl," Reverend Tim whispered, his hand on her back. "Just let it all go."

He turned away, leaving her with the thrill. Letting her have it all to herself. And maybe he saw the tears. And shaking his head because she had done it and maybe he couldn't believe it, a hole in the cheek, in the shoulder, in the fleshy excess of the abdomen. He laughed like a proud father. "I had a feeling you were going to be good at this."

37

THE PARCEL SAT on their doorstep. Annie picked it up. It was addressed to her. The return address was from the catalog company McMillan & Taft, a favorite among her students. Unwrapping the brown paper she felt a tingling in her legs, a rapacious anticipation. Her eyes met the lavender tissue paper, folded neatly around the mysterious gift and sealed with a sticker that said *Delectable Intimates*. Her fingers tore apart the sticker and ventured under the paper into the slippery undulating folds of a satin negligee. Her heart began to pound; there wasn't any card.

Of course it had to be from Simon, she thought, suddenly famished for his touch. The negligee was the palest shade of pink, like the inside of a shell, and, she thought, in very good taste. Alone in the house, she decided to try it on. Upstairs, she went into the bathroom and took off her clothes and slipped the negligee over her head. The fabric slid over her body like running water, hugging every inch of her. Annie looked in the mirror and saw herself anew. From housewife to temptress in a matter of seconds. She felt like one of those Hollywood actresses in an old movie, beautiful and misunderstood, gliding through the room clutching a cigarette case and a highball.

That afternoon, after her Intro to Journalism class, she drove out to the motel. She tried the room; it was locked. She went down to the office and tapped the little bell. The manager came out from the back room, slid the key across the counter. "He's not here yet."

"Oh. Well, thank you." Awkwardly, she took the key. On quivering legs, she walked down to the room as if she were high on a rope bridge over a deep ravine. Simon was always there first, waiting for her, which made the whole situation so much easier. Unlocking the door, she considered the strange reality that her secret union with Simon was the first thing she had done on her own, entirely for herself, since the day she'd married. Even her decision to marry Michael had been prompted and promoted by others for as long as she could remember. Like fulfilling some subliminal family contract, Annie had done all the right things. She'd married in her twenties—a *doctor*—had had children before it was too late, and had salvaged something of her career. But when she was honest with herself, Michael's profession had proved to be a disappointment. His career had chipped away at the compassionate young man she had fallen in love with and had turned him into a weary, desensitized workaholic. The change had been a tedious betrayal that took greedily from him, *from both of them*, without remorse. On the surface, Michael was handsome and successful and Annie could easily rationalize his neglect, overlooking the emotional toll it was taking on her. But now she had changed. She couldn't do that anymore.

During the few hours a week she spent with Simon Haas, she had blown the dust off her prim middling self and gotten reacquainted with the woman underneath, a slippery, lithe, ravenous animal—the woman Michael had been ignoring for too long. The awful truth was that, at some point soon, she would have to banish her again. She knew this. And she would miss her profoundly.

The little room was cold and seemed haunted with the ghosts of dissolute guests. She sat down on the bed and waited. An hour passed. Maybe something had happened, she thought. His wife, perhaps. Maybe something had happened with his wife and he couldn't call her. Or maybe he'd decided to end it. It was too painful waiting here, not knowing, and she felt foolish in the negligee. She couldn't stand it another minute. She decided to leave a note with the manager, but where was a pen? She looked around the shabby little room. It was dark and pathetic, as was their alliance. Guilt bullied its way into her heart, and for the first time she felt ashamed. She should have just ended it, she thought. Her marriage was already in jeopardy. Who did she think she was, having an affair? She was not the sort of woman who did this kind of thing.

Resolute, she decided to write a letter to Simon explaining her feelings. She didn't want to hurt him; no, that was the last thing she wanted—in fact, her feelings for him were very deep—but the affair would have to end. Yes. She would have to put aside her desire for him for the benefit of her family. It was the right thing to do, *of course it was*, and he would understand. If he wanted, he could find another writer for the article. There was still time, if he felt that was necessary.

Strangely relieved, Annie grabbed her bag and opened the door only to find her lover standing on the other side of it, the key poised in his hand like a weapon.

"Don't bother, I'm leaving."

"I'm sorry I'm late."

"No apology necessary." She attempted to get around him but he held her arm and pushed her back into the room rather violently and closed the door. Her heart began to pound.

"Stop this nonsense. Take off your clothes."

"And what if I don't?"

"You'll be sorry." He smiled. And then, unwittingly, she smiled, too. "I'll have to give you a spanking."

She could feel her face flushing red. "Where were you? It wasn't nice of you to keep me waiting like this."

"I know," he said softly. "I was painting, Annie." He opened his hands, revealing the splotches of color. "It's because of you." He came toward her.

"Look, Simon. This isn't right. We can't keep doing this. Even though I want to. You know I want to."

"I don't know why you do this to yourself."

"What we're doing is wrong. You know that."

"We have this incredible thing, Annie. We have this, this *heat* between us. It doesn't happen every day. It's a gift. You think I've ever had this?"

She desperately wanted to believe him.

"You think I have this with *her*?" He sat down heavily on the bed. "I'm trapped," he said. "Her and me. We're both trapped." He sighed deeply. "I never meant . . ."

"For this to happen?"

"I never expected to feel like this." He looked at her. "I never expected to feel this way about you."

"Me either."

"I love the way your hair falls down your back, for example. Your hair." He ran his hand through her hair. "It's like ink spilled out all over the place, it's like a whole bucketful of water. Cold river water. Or the mane of a horse." He grabbed her hair like a tail and pulled on it hard. "You are my wild horse."

It was true that he loved her and that she loved him, it was all true yet there was nothing either could do about it. There was no future for them, nor did they have a past. She could not call him whenever she wanted, or see him whenever the spirit moved her. And yet, in so many ways, he was the one person who seemed to know her best. He was the single person on earth she wanted to be with.

It seemed to her that life was full of missed opportunities, that nearly every moment in a day contained fragments of loss.

She loved his painter's eyes, the moody complexity of his mouth. And she loved the boy that lingered there, the sad boy in his fingertips as they ran their lovely rain across her back.

"Come here, let me kiss you." He reached out for her, unbuttoning her coat. When his hands came in contact with the satin fabric of the negligee his face opened with surprise. "What do we have *here*? Is this for *me*?" Kissing her face, her neck, he ventured beneath the raincoat to the negligee below. "Lovely." He kissed her wrists and elbows and shoulders and neck. Her thighs, her knees, her long calves. Her toes. They moved back on the bed, spinning inside each other's arms, and she closed her eyes and indulged in the commotion of desire, holding on to him very tightly as if in the midst of a terrible storm. In his arms, she had found a quiet place, far away from everything she knew, and for the first time all day she could breathe.

38

THEY HAD LAIN THERE for a long time, watching the rain. Simon sensed her uneasiness, as though she were playing out some premonition in her mind. He rolled onto his side and put his arms around her. She turned her head and smiled at him. She said, "You shouldn't send things to the house. I mean I love that you did, but you really shouldn't."

He looked at her. "What are you talking about?"

"This," she said, touching the negligee on her body, "I'm talking about this."

He saw in her face that she'd thought he'd sent it.

"A bit conservative for my taste, don't you think?"

"What? You mean you didn't send it?" Her skin turned a queasy pea green.

He shook his head. "Maybe your husband's trying to tell you something."

"Tell me what?"

"Well, I assume you're not sleeping with him terribly much."

She didn't like the comment, but she did not deny it. "I have to go." She got up and went into the bathroom and turned on the shower. He could hear the plastic curtain sliding across the rod. He went into the bathroom and picked up the negligee off the floor. If her husband *hadn't* sent it, who had?

The tag said *Delectable Intimates,* but that meant nothing to him. He wasn't the sort of person who knew about things like tags and designers.

He yanked on the shower curtain and appraised his lover's shape. "Hello there."

"Hello."

"I was just wondering. Do you come with the room?"

"Go away." She slid the curtain back.

He yanked the curtain open. "I was hoping for a little room service."

"Room service?" she asked, her grin an invitation.

"I hope you don't mind." He stepped under the hot streaming water. "I've got a very big appetite."

She opened her arms. "Help yourself."

With the retrospective looming, Simon had begun to paint regularly in his studio. Besides the motel room with Annie, it was the only place he wanted to be. He knew, however, that he could not afford to abandon his wife just now. On her last visit to the psychiatric hospital they had diagnosed her with severe cyclical depression that required careful monitoring. They'd set her up with a local psychiatrist, but Simon suspected that she didn't keep her appointments. Now he feared that the cycle had returned, and that without the proper medication, she would be swept up in an emotional tornado that had the potential to wipe out whatever it came in contact with.

To the outside world, Lydia exuded a modesty and temperance. Simon knew that, as an employee at the catalog, his wife was tirelessly reliable. He also knew that the people she'd entertained from church saw her as a veritable saint. All those happy people who sat in his house around his kitchen table talking about the great Lord Jesus and His wondrous deeds. It gave him a headache just thinking about it.

When he returned home from the motel that afternoon, he took it upon himself to search through her things. He did so methodically, like a detective would, craving an understanding of the woman he called his wife. His instincts told him that she was up to something ugly. Her world, it seemed to him, was that of a teenager's, full of high peaks and dramatic valleys, but her sordid pathology made it impossible for him to predict her behavior. Her bureau was crammed with bowls of bracelets, childish bangles and necklaces adorned with charms of the day, such as peace symbols and crosses and words like *Happiness* and *Tranquillity*, two things his wife knew nothing about. There was an assortment of religious objects, crucifixes and candles and small figurines of the Virgin Mary. *Garbage*, he thought, fighting the impulse to sweep the surface clean.

He tugged open her underwear drawer, stuffed with little white panties that had at one time been the prurient substance of his affections. He picked up a pair of panties and examined them, amazed to see that their tag read *Delectable Intimates*. Fiercely interested, he searched the entire dresser, but found nothing more with that label on it. Perhaps it was a popular brand, he thought, and moved on to the closet. The closet was full of new clothing still fastened with tickets from McMillan & Taft, clothing, it seemed, that she had no intention of wearing. He wondered if she had stolen it. Sitting on the top shelf was an old sewing box that he vaguely remembered from her father's house. The box was oval in shape and had a cloth exterior that portrayed a scene of children at a skating pond. He took it down and lifted off the lid, under which was a tangle of embroidery thread and a piece of fabric that resembled burlap—a sampler, folded neatly across the top of the box. He removed the sampler and examined it and saw that Lydia's mother, Frances, had stitched it when she was a child. It showed a little red barn, four white chickens, and a yellow-haired girl tossing feed. He turned his attention back to the box, where he found the white Bible Lydia had received from one of the nuns in school, a dour Sister Louise he had met only once, and a leather-bound volume of nursery rhymes that was so old the pages had come loose from the binding. Gently turning the brittle pages he discovered an inscription from Lydia's mother. *To my darling daughter, Love, Mama,* she had written in ornate script. Taped to the page beneath it was a small photograph of the woman and child; Lydia's mother, Simon presumed, and Lydia as a little girl.

Simon sat down on the bed and sighed, all at once overcome. He studied the photograph. At three years old, the child was already exquisite, a rare and dazzling jewel. Why had he been the one to find her? And what would have become of her if he had not?

He was putting the book away when an envelope dropped out. The envelope was full of cash: an assortment of bills, ones, fives, tens, twenties, and a fifty, totaling nearly six hundred dollars. He wondered where she'd gotten it. Simon deposited all of her paychecks and had sole control of their checking account. He gave her a weekly allowance for groceries and whatever else she needed. In truth, his wife was innately penurious. She spent modestly. The perfect match for a fledgling painter, although, as it had turned out, he hadn't struggled for long. Money had never particularly interested him; it had certainly never motivated him. As long as he had paint and canvas and food in his belly, that's all that had ever mattered to him. When he'd hit it big in the art world and the money had gushed in like a river tainted with pollutants, he couldn't wait to get rid of it. Unbeknownst to her, he'd stashed most of it in a private account and had hired a local management firm to invest a portion of it in the stock market. The rest of it he'd spent quickly, foolishly, and when there was little left he did not regret it.

When Lydia had told him she needed to work to pay off creditors (he was terrible at paying the bills), he had acquiesced, wanting to promote in her mind a sense of responsibility that she was contributing to the family till, so to speak. But this money, this money she'd been saving. Perhaps she'd gathered it like a little squirrel, loose change left around the house, piling up in the ashtrays, ceramic bowls, five dollars here, ten dollars there. He supposed it added up. But to this amount?

The dogs began to bark and a moment later he heard her car pulling into the garage. Swiftly, he put everything away exactly as he had found it. He hurried downstairs to the kitchen, put up water for tea, and situated himself at the kitchen table with his small sketchbook and charcoals, as though he'd been there all afternoon. She came in through the side door, the fire of winter in her eyes. In their early days together, she'd liked interrupting his work. On some occasions, she would spend whole afternoons watching him work, content to just sit and see the thing come to life before her. It was an aspect of their lives that had come to an end when he'd stopped painting. He knew she blamed herself. He ventured that she believed he no longer painted her because she'd grown hips and breasts and the fertile intelligence of a woman. He could see this in her eating habits, which verged on anorexia. It seemed to him that she no longer knew where she stood in the world now that her body, her persona, was no longer on public display, vulnerable to the malicious interpretation of strangers. And not knowing drove her mad. It made her do things to herself.

"How was work today?" he asked her.

She turned around, startled by the question, her long yellow hair rushing over her shoulder. "Fine." The teapot whistled and she took it off the flame. "Would you like me to make it for you?" Not waiting for his answer, she began to fix him a cup. Then she brought the two cups over to the table, her face bright with expectation like a little girl at a tea party.

"Do you like it?" he asked.

"Do I like what?"

"The job. Working there. Is it a nice place to work?"

She shrugged. "It's all right. I'm on the phone all day. Taking orders. It's nothing great."

"What do people order usually?"

"Clothes, of course. From outerwear to underwear," she said in a charmed voice. "That's the company motto."

"Underwear, too?"

"Why all this sudden interest in my work?"

"Just wondering, that's all. Just wondering what my wife does all day. Isn't that all right?" He manufactured a tone of propriety. "Doesn't a husband have the right to know what his wife does all day?"

Her eyes looked glassy. She smiled, seemingly pleased by his attention, and her face bloomed like a flower, a dahlia with its crimson secrets. "It's really very boring."

"Have you made any friends?"

"Yes. A few. From church. We eat lunch together in the lunchroom. We talk about our work. Our charity. But you wouldn't know anything about that, would you? You don't give of yourself, Simon. It's not your nature."

"No," he said softly, slightly spurned by the comment. He'd given to her, hadn't he? He'd saved her. He'd given her plenty. But he said, "No, Lydia, I suppose it's not."

"But you're an artist," she reminded him. "You give differently."

"How very generous of you to put it that way."

She flashed a grin and sipped her tea.

"You look very pretty today. It's a pity I never see you."

She smiled richly, obviously flattered. "I work like everybody else," she said, her girlish enthusiasm betraying every attempt at seeming womanly. "That's the best part. I'm just another employee, not Simon Haas's wife. It feels good to just be me for a change."

He nodded, uncomfortable suddenly. "And after work. What takes you so long to get home?"

"Church meetings. Stuff like that."

"What stuff?"

Her eyes darted this way and that, minnow-quick. She was deciding whether or not to tell him the truth. It was an expression he knew well when it came to his wife. "You may as well know I'm part of Life Force, the pro-life movement."

"You mean those people who protest in parking lots?"

"We fight for the lives of the unborn." Her voice sounded dead.

"What the hell for? What interest do you have in that?"

She summoned tears to her eyes. "We could have *had* that baby, Simon."

"Don't bring that up. *Jesus.*"

"We didn't have to kill it."

"Oh yes we did."

"You made me do it. That awful woman. What *was* she, a prostitute?"

"A dubious line of work, but it pays."

"You *forced* me."

"The hell I did. You were *fourteen.*"

She shook her head, tears falling thickly onto the kitchen table. "We could have saved it. We could have taken care of it."

"For Christ's sake, Lydia, you were *raped.*"

Her back went stiff and she gazed at the window, where darkness had pulled down its heavy shade and only a sliver of orange remained.

"I could have taken care of it." Her voice quavered. "That place she took me to. It was *horrible.* It was the worst experience of my life."

"Worse than being raped?"

"It was a *life,* Simon. It was a *gift.* How it got there makes no difference."

"Boy, they've done a good job on you."

Furious, she shoved the chair violently against the table. For a moment she just stood there, as if she was surprised at herself, amazed even, her chest heaving with anger. Then she raced up the stairs and slammed the door. A moment later he could hear music playing, some Christian rock group, so loud that the walls trembled. He sat for a moment, but the music annoyed him. *How dare she,* he thought. Climbing the stairs, he wondered what he would find behind the door of their bedroom. He opened it, but the room was empty, and he walked in searching for her but found himself alone. She'd opened all the windows and the cold air blew in, swirling the curtains. He turned off the music and closed the windows. A moment later he heard a door slam downstairs. How she'd gotten down without him seeing her eluded him. He glanced out the window and saw the flash of her taillights as she turned the corner and vanished behind the trees.

Where in hell was she going? he wondered.

Back in the kitchen, he made himself a supper of bread and cheese and poured himself a glass of whiskey. He noticed her canvas bag on the back of the chair, full of newspapers and magazines, all rolled up together. Curious, he shuffled the papers out onto the table and put on his bifocals. There was a *Time* magazine, the cover of which showed Wally Nash and the president at their debate podiums. Lydia had drawn the horns of the devil on the president and an angel's halo above Nash. Rolled up inside it was a catalog from McMillan & Taft. On its front cover, which showed an oppressively happy couple strolling in the autumn woods, was a little cloud containing the words *Delectable Intimates*. He scrambled through the pages to the very end, amazed to find a whole section of photographs of models in high-end lingerie. It did not take long to find the identical negligee that only hours before he'd admired on his lover's body. Someone had circled it with black pen. Suddenly, his appetite was gone. The spit of rage filled his mouth.

Lydia had sent it to Annie. He was sure of it. She knew.

39

LYDIA'S FATHER had compared the sensation of dying to that of falling into quicksand. Over and over again during those long months, she imagined the gritty warmth enveloping him, suffocating him. He lay in bed, thin as a bundle of sticks, his skin the color of mustard. His manner was caustic and disagreeable, as if he'd swallowed lye. She fed him whiskey off a spoon, but that only made him sicker. Sometimes she dreamed of smothering him under his pillow. She'd play it all out in her head. Putting the pillow over his trembling face. The terror in his eyes. The way his legs would twitch and go quiet. Finally, she called a doctor, who came over at once. The doctor wanted to put him in the hospital, but her father wouldn't hear of it, brandishing a flyswatter in the man's face.

With her father sick and unable to work, there was little money. Lydia's teacher, Sister Louise, secured a job for her at the nursing home in Gloversville. They paid her four dollars an hour under the table, since she was underage. Each day after school she rode her bike to work, where they used her in the kitchen to help prepare the meals. There was the red-faced cook with his bloodsucker veins. The smell of boiling sugar beets, wilted onions. Salisbury steak and peppers. Other girls worked there, girls like her, who were poor, who at the ages of fourteen and fifteen were already brittle and indifferent. Lydia would smoke with them on break among the old people drooping in wheelchairs. Sister Louise believed Lydia was performing a godly task. She said Jesus had chosen Lydia, but on some days it was hard for Lydia to see the benefits of her service. Pushing around the cart at feeding time, tying on the bibs, forcing the cook's slop down their throats. The black-skinned women who cleaned the bedpans, murmuring complaints, the scandalous odors of the body's decay permeating the walls.

One afternoon Lydia discovered the small room where they kept the medicines. She soon realized that it was not difficult to slip a bottle of aspirin into her pocket, or even the tiny yellow pills they gave to the more disagreeable patients. When she got home, she crushed a few of the pills into her father's food, in an effort to ease his pain, and he never suspected. The pills gave him an easy, glassy-eyed look, and he didn't bother her so much, didn't scold her. He'd gaze out the window at the fields, or stare blankly at the television. Weeks passed, and little by little the hard lines of her father diminished, and he became someone else, a befuddled stranger. Without him bugging her all the time, she felt a new sense of freedom and now it was she who snapped at him, tugging at his sheets, shutting off the TV. Sometimes she even got lazy and would forget to feed him, or change his clothes, which had the foul odor of his excrement, but he never complained, not once.

The cook singled her out to do certain tasks. He made her clean the ovens, and he would supervise her and inspect her work and if it was not done to his satisfaction he would make her do it again. One day after work he called her into the kitchen. He took her hand and brought her into the pantry. She did not like the look in his eye, sweat forming quickly on his brow. He grabbed her knapsack, rifled through it, and pulled out the stolen pills. Almost instantly she began to cry. "Do you know it is a crime to steal?" he asked her. "These are narcotics, Miss Crofut. Do you know you've committed a federal offense? I could turn you in. I could have you arrested." She cried, dropping to her knees. "You've caused me nothing but trouble," he told her. "You're a foolish, insipid girl and you'll never amount to anything. You don't do anything right. Even the simplest tasks." He took down a can of lard and opened it. He shook his head as though he were sorry for her. He grabbed her and lifted her skirt and bent her over the piled sacks of flour, roughly tugging down her underwear. He used the lard, smearing it liberally the same way he greased the pans for corn bread, then took her with a brooding force. When he finished, he withdrew from her, wheezing and stumbling, and fired her. "One word about this and I'll call the police," he said. "I'd hate to see a young girl like you spend the rest of your life in prison."

Riding home on her bike, she found it too painful to sit down on the seat. She could hardly see through the blur of her tears. The gray houses tumbled behind her. She did not understand why the man had done such a thing, but she knew it had been a sin, a terrible sin. The next day she concentrated on chores, ignoring the pain the man had caused. Trying to forget it. To stuff it deep in her heart where she'd never look again. First she mowed the lawn. It was hard work, the sweat pouring out of her. Then she washed her father's sheets, soiled with sweat and piss. She filled the washtub with water from the hose and let it warm in the sunlight. Then she gathered the sheets and brought them outside and pushed them deep underwater, holding them there, holding her breath. She could not go on like this much longer. Taking care of him. She could not. She pinned the sheets on the line. Wet, they reminded her of the cool damp skin of her dying mama, and she wrapped herself up like a mummy, waiting for her mama to whisper. *If only she would,* Lydia thought. *If only.*

Shortly after the rape, Lydia went to confession and told the priest of the awful event. Afterward, the priest sighed and spoke in a doleful voice. "You will spend your entire life trying to rectify this act."

Lydia went home and looked the word up in the dictionary. *To set right; to correct. To correct by calculation or adjustment. To refine or purify.* Lydia did not have any idea how she could possibly do any of those things and lay awake every night going over the incident in her head. Had it been her fault? Why hadn't she done something—why hadn't she fought back?

Oh, yes, Lydia knew about sin. Jesus had never forgiven her.

A week later Simon Haas knocked on their door. The minute she saw him she knew that he would be the one to save her.

They'd buried her father in the cemetery, next to her mother. After the burial Simon moved in with her. He'd brought his things from the city. He didn't have much, just his paints and a small suitcase, two pairs of trousers, three shirts, four pairs of socks. He set his few belongings out on her father's dresser: a leather pouch that contained his money and a small, ornate box that had been his mother's. He had in his possession a small green bottle of aftershave, a razor, a tortoiseshell comb with several teeth missing, and a tin that contained a special tobacco that, he said, he used to calm his nerves. People thought they were related, that's how he got them to stay away. And they lived like that. He said he was willing to keep her, to take care of her like a relative, in exchange for almost nothing.

Simply the opportunity to paint her.

Routinely, he woke early, before dawn, and went walking in the long grass behind the house. He liked to witness the rising sun and the wailing geese crossing the red sky. Lydia would watch him through the kitchen window, a large man in a leather coat, confronting the new sun like a dare. During those moments, when they were separate, she tried to understand him, to get inside his mind. But he had told her nothing of his life or his past. He'd come in and shake off the cold, hang his coat on the hook, and wait for her to serve his breakfast. He liked strong black coffee with sugar, and took his bread dry, without butter or jam. He moved slowly through the day, observing the various details of their life in the house. The way the cream fell from the pitcher. Her hands as they poured his coffee. He said her hands reminded him of birds. He'd take them in his own and warm them at his mouth. Or the sun crawling across the table. The light attracted him as much as the darkness. Each was important, he told her, and one could not survive without the other.

He followed her around like a lost dog with his paper and his pencils.

His charcoal. Her only escape from him was the bathroom, the narrow room that dripped and hummed. The little birds in the tree by the window. The smell of peppermint soap. Sometimes she would stay a long time just to torture him, to make him wait for her, and when she'd finally emerge he'd study her as though she had changed somehow, as though she'd transformed in some powerful way.

Afternoons, he sketched her all around the house. At the window, looking out at the trees. At the table buttering bread. The time dragged, and she longed to be back in school, but Simon wouldn't let her leave the house. He told her he couldn't bear her being out of his sight. At first, she felt special and important, almost like a princess. But then she saw his obsession, she saw that he was using her, and she began to hate him for it.

To occupy her, he gave her chores. He taught her things: how to stretch the canvas, how to prepare the colors. Dissatisfied with the paint he brought back from the city, he took to concocting his own pigments and taught Lydia how to mix them, too. She didn't mind mixing colors. She liked the way a color could make her smile. He was particular when it came to his supplies and she'd dutifully stand at the sink, scrubbing his brushes until they shone, the turpentine ripping up her hands, the colors running off her fingers like blood. After what she'd done to her father, she knew her life had become the consequence of that awful sin, and she believed this with all her heart. Jesus was letting her off easy.

Simon ripped down the velvet drapes that her mama had sewn and burned them in the yard with all her father's things. Now the sun filled the old house. His easel and his paints all over the living room. He was not a good housekeeper; she found herself picking up after him endlessly, his plates left on the couch, a banana peel in the bathroom, a bottle of milk spoiling on the back porch. He painted constantly. He painted whatever he saw that interested him. If she ate an apple he painted the core and the pits and the bruised petals. He painted her father's house from every angle, the windows and their changing light. He painted the old wrinkled woman who walked the road in her black coat, pulling her three-legged dog. The men in flannel shirts, painting the barns. The smirking redheaded boy who mowed the big field across the road, high up on the big green tractor.

Two months later she took ill. She couldn't eat, couldn't sleep. She knew there was something wrong with her, and she suspected it had something to do with the cook at the nursing home, but she didn't dare tell him. One afternoon Sister Louise came to the house for a visit. Simon answered the door in his undershorts, his naked chest covered with paint. He had a look in his eye all the time, a madman. "There's something wrong with her," Lydia heard him tell the nun. "Maybe she'll tell you."

Sister Louise came into the room and shut the door. She had a long face; she rarely smiled. Like Lydia, she had grown up without her mother. At school, Lydia had been her pet and Sister Louise used to bring her presents. Once she gave her a tin of shortbread. She sat on the edge of the bed and took Lydia's hand. "Lydia, tell me what's wrong?"

Lydia broke down and told Sister Louise about the cook and what he'd done to her.

Sister Louise's face went pale and her blue lips trembled. She called Simon into the room and told him what had happened. "She'll have to go to a home for unwed mothers," she said. "Take her to a doctor at once. If you don't, I'll call the police and they'll think it's yours. You'll go to jail. It's still against the law to have relations with a minor." With that she left.

The next morning they closed up the house and left for New York. "I don't want to go to a home," she kept saying.

"You're not going to any home," he told her. "I'm not putting you in a goddamn home."

He took her to his friend Grace's apartment. It was a tiny room that smelled of sweat and lilacs. Grace looked at her and shook her head. "Naughty boy," she said to Simon.

"It's not what you think," Simon told her. "Somebody else did this."

"Sure they did, honey, sure they did."

That afternoon Grace took Lydia to a clinic that was located on the third floor of a building with no elevator, over a veterinary hospital. Lydia could smell the dogs and cats as she climbed the stairs. They had to wait two hours. Lydia had to answer questions. She had to lie about her age. Then Grace paid them in cash. They took Lydia into a small room and put her feet up and spread her legs and took the thing that was making her sick out of her body. They sucked it out and she could hear it getting sucked, like a vacuum, and it made her sick, too, the idea of it. She could still remember the Oreos they gave her afterward, and berry punch. She was crying. She didn't know why she was crying but she couldn't stop. It wasn't that she wanted it, really—she didn't know what she wanted. But still, she felt sad. Deep, deep sad.

"You'll get over it," Simon had told her in the car. But she knew she wouldn't. They were living out of his car. It was just three days later when Simon sold his first painting to a woman named Norma Fisk. With the money they rented a furnished room with a hot plate and a small refrigerator. She'd stare out the window all day long at the city streets. He'd give her pills that he bought on the street. Sometimes they made her feel better. Sometimes they made her sick. He'd paint constantly, as if it was the only thing that could keep him from touching her. She knew he wanted her in a sinful way and it tortured him. He would sink into a dark mood and drink and avoid her. She told him she wanted to go back to school, and he yelled and screamed. Perhaps her father had been right, he said, perhaps she was lazy and ungrateful. *Get me the phone, I'm calling that orphanage. Let them deal with you.* Once, he became so enraged that he packed her things in a suitcase and put her in the car. "I'm not cut out for this," he said. "I can't take it anymore." She cried the whole way up the Northway, until he pulled up in front of a dreary house with a sign out front, Bard's Children's Home. "Out of the car, get out of the fucking car!" And she cried and screamed and twisted on the seat and then he kissed her. A surprise of moisture on her mouth. And he looked into her eyes. "Don't you know I love you," he said. "Can't you see that you're everything to me? I'd fucking die without you."

And it was then, with his face inches from hers, that she made her first fatal mistake; she believed him.

40

THERE WAS SOMETHING heartbreaking in discovery. You had to let go of the past and that wasn't easy, no matter how much you wanted to. Earlier in the evening, when Simon had followed Lydia to St. Vincent's, he'd discovered that she had a whole other life outside of the tight formality of their marriage. Much to his bewilderment, they'd enlisted his nut job of a wife to man the Crisis Hotline, advising strangers on what he imagined were a variety of domestic travails; it baffled him to think that she could handle the task. Yet he'd spied her through the glass window in her little pink coat, handling the calls with apparent ease, a flush of importance on her cheeks. He had loitered for two hours in the corridor near the candy machines, drinking sour coffee and sketching people on paper towels from the men's room. Finally, she'd emerged from the small office, accompanied by a man with a limp, and he'd known at once that it was Tim Hart, the minister from her church. Around his very own kitchen table, Simon had heard many a dewy-eyed devotee speak, in somber tones, about the man's unfortunate disability. Unimpressed, Simon had refused to get swept up in the evangelical gusto of the New Birth Church, but had, in his guilt, donated hundreds of dollars to its discretionary fund with the blessed hope that this man of enlightened sensitivity could keep his wife on an even keel.

He had clearly done more than that. There was this look on her face, like she'd walk through fire for him. Simon unwittingly felt betrayed, even though he knew he had no right. It wasn't like she was fucking the man.

The minister was driving a black Cutlass and Simon's wife was inside it. They were heading into High Meadow and Simon was in an old Dodge Dart behind them. He had borrowed one of his student's cars, explaining that his own had broken down. A predictable excuse that sufficed. It was not fast, but they would never suspect they were being followed.

They exited the interstate at Nassau, then wound their way down dark roads into High Meadow. He could not imagine where they were going now. The minister slowed down and turned onto a narrow dirt road, cutting his headlights. Simon did not turn into the street after them. Instead, he pulled into a cluster of bushes and got out and walked.

Down the road, he could see the two of them getting out of the car, walking around to the back of a house. It chilled him, seeing this. *That's my wife*, he wanted to scream. *That's my fucking wife!* After several minutes, Simon saw them return to the car. He ducked into some bushes and watched the car crawl down the road and turn the corner.

He waited on the dark road, unable to stop his pounding heart. Gradually, as he neared, he began to hear music coming from one of the houses. Was it *La Bohème*? With a sinking apprehension, he walked toward the house, knowing somehow what he would find when he got there. Her Volvo in the driveway, for instance, did not surprise him, nor did her beautiful house, which was more impressive than her description of it had been, with big windows, all lit up inside. She was just the type to waste electricity, he thought. The whole house seemed to glow from within—because of her, he thought. *Her* light. It was exactly the sort of house he'd imagined her in. Standing there in the dark he felt cheap and loathsome, like a Peeping Tom.

He remembered their lunch together at the museum, how she'd confided in him about the threats. It was Lydia's church, he realized, that fanatical Reverend Tim. Why else would they come out here together in the dark?

Sweat coated his skin and he felt sick to his stomach. He did not know what he would do if they hurt Annie. He needed to see her. He needed to make sure she was all right.

Like a thief, he walked around to the back of the house. His hands felt heavy, useless. The wet grass seeped into his shoes. A chill went all through his body and for a moment he entertained the theory that he'd been marked by destiny in some way, that he was a flawed man and would perish for it.

The deck ran across the back of the house and he stepped up onto it. The blinds had been pulled down over a large picture window, but he could easily see through the slits. He knew Annie was unaware of this, and he would never be able to tell her. He saw a family room off the kitchen. The TV was on, and he stood there for a moment watching it flash, thinking distantly of his own home and the dark mood that washed through it like a sloppy watercolor. Annie came into the room, suddenly. To his relief, she looked content in a white bathrobe and bare feet. She sat down on the couch. The only thing between her and him was the cold glass of the window, and he put his hand upon it as if upon her back. Her hair was wet, scattered across the green pillow like twigs in the grass. She picked up the newspaper and began to read. She was extraordinary, he thought. This woman whom, with his own hands, he had vigorously explored. This woman whom he had begun to love.

A day passed and he hadn't left his house. "What's wrong with you?" his wife asked that morning.

"Touch of the flu," he told her.

Lydia scowled. "You're never sick."

"I am now."

"You have a class this morning."

"I've canceled it."

She bristled slightly, buttoning her blouse. "I'm going to work. I haven't fed the dogs."

"I'll do it. And Lydia, I'd like you to come directly home after work."

A smiled eased across her face. "What for?"

"I'd like to spend some time with you."

"Really?"

"Is that so surprising? A husband wanting to spend some time with his wife?"

This made her laugh. "Sorry, old man. I've got plans."

He could hear her galloping down the stairs. I've lost her, he thought. "Lydia!" he called out. "Just a moment. *Lydia!*"

But she was already out the door.

Standing at the window, he watched her get into her car. She'd put a bumper sticker on the rear bumper: BELIEVE IN YOURSELF, CHOOSE LIFE. The sticker embarrassed him. He didn't like bumper stickers or the people who used them. He didn't like people blasting their opinions all over the place. And since when did his wife have any opinions. The idea that she was so shamelessly involved with that minister gave him the creeps.

Should he tell Annie, he wondered. Should he *warn* her? He could forbid Lydia to see Reverend Tim, he thought. He could threaten her. Lock her up in the house. Commit her to Blackwell.

The phone rang, trilling through the house. It was the museum curator's secretary, a young man with an Australian accent. "Just checking up on you, Mr. Haas. How are the paintings coming?"

"Quite fine," Simon told him. "Don't you worry, you'll have what you want." And they would. Yes. They'd have their lousy paintings and they would make him famous once again. But for what? For what, *for whom*, he did not know. Annie, maybe. Yes, he thought, perhaps he was painting for her.

He hung up on the man and left the house at once. The brisk morning air smacked his face and he gathered his skimpy coat around himself. The sun was still weak, the sky a fresh bruise. He walked into the woods, the dogs loping at his heels then scattering among the fallen limbs and hills of dead leaves. He walked and walked for over an hour, hearing the rushing of the lake. It suddenly occurred to him that he was alone; the dogs had vanished, and he did not hear them barking. Disoriented, he searched the black trees, looking for landmarks. There were none. He was completely lost. His eyes began to tear and his throat went dry. Trudging uselessly in one direction, he roamed through the stifling maze of his past where it was so dark, and he was so lost, that there seemed no escape. One poor decision after another, constructed out of flimsy, dishonorable intentions. For a moment he was overcome, and dropped to his knees in the cold leaves and wept.

The sound of a gunshot broke open the air. He heard his dogs barking wildly and remembered that it was hunting season. It was dangerous to be walking in the woods. Slowly, he got to his feet and started toward their noise, grateful that at last he would find his way home.

41

LYDIA PARKED in the visitors' lot just inside the main gates. The man in the little white booth gave her a map and she found the registrar's office easily. The campus seemed quiet, students scattered on benches here and there across the quad. It was a bright windy day and she took her time, walking slowly behind a group of girls in bright ski jackets, eavesdropping on their conversation about a class they were taking. They were so pretty and smart, smelling like flowers, strolling along as if they didn't have a care in the world. An old anger surged through her body and she quickened her pace.

Luckily the registrar's office was quiet, and the woman behind the counter looked nice. Lydia went up to her and explained her situation. The woman behind the counter had her hair pulled back in a tight bun and was wearing a pin that might have been made by her daughter or son, constructed out of cardboard and a safety pin. The woman frowned, pursing her lips. "The semester started over a month ago. I'm afraid that class is closed."

"Do you have any idea who I am?"

"No, I can't say that I do."

"I'm Lydia Haas."

The woman in the registrar's office looked perturbed, then embarrassed. "Of course, Mrs. Haas. Forgive me. I didn't recognize you. Let me see what I can do."

The woman behind the counter disappeared through the door behind her. *Of course, Mrs. Haas. Forgive me.* Lydia waited for nearly fifteen minutes. Finally, and with hasty impertinence, the woman returned, offering Lydia a stack of papers that needed to be filled out. "You're welcome to audit the class," the woman told her, "but the professor will not be required to submit a grade."

"Is there a charge?"

"No, no charge for spouses of faculty members. The class meets in Hillard. Monday through Thursday, at noon."

Lydia forced a smile. She left the building quickly and ran all the way to her car. Driving home she had an intense craving for prunes, and she pulled into Brewster's and purchased a canister and ate them quickly, spitting the pits out her window. When she got home she had to run into the house to use the bathroom, and she was in there for quite some time. She got into bed in her clothes, pulling the covers up to her chin, and stared out the window, watching the trees dancing in the wind. She lay there all afternoon and into the evening. She saw no reason to get up for anything.

When she woke in the dark room, her husband was shuffling in, wearing some kind of costume. At first she thought she was dreaming. She could see that he was drunk, stumbling around, spilling his drink on the carpet. He went into the bathroom and urinated, then washed his hands. She sat up in the bed and watched him as he began to undress.

"What's that you're wearing, Simon?"

"A costume. From fucking Shakespeare. I stole it from the Theater Department."

"What for?"

"What for?" He grimaced. "Fucking Halloween, that's what for."

"Oh, I see."

"There was a party."

"I'm sorry I missed it."

"You didn't miss anything."

The wind had picked up and she could hear her chimes clanging on the porch. He sat down heavily on the bed and wiped his face with his hands.

"I see you've had some whiskey."

He nodded. "More than some."

She stood up in the dim room and took off his shoes and socks. Then she helped him back onto his pillow. Swiftly, he fell into a deep sleep. It was almost midnight. His face in sleep looked boyish and vulnerable and she had the most intense desire to slap it. For a moment she indulged in a fantasy of slapping his face over and over again, one cheek and then the other, alternating until they were bright red. It made her a little wet, thinking about it, and she began to undress, slowly, sleepily, then stood naked beside the bed, feeling the thrill of a draft, hearing the rain beating on the roof then running through the gutters like hundreds of coins. Her heart was beating fast and she did not know what she would do next. She did not know what she would do to calm herself down. She took his hand and wriggled it, trying to rouse him, but he did not wake up. She sat down beside him thinking *Little Miss Muffet sat on a tuffet,* and put his hand on her breast, molding it around the circle of flesh, and still he did not wake. She took his fingers in her own and squeezed her nipple like a cow's teat until it hurt, until she gasped out loud, until the sweat prickled her neck like thousands of tiny pins and her eyes began to tear and *still* he did not wake up. She picked up her pillow and put it down softly over his face *like a cloud* and thought, *How easy this is. How perfectly simple,* letting the picture of his inevitable suffering fill her head, his struggling, his twisting and turning under her hands, his squirming feet.

Feeling the pressure, Simon coughed and turned onto his side, powerfully, knocking the pillow to the floor, and the idea, entertaining as it was, flew out of her head.

Exhausted, she crept into bed and lay on her stomach, turning away from his sour breath, and went to sleep, hating him slightly less than before.

Lydia did not tell her husband that she would be taking Annie's class. In fact, she said very little to her husband, as little as possible. With him painting again more intensely than ever, perhaps he was relieved. Anyway, he was too busy to take notice.

Too busy fucking Annie Knowles.

That morning she dressed for work as usual, but paid special attention to her hair and makeup. She even sprayed a little cologne on her neck. She hoped Simon would notice, but he scarcely looked up from his bowl of oatmeal. At eleven-thirty she left work and drove to the college. Reverend Tim had given her some special pills for her nerves and she took them now to calm down. She parked in visitor parking, wanting to keep her little secret from Simon. Well, he would find out soon enough, she guessed. She bought herself a cup of coffee in the little café on campus, and waited until it was time to go to the class. The classroom was located in a small octagonal building just a short distance from where her husband taught his classes in the art building. Walking toward the door, she swallowed hard, her throat parched from nerves. It had been ten years since she'd been inside a classroom. She hadn't been much of a student, and she had never liked the other girls, the vicious scrutiny of the nuns. So when Simon had put an end to her education, convincing her that life on the road with an artist would teach her everything she needed to know, she hadn't argued. Years later, after they'd moved to High Meadow and he'd gotten the job at St. Catherine's, he suddenly became eager for her to know more. Simon Haas needed a smart wife. "Your ignorance is an embarrassment," he'd told her once when he was drunk. He'd been the one who'd sent for the application for the high school equivalency exam. He'd helped her study. And when she'd passed, he'd bought her the Mercedes.

Entering the building she encountered a small group of students, waiting outside the classroom with their bags and books. They all looked smart, involved. She hovered near the drinking fountain, hoping no one would notice her. Even with the pills, she felt desperately anxious; her hands were sweaty and cold, her throat dry no matter how much water she drank. Annie Knowles came through the big noisy door at the other end of the hall and rushed toward them, her enormous leather bag swinging wildly from hip to hip. Her coat was open, as if she had put it on hastily, and she wore a silly wool hat, pink as a snow cone. She didn't seem terribly organized, Lydia thought, not like the nuns at her old school. In fact, Lydia thought, Annie Knowles seemed more like a student than a professor. She found it amazing that the girls were so enamored with her.

Annie Knowles didn't notice her at first, and Lydia followed the other students into the classroom, where they took seats around the table. There were fifteen students in all, most of whom were now seated and waiting expectantly. Lydia advanced toward her husband's lover, who was already busy talking to another student, and suddenly the whole world slowed and went quiet and all she could hear was the wind inside her head and the howling of her own heart. She felt, at that moment, that she could do anything, even kill.

The professor looked up, confused by Lydia's approach, her forehead as wrinkled as a basset hound's. Their eyes locked, and in those fleeting seconds so much seemed to pass between them. Lydia reached into her pocket and everything slowed down to a whisper. Annie Knowles turned white and her lips trembled slightly and her long white arm went stiff on the tabletop, as if to ward off evil. *It's not a gun, stupid, not yet,* Lydia thought, and it was in this potent and silent exchange that she realized all she was capable of.

42

IN A FLEETING SPASM of panic, Annie imagined her own death. Simon's wife reached into her pocket slowly, deliberately, then pulled out what Annie thought was going to be a gun. It wasn't a gun, of course. It was a pink slip, an add slip for her course. Annie took the piece of paper and excused herself and went into the bathroom to wash her face. In a matter of seconds, her shirt had been soaked through with sweat.

When she returned to the room, Lydia Haas was sitting at the table, doodling on a pad of paper. "Excuse me, Mrs. Haas, but this class began over a month ago. There's no way you can possibly catch up. I don't know how they could have let you in."

"I'm only auditing the class," she said. "They told me I could do it."

The room had grown quiet. The other students watched the famous artist's wife with dire fascination. Annie was acutely aware that they were watching her, too. Annie knew that her handling of the situation was critical.

"Do you have any writing experience?" The words stuck to Annie's tongue like Velcro.

"Yes," Lydia Haas answered tentatively, but Annie doubted that she'd ever taken a serious class.

"Are you a degree candidate?" Again the confused expression. "Are you working toward a degree?"

"No." She paused a moment. "Not officially."

Annie felt the sweat trickling down her back. *Does she know?* She wondered if Simon had mentioned the article for *Vanity Fair* to his wife. Perhaps his wife admired her work; perhaps she should be flattered. No, Annie thought darkly, she should not be flattered. Lydia Haas exchanged shy smiles with the other girls. The fact was, she might have been one of them, yet she had a sneaky, sly demeanor that thoroughly disarmed Annie. Lydia's complexion was sallow, sickly, as if she lacked fresh air. Sitting there with clasped hands she looked as if she were calculating some elaborate scheme. "Well, then," Annie said, "welcome to the class, Mrs. Haas." She tried to smile at her, but Lydia did not smile back. The other students gazed at Annie attentively, waiting to hear her opening remarks. Acutely aware of Lydia's presence at the table, Annie awkwardly reviewed the last assignment, then launched into a meandering lecture on the elements of writing the personal essay, encouraging them to dig into their own lives as a means of producing effective social commentary. "I'm looking for essays that tell the stories of how we live, stories that attempt to provide a context for the way we behave." Hearing her own words, she began to formulate an idea. "I'd like you to try a writing exercise at home tonight. Write a page or two describing a close friend, someone who means a lot to you. It could be a sibling. Or even a parent. Or, in your case, Mrs. Haas, a spouse."

Their eyes locked for a daunting moment, until Annie looked away. The classroom emptied. Lydia Haas was the last to leave the room.

Annie had a date with Simon that afternoon and considered breaking it. Did he know his wife was taking her class? If he *didn't* know, she reasoned, she could possibly use it to her advantage by keeping it a secret, glimpsing the Haas household from the tormented wife's perspective, if she *was* in fact tormented. *Thinking like a true journalist again,* Annie thought with irony. Perhaps she was getting her fangs back after all. Annie remembered Simon's treatment of Lydia at the Spaulls' party, his apparent violence, and she had sensed in his lovemaking a power that could do great damage to someone if he wanted to. *Don't be shy,* she remembered her editor at *Vanity Fair* saying.

Simon's car was parked in the motel lot. Still uncertain of what she would say to him, Annie went to the door. Music surged within; was it Mozart's *Requiem*? He'd pulled open the curtains and she could see him through the window, sleeping on the bed. He was fully dressed, hadn't even taken off his shoes, listening to the music so intently that he had no idea when she entered the room. On the table was a bottle of wine, half empty, a baguette, a saucer of olives, and a small blue bowl full of figs.

For a moment she just stood there, watching him, as if he were the subject in one of his own paintings. A still life. *Still Life with Figs,* she thought. Now she, too, was in the painting. *Lovers,* she'd call it, or *Afternoon Tryst.* Annie tossed her keys down on the nightstand and Simon woke with a start. "You're late," he said, reaching out for her hand.

"I know. I'm sorry. My class ran over. I had a new student."

Simon looked surprised. "A new student? Mid-semester?"

"Someone very unique, in fact."

"They can't do that to you. Kick her out!"

Obviously, he had no idea that his wife was taking her class. "Oh, this student is very dedicated."

"Are you all right? You're pale."

"I have something to tell you."

"What? What is it?" He looked at her, waiting, his face shaped with concern. If only she didn't love his face. If only she didn't want to kiss him.

Tell him, she thought, but instead she whispered, nearly inaudibly, "Kiss me." Simon pulled her down gently onto the bed and kissed her and then she kissed him back, their kisses rushing at each other with urgency, and then they were rolling around like two boys in the grass, two boys wrestling, and she pulled on his hair and laughed a little wickedly and he pulled on hers and laughed, too, and then his mouth covered her neck with kisses. His mouth covered her shoulders and breasts and belly and thighs with kisses. *Fuck you, Lydia Haas!* she thought gleefully, clinging to his back. She wrapped herself around him so hard that neither of them could tell where one body began and the other ended, and they were one as they fucked, they were one, and tears fell from her eyes onto his face and became his tears. *Requiem,* she thought, the music storming through the room, thinking of the painting their bodies made. *Requiem for Two Lovers.*

She didn't want it to be over, no, she didn't want it to end, but she knew it must. *I must end this now!*

But she didn't.

The chorus sang its desperate chant of loss and it was her loss, too, it was both of theirs, and they would both suffer for it. Oh, they would suffer.

She looked at him in the gray light. He had fallen asleep. It began to rain, the drops twitching on the window. "I have to go," she told him.

His hand slid down her naked back. "So, go."

She dressed quickly, feeling his eyes on her, watching her. There was a taste in her mouth, like copper, like blood, and she wondered if perhaps he had bitten her.

"I'll miss you," he said.

"Me, too." She looked at him directly, wanting him to read her thoughts, all of their unspoken words crushed together inside her head. She leaned over and kissed him and left him alone.

The air stank of rain. Crossing the parking lot, she noticed a white car parked near her own. A Subaru. There was a woman sitting in it. Just sitting there. The woman had on big sunglasses and a ski hat. Annie saw a little girl playing in the backseat. The car seemed familiar to her. *Was it Christina's mother?* What her babysitter's mother would be doing at the Hum Drum Motel at two-fifteen in the afternoon Annie could not imagine, so she quickly discounted it. Suddenly, the Subaru started up and drove away. The car had a bumper sticker: BELIEVE IN YOURSELF, CHOOSE— but the rest of it had been scratched away. Standing alone in the empty parking lot with the rain falling down her face, Annie wondered what to do next. *Go to your children,* a voice told her. *Call your husband.* But she suddenly could do none of these things.

Her cell phone rang, startling her, and she ran to her car and answered it, the rain pounding down on the windshield. "We know what you're doing," a man said, "we've been watching you."

"Who is this?"

The man said nothing, but she could hear his breathing, the sound of the rain, a car horn in the background.

"I asked you a fucking question," Annie shouted.

"I don't talk to whores," the man said, and the line went dead.

43

JUST TO TORTURE HIM, Lydia worked on the assignment at the kitchen table. Simon stalked the room with his mug of tea, squinting down at her work with perturbed frustration. Deciphering her handwriting was a near impossibility, according to the nuns at her old school. Sister Eleanor, the cruelest sister, with eyes black as prunes, had bound her hands with surgical tape when Lydia had failed to write in the proper position.

"What are you writing?" he finally asked.

"Oh," she sighed in a voice light as meringue, "just an assignment for a class I'm taking."

"What?"

Just as she'd thought, Annie hadn't told him anything during their fuck session. "Don't worry, Simon, you don't have to pay for it. Actually, it's free. All the spouses are allowed to do it."

The look on his face was priceless. "You're taking a class at St. Catherine's?"

"Is something wrong?"

He'd broken out in a sweat. "I just wish you'd told me."

"I'm telling you now. It's a writing class. The art of the *personal* essay." She emphasized the word *personal*.

"A writing class? What in hell for? You have no interest in writing."

"Matter of fact, that friend of yours teaches it." Quivering lips, twitching shoulder. An old man, she thought. A disgusting, horny old man. "Well, it's been nice chatting." She grabbed her bag and started for the door. He grabbed her violently.

"What do you think you're doing, Lydia?"

"What do you think you're doing?" she repeated derisively.

"Answer my question!"

"I don't have to answer to you." Roughly, she pulled away and walked out. It wasn't until much later, when she'd driven into town to solemnly walk the aisles of the supermarket, that she realized she'd left her assignment on the kitchen table.

44

SIMON IMMEDIATELY TRIED calling Annie's cell phone, but she didn't pick up. He left a message on her machine at the college, begging her to call him, but he knew she wouldn't. He also knew that she would end their affair; perhaps, in her own mind, she already had. *It's over*, he thought, a sinking feeling in his chest. His stomach on fire. Over.

He would go to the registrar's office in the morning, he decided. He would have Lydia's name removed from Annie's class roster. He would explain to the forlorn woman behind the counter that his wife was delusional, thinking she could handle a college-level class, and would not be attending any more of them.

The idea of never seeing Annie again, of never touching her, filled him with the deepest sense of anguish. He would go to her office in the morning, he decided. He would explain the situation. He would find a way to reach her.

But when he went to the college the next morning, Annie's office was locked.

"Where's Professor Knowles today," he asked Charlotte, the department secretary, in as casual a tone as he could muster.

"Called in sick."

"Oh?"

Charlotte gazed up at him. Her pencil, he noticed, was all chewed up on the end of it. "You look rather disappointed, Professor Haas."

"Well, as a matter of fact I am. We were supposed to have lunch today."

"Lunch?" Her big brown eyes widened suggestively. He didn't appreciate the suggestion.

"Yes, Charlotte, we were going to *masticate* together."

Charlotte's face simmered. "Oh?"

"You might want to look it up." He grinned. "Masticate."

She gulped. "Okay."

"Has she canceled her classes?"

"Professor Wendell is covering for her this afternoon."

"Thank you, sweet Charlotte."

Halfway out of the room, he heard the thump of her dictionary.

Felice Wendell taught all her classes in Briggs Hall, on the north side of campus. Felice was in the midst of lecturing when he slipped into her room, inspiring a ravenous eruption of whispering among her students. Felice flushed and smiled at him. "Well, now, what an unexpected delight. Hello, Professor Haas."

"Hello, Felice. Ladies." He sported a charming grin. "May I have a word with you, Felice? Won't take a minute."

"Of course." She walked over and put her hand lightly on his shoulder. "What could possibly be so urgent?"

"I just spoke with Annie Knowles," he lied ruthlessly. "She mentioned you were teaching her class this afternoon. Look, I'll teach it. I don't have anything this afternoon."

Felice scoffed, "Be my guest. I was doing her an extreme favor."

"I realize that. I'm happy to do it."

"Well, isn't that nice. You know I'd never refuse *your* services, Simon," she said dramatically, loud enough for the students to hear. "But who's doing *whom* the favor? That's the real question, isn't it?"

He cracked a smile. "Good afternoon, ladies." He bowed slightly and walked out.

Felice called after him. "They're reading their essays aloud, something about lovers and enemies. I gather it's a subject you know something about?"

Without turning around, he answered, "Yes, I know something about that."

At noon, he entered Hillard and located Annie's classroom. He was a few minutes early. He couldn't wait to see the expression on Lydia's face when she found him sitting here. Contrary to her devious little plan, she would *not* be reading her essay, which was chock-full of slanderous untruths. *My husband is an abusive man*, she'd written. *Once he locked me up in a closet. I didn't eat for four days.* This, of course, was entirely fallacious. *He has the sexual needs of a predatory animal.* Well, perhaps that one he would allow.

Ah, here they were now. Lovely girls with swinging long hair and fresh faces, unlike his tormented Lydia. Sylvia Wheeler, one of his art students, took a seat at the table. "Hello, Professor Haas. Where's Ms. Knowles?"

"She couldn't make it today. I'm filling in for her."

"Groovy."

"Ah, here's the little woman now."

His wife appeared in the doorway, her face flushed persimmon. She looked positively mortified. Her lips began to tremble, and he thought she might burst into tears, but she didn't. "Don't worry, love, I've got it right here." He waved her assignment in the air like a handkerchief. "You won't be marked off, if that's what's troubling you."

He could feel her desire to run out, but something kept her there. She hesitated in the doorway while the other girls leered with fascination.

"Moving right along. This may be fun, actually. I've never taught around a table before. Something like *duck duck goose,* I imagine."

Some of the girls snickered. Lydia took her seat, her yellow fingertips scrambling to button up her cardigan. He observed her complexion, sallow and agitated.

"As some of you may know, I'm Simon Haas, and this"—he pointed to Lydia—"this is my *wife.*"

The girls shifted in their chairs, stifling giggles.

"We've been together for a long time, haven't we, Mrs. Haas?" He tossed her a smile. "Now, as some of you know, for many years your classmate here was the subject of many of my paintings, which turned out, in some instances, to be difficult for both of us. People look at the work and think what they want and feel what they want."

The students shifted in their seats, eyeing him uncertainly.

"Now, then, when you write these autobiographical pieces about your lives, *writing from the heart,* as Ms. Knowles calls it, it's important to understand that people will interpret your work any way they want to. Strangers. It's every artist's dilemma and we have little control over it. And it can be very painful for you, as well as for the people you write about, so I warn you to choose your subject matter with care." He shot Lydia a cold look. "You see, it's easy to call a man like me an asshole without really filling in all the gray areas. Like the lines in a drawing, black and white makes a picture; no matter how crude, it's still recognizable in some way. It's the framework, the *architecture,* so to speak. But then there's *gray,* and that's the heart of your work. Gray is where you want to get to, but it's difficult. Anyone can take a piece of charcoal and sketch a figure; even a stick figure will suffice. Anyone can write a sentence that describes a person doing something. But it's the gray area that beckons the true artist. It's the place that lures us, frightens us, and even deceives us. It's the place that drives us to do things. Awful things."

He took Lydia's assignment and flattened it on the table before him. Folding it, he fashioned it into a paper airplane. He knew he was being cruel, but he couldn't help himself. "You will discover that, in order to learn, failure is often necessary. But even the worst material can often be put to use."

He sailed the plane through the air toward the wastepaper basket.

With perfect aim, it nose-dived directly into it. He met Lydia's eyes. Hers burned with anger.

"That's all for today," he said with a smile, then walked out.

45

ENTERING THE SOUTH COTTAGE the next morning, Annie noticed that her mailbox was crammed with papers. The papers had been carelessly torn from a notebook and were filled with sloppy cursive handwriting that resembled Henry's. In lieu of a paper clip, the student had used a safety pin. The name in the upper-right-hand corner was Lydia Haas.

My husband has eyes like soda tin and a heart like a black stone. He likes to have sex with me whenever he can. He is a magnificent lover. I give myself up to him. He brings me little presents. Sometimes he likes to use sex toys that drive me crazy. Once, he took me to a shop on Lark Street and made the shopkeeper explain how to use the bondage toys. Right there in the store, with people coming and going and me down on my knees, the manager showed my husband how to turn me into his love slave. I am completely at his disposal. I satisfy all his whims. I tremble in his hands. He likes me to put on outfits. Sometimes I put on my Catholic school uniform and show him my dirty white underpants. Sometimes he will tie me to the chair and feed me yellow custard . . .

Annie could read no further. She crumpled the paper up in her hands. She wanted to burn it, but she knew she could not. Furious, she went into her office and shut the door and burst into tears. *Never again!* she thought. Never would she let him near her.

Disgusted, she opened her window and gulped the cold air. How could she have been so stupid? Now she was feeling nauseous. What could she have been thinking? She had gone blind, she decided. She had forgotten who she was.

Shaking, she ran into the bathroom, bracing herself over the toilet, but nothing would come up. She had been foolish, she had been manipulated. *How pathetic,* she thought, full of self-loathing. Bristling with shame. She had spilled her blood into his waiting hands.

Afraid of running into him, she hid in her office all morning, and when the phone rang she did not answer it. She considered telling Charlotte she was sick and had to go home, but it wouldn't look good to cancel classes two days in a row. At ten minutes to noon, she crossed the muddy quad to Hillard. Wet piles of leaves gave off a moldy, putrid odor. Her head was beginning to pound. She didn't know how she could possibly go through with teaching the class.

The girls were waiting for her. Lydia Haas sat tall in her seat. Unlike the other days Annie had seen her, today she was wearing makeup and her hair had been neatly tied up in a bun. Annie sat down and tried to begin, but her head was spinning.

Lydia Haas smiled at her, an eager pupil, and her assurance thoroughly disarmed Annie. Annie struggled to collect her thoughts, to broach a topic, but all she could manage were stutters. The girls shifted in their seats. The silence blared. Her head throbbed. Abruptly, she stood up. Offering no explanation, she left the room.

46

ALONE IN THE KITCHEN, Simon poured a generous glass of whiskey. He felt himself sinking into a dark place where drinking was a necessary distraction. Dishes were piled in the sink. Large bowls encrusted with a brown batter, wooden spoons thick with chocolate frosting. His wife could barely get dressed in the morning, yet she still came through for her church bake sale. This outward gesture of goodwill baffled him. Did they know how she fell apart when she came home? How she plunged into sleep like a child, sleep being her only accessible refuge? The faucet dripped into the bowl of muddy water and he thought perhaps he should wash it. Load the dishes into the dishwasher at least. His wife had stopped cleaning the kitchen. The entire house seemed topsy-turvy.

After his second drink, he rinsed the dishes in the sink and stacked them in the dishwasher, gazing out the window with numb preoccupation. When he finished loading the dishwasher, he took out some scouring powder and cleaned the countertops. It felt good, cleaning. It made him feel more in control. He felt as if everything around him had gone slightly out of focus, and putting things away, creating order, gave him hope.

Lydia's Mercedes churned up the driveway. Through the window over the sink, he watched her pull up and park. For a moment she studied her face in the rearview mirror. Then, appearing satisfied, she pushed the mirror back in place and got out of the car.

She looked rather pretty, he thought.

He continued wiping down the countertops as she unlocked the front door.

"My, my, aren't we spiffy," she said dryly. "Do you do windows, too?"

He turned and looked at her. She was wearing makeup, her lips painted a deep crimson—the sort of lipstick Annie wore. "Hello, Lydia."

"Hello, Grumpy." She dumped her pocketbook on the floor and retrieved a glass from the cupboard. She poured herself a drink.

"How was school today?" he asked in the tone one might use with a small child.

"Boring."

"Then why keep at it?"

"I want to get my degree," she said seriously.

"Oh. Whatever for?"

"I don't know yet, but I'm sure I'll think of something." She swallowed the whiskey in one gulp. "That friend of yours should find a different line of work. I've never been so bored in my life."

"Drop the class then."

"I just might do that." She poured herself another glass. "Oh, yes, I might do just that."

"I wonder if you should be drinking."

"Why shouldn't I?"

"Are you taking your medication, Lydia?"

"What in hell for?"

"Well," he explained gently, "when you don't take it, you get all confused. You get very sad, remember?"

Her foot began to wiggle. "I don't care. I'm already sad. I'm sad all the time." She looked at him. "You have no idea who I am."

The proclamation frightened him because he sensed she was right.

"You have no idea who you're dealing with."

"Don't I?" He nudged the bottle closer. "Go ahead, have another."

She grinned, madly. "You wouldn't believe some of the things I've done."

"Tell Papa all about it."

"I've got something really special planned for you, lover boy."

Simon watched her closely, the way she moved, like a cat. It came to him that she was completely delusional. He considered luring her into the car and taking her to the hospital, but he did not move.

"Why don't you tell me all about it, Lydia."

"Oh, no, I wouldn't want to spoil the surprise." She finished off her drink and threw the glass into the sink. It shattered, surprising both of them. "One less to wash," she said, and went upstairs.

The next morning he went to the college especially early and found Annie in her office, working with deep concentration at her computer. His presence seemed to startle her, and her face went white. Immediately, she closed the window on her monitor and the screensaver came on.

"I can't see you now." Her eyes flashed. "You'll have to leave." She seemed nervous, uneasy.

"What? Why not?"

"I don't want to talk to you right now."

"What's the matter?"

"Simon, I'm exceptionally busy."

"I have something important to discuss with you." He stepped inside the room and closed the door. She stood up and came toward him, her hand extending toward the knob. He grabbed her wrist, harder than he intended to, and she retracted, wincing. "You've been avoiding me. I want to know why."

"Please let go of me, Simon. My life is extremely complicated right now."

"I'm sorry to hear that. Let me help to simplify things."

Her face opened up for a moment like a window full of spring air. "Simon, listen, we had something great. But it's over."

"Why the big change of heart?"

Now she tugged free of him and went to her desk and sat down behind it. "I think you've got some things to work out."

"What are you talking about?"

"I don't know how you live with yourself. Whatever goes on with you and your wife . . ." Her voice trailed off.

"Annie, please. I don't understand."

She shuffled a stack of papers. "Look, I don't have time for this right now. I've got a stack of midterms to correct. I'm trying to finish the article."

"How's it coming anyway? Chock-full of grotesque insinuations, I hope?" It was meant to be a joke, but she only glared at him.

"No," she said finally. "No insinuations."

"Tina Chase likes the dirt, you know."

"There's plenty of that. I'm sure she'll be very pleased."

"What about me? It's my life, isn't it? I have a right to see it before you send it in."

"You have nothing to worry about. It's the truth."

"According to who?"

She didn't say anything, busying herself with her red marking pen. It occurred to him that Lydia might have said something to her.

"I'd make sure to check your sources," he said. "Slander can be very costly. You wouldn't want to get into a legal thing at this stage in your career."

"There's nothing slanderous about it."

"She's really gotten to you, hasn't she?"

"What?"

"My wife."

"You obviously have some serious issues, Simon. You really ought to see a therapist."

"Annie, look, I have no idea what you're talking about."

"It doesn't matter anyway."

"Yes it does. It matters to me."

She unlocked her desk drawer and took out some crumpled-up notebook paper. "Maybe you can explain this."

He read the page of his wife's handwriting with his insides twisting. For a moment he could do little more than stand there with his mouth open. The lengths she would go to, he realized, were boundless. "Oh, my love, you've been had."

"You obviously have a very interesting sex life at home. I can't imagine what perverse notion you've been entertaining with me."

"This is totally absurd. Annie. Please. My wife is a very sick woman."

Annie stood up, her body poised defensively. He could see the swimmer in her, the lithe athlete. "I don't know, Simon. I don't know what to believe anymore."

"It amazed me, actually, that she had the audacity to take your class, that she was that determined. I can't imagine why she would do such a thing."

"Because she loves you, that's why." Annie looked at him somberly. He desperately wanted to kiss her.

"Annie, these are all lies." He tore the paper to shreds. "The only time my wife's been tied to a chair and fed custard was as a patient in a strait-jacket at Blackwell." But still she did not seem convinced, a glimmer of suspicion in her eyes.

"You need to go now, Simon." Annie opened the door.

He grabbed her arm, violently. "For Christ's sake, Annie, I'm in *love* with you."

"You don't know what love is." Annie pulled away just as Charlotte Manning was walking by the office. Charlotte pretended not to notice, but Simon imagined that her interpretation of the scene would be making the rounds by late afternoon. "Now, if you'll excuse me, I have work to do." Wearing an expression of disgust, Annie ushered him out and firmly closed the door.

47

LEANING AGAINST the door, Annie held her breath. She felt queasy, belea-guered. She'd finally done it, she realized. She'd ended it. But instead of feeling relief, she felt complete remorse.

She went to her computer and opened the article for *Vanity Fair.* The article had been his bait, she realized, and she'd willingly taken it. And in her gratitude, she'd given him her body, *her love,* in return. He'd made out just fine. What he didn't know was that the story she'd written about him, with great tenderness she might add, had little to do with his wife. It was a gloomy tale about a sad little boy with an incredible talent who had grown into an emotionally disabled adult. Alone from the start, he was alone now. She printed out the article, put it in an envelope, and sealed it. Tina Chase, she ventured, would hate it.

A week passed and she did not see him and she did not call him and he did not call her. For the first time in her life, she knew real depression. Like a drug addict, she ached for him, and it cast a hue of malaise over everything she did. Cooking meals, washing dishes, doing laundry, helping the children with homework—all became a cycle of oblivion. She felt enervated beyond description, and in the afternoon she would climb the stairs to her room and crawl into bed, shaking into her pillow. It was like mourning a death, she thought.

"You sick?" Michael asked her one morning, his hand on her forehead. "No fever."

"Yes," she told him. "I'm not myself."

"What are your symptoms?"

My heart aches. "I'm sick. I can't eat."

"Must be a virus." He leaned over and kissed her forehead. "You going to work today?"

"I'll try."

Their eyes locked for a moment. What did her expression say to him? Did her eyes reveal that she had betrayed him? She hadn't asked for this. She hadn't wanted it, not any of it, yet it had come. Now consequence traipsed through her life like an interloper, leaving its sticky fingerprints on everything she knew.

Somehow she clambered from the bed into her clothes and maneuvered the children through the morning routine. As she was driving them to school, Rosie asked, "What's wrong, Mommy?"

"Nothing, honey, why?"

"You look different."

"What? No I don't."

"You're acting funny."

"Rosie! I am *not.*"

"She's right," Henry said. "You are."

"I don't know what you're talking about."

Annie pulled up to the school. "I want my old mommy back!" Rosie yelled, slamming the door and storming into the building.

Henry stuck his head in the window. "I have soccer practice."

"I know, honey."

"We have a game on Saturday. Can Dad come? Coach says I'm gonna play."

"You know he works on Saturday, Henry. How about if we make him a video?"

"Forget it. It's not the same." Henry trudged up the walk.

"I'll talk to him, Henry," she called after him. "I'll tell him he has to."

"Don't bother." The boy waved her off and disappeared inside. Annie sat there for a moment, disturbed by the fact that her son, at the age of ten, already understood the insult of compromise.

48

AT NINE O'CLOCK on Saturday a woman with a familiar face came to see Michael at the clinic. When he entered the examining room he was struck with her beauty and had to suppress his reaction. She had startling gray eyes and blond hair down to her shoulders. The nurse had prepped her for an exam, and she was naked under the white paper sheet. He had a moment with her alone, before the nurse came in. He was certain that he'd seen her before and glanced at her chart hoping to connect with a name, but they'd written Jane Doe on her file, which meant she'd refused to tell it to them. This happened on occasion, usually when a woman had something to hide. "Good morning, I'm Dr. Knowles. I see you're a new patient."

The woman nodded, her lips tight.

The assisting nurse entered the room. "We're doing a routine checkup today," she said.

"I haven't been to a doctor in ten years," the woman offered. "I was fourteen."

Michael and the nurse exchanged a look. "Well, we'll do a couple of tests just to make sure everything's okay, and then I'll give you a pelvic exam."

"What's that?"

"I examine you internally."

"Only takes a minute," the nurse said.

"Will it hurt?" the woman asked.

"It shouldn't," he said. "I'll do a breast exam as well."

The woman cringed noticeably.

"Are you sexually active?" the nurse asked.

She hesitated. "My husband likes it."

"Meaning?" Michael wanted more information. Her behavior was suggestive of a woman who had been abused. The woman went pale, discomfited as a nun in a bikini, and didn't answer. "Do you have any other sexual partners?" he pressed.

She shook her head. "No."

"Why don't we just take a look, all right?"

"Lay back. Put your feet right up here." The nurse gently instructed the woman to place her feet into the stirrups. Michael sat down on his stool and turned on his headlight. He pulled on his gloves and inserted the speculum into her vagina. Her body went tight. "Just relax," he said. "You have a bit of scar tissue here."

"I had an abortion once," she blurted.

"Not necessarily related." He did a Pap smear while she lay rigid, as if she were holding her breath. "Just breathe," he said. "We're almost through." He removed the speculum. "Are you planning on having children?"

"No," she said firmly. "Are we done?"

"Just lie back a second so I can check your uterus."

With his fingers up inside her, it came to him who she was. He had met her at Annie's faculty party. This was the artist's wife, Haas. Yes, yes, he was certain now. Perhaps she'd withheld her name because she was married to a famous man, he reasoned, but why hadn't she reminded him who she was? Surely she recognized *him*. Well, he had learned over the years to respect a woman's privacy. It was up to her to say something.

He pulled out his fingers and ripped off the gloves. "You've got a tipped uterus."

"I do?"

"Yeah, it's no big deal, it's just your anatomy."

"My what?"

"The way you're built." Quickly, he checked her breasts. "Are you using birth control?"

She shook her head. "They told me I couldn't get pregnant."

"Who told you that?"

"A priest. He said I'd had my chance and squandered it."

Michael and the nurse exchanged another look. "I doubt God holds it against you."

"Jesus remembers everything," she said.

"But he forgives, no?"

She shrugged him off. "My husband doesn't want a baby."

"You've got time. Maybe he'll change his mind."

"He won't."

"We're all done here."

"Can I get dressed now?"

"Yes, ma'am," he said. "Stop back and see us next year, all right?"

She nodded and he left the room.

49

THE MOMENT Michael Knowles left the examining room Lydia got down off the table and dressed. She could just walk out, she realized. She didn't have to go through with it. Still, her fingers fumbled in her pocketbook for the device. *Walk out and never look back,* she thought. *Drive and drive till nothing looks familiar. Leave everything behind. Start over.* No, she didn't know how to start over. With trembling fingers she opened a cabinet and put the device inside it and set the timer, just as they had shown her. It made a little noise, and a red light began to blink. It was a small bomb, but according to Mack Johnson, a member of their church who had made it, it would take most of the building down. Johnson, who was an engineer by day, had constructed the bomb in the loft of his garage late at night when his children were sleeping. On her way out, she retrieved the doctor's gloves from the trash and shoved them in her pocketbook, then walked to the front desk and paid for the visit with cash.

Driving home, Lydia could still feel a pressure in her abdomen from the examination. When he'd been inside her, she'd concentrated on the image of his wife lying beneath Simon. It had filled her with a certain ticklish hatred. In a small way, unbeknownst to the good doctor, she had gotten even with Annie Knowles.

The memory of her abortion swam around inside her head like a fat trout. A year after Simon became famous, his friend Grace had called a magazine and told them about Lydia's abortion. She told them that Simon was a sick man who liked little girls. The paper wrote all about it. They called him a pervert. They said he'd exploited her, the poor dumb girl. They said he should be put away.

The real truth was, he'd never even touched her.

They left New York after that and traveled all over the country, living out of his car. On her nineteenth birthday he asked her to marry him. She shrugged and said, "Okay," and he put a ring on her finger. It had been his mother's.

They were married in a wedding chapel in Fresno. It cost them forty-seven dollars. Afterward, they shared a plate of spaghetti and went skinny-dipping in a lake. They made love for the first time in the backseat of the car, her bare back getting stuck on the hot vinyl. It had been the first and only time she'd told him she loved him.

Lydia turned into the parking lot of a Price Chopper and sat there for several minutes just watching people get in and out of their cars. The low sun was bright in her face. A dog barked wildly in the locked car beside her. She watched the barking dog for a long time, and she understood how it felt. All locked up. No way out.

50

SIMON HEARD THE NEWS on the radio on his way home. Briefly, he fantasized that Michael Knowles had been killed, imagining the entire dilemma in Technicolor splendor: the clinic in ruins, the doctor's destroyed body, a hysterical Annie being pulled away. Of course, Simon would be there for her. Anything she needed. He'd escort her to the funeral, a dear family friend. Holding her hand, offering her handkerchiefs. Carrying her little daughter on his shoulders in the cemetery, holding the hand of her son. Picturing his lover in a black dress, glistening black stockings, he felt gently aroused. Did he even own a black suit? he wondered idly. Yes, *yes*, it was upstairs in the attic closet.

But, as the news reported, Knowles had not been killed. Nor had his notorious associate.

Arriving home, he saw his wife's car parked haphazardly in the driveway. Seeing it made his head ache; he didn't know why. The dogs were nowhere in sight. As he approached the house, he could hear them whining in the cellar. He unlocked the door and went inside and immediately let them all out. The dogs were relieved to see him, prancing about with their tails whipping the air and their snouts steaming. Back in the foyer, he called out for Lydia, but there came no reply. He climbed the stairs and found her in bed, delirious. A bottle of Valium sat on the nightstand. Yet her face was not at peace. She struggled, as if in a nightmare, twisted in the sheets, soaked in her own sweat. "Lydia," he said, trying to wake her, but she only groaned. "Lydia, wake up." But there was no rousing her, and he was momentarily startled by her deathlike stillness. Arms and legs thrown asunder, the creamy folds of her nightgown. With growing concern, he wondered if she'd taken too many pills. He held her head in his hands; he considered slapping it but couldn't bring himself to do it.

It was only midafternoon, but he felt the need for a drink, a stiff one. He opened the drawer in the nightstand and helped himself to some whiskey. He noticed her pocketbook on the floor, beckoning his inquiry, and he picked it up and dug his hands into it, tangling his fingers in her rosary. Crammed in a side pocket were two neatly folded pamphlets from the Free Women's Health and Wellness Center on South Pearl Street. One described various methods of birth control, and a second provided information on sexually transmitted diseases. Further inspection exposed a pair of plastic gloves, the sort a doctor wore.

Had she been down to that clinic? Had she been to see *Knowles*? And then he imagined the unthinkable.

Standing over his wife he suddenly felt dizzy. He staggered through the hallway as if crossing the deck of a reckless ship, and sought refuge on the bed in the guest room. He didn't want to think anymore. His thoughts only brought him pain. Maybe he would just stay in bed for a while. Nobody would miss him. Not even Annie.

51

IT WAS HENRY'S big day on the field and Annie and Rosie were his loyal fans, even though the temperature had plummeted since morning. Now it was almost noon and they were huddled together on the bleachers under an old plaid blanket. Like the other parents, Annie belted out her support for Henry's team, but under that wholesome, maternal facade her mind wound tight around her memories of Simon, the prickling reality that she had not gotten over him.

Henry's team scored a goal and everyone stood up, wildly cheering. Rosie climbed up on the bleachers and jumped up and down, clapping for her brother. Annie felt someone's arms go around her and turned to see Michael, his face in silhouette with the bright sun behind him. "Michael! What are you doing here?"

"Daddy!" Rosie threw her arms around him.

"Rosie girl."

"What happened, Daddy? You're bleeding."

There was blood on his forehead, dust on his clothes, and pieces of plaster in his hair. "Oh, my God. Michael, what happened?"

"Somebody bombed the clinic," he told her. "I'm all right." He held her close with Rosie clinging on, the three of them locked in a huddle. For a moment they didn't move, and she could feel him shudder slightly. "I had just finished an exam and this blast went off. It threw me across the room. The whole front of the clinic's been damaged. Luckily, nobody was killed. Our security guard's in critical care. Anya, the receptionist, got pretty banged up."

"And Celina?"

"She's already on the phone with contractors. The woman's relentless."

"Are you sure you're okay?"

"I got out. I'm fine."

He didn't look fine. He picked Rosie up in his arms and kissed her and squinted down at the game. "How's Henry's team doing? They gonna win this thing, or what?" Annie sensed that he couldn't look at her just now because in looking at her he would have to admit how sorry he was for getting involved with the clinic. How sorry he was about what it had done to their lives. But then, incredibly, he said, "I'll never give in to those bastards now."

The comment burned through her. His arrogance.

Rosie shook the sleeve of Annie's coat. "Mommy, *look!*"

Henry had the ball. He was kicking it toward the goal, followed by a throng of players. Henry was not an especially good athlete, but, she had to admit, he had tenacity and at this moment in time it seemed to be paying off. "Go, Henry!" they all screamed at once, standing up and clapping their hands, and Henry miraculously kicked the ball into the goal. It was his first goal of the season. His teammates swarmed him, and all the people in the bleachers stood up and cheered. Michael and Annie joined in, shouting as if their lives depended on it until their throats were raw. They were shouting for Henry, and they were shouting because it was the only thing left to do that made any sense.

52

"I WONDER HOW your friend's wife made out," Michael said to her later that night in their kitchen. They were drinking a bottle of wine together at the table after the children had gone to bed. All the drapes in the house had been pulled, the shutters tightly closed, the doors dead-bolted. It was a terrible thing, not feeling safe in your own home. At his feet was his canvas bag, the one that contained the gun. He would use it, he decided. He would use it if it came to that.

He watched his wife across the table, her cheeks ruddy as a cheerleader's after a game. God, she was pretty, he thought. She had a certain wholesome radiance. It had been a long time since they'd sat down together for a drink. Weeks, months even. It felt awkward sitting here with her now. Something tight about her, something concealed. It was just a hunch, but he had come to know when a woman was hiding something; he'd seen it enough in his practice, a certain withholding, a passive gaze of apology. For what, he did not know.

He swallowed more wine, wanting to get a little drunk tonight. *I've been granted mercy,* he thought dully, reflecting on the explosion, knowing that you didn't get mercy without guilt. It was too late for guilt, he realized. Guilt wouldn't get him out of this alive.

Annie touched his hand. "What did you say?"

"Your friend the painter. Haas? His wife came to see me this morning." He did not mention the fact that Lydia Haas had not given her true name; he intended to call the police with that scrap of information.

His wife stared at him. "Lydia Haas came to see you at the clinic?"

"I figured it was because of you."

"Because of *me?*"

"You know. Because of Haas. The article? I just assumed he recommended me."

She was squinting at him fiercely. "What did she come in for?"

"A general checkup." He paused. "She hasn't been to a doctor in ten years."

"I wonder why she went to the clinic? Why not your office?"

"Maybe she didn't want to wait. There's a three-week wait for a routine checkup on Hackett Boulevard. At the clinic, you can get in the next day."

"Why the big rush?"

"What?"

"You just said she hasn't seen a doctor in ten years. She couldn't wait another three weeks?"

Michael shrugged. "Don't know."

"Was she all right?"

"Sure. Yeah. A little freaked out, but other than that."

"Freaked out?"

"Uptight. She had . . ." He hesitated.

"Had what?"

"Scars. On her thighs."

"Scars?"

"I shouldn't have told you. I just assumed—"

"Assumed *what*?"

"Well, because of him. Anyway, I met her once. Remember? Jack's party."

"Oh, yes, I remember."

"When you and her husband were off in the woods together."

Now she looked the other way. "We got lost, remember?"

"Yeah," he said. "I remember." And he left it at that.

"Don't tell me you're going in," she said to him the next morning. "How can you possibly go in today?"

He stood there, tying his tie. "Why shouldn't I? I have patients. I have rounds. It shouldn't take me long."

She was up, pulling on her robe, yanking the belt into a knot. "Michael, they tried to kill you. They bombed the clinic. Not just to destroy the building, but to destroy you, honey." She tried to take his hand, but he wouldn't let her.

"Annie, it's what I do, all right? I don't know how else to explain it to you."

"I *know* it's what you do, Michael. Believe me. Nobody has to tell me because you know what? You know what? I've been *right here*. I've been *right here* the whole time. So don't tell me it's what you do."

I don't need this. "I'll be at the hospital. Page me if you need me."

And he left her there.

53

THROUGHOUT THE WEEKEND, Simon stayed in the house, tending his wife. Her condition had not improved. He brought her food on a tray. He changed her sheets and helped her to the toilet. He even showered her, squeezing the soap through her long yellow hair. Stroking her back, feeling the swell of bones underneath. In her dark glittering eyes they silently shared the awful thing she'd done. While she slept, he sat in the den gazing mindlessly at the news, the pervasive coverage of the bombing. He did not rebuke her for it, and he did not call the police.

Monday morning, at seven o'clock, there came a knock on the door. It was a cop. Simon's heart rushed to his feet. He opened the door a crack, grateful that the dogs were in the cellar. Sensing an intruder, they began to bark.

"Hello, Officer," he said, trying to sound amiable.

"Mr. Haas, is it?"

"Yes?"

"Is your wife at home?"

Simon felt himself hesitate. "Yes?"

"I'd like to ask her a couple of questions if I may."

"About what?"

"Sorry, but I need to speak with her."

"I'm afraid that's impossible," he heard himself say.

The cop's head tilted and he smirked. "Why's that?"

"She's ill. It's a"—he coughed into his hand—"a female problem. You know."

The cop nodded as if this made perfect sense. "That's along the lines of what I wanted to talk to her about."

"Oh?"

"She had an appointment Saturday at a clinic downtown. You might have heard about it on the news?"

"My wife told me all about it. In fact, she was so frightened that her condition seems to have worsened."

"I'm sorry to hear that."

"She's upstairs, in bed." It was all the truth, he realized. "Would you like to come and have a look?"

"No," the cop said carefully, then added, "I believe you, Mr. Haas."

"Maybe when she's feeling better? I could have her call you."

The cop stole a look past Simon, briefly rising up on his toes. Simon hoped he hadn't seen Lydia walking around. A tense moment festered. "I heard about your dogs," the cop said finally. "Great Danes are they?"

"Misunderstood animals. It's their size, you know."

"Yeah, well. We'll stop back later in the week."

"Good. That would be very good."

Then, as an afterthought, the cop added, "She went as a Jane Doe, in case you're wondering."

Simon tried not to look surprised. "Excuse me?"

"You being a big shot and all." The cop cocked his head, but Simon said nothing. "You people always have secrets, don't you?"

Better to let that one go, Simon thought.

The cop walked back to his car, taking his time, then turned and looked up at the windows on the second floor. He hesitated, and Simon feared he'd caught sight of Lydia.

"You ought to get those gutters cleaned."

Simon stepped down off the porch and had a look. "Oh, yes, you're right."

"Full of leaves. Winter's coming, you'll have yourself a big problem."

"Yes, you're right, Officer. Thanks for the reminder."

The cop patted the hood of Lydia's car. "Inspection's out of date."

"Really? I hadn't noticed. That's my wife's car."

"Well, she's a month overdue. That's a thousand-dollar fine you get caught, did you know that?"

"Wow, that's pretty steep. We'll take care of it."

The cop nodded and said nothing more. He got into his cruiser and pulled away.

Simon stood there for several moments, feeling the sweat run down his back. He didn't know why, exactly, he was protecting her. And the fact that he had, the fact that he knew and had chosen to keep quiet, meant that he, too, had broken the law, and that, in all likelihood, he would eventually pay for it.

It was his guilt, he realized. His heart was tangled up in guilt, making it difficult to breathe, and he'd grown used to it, as if it were some sort of incurable medical condition. He had learned to live with it.

Heady with regret, he went into the house and climbed the stairs quickly, expecting to find Lydia asleep, but he heard the shower running. She was up.

He went into the bathroom. "Are you feeling better?"

"Yes, yes, I'm fine. I'm much better."

"A cop was here."

"What?"

"I said a cop was here. Just now." She turned the shower off. "He wanted to ask you some questions."

She stepped out of the shower and for a moment he stood there, struck by her dripping-wet nudity, the heat coming off her body like steam on a city sidewalk. He had known from the beginning, from their first peculiar day together, that she would be his ruin. And now they were standing at the threshold of it, looking into the swollen darkness that would be their future.

"He wanted some information," he repeated. "He wanted some answers."

Brushing past him, she pulled on her robe and tied the sash tightly around her waist. "About what?"

"You had an appointment at a clinic Saturday, downtown?"

"So?" She opened the drawer, looking for a pair of underwear.

"Did you plant that bomb, Lydia?"

She stopped moving and she stood very still with her back to him.

"Let me rephrase that: I know you planted it."

Without turning around she answered him. "I don't know what you're talking about."

"I saw the things in your purse."

"What things?"

"The plastic gloves."

Now she turned, her face crimson. She took up an old glass of water and drank it down. Stalling. "You're right. I went to the doctor. I haven't been feeling well, all right, so I went."

He found himself wanting to believe her. "What's wrong with you?"

She didn't answer him.

"What doctor did you see?"

"I don't remember." He grabbed her by the wrist and twisted her arm up behind her back. She winced. "You're hurting me. Please, Simon. You're hurting me!"

"I'll fucking break your arm if you don't tell me the truth." He yanked her arm up another inch and she started to cry. "It was Dr. Knowles, wasn't it? Wasn't it?"

When she didn't admit to it he shoved her hard across the room, harder than was necessary, but he wanted to hurt her. She crumpled to the floor, weeping. "Do you have any idea what you're doing, Lydia?"

She groped to her knees, hysterical now. "You don't love me. You never loved me. You just used me. That's all you did, Simon. You used me."

"Let's not forget the circumstances of our meeting," he said evenly. "Let's not forget poor Daddy."

"You *bastard!*"

"The day I showed up was the luckiest day of your life."

She stood up, grabbing for her clothes, pulling them on. "I have to get out of this house," she said, hurrying out of the room, down the stairs. He went after her, but she would not be detained. She grabbed the keys off the table, shuffled into her shoes, and ran out to the car. A moment later, she was gone.

Simon stood there for a moment, feeling his feet pressing into the floor. *Where the hell is she going?* His keys beckoned him on the hall table. He grabbed them and went to his car. He drove down the long driveway, trying to ascertain which way she might have turned. He went right, down the dirt road toward town. A half mile up the road he saw her car rising up the hill. It was a quarter past eight, the sun indifferent, people on their way to work, driving sluggishly after the weekend. But his wife was a reckless driver, and he was speeding just to keep up with her. They came into town, heading south on Main Street, where the speed limit was strictly enforced. There were three cars in front of him, and then Lydia's blue Mercedes. He remembered buying her the car secondhand from a dealer in Albany. She'd been thrilled by the gift, he recalled, and they had taken many rides together after that. That was a long time ago; things had changed.

She stopped at the stop sign and made a right. The cars ahead proceeded, each stopping at the sign and then going on, but he was stymied by the Explorer in front of him, which wanted to turn left against a stream of oncoming cars. Simon waited, frustrated, certain that, by now, he'd lost her. When at last he finally turned, her car was nowhere in sight. Puzzled, he drove down the narrow streets of the village, which were cluttered with turn-of-the-century homes. Everywhere he looked he saw posters for Wally Nash. Wally Nash, with his shiny hair and chalk-white teeth.

A yellow school bus caught his eye and he followed it down Baker

Street, toward the grammar school. Lydia's car was parked in a driveway across the street. He slowed down, pulled over to the side, and waited. He didn't know who lived inside the house. It was sunny now, and children were playing in the schoolyard, behind the high metal fence. He turned his attention back to the driveway where his wife had parked and the tidy white clapboard house with yellow shutters. The curtains in the front window drooped awkwardly, wrinkled as a worried face. A spotless white Suburu sat in the driveway, beside Lydia's car.

Curious, he got out of the car and walked down the sidewalk toward the house, hearing the shrill whistle of a teacher across the street. The house was surrounded with shrubs, making it easy to duck into the backyard without being noticed. He glanced into a window and saw his wife sitting on a couch, crying. Another woman sat next to her, comforting her, and still another woman brought her a cup of tea. There were a few other women sitting around a living room. Most of them were knitting sweaters, tiny pink and blue sweaters for infants. His wife, evidently sufficiently comforted, took up a ball of yarn and a little pink sweater, and began to knit. He didn't even know that Lydia knew how to knit. He saw a little child taking cookies off a plate. The girl had a wide strange face and small black eyes.

Who the hell are these people, he wondered fiercely.

Having had enough, Simon crept out of the yard and back to the street. He walked around the corner, past other orderly, wretched homes, each with its own wretched story, and retreated into the darkness of a bar. He took a stool and ordered a double shot of Scotch. The bar was dark and empty and he liked the quiet mood of the place, the crackling radio, the skinny dog asleep in the corner, the old bartender with rotten teeth, playing dominoes on the bar. A lugubrious mood swept over him. He had wanted to tell Annie about his wife's involvement with the anti-abortion group, he had wanted to warn her that her husband was in danger, but he hadn't and it made him feel monstrous. The risk of losing her had felt too great and now he'd lost her anyway. His Annie, whose battered, unstylish clothes carried the scent of her mothering. She was like a good soup simmering all day. She appealed to the small boy within him, crouching in the dark space of his aching heart. Lamenting the fact that destiny had not brought her to him sooner, that their future was now doomed, he sat there all day, drinking whiskey, until the corners of the room had filled with darkness, and there was no place left to go but home.

54

"YOU ARE NOT to leave this house," Simon ordered her. "If you don't co-operate, I'll have to lock you up." She sat there gazing up at him with her little-girl eyes and when he handed her the pills she took them. He turned on the television, one of the morning talk shows. "Now sit here and don't move. I expect to find you here when I get home."

He'd been his usual disorderly self that morning, trying to get out the door to teach, and he'd forgotten his sketchbook on the kitchen table. While having her morning coffee, she found herself idly flipping through it. There were drawings of hands and feet. Faces. All kinds of faces. And bones. A skeleton. And then there was Annie, naked.

Much later, she woke on the floor in a fetal position. How she had got-ten on the floor escaped her. It was four o'clock in the afternoon. She crawled onto her knees. She prayed with her head on the carpet. At a loss, she drove down to the Life Force headquarters and found Reverend Tim studying the Scriptures. He gave her a worried smile and stood up abruptly, as if she had walked in with a gun. "What is it, Lydia? What's wrong?"

"My husband's in love with that woman." She blurted the words like something foul in her mouth. She took the drawing out of her purse and showed him the sketch of Annie Knowles.

Reverend Tim studied the drawing for what seemed like an eternity, then folded it up into a small square. "Save this for a rainy day." He handed it back to her. "It may come in handy."

He reached into his pocket and pulled out a bottle of pills. "These are for you. To keep you calm. Take one or two when you're feeling anxious. They may help. They have helped me in times of duress."

Back in her car, Lydia put a few of the pills into her mouth. She turned on the radio, loud, and opened all the windows. Reverend Tim was the only person who understood her, she thought. She drove for a long time on the back roads, her foot hard on the pedal. Just for sport, she took

Valley Road, with its deadly turns. There were no police out here. She could drive as fast as she wanted. There was nothing better than driving at a dangerous speed when you felt your life was about to end. Conquering a vicious turn at eighty or ninety miles an hour without even breaking a sweat only assured her that she could handle whatever came next. Putting the bomb in the examining room had not been her idea, and she did not consider herself a murderer, but now she wasn't sure, and the uncertainty nagged at her like a toothache.

Driving up the long road to the house, she saw a light in the living room. It was only eight o'clock, but the sky was richly dark. She found Simon in the old wing chair, asleep, his face red and creased, the newspaper open in his lap. They'd bought the old chair at an estate sale. It was upholstered with a faded blue-and-white toile that depicted men and women frolicking about. Chubby women with ribbons in their hair and doting men in waistcoats and knickers. She had always liked the chair because the people looked so happy, even when her big nasty husband sat all over them, as he was doing now. Wood smoldered in the fireplace, suggesting that he'd been sitting there for a long time, several hours perhaps. She stood over him in her coat, the cold melting off her, until he opened his eyes. She stood there and waited for him to speak. She couldn't tell if he was mad or not. He didn't look especially mad, but you could never really tell with Simon. She wanted to say to him, *Please don't see that woman anymore,* but the words were stuck in her mouth.

"I . . . I ran out of cigarettes," she stuttered. "I was only gone a few minutes. "

He didn't say anything to her, staring into the fire. "You didn't feed the dogs."

"They didn't look hungry," she said stupidly.

He tilted his head, eyeing her. "How are you feeling?"

She shrugged, wondering if it was a trick question. "Okay."

"I've made an appointment for you."

"What?"

"Think of it as a reunion with some of your old friends."

This meant the hospital.

"They're looking forward to seeing you."

"I don't want to go," she muttered in her little-girl voice. "I won't."

"Next week. We'll take a drive up there."

"I'm not going."

"It'll be fun. We can bring a picnic."

"No, Simon."

"I've made the appointment." He looked at her. "I'm not canceling it."

Lydia felt her lower lip trembling and bit down on it to make it stop. "We'll see about that." She smiled for him, just a quick flash, and turned and went up the stairs and closed the door. Ten minutes later she heard a car pulling up out front. It was a police cruiser. *Had Simon called the police?* A cop got out and knocked on the door. He was different from the first one.

She heard them talking. Then Simon called, "Lydia! Come down here, please!"

Lydia reeled, glanced in the mirror, slid some lipstick on her lips. A safety pin on the dresser caught her eye and she picked it up and unfolded it. "Just a minute!" She took the pin and pushed it into the fleshy palm of her hand. Deeper, *deeper,* until blood spurted out.

"Lydia!" Simon shouted, and she pulled out the pin.

Trembling, she descended the stairs. "This is Detective Bascombe," Simon told her. "He wants to ask you some questions."

She could feel the man studying her the same way people studied Simon's paintings, with stifling fascination.

"I'm following up on an investigation about the bombing at a women's health clinic."

"He means the abortion clinic, Lydia," Simon said eagerly.

Lydia swallowed, shifting on her feet. "I was sick. I needed to see a doctor."

The detective wrote something on his pad.

"I just had an appointment that day," Lydia told him. "I didn't see anything." She shrugged, wobbly. "I just had a regular appointment."

"She wasn't there for an abortion, is what she means," Simon clarified.

Lydia's throat dried up. "I don't know anything about the bombing."

"I see, uh-huh. If you don't mind my asking, why didn't you give the receptionist your name when you made the appointment?"

"Some things are private," she managed. "I'm a very private person." She looked at the cop meaningfully.

"My wife is a very private person," Simon repeated in a mocking tone. The detective scrawled notes on his pad.

"Tell him about the man with the limp, sweetheart," Simon persisted in his phony loving-husband voice. "You told me you saw a man with a limp."

The detective looked at her, waiting. *Had she mentioned Reverend Tim in her delirium?* "I don't remember saying that," she said softly.

"Yes, yes, yes," Simon patronized, "you said you saw a man with a limp coming out of the men's room."

"I don't remember," Lydia said.

"All right, let me get this straight," the detective said to her. "You saw a man with a limp come out of the men's room just before the bomb exploded?"

Lydia swallowed but nothing went down.

"A limp? Well, that's a helpful detail."

"My wife was very troubled by it. No doubt one of those anti-abortion fanatics," Simon said. "Write that down in your little book."

They stood there watching the detective get into his car. Simon closed the door and smiled at her. She raised her hand and slapped his face as hard as she could. It felt good doing it, and she didn't care if he hit her back.

55

WALKING OUT of the office that evening he felt as though the world had slowed down, and like a silent movie, there was no sound. Nurses streamed past without acknowledging him. Finney walked right by him in the corridor and said nothing. *Asshole*, Michael thought. Ever since the news coverage had appeared on TV, where one of the cameramen had caught Michael rushing from the burning clinic in his scrubs, his partners weren't speaking to him. Everyone seemed to know that he was the targeted abortionist. He was the one the Lifers wanted, and before long they would get him.

Celina seemed to be his only friend in the world. After work, he drove over to the clinic and found her in her office dictating charts. "You want to get something to eat?"

They walked around the corner to the pizza place. Michael could feel the gun in his pocket. He'd taken to carrying it wherever he went, although he questioned his readiness to fire it. Marie's Pizza was a smoky place with dim lighting and pizza boxes stacked to the ceiling. They sat in a booth against the wall. The waiter took their order and brought over their beer. Michael sucked down half the bottle, hoping the alcohol would quell his anxiety. No such luck.

Celina studied him, frowning. "Okay, I'm waiting."

"Waiting for what."

"For you to tell me what's wrong. You look like shit."

"It's Annie. We're not getting along. I get the feeling she's ready to bail."

"I don't blame her."

He just looked at her.

"Look, Michael, you need to stop now. No more of this hero stuff."

"I'll never give them the satisfaction."

Celina took his hand and held it dearly and repeated the phrase slowly, emphatically. "Michael, you need to stop. It's getting worse. It's going to keep on getting worse until they get what they want. So, go, you have my blessing."

"Go where? They're all over the country, this group. If I give up, it's like an admission of guilt. I won't do that. I won't do that, Celina. Not for them. Not for anyone."

"What about for Annie?"

He heard her but made no comment, and then the waiter brought over the pizza. He sat there, looking at it. He suddenly could not eat.

"Look, Michael. I want to thank you for everything you've done."

"You don't have to thank me. I should be thanking you."

She looked confused. "For what? For totally screwing up your life?"

"For opening my eyes."

Celina shook her head. "Do me a favor, honey. Open them a little wider and *stop*."

The rain fell in torrents as he drove home. When he got there, he found the children in the family room watching TV in their pajamas. They were

making posters with crayons and paper, LOST, MAGNIFICENT GOLDEN RE-
TRIEVER, SWEET AND KIND—PLEASE RETURN HER—DOGS CAN'T TELL YOU HOW THEY
FEEL! They were so intent in their work that they hardly seemed to notice
him when he came into the room. "Hey, guys."

"Hi, Daddy," Rosie said. He could always count on Rosie for a proper
greeting, whereas Henry hardly looked up. "Look, Daddy, we're making
posters for Molly."

"Great idea."

"Mommy's really mad at you," Henry said gravely. "We heard her
crying."

"Well, I better go see what's upsetting her."

Reluctantly, Michael climbed the stairs, regretting that he hadn't called
her to say he'd be late. Annie was in bed, surrounded by crumpled tissues.
"Hey."

"Where've you been? Forget it, I don't even *care* where you were."

"I had dinner with Celina," he told her, watching her back go stiff, a
look of disgust cross her face.

"I never liked her," she said. "I've never trusted her."

"It's not like that, Annie, and you know it. I just wanted to make sure
she was okay. Safe."

"So you had dinner with her?"

"We grabbed a bite. No big deal."

"What about *us*?" She spoke so softly he could barely hear her. "What
about *our* safety?"

"I know. I'm sorry," he said.

"Sorry isn't good enough." She got out of bed and put on her robe.
"The fact that you survived that bombing was just dumb luck. Next time
it'll be your life. I'm tired of waiting around for you, wondering if you're
alive. Wondering if they've finally gotten you. I've had enough, do you understand. I've had *enough!*"

He took her hands and held them tight. "Annie, think about it. Think
about what they're doing to us. You're letting them win."

"I'm not playing, Michael. It's your game, not mine. You don't seem to
get that."

"Here's what I don't get: I don't get *you*. I thought you'd be on my side
over this. You call yourself a feminist. That's a joke. You used to be differ-

ent. You'd take the subway up to Harlem at three o'clock in the morning if you thought you'd get a good story out of it. You weren't afraid of anything."

"That's because I had nothing to lose." Her lip started quivering. "But now I do. And it's gone too far. I don't want to fight these people. I just want out. I just want to be left alone."

"They have no right to threaten our lives because they don't support what I do. *That's* against the law. What I do isn't. If I succumb to them, who am I?"

"If you don't protect your children, who are you?" He looked at her worried face and realized she was right. "Don't you see what's happening to us? I don't even know who you are anymore."

"That makes two of us."

She gave him a dumbfounded look. "You won't even stop for me, will you? I guess I'm not important enough to you."

"That has nothing to do with it."

"I'm ready to leave you. Is that what I have to do to make you understand?"

"Is that what you want?" Tears ran down her cheeks, but she didn't answer him. He asked her again, "Is that what you want, Annie? You want to end this? You want to break up this family?"

"You've already done that." She gave him a look and left the room.

56

THEY HADN'T SPOKEN for over a week. She felt bereft, lost. The idea of never seeing him again made her physically ill. Finally, she broke down and called him. "I need to see you."

The air was cold, the sun cruel and bright. The lake shimmered behind the motel. He was waiting for her when she arrived, sitting on the edge of the bed with the radio playing. He gazed at her dispassionately. "I thought you never wanted to see me again."

She stood there, awkward. "Your wife went to see Michael. She went to the clinic."

"Yes."

"Why?"

"She didn't tell me."

"She knows, doesn't she? She knows about us."

He looked at her. "No, she doesn't know."

But Annie didn't trust him. "I think she's dangerous."

"That's ridiculous."

"I'm afraid of her."

"Why?"

"Just a feeling I have. I can't explain it."

"You have nothing to fear." He patted the mattress. "Come sit here next to me."

She went and sat down on the bed, but she did not remove her coat. "I'm sick."

"What is it?"

"All the time. I just feel sick." She wiped her tears. "It's hard for me. This whole thing."

"It's hard for me, too."

Annie nodded, her heart twisting.

"I can't leave her, Annie."

"I never expected you to." The comment made her angry. It wasn't that she wanted him to. She didn't know what she wanted. She had gotten herself into a situation and now she did not know how to get out of it. *Walk out,* a voice told her. But she didn't. She couldn't.

"You said it yourself. We would never work out together."

It wasn't what she wanted to hear. "This was a mistake. Admit it. Admit that you regret it."

"I don't."

"It was a stupid thing to do."

"It changed you, I can see that. You're a different woman. We've both changed."

"Not for the better."

"I know you don't really believe that."

"I don't love you," she lied.

"Love has nothing to do with it. It never does."

She didn't know what he meant, but it made her stomach tight. "I should go. I shouldn't be here with you." *I hate you now.*

Then he kissed her hard, angrily, and she kissed him back with equal vigor, and they fell back on the bed and he climbed on top of her. She wanted to feel his weight on her, even though it made her insides squeal, even though it made her guilt fester. But as she lay beneath him his eyes seemed distant, his movements mechanical. "Let me up!" She shoved him hard, but he would not be deterred, and his hands worked swiftly, opening her blouse, snapping off her bra, and she hit him, she slapped him all about the face and chest, and she cursed him, and he cursed her back with his spit flying, and he grappled to contain her, capturing her wrists and holding her still until she looked at him and he looked at her and their eyes did not waver. "Let me up! I have to go."

"You're not going anywhere."

It was almost dark when she finally left the motel room. Driving out of the lot, she noticed a red pickup truck in the parking lot. There was a man sitting in it, wearing mirrored sunglasses, and just as she turned the corner she saw him raise the long lens of a camera and take aim.

Halfway home, she stopped at a gas station, overcome with a spell of nausea. She retreated into the bathroom to be sick. What a time to get the stomach flu, she thought. But afterward she joined the dinner crowd at the fast-food restaurant next door. With the abandon of a teenager, she ordered a cheeseburger, French fries, and a strawberry shake and consumed the entire meal in less than five minutes. When she was finished, she sat in the plastic chair, watching the people come and go through the glass double doors. Queasy again, she walked out to the parking lot for some air. A minivan pulled into the spot next to hers and a man and his pregnant wife got out. Annie had to wait for the woman, who was so big she needed to open the door all the way. Drawn to the woman's belly, Annie suddenly realized what was wrong with her. It wasn't the stomach flu after all.

57

WHEN SIMON GOT HOME that afternoon, wearing the scent of his angry lover, he found Lydia waiting for him in the kitchen, a glass of Scotch before her on the table. The room was dark, she hadn't bothered to turn on a light, and he could see she'd been crying. The wind had picked up and he could hear her chimes wrangling on the porch. "I know I haven't been much of a wife," she said.

He waited.

"I know you've never really loved me."

"That's not true."

She finished her drink. "I know about Annie Knowles. I've known for a while."

Methodically, he went to the cupboard and brought down her pills and filled a glass with water. He set the pills and the glass down before her. "You're delusional," he said. "You'd better take your medication."

"You're going to be sorry, Simon," she said. "You're going to be very, very sorry."

He walked out and was not the least bit surprised when she threw the pills at his back and they fell out, like rain, all over the floor.

PART FIVE
Prayers

58

THE BOYS WERE HAVING more fun than the girls. Now, why was that? Lydia loved watching the boys as they ran across the muddy field, leaping over puddles, grabbing hold of one another with their heads thrown back in the sun. She loved the boys. She loved watching the boys. But the girls just stood around in circles. They stood around, staring glumly at the dirt, secret thoughts tingling with judgment. She felt a memory of her own school days creeping in, the schoolyard full of callous girls in faded uniforms, scheming hateful tricks to play on her. Lydia squeezed her brain shut and concentrated on little Rosie Knowles, skipping around the puddle with her little friend. *Ring around a rosie, pocket full of posy.* The child resembled her mother, Lydia noticed, with her gangly legs and wild hair. Absently, she wondered what it was like being Annie and having the little girl for a daughter.

The school bell rang and the children began running into the building. The two teacher's aides who covered recess had moved to the doorway and were waving the children inside. Lydia started down the grassy hill toward the playground. She only had a minute or two before the aide would notice that Rosie had not come in with the group. Lydia felt a smile filling up her mouth like too much chocolate. She took the picture of the Knowles' golden retriever out of her pocket and held it up. "Hey, Rosie," she called out.

Rosie stopped and looked at her, confused, but then she saw the picture of her dog and smiled and ran over to her. "Did you find Molly?"

"Yup. Want to see?"

Rosie glanced around uncertainly.

"She's right up the hill. See that car over there?" Lydia pointed to the white Taurus she had rented for the occasion. It was parked at the curb. "Let's don't stand around talking about it. Don't you want to see her?"

The little girl nodded. Lydia took her hand and led her up the hill to the car. The little hand in her own was small and perfect.

"I don't see her," Rosie cried.

"She's hiding. Get in the car."

"Why?" She started to cry.

"Just get in, Rosie. Just do what I tell you."

The child studied her face.

"Don't you want an ice cream?"

"Okay."

Lydia helped the child into the car and strapped on her seat belt. The key turned and the engine started. Lydia tried not to look at the little girl, who seemed so small all of a sudden. She was whimpering a little, tears running down her cheeks.

"Don't cry."

Fists rubbing her eyes. "You said you had my dog."

"I do. Not in the car, you misunderstood me. Don't worry, she's safe." Lydia sniffed. "Just sit back and be quiet and try not to make me mad."

The pills she'd taken before this little excursion were making her nose run. Rosie Knowles was crying. It made Lydia think of a sick pig. "Stop your crying!" she shouted. "Stop or I don't know what I'll do next."

Rosie Knowles sucked the air, she squealed like a little dying pig.

The Dairy Mart was down Holby Road. Reverend Tim had taken her there once. Lydia pulled into a parking spot on the side. "What kind do you want?"

"Kind of what?"

"What flavor?"

"I'm not hungry."

"Don't be impolite. I want to buy you an ice cream. You say, 'Yes, thank you, I'd like strawberry, please.'"

"I don't *like* strawberry."

Lydia took a deep breath. *Spoiled brat.* "What do you like?"

"Chocolate."

"Stay here, or you won't get your dog."

Lydia got out. She stuck her hand through the handle of her pocketbook and shoved the purse up her arm. She flipped her hair back behind her ear. It was something she'd seen Annie do in class. She flipped back her hair and went up to the counter, where a pimply-faced boy scooped the ice cream. Lydia ordered a chocolate cone and paid the boy. "Excuse me, ma'am, but there's something wrong with your nose."

"What?"

"It's bleeding."

Connecting the dots of his pimples she said, "What did you say to me?"

"Your nose, ma'am." He handed her a tissue.

"Oh, my *goodness*," she said, the blood dripping onto her blouse, the tissue soaked with blood. She hurried back to the car. "Here you go."

Rosie's eyes were red. She took the cone with a face that said she didn't want it.

"You eat that cone, miss," Lydia said.

Rosie started eating it and Lydia slipped back behind the wheel but didn't start the car. She stared ahead out the windshield at a garbage can overflowing with trash. Why hadn't somebody emptied it, she wondered.

"Can we go now?" Rosie squeaked.

"I just have one thing to do," she told her. "With this red marker. See? Then we can go. Do you like tattoos?"

Rosie shrugged.

"I want to give you a tattoo. It's just something I want to do. Okay?"

"And then what?"

"And then we'll see."

"What kind of tattoo?"

"A present for Jesus."

"Okay." She reached out her hand.

"Not there. On your tummy."

"Why?"

"It's a good place to do it. That's where Jesus wants it."

The little girl thought for a moment. "How do you know?"

"Because I work for Him. He's the one I answer to. Now just lift up your shirt and we can do this and then I'll take you back."

Rosie lifted up her shirt. Lydia took her red Sharpie and drew a red cross. She'd learned how to draw a three-dimensional cross in eighth grade, Sister Louise had taught her, and she did it now on the child's stomach, and it came out good. Big and red. It took a few minutes to color it in. "There," she said, and capped the pen.

"I want to go now."

"Be quiet and eat your ice cream."

Lydia started the car and drove back to the school. She was right on schedule. School would be over in fifteen minutes. Someone would find the child and scold her for hiding instead of returning to her class like she was supposed to. *We've been looking all over for you!* When Lydia had been in school, she'd had Sister Eleanor to contend with, who used to lock her in the closet with the spiders.

She pulled up to the curb near the playground. "Run along now," she said.

"What about my dog?"

"I lied to you. I don't have your stupid dog."

Rosie wiped her eyes again.

"Don't you tell anybody about this. Or I'll come back and get you. And I'll make you eat worms."

The child's eyes went dull with fear. "You're not very nice," she muttered and scrambled out of the car and ran down the hill back into the school.

Lydia reached across the seat and closed the door. Then she pulled away fast, her tires screaming like the small voice inside her heart.

59

SNOW FELL from the heavens that afternoon. It was a fluke, the weatherman said, so early in the season. There would be sixteen inches by noon tomorrow.

The bell rang inside the school. A moment later the doors opened and the children spilled out, rejoicing in the snow, twirling through the thick flakes with their heads thrown back and their mouths open wide. Even Henry looked happy, tossing fluffy snowballs into the air. But when Rosie came toward the car, Annie saw that something was not right. "Hi, Rosie. Look at the snow! Isn't it beautiful!"

Rosie just stood there.

Henry, a devoted snowboarder, pressed his hands together in mock prayer. "Please, God, give us snow! Lots and lots and lots of it!"

"Rosie, come on, get in, sweetie."

Rosie hesitated. "What's your problem, Rosie?" Henry grabbed her coat sleeve and pulled her into the car. Rosie twisted away from him and stared out the window.

"Rosie, what's wrong, honey?" Annie asked, but Rosie didn't answer. "Had a hard day?" Annie studied her daughter in her rearview mirror. Her hair was a little mussed and there was some chocolate in the corners of her mouth that made her look as if she were frowning. "Rosie, are you sad?" she asked.

"Leave me *alone!*"

They drove the rest of the way in silence. When they got home Rosie ran up to her room and closed her door. Annie and Henry exchanged a look. "I'll go," Henry volunteered.

"All right."

Annie waited at the foot of the stairs while Henry went up and quietly entered Rosie's room. Moments later he called for Annie. Worried, she went upstairs and opened the door, only to encounter her tearful little girl holding up her shirt and baring her naked midriff, where a large red cross had been drawn.

"Who did that to you, Rosie?"

"Someone."

"A man? A woman?"

"A lady at school."

Suddenly weary, Annie sank to her knees. She opened her arms to Rosie and Rosie came over and crawled inside. "Tell me, honey. Tell Mommy what happened."

"She said she had Molly. She took me in her car and got me ice cream."

This was no time to admonish Rosie for getting into a stranger's car. "Have you ever seen her before?" she asked gently. Rosie shook her head.

Annie swallowed her tears; she did not want to cry in front of Rosie. She would do it later, in the privacy of her room.

"What kind of car was it?" Henry asked.

"White. I got to sit in front." She paused for a moment, her eyes filling with tears. "She didn't have Molly. She said she did. She lied."

"What did she look like?"

"Black hair. Her nose was bleeding." Annie imagined some demonic creature. She waited for Rosie to give her more description, but the child climbed back onto her bed and curled up, hugging the doll she had saved from the mailbox. They had something in common now, after all, Annie thought.

"I'm going to call the police. Henry, stay with Rosie."

Henry sat down on the end of Rosie's bed and began to read to her from one of her books. Annie went into her bedroom and made several phone calls. First, she called the school and explained what had happened. The principal questioned one of the teacher's aides who'd been on duty at the time. The woman claimed that Rosie was with the group the entire time. Annie became so incensed that she hung up on the man and called the police. The female officer on the other end listened to her story. "I'll send somebody out there to write up a report. Of course with this weather coming, it may take a while."

"Please, tell them to hurry."

"They'll be there just as soon as they can."

Annie hung up and paged Michael and when he called back she told him what had happened. For a moment he said nothing. "Michael?" She could only hear his breathing, erratic gasps of rage. He told her he would be home within the hour and hung up.

Rosie came into the room. "I want to wash it off."

"We have to show it to the police," Annie explained. "Just keep your shirt down and pretend it's not there."

"It's a present," Rosie said. "For Jesus."

"Is that what she told you?"

Rosie nodded.

Annie took Rosie onto her lap and held her and rocked her as tears fell from her eyes. "Don't cry, Mommy," Rosie said. "You don't have to cry."

"I won't, Rosie, I won't cry," she said, but she could not seem to stop, and she held on to her little girl tightly, as if the child was the strong one, not her. They sat there like that for a long time as the windows filled up with darkness. Neither of them made any effort to move.

60

EVEN THOUGH he'd promised, Michael would not be home within the hour.

He left the office at once and drove to St. Vincent's. He parked his car in the loading zone in front of the hospital and went into the page operator's office. The woman on duty was frail and white haired. An open box of candy sat on her desk. She'd taken bites out of several pieces and the small brown wrappers held remaining half-moons of chocolate. "How you doing today, Lorna?" he asked, reading her name tag. "I need a favor."

"Why sure, Doctor. What can I do for you?"

"I want to send something to one of the chaplains, but I don't have his address. I don't even know his last name."

"Oh, certainly. Who is it?"

"Reverend Tim."

"Oh, yes, Reverend Tim Hart." Her face lit up. "He's a wonderful man, isn't he?"

"Oh, yes. Yes, he is."

She flipped through her Rolodex and wrote the minister's address down on a Post-it: 23 Dove Street. "Why, that's right around the corner, isn't it?"

Michael left the hospital and walked toward the park. The snow was falling heavily. As it landed on the tops of things it dazzled in the twilight. It made the world quieter, he thought. Michael wasn't sure what he would do to the man once he got there, but he knew that he would have to use his gun. Dove was a cobblestoned street flanked with brick town houses and brownstones and small shops. Number 23, a brick walk-up, housed a hardware store on the ground floor. A big hammer hung on the outside of it. Michael stood across the street from it, looking up at all the windows. The windows above the store were dark. The street was crammed with parked cars and the snow was beginning to pile up. A little bell rang and he turned toward the sound of it and saw a man coming out of a shop, closing and locking the door behind him. The shop owner grunted a greeting and walked on down the street. Michael glanced in the large window of the shop and saw an array of animals, real animals that had been stuffed—a taxidermist's shop. There was a wild boar, a tiger, a zebra, and beyond that, in the back, the unmistakable yellow fur of a golden retriever. Michael stood there, incredulous, and moved closer to the window to get a better look, focusing on the collar around the dog's neck. Sure enough, with bizarre clarity, he saw the name on the tag. MOLLY.

Michael entered the vestibule and found Reverend Tim Hart listed on the registry, Apartment 2B. Feeling the gun nudging against his ribs, he climbed up the stairs. He stood at the door. There was the sound of a vacuum running inside. He tried the knob; it was unlocked. He opened the door slowly and stepped into a dark foyer. Beyond the vacant living room he saw a heavyset black woman vacuuming a bedroom. Michael stealthily entered the living room, taking in the surroundings. The room was modest, exceptionally neat. A white cat slept curled up on the couch. The cat looked up at him moodily, then settled back down to sleep. Michael had never liked cats, really. *I'm not a cat person,* he often told people. The vacuum went off for a moment and the woman said, loudly, "Stop your fussing, I'll be done in a minute!" Michael noticed an oxygen tank against the wall, the line of which was attached to someone in the room, obviously not the minister. The vacuum went on again, and the woman continued her work, shaking her head angrily. All the other rooms in the apartment looked dark; Tim Hart was not at home. Michael searched the living room for something of value to destroy, but nothing really stood out. There were several books on the shelves. An oil painting of the Virgin Mary. A small photograph of a woman, perhaps the man's mother, on the table. There was nothing that connoted a dangerous man. Nothing that implied a person who was behind what had happened to Rosie that afternoon. The cat meowed and stretched and Michael found himself studying the animal strategically, trying to convince himself that killing the cat would be the ultimate retaliation for what he believed had happened to Molly. If he killed the cat, he thought, Reverend Tim would get the message not to fuck with him anymore. The cat was an easy target, he thought, just as Molly had been for the minister. Surely, he could shoot it.

He took out his gun and put it right up to the cat's furry head. The cat nuzzled its head against the short barrel of the pistol. *Stupid cat.* He clicked off the safety and took aim, but his hand began to shake. *Coward,* he goaded himself. *After all they've done to you. After what they did to Rosie.* Anger burned through him, yet he could not go through with it. He clicked the safety back on and returned the gun to his coat.

The vacuum went off again and the woman walked across the doorway, complaining, "Now, what you go and do that for? How many times I told you not to pull that thing out. You won't be able to breathe, honey. That what you want?"

It was time to go, he realized. Any minute the cleaning woman would come out and see him and he did not want that, no. He did not want that at all. Looking back at the cat, he was struck with a new idea. He picked the animal up and put it inside his coat, then stepped out into the hall, closing the door soundlessly behind him. He hurried down to the street. In just a few moments, the snow had grown deeper. Cars moved sluggishly down the street. He drove home slowly with the cat on the seat beside him. He would not say a thing to Annie about where he'd been that night or what he'd done. He would say he found the cat in the hospital parking lot. The cat would serve a dual purpose. It would distract the children from the loss of Molly. And it would befuddle Reverend Tim.

61

MICHAEL HAD SAID an hour; now it had been three and he still wasn't home. Sheriff Baylor had come out to take Rosie's statement, but when Annie asked Rosie to lift up her shirt to show him the cross, Rosie started to cry. She ran up to the bathroom and started to wash it off. Baylor stood in the hallway waiting while Annie tried to change Rosie's mind, whispering through the door, begging Rosie to come out and show him what had happened. But Rosie would not come out. "Unless I see it, Mrs. Knowles, it's kind of hard to file a complaint," Baylor said.

Annie remembered a throwaway camera she'd used a while back; there were a few shots left. In the privacy of the bathroom, Rosie let her take pictures of her stomach. Rosie had scrubbed herself raw, but the image still showed through.

Annie gave Baylor the camera and he left, the chains on his tires clinking into the night. Then Michael's headlights flashed across the walls. Furious, she was ready to let him have it, but he only smiled at her. He unzipped his coat and pulled out a fluffy white cat. Her mouth fell open.

"What? Where did you get it?"

"Found it in the parking lot."

"What a miracle." Annie took the cat into her arms. "What a pretty kitty."

"I stopped at PetsMart and got some cat stuff. That's what took me so long."

They brought the cat up to Rosie's room. The children were thrilled. "But you're not a cat person," Henry said rhetorically.

"I'm a changed man," Michael said.

"I love you, Daddy." Rosie kissed his cheek.

"Is it a boy cat or a girl?" Henry inspected the cat. "Girl," he announced like a proud father.

"Let's call her Snowflake!" Rosie said.

"Snowflake it is." Michael kissed Rosie and held her tight. "What happened today wasn't because of you, Rosie. Do you understand? It wasn't your fault."

Long-faced, Rosie nodded, and Michael tucked her into bed. "You and Snowflake get some rest, okay?"

Later, in bed, Annie said to him, "When the weather clears, I'm taking them to my parents." Michael consented with a nod, but said nothing. They lay there for a long while in silence. Finally, she turned and looked at him through the dark. "I have something to tell you."

"What is it?"

And then she said it, because she could not keep it to herself any longer. "I'm pregnant."

Michael turned on the light and reached for his glasses and put them on. He studied her carefully with the scrutiny of a seasoned physician. "What?"

"I did the test this morning."

"Are you sure?"

"Yes." She paused, her guilt blazing like a rash. "I'm not keeping it," she said quickly. "Not like this. Not now, after what happened to Rosie." Although she wanted to tell him about Simon, to come clean, she knew she could not. She wouldn't tell him that the baby inside her might not be his. She could not bear to speak the words aloud. "I'm not keeping it," she said again, as if to convince him of her conviction. "I've already made the appointment."

Snow brought peace to the house, and when they woke the next morning the land was covered with it. The trees stood white and silent. Nothing moved.

Annie crept out of bed and went to check on Rosie, relieved to find her sleeping, the white cat curled up at the end of her bed. She said a prayer, thanking God that her daughter had been safely returned. Back in their room, Michael was awake, already on the phone. He'd put on a pair of jeans and his old Lacrosse sweatshirt. Seeing him there, like that, made her want to cry, she didn't know why. Maybe because the sweatshirt was proof of their history together. They'd come this far. And now, like two explorers, they'd lost their compass. They had no map. "Just covering my tracks," he explained, hanging up. "Everything's been cancelled."

She stood there. She said nothing.

"I know things have to change, Annie."

"I'm not going to live like this anymore."

"I don't expect you to. Give me time."

"I don't know, Michael."

"We'll move somewhere."

"There's no escaping these people."

"I'll do whatever it takes."

She was struck with the sense that they'd reached the end of something and that everything would be different from now on. She wouldn't tell him the truth, she decided, because it wouldn't accomplish anything. He would never be able to understand that sex had not been her motive for the affair. It had been about so much more. The unspoken rhythms of her heart, the voice deep inside her that Michael had never been able to hear.

Maybe now he could.

Exclamations of glee sounded in the hallway. "No school today!"

Michael smiled at her, and she smiled back—a knowing exchange between parents—and he seemed reassured, content. The kids charged into the room and jumped on the bed. "What do cats eat for breakfast?" Rosie asked, holding the cat. The two had become fast friends.

"Pancakes, of course," Michael said, getting out of bed. "Where's my assistant chef, Monsieur Henri?"

"Voilà!" Henry jumped off the bed, and they all went downstairs to make pancakes.

The snow fell hard, buckets and buckets of it. All morning, they lingered together as a family, quietly, gently. It seemed so quiet, as if the outside world had disappeared. As if they were the only ones left. Annie looked outside at the seamless white fields. No footprints. No car tracks. They were completely alone. For the first time in months she felt safe.

They played Monopoly for hours, during which Henry's contemplative, frugal nature made him rich and Rosie's whimsical spontaneity made her poor. Afterward, Michael dozed on the couch with the cat on his lap. Annie sat in the big easy chair watching him sleep, wondering what tomorrow would bring—would he go back to work? She tried to read but couldn't concentrate. The incident with Rosie preyed on her mind, the most disturbing aspect of which was the fact that a woman had taken her. She couldn't help thinking of Lydia Haas.

She covered Michael with a wool blanket and waited a moment, making sure he was in a deep sleep, then went into the kitchen and dialed Simon's number. It rang and rang. Finally, to her relief, Simon picked up. "Yes?"

"It's Annie."

"Hello, Annie." His tone was distant. Or was he contrite?

"Something happened to Rosie. I wanted you to know." She told him the story.

At length, he said, "My God. That's awful. I'm sorry."

"It's someone from that group," she taunted. "Someone with a major problem." She could hear him lighting a cigarette and pouring something over ice. Was he drinking at this hour? It wasn't even noon. "It was a woman who took her."

He said nothing to this.

"Simon? Are you there?"

"Yes, I'm here."

"Are you all right? You sound a little down."

"I'm sorry to be so obtuse, Annie, but please don't call here anymore."

"Simon—"

"You were right, she knows. She knows everything. Things have been difficult."

"Oh, I see."

"I'm sorry, Annie. I have to go." The line went dead.

Annie stood there in the kitchen with her heart beating. *What about me?* It wasn't that she *wanted* him—she knew it was over; it had been *she* who had ended it—but now, in light of the fact that she was pregnant, and that the baby she carried might be his, she could not help feeling betrayed. No matter what he'd told her, it was clear to her now that he still had feelings for his wife. There was some intangible element that seemed to bind them together, she didn't know what. And then it came to her. It was fear.

In the afternoon the children wanted to go sledding. With the roads closed, there didn't seem much chance of danger, and like astronauts preparing for a launch, they all pulled on snow pants, boots, ski jackets, hats, and mittens, and ventured out into the dazzling white world. Henry started a snowball fight and they ran around, dumping snow on each other. Then Rosie wanted to make an igloo. They went sledding down their long hill, laughing together as if none of the awful things had happened, as if they lived a charmed existence, free of danger of any kind.

But by four o'clock the air had warmed, and the snowplows had made it out. The plows roared down the main roads, putting her in mind of army tanks in an occupied country. The gunshots of deer hunters echoed in the neighboring fields, completing the eerie suggestion. It felt like an omen.

"Hunters," Michael said. "The roads must be clear."

They went inside and locked all the doors and pulled down all the shades and closed all the drapes. Michael made a fire and they sat huddled together, all four of them, on the living room couch, watching the flames jump and snap. They cooked dinner together like they used to. Annie made a roasted chicken and baked potatoes, while Michael and the kids made a salad. Henry chopped the cucumbers and Rosie, for her part, ate them.

Over dinner, Henry entertained them with his repertoire of terrible jokes. Rosie served dessert, having a splendid time with a can of whipped cream. "How about a little ice cream with your whipped cream, Rosie?" Michael said. When they'd finished, the kids escaped into the family room to watch TV. Annie poured Michael a cup of coffee.

"I've been thinking it over," Michael said. "I want you to cancel that appointment. Will you think about it?"

She nodded that she would, but she had already made up her mind.

"Don't you know that I love you, Annie?"

Silently, she nodded, but she wondered if love was enough.

"For Christ's sake," he whispered, "every move I make is for you."

Annie cleaned up the kitchen, taking comfort in routine tasks, and Michael put the kids to bed. When he came downstairs, he offered to take out the trash. "There may be some mail out there," she said.

"I'll check."

He went outside with the garbage. As she sponged down the countertops it occurred to her that he'd been out there for a while. When he finally came back inside he looked pale.

"Any mail?"

"Just junk." He tossed the pile into the trash.

"You all right?" she asked. "You look pale."

He said nothing.

"Is it cold out there?"

"It's cold."

She stood there. "Want to go to bed?"

"No."

"Michael?"

He seemed suddenly distant. "I'm going to stay up for a while. I've got things to do in the study."

She waited for him to say more, but he didn't. He turned, and left her standing there. "I'm going to bed," she said to his back.

"Go ahead."

"You sure you're okay?"

At the study door he looked at her and nodded, but his face remained cold. Without another word, he went into the room and closed the door. Annie climbed the stairs like a child who'd been sent off to her room without dinner. She felt empty again. Lost.

An hour or two later, she woke up to the remote sound of his beeper. Where was he, in the study? He hadn't come to bed. Annie sat up, listening. He was in the study on the phone. It was after one A.M.

Then she saw it.

Tacked to the wall was a drawing of her. Simon had done it one day at the motel. She was sitting in a chair naked. "I'll call this one *Just Fucked*," Simon had said, and now she saw those words scrawled in Simon's hand on the bottom of the page.

Her heart began to pound.

Now he was coming toward the door. She jumped and slipped back under the covers and closed her eyes as he entered the room. He was pulling on his scrubs and a heavy sweater, tossing things noisily into a bag. He was going in.

Why, she wondered? He wasn't on call. Why were they paging him?

She didn't dare open her eyes, terrified of what he might say to her. She could feel him standing there, watching her, and she could sense his anger in the way he moved. He jerked open the nightstand drawer, scrambling for a pen; he was writing her a note. He turned off the light. And then he was gone.

Panting with shame, she began to cry, gulping the air. She ran downstairs hoping to stop him, to tell him she had made a mistake, a terrible mistake, and she'd felt nothing for Simon Haas, nothing! But she was too late. He had already pulled out of the driveway and turned onto the road.

Weak with apprehension, she gripped the banister and climbed the stairs to her room. Annie ripped the drawing off the wall and crumpled it up. She crawled back into bed, weeping, turning in on herself, unable to find comfort in the soft pillows, the warm quilt. Her whole body ached with fear, sensing danger like an animal keen to its scent, tasting it in her throat, on her teeth, expecting it yet having no idea of how to tame it.

PART SIX
Extremities

62

TWO DAYS HAVE PASSED and now it is the third. Something has happened to his eyes. The world comes in a blur. There are no windows, no lights, only a smear of daylight. His body is heavy and dense, like he's been covered with stones. A grave, he thinks, shivering. He did not think it would be like this, his death. From time to time he would imagine it as he does now, picturing himself in a room with a bed, a pink blanket, perhaps, a window where the wild sun beckons him, the distant sound of children running through the house—not his children, but his children's children. And music, of course. Italian opera filling up the halls, roaming into rooms with unmade beds. Something delicious cooking on the stove, the tantalizing smoke rising up through the banister to his waiting nostrils. A hand turning a wooden spoon, contemplatively, knowing that his death will arrive at any time. And waiting for it. The whole house waiting for it. The chairs in the living room waiting for it. The piano with its grinning white keys. The bowl of pears on the table. Even the dripping gutters waiting for it. Sensing it like a disastrous storm. He has imagined his old man's hands like the gnarled roots of a lilac bush, quivering a little, covered with liver spots. And Annie's hands, he has imagined them, too, graceful and warm, unhindered by age. In his dreams, he has seen her taking up his hands like summer earth, the way she knows to turn the soil, and he remembers her now in her big straw hat, making the flowers come up all around the yard. She would come to him, he thinks now, she would hold his hands, she would wait with him to face the worst.

He imagines his house in the country in total disarray, Annie trying to cope with her ordeal. She will take the kids to her parents', he knows; that's where Annie goes when she needs to hide. He pictures his kids sullenly playing chess on the priceless Sarouk carpet in the living room. Henry will be angry when they make him tuck in his shirt, and Annie's mother, perennially obsessed with order, will insist that Rosie brush her hair. No taming *his* children, he thinks a little proudly. The image brings him a surge of relief, but it doesn't last, and he is almost too frightened to think. *Your life is over.*

The wind mutters all night long. He can hear the wind rippling the window screens. He can hear the wind groaning like a man with a broken heart. Something drips. He hears the tidy scuffling of squirrels and wonders if they've gotten into the cellar. In his dreams he sees their long furry tails. "Squirrels," he tells the woman when she comes to tend him, but she refuses to admit it, hastily wiping the feverish sweat from his face. She comes and goes like a vision in a nightmare. She keeps him drugged, but he does not refuse her, taking the warm broth into his mouth, bitter with codeine, dense with salt, his head in her lap like a child's. His pain is voracious. There is nothing he can do but accept her care. She is the healer now, this strange woman whom destiny has cruelly paired him with.

The room is damp, insalubrious, and makes his throat sore. The mattress upon which he lies is wet under his back, but he will not tell her this. The old wool blankets stink of mothballs, but he has convinced himself that it will keep away the squirrels, because he knows they are there, fussing in the dark, an ominous vigil with their tiny yellow eyes.

Like a blind man, he tries to read the subtle variations of the dark. Once, he asks her to turn on a light, but the question enrages her. "Don't you *get* it, Michael? There's nobody here. There's nobody *living* here. Why would I turn on a light if there's nobody here?" She starts to pace nervously, lighting a cigarette. "Do you want someone to show up here? Is that what you want? Because the minute that happens, you're dead, understand?"

She takes out a little box of pills. "I've got to *calm down*. You've gotten me all upset." Swallowing a few of the pills, she comes up close, standing over him. "You think this is easy for me? Huh?" She kicks his leg and he recoils, turns inward. "You think I *like* being here?" Another kick, only harder. "You think I like the fact that I had to do this?"

Shaking, he braces for another kick. A moment lingers between them. He feels her watching him, making up her mind, sensing her power over him. The kick does not come, and he turns slightly to see her circling the room, mumbling to herself. Round and round and round in a tight circle.

She crouches down, hugging her knees. "I'm sorry I kicked you. I'm *sorry, okay?*"

She looks at him, waiting for him to forgive her, but he does not and she starts to cry.

"Nobody sees me," she whispers. "I'm a ghost. I'm invisible."

"I see you," he answers at length. "You're right there."

Flashes of the accident come back to him with visceral clarity. He remembers her voice, insisting on the seat belt. *He wouldn't drive without one,* she'd told the men. *It will look suspicious to the police.* Now that he thinks of it, that seat belt was what saved him. There was the deafening slam of the car door, the man's farewell—*See you later, asshole*—and then the rolling car, the bristling feeling in his belly, the anguished uncertainty of a carnival ride as the car soared through the air then dropped to the ground below. *Let it go,* he remembers thinking, feeling his body fall through space. *Let it all go.*

Numb is what he is, he thinks, in a state of shock. A womblike sensation of nothingness. A state of being—empty. He gives himself up to it. He gives himself up to it because there is nothing else.

Time drifts. His head fills with snakes. Now they are spiders. His head spins a web of fury. He doesn't know. *I want my wife,* he thinks. *I want my Annie.* The floors squeak overhead, back and forth and back again. There is the sound of heavy rain. No, it is not rain. It is the woman crying. She frees his hands and he brings them to his face, he covers his face like a shield. He cups his hands together, he braids his fingers, he whispers to his thumbs. *Here is the church, here is the steeple, open the doors and see all the people.*

She has chained him to the furnace. There are two separate loops around each ankle, old-fashioned bicycle locks attached to steel cables, the sort he had as a boy, encased in thick yellow plastic with cylindrical combinations. The cables are locked to a larger chain, the sort you'd use to tow a car, which snakes across the floor and is padlocked to the furnace. The chains dishearten him; he has no idea how to free himself of them. Yet if he could find something sharp, a pair of pliers even, he might be able to cut them. In the dark, gasping and spitting, he crawls across the cement floor, hoping to encounter something he might use to cut through the plastic, but the cellar floor is a vast wasteland and he encounters nothing. On his hands and knees he is a wounded animal, an animal shot in the leg, an animal whose hand had been severed by a trap. It makes him think of poor Molly. He finds himself overcome with a fierce rush of anger. The feeling depletes him, and suddenly exhausted, he drags himself back to the mattress. He begins to shiver, his teeth chattering. A fever coming on, he realizes. Before long, his body simmers in the dampness. He must stay focused, he thinks desperately; he must methodically plan his escape.

She comes down later with her usual tray. He isn't interested in the food. What he wants are the drugs. Something to temper his pain. Something to stop the infection. "I need an antibiotic," he insists.

"You've been taking one."

"It's not enough."

"Are you all right? You're shaking."

"No, I'm *not* fucking all right. I've got an infection! I've got a broken fucking hand!"

"Here." When she hands him the pills, their skin touches. Hers is softer than his, and warm, and it alarms him. It alarms him because he was not ready for her. He was not ready to grab her wrist, her arm, her fucking neck. He was not ready to throttle her senseless. He takes the pills and drinks down a glass of water that tastes like rust. He wipes his mouth, looking at her, trying to figure out where she's put the gun.

"It's right here," she says, answering his thoughts. She takes out the gun, proficiently opens the cartridge, then snaps it back into place. She just stands there watching him. "I'm a very good shot, actually. In case you're wondering."

"I don't care about your gun," he lies. "I'm not afraid of you."

She flashes a bitter smile. "Shucks."

"I'll give you whatever you want. What is it you want? There must be something. Is it money? Tell me. I can get you money."

"No one can give me what I want." She sulks.

"Let me try."

"You're not ready. You need to rest. You need to heal."

"Take me to a hospital."

"That's not an option. At least you're alive. Try to be grateful."

"Barely alive," he grunts.

"You look better today. Much better. I can see a big difference."

"I told you. I'm very sick. I'll die here. My eye, for one—I can hardly see out of it. And my hand. If it's not set properly, if it's not put in a cast, I'll never be able to practice again. I'll never be able to deliver a baby. Is that what you want?"

She says nothing to this.

"Look how I'm sweating. I'm burning up! For Christ's sake! Please! Out of human decency! Take me to a hospital!"

"I know what you're trying to do. You're trying to scare me."

"I don't want to die!"

"I have to go now." She starts for the stairs.

"Please don't go," he begs her. "Don't leave me here."

"Try to eat. You need your strength."

"I'll never eat for you." He hurls the bowl of oatmeal after her. "I'll never fucking eat!"

He hears her upstairs, running across the squeaking wood planks out into the world beyond, a world he does not imagine he will ever see again. The hours twist and turn and his mind careens through a tunnel of desperation. She does not return for what seems like days, and he craves the drugs she's been feeding him, craves them feverishly. His hatred of her taints his blood like a poison, yet she is his only way out of this awful place. His heart spins with dread. He must somehow convince her, he realizes, to let him out.

He wakes hours later in a cold sweat. On the tray next to his bed there are several Baggies full of pills—unlabeled—he cannot possibly identify them—and a large bottle of water. She must have bought them on the street, he surmises. Or stolen them from the pharmacy. Even in his pain, he knows better than to take the pills without knowing what they are. Better to be especially cautious now, he thinks. Better to be ready for her. Even with only one good hand, he is angry enough to rip her throat out the first chance he gets. Something on the tray catches his eye and he fishes out a large manila envelope. Inside the envelope is a pair of glasses, cheap drugstore bifocals. He puts them on, relieved that his vision is slightly improved. There's more inside the envelope: photographs. Pulling them out with curiosity, he finds himself looking at pictures of his wife and Simon Haas. They are naked on a bed in a motel room. Gasping, his mouth watering with rage, he witnesses their lovemaking in black and white, noting the variety of positions, a sordid erotic display. How could this be? he thinks. How could she do this?

Examining the photographs, he feels light-headed. Weak. It's not the sex that bothers him most, he realizes. It's the expression on her face. The way her head is thrown back with her eyes closed and her mouth open as if a languorous sigh is coming out of it. An expression of utter joy, he decides, and one that he cannot recall ever seeing in his own bed.

63

ON MONDAY MORNING, Lydia unlocks the cellar door as if it were the cage of a wild animal. She sinks down each step, slowly, with trepidation, as if any moment the wild beast will break free of its chains and rip her to pieces with his teeth. Descending into the dampness, she can smell his awful smell. Like the stink of her dying father, he is not particularly fastidious when it comes to hygiene. It is deliberate, of course. He thinks it will keep her away from him. He doesn't realize her level of tolerance. He doesn't realize how important he is to her.

She hears the wind. The wind is great. The wind is magnificent. The wind has filled her with spirit. Driving here in the early evening she'd marveled at the trees moving their black limbs all at once against the copper sky.

"Our Father, who art in heaven," she blurts out, going down the steps. "Hallowed be thy," but she can't seem to finish. He lies there in a fit of despair. He has not touched the water by his bed, nor has he eaten any of the food she's left him. If things go on like this he will die, just as he has warned, and her plan will have been a failure. Lydia did not anticipate this kind of reaction. She does not know what to say to him; she does not know how to cheer him up. If only he would take the pills. They were very expensive and they are very good; she has sampled several of them herself. Scattered across the floor are the photographs of Annie and Simon, ripped to shreds. As she nears him, she sees that he is crying, his whole body shaking. It puts her in mind of her father, at the very end, when he would lie there and weep with the TV blinking and all the wild pussy willows clawing at the windows.

Lydia stands there holding the tray, and she is shaking, too; they are shaking together. They have both been spurned; they have both been betrayed. This is something they share, like a death, and they shake mournfully. They mourn together. The teacup rattles on its saucer. Without a thought, she lets it all go, just drops the tray to the cement floor without a care. It makes a loud noise when it hits and the plate breaks and the little cup rolls and they are both startled by it, by its deliberate intrusion. And in the moments that transpire he turns and looks at her and sees that she, too, is crying. And she thinks that perhaps he knows her with a perfect clarity, the keen song of a loon, perhaps, as it calls to its lover across the lake. The moment ends and he does not take his eyes from hers, and it is as if something new has been established between them and it makes her cry a little more as she kneels down and scoops up the broken china as quickly as she can. Trembling, she welcomes the small cuts and slivers, she deserves them. *I will not cry in front of you*, she thinks, clutching broken pieces of china in her bleeding hands, and runs upstairs.

64

THE HOURS DRIFT and sigh. He spins like a meteor through space, dreaming of Annie. Her fingertips, like raindrops. There is the sound in his head of his children laughing. Upstairs, he hears the radio. Now and then, the weather report comes on, the man with the sensible voice: *Expect snowfall today, reaching over six feet in the higher elevations, two or three inches in the Capital District.* He thinks he can hear the snow. The sound of it falls like the whispering of children. The whispering of children in a dying man's room. He wonders what time it is. What the day is. He has lost track.

Michael hears the locks and rouses himself to a sitting position. His mouth is dry. When the door opens, the yellow light in the hall quivers behind her. Big blue hydrangeas on the wallpaper like the backdrop in a play and he is deep in an audience, watching a madwoman. Her boots are rubber, caked with mud, and they descend one after the other slowly, feebly, like a person in pain. She wears her pathology like a heavy coat.

"We need to talk," she says. Like the steps to some bizarre primal dance, her body guides him: the white drifting smoke from her cigarette, her eyeglasses swinging on a string around her neck. The apron she wears, tied in a bow around her waist. The gun jammed in the right pocket. She lights the oil lamp and he blinks. She takes her gun and sets it down. "I realize what you're doing," she says, lighting a cigarette. "The fact that you're not eating or drinking will get us nowhere. I'm sorry about the photographs. I felt you should see them."

He nods. "It's not just her fault," he manages. "It's all of ours. You can't just blame Annie."

"Oh, yes I can," she says. "I can blame her all I want." She rifles through her bag and pulls out some whiskey and a bottle of pills. "You can talk yourself into thinking it's your fault, Michael. You can talk yourself into it all you want. But we both know it's not true. We both know your wife is a whore." She swallows a glassful of whiskey. "I'll have to kill her if she doesn't leave him alone. I'm just telling you now. I'm just telling you so you're prepared."

It is only now that Michael fully understands the extent of his dilemma. "That won't be necessary. I promise you that."

"How can you be so sure?" She laughs, filling up her glass.

"Because she's my wife. I know her better than you do."

"I hope you're right. Because I'm very angry with her."

"I know you're angry. I'm angry with her, too."

"I've had to work very hard to control myself. It makes me sick to think about all the things they've done together. Like animals. Nasty, nasty, nasty. It's amazing what people do when they get between the sheets, isn't it? You of all people should know that, Dr. Knowles. Perfectly respectable people by day, but in bed—I can't even talk about it without feeling like I'm going to puke. He's all I have! I don't have anyone else! He's all I have! And she stole him from me! She stole him. And I want him back! Do you hear me?"

"Lydia, please try to stay calm."

"I've thought of killing her. I've thought about it many times. When I first found out. I went through all of the steps in my head. Just how I'd do it. It's not that difficult. It's not as hard as you think. I'd go into your house when she's at work. I'd poison the wine she drinks at night, the cream she dumps in her coffee. Splat, there she goes! *Splat! Splat! Splat!*"

"You touch her and I swear I'll kill you. I'll fucking rip you apart!"

"I think the back field will do nicely," she says lightly, like a woman planning a garden party. "I'll need help, of course, with the body. Dead bodies are awfully heavy! But you'll be here for that. We'll dig a nice cozy grave and put poor Annie into it. I'll even plant flowers all over it in spring. All kinds of lovely flowers."

"You're fucking twisted, you know that?"

"I'll take that as a compliment."

He shakes his head. If only he could wrap his hands around her throat. He'd throttle the air right out of her. "One of these days someone's going to figure this out, Mrs. Haas, and when they do, when they find you, and they *will* find you, they're going to wrap you up in one of those straitjackets and cart you off to the state hospital. You ever spend any time in a straitjacket? It's not a whole lot of fun. Of course the drugs aren't too bad, if you don't mind drooling all over yourself, shitting your pants."

She raises her gun, swift as a bird, and takes aim at his head.

"Go ahead. Shoot. I dare you."

"I will if you don't shut up."

But he can see she's bluffing. The drugs she's given him are starting to kick in. They make him brawny, shameless. He spreads his arms, rattles the chains on his feet. "Shoot me, goddamn it! Come on, *Mrs.* Haas, put me out of my misery! You fucking insane woman! You fucking lunatic!"

The blast comes louder than he ever imagined, like a wrecking ball making impact in the cinder block behind his head. His whole body quivers with the aftershock, his ears rendered useless. The woman rises like a ghost in the drifting smoke. "Drooling and shitting your pants," she says softly. "I guess you know something about that now."

And then she's gone.

65

BOILING MAD, Lydia drives to the doctor's house in the rental car. The rental car is good, she thinks, popping a few more pills into her mouth. The rental car is very good. Roomy. American. Driving it, she feels like another sort of woman, not a woman with a husband who betrays her. No. Not that sort of woman. Someone clean. Someone with an orderly life. Someone who moves quickly through life and offends no one. Someone pure.

Lydia finds the street easily and creeps up slowly, as if she is uncertain of an address, as if she is lost. A squall of black crows crosses the field. Annie's Volvo sits in the driveway. Lydia passes the house and parks down the street behind a witch hazel bush. She dials Annie from her cell phone. Annie's voice comes hollow and tentative, like the other end of an echo. "Who is this? Who *is* this?"

Although it is not smart to be there, Lydia is in no particular hurry. Killing time, she puts on more makeup, gobs of it. Finally, Annie appears on her driveway, nervous, pale, urging her children into the car, squinting in the bright reflection of snow. The boy carries a violin case and a floppy stuffed dog; the girl clutches a fat white cat. Swatting tears from her face, Annie tells the children to hurry up, to get into the car. What does Simon see in her? Lydia wonders. *What does he see in her?* Lydia takes a deep breath, concentrating on controlling herself, tempted to step on the gas and run the woman over.

Annie balks and jitters around her children like a nervous chicken. Pretending that they are just going to Grandmother's house for an ordinary visit. Throwing in knapsacks and books, stuffed animals, a haphazard pile. Annie hauls her bossy breasts up the driveway, plump, logy breasts that have been fondled and pinched and sucked by Lydia's husband. Annie slips behind the wheel with her cunt that has been pounded and prodded and savagely fucked by him as well. *Hammered,* she thinks with vulgar delight, *corked, rammed, pounded.* Thinking about it makes her mad all over again, steaming mad, but there they go now, backing out of the driveway, and she remembers that it's time to focus. Work to be done, work to be done, she thinks frivolously as Annie races down the road with the children still grappling for their seat belts, a look of vacant determi-nation on her face. She is pathetically oblivious to Lydia, who simply gets out of the car in her black wig and sunglasses and walks toward the house thinking, *I am invisible.* The street is empty, the house set back from the road; isolated. *Isolated,* what a stunning word. That's what you want when you live in the country. You want land. You want space. You want to be left alone.

Leave me alone!

Lydia wanders up the driveway, around to the back. Takes the doctor's key out of her pocketbook and opens the door, steps into the bright chaos, so different from her own life, her own dead kitchen. The glaring window light floods in like a spectator. All through the house is the pres-ence of the children, their scattered shoes and woolen hats and mittens. Their bright paintings of big skies, enormous suns, brown trees, purple flowers. And Annie's things, the blue pitcher full of wooden spoons, the cracked green vase, the clay bowl full of coins, a pair of earrings left on the counter. Envy swarms her heart like a hive of bees. She scoops the earrings into her pocket and goes upstairs, the carpet plush under her flats. The house hums, it has a heartbeat. She hurries past the children's rooms, stuffed with toys, because she knows they will depress her, and she tries to squeeze out the memory of her own childhood room, the stained yellow walls, the bed with its awful creaking springs, but she cannot. A darkness whirls up in her body, a darkness like ink spilled on her soul so deep and wide there is no containing it. The only refuge from it is hate. Hating Annie.

Wandering into the couple's room. The *bedchamber,* she thinks, but the room is simple and ordinary. Only the skylight draws her interest, the weak sun pouring down. Annie's things scattered on the mattress, her makeup, and the lipstick she favors, like garnets. The fat candle on the nightstand. Books scattered like flat stones across the floor. The bathroom smelling of lavender, vanilla. Her cologne from Paris. Lydia opens the small blue bottle and dabs its tiny mouth, glides her sticky finger down her neck. It's not enough, she thinks, wanting to reek of her, and she pours some more into her hands, splashing the wanton smell over her breasts.

Smelling fervently of Annie, she returns the Taurus to the rental agency, appreciating the fact that she doesn't have to speak to anyone. Wearing the black wig, she hands the attendant the keys. They already have the credit card. Not her own. Several days earlier, she'd gone to the public library in the center of town, the children's section, where the women were always dumb with trust. A woman's pocketbook sat on the floor, next to a toppled pile of blocks. The woman was tending to her crying child. It had been the easiest thing, slipping her hand into the purse and retrieving the wallet as if it were her own. Fussing through it, selecting the Visa and driver's license, putting the wallet back, safe and sound. It hadn't taken her long to assume the woman's persona. She'd purchased a wig at a shop on Wolf Road. *I always wanted to be a brunette, she had told the woman. Everyone knows brunettes are smarter. They exude intelligence, whereas blondes are just plain dumb.* "Thanks, Mrs. Wilson," the boy says to her and for a moment, just a split second, she is somebody else.

Lydia walks briskly back to the commuter parking lot where she left her car and gets in and turns the radio on loud. There is nothing so pleasant as blasting a radio when you are fucked up out of your mind. *Be a good wife,* Reverend Tim had told her, so on the way home she stops at the market and buys two steaks, salad fixings, a box of rice. Two chocolate brownies. A bottle of Jim Beam. *I am the perfect wife,* she thinks, driving home to her big silent house. The dogs sniff at her curiously. Simon is sitting at the kitchen table, reading the paper. Waiting for her.

He snaps the paper open, startling her with the face of Michael Knowles blazing across the front page. The headline reads: "MED CENTER DOCTOR DISAPPEARS: Drifter Found Dead in Doctor's Car, Investigation Under Way."

Simon folds the newspaper back up and slaps it on the table. "Where've you been, Lydia? We had an appointment at Blackwell today."

"I'm sorry I've been so awful, Simon. I'm sorry." Unsteady, she leans against the counter, the glorious drugs rushing through her, making her breasts full and warm like Annie's, making her belly quiver.

"That's not good enough," his voice drones.

"I want to make things up to you." She sinks to her knees before him, putting on her little-girl face. "Let me try, please. *Please let me try.*" Her tongue is big and thick inside her mouth. *Better to eat you with,* she thinks, and laughs out loud.

He studies her over his bifocals. "You're in a mood tonight."

"Let me make you supper, all right?" *Let me suck your cock.* "Let's just sit together and have dinner. In the spirit of Thanksgiving."

"All right," he says evenly. "I suppose we could do that. But what are we giving thanks for?"

"For each other. For having each other." She looks up at him cautiously, afraid, and he looks away just as she knew he would. He is not thankful, she realizes. He is not grateful that she is his wife.

"Give me a chance, Simon. We need to *be* together. We need to talk like a normal married couple."

"There is nothing normal about us, my dear. Never has been."

"We need to try," her voice begs, weepy. "Please. Can we please try?"

He reaches out and takes her hand and pulls her gently onto his lap. He studies her the way he used to when he'd paint her. "All right, Lydia. We can try." *Yes, yes, Lydia, you can suck my cock.*

She concentrates on making the meal, sensing that he is watching her every move. The smell of the meat fills the small kitchen and her mouth waters for it. *Drooling all over yourself,* she thinks of the doctor. On the table her pocketbook waits, a loyal subject. It holds three things of interest: the scent of her husband's lover, the lipstick that has roamed his lover's lips, and the fat candle that she stole from his lover's bedroom, which she will light later, when she lets him fuck her.

66

SIMON FINDS THE WIG by accident. Tuesday morning, before Lydia wakes, he takes her car to be inspected. It happens at the garage, when he opens the glove compartment to find her registration and there it is, shoved in like a furry black kitten. He jumps back in fear, not knowing what it is. He pulls it out and curls it around his fist.

He realizes that Lydia has become completely delusional. In a manic fury, she had begged him to have sex with her the night before, all part of her merciless plot to make him want her again—that would never happen. Sickened by her behavior, he'd gone to sleep in the guest room. He has decided to call Blackwell and have her committed.

With the new inspection sticker, he drives home and finds her in the kitchen, drinking coffee, dressed for work, looking like any bushy-tailed psychotic. The memory of the wig swirls back and he can hardly look at her. As it turned out, it wasn't the only suspicious thing she'd shoved into the glove compartment. There was a red marker in there, too, a Sharpie. It was the same kind of red marker that an unidentified woman had used to draw a cross on Rosie Knowles.

67

ANNIE WAKES from a deep sleep in her childhood room. Sunlight pours through the shutters. Her eyes drink in the beauty of the room: the rose-bud wallpaper, the magnificent Chippendale highboy, the small mono-grammed handkerchiefs that her mother set out for her on the nightstand in lieu of ordinary Kleenex. Annie is continually amazed by the plush civility of her parents' home, a quality of life that she and Michael could never duplicate.

"You'll be fine, sweetie," Annie tells a tearful Rosie as she hugs her good-bye after breakfast. They're standing in the foyer. Annie takes Henry's shoulders because he does not seem to want to hug her. "I'll find him, all right? I promise." He nods, but she knows he doesn't believe her—he doesn't trust her. He thinks it's all her fault.

"They'll be just fine," her mother interrupts, flapping the back of her hand at Annie. *Go!* "Who's going to help me make the pumpkin pie? We have a lot of cooking to do before Thursday."

Rosie immediately volunteers. As usual, Henry pretends he isn't interested. Annie watches her mother guide the children through the swinging door of the kitchen. She peers through the oval window and watches as they begin to make the pie. Even Henry helps, scooping the sloppy seeds out of a pumpkin. Annie is grateful that her parents have this beautiful home, grateful that she could bring the children here, where they are safe.

She steps outside and walks down the circular driveway to her car. As much as she has tried, she cannot seem to warm her bones. The air seems colder today, it cuts right through her. Her head hurts and her breasts ache. Her nipples feel raw. Even the hot tea her mother made for her and poured into a thermos does not warm her. *If I begin to cry,* she thinks, *I will never stop.* She does not mind the two-hour drive back to High Meadow. It is the first time she's been alone for days, and it makes her sad and a little frightened. Where is Michael now? she wonders. A feeling of dread comes over her. She can't help feeling as if God has taken him from her to teach her a lesson. *Selfish wife,* she thinks. He was selfish, too. They are *both* at fault, she argues to the heavens. And no amount of apologizing is going to change anything.

Crossing the river under a dusting of light snow, Annie sees the gushing smokestacks of the chemical plants down by the port, fat yellow clouds rising into the sky. The river is black and the scrawny trees on its shore grieve for the distant sun. The streets of Albany are slippery at this hour, a pandemonium of school buses and pedestrians and early rush-hour traffic.

When she gets to South Pearl Street it begins to snow again. She parks and enters the clinic, happy to see that Anya, the Russian receptionist who was injured in the bombing, is back at work. Anya puts down the phone and comes around the counter to greet her. "Annie." They hug. "How are you?"

"Not so good."

"Any word? Anything from the police?"

Annie shakes her head.

"How are the children?"

"With my parents."

"Take a seat in the waiting room. Dr. James will be with you soon."

Annie waits in the crowded room, wondering how all these people can possibly be seen. Without Michael, she knows, they will have to wait longer than usual. She looks around at the faces in the room. A young couple sits across the room, each in headphones, plugged into a shared Walkman, moving to the same beat in exactly the same way, their eyes half-moons of tranquillity. Next to them, two women, a mother and daughter, jerk and twist with impatience. The daughter, a teenager in studded blue jeans and a Puma sweatshirt, holds a swaddled infant with pierced ears. The girl diligently chews on a wad of bubble gum, blowing bubbles for her baby. The baby stares blankly at the expanding pink bubble until it pops. "Pop!" the girl says. The mother, who wears a Proud Grandma T-shirt, irritably flips through *Good Housekeeping* magazine and continually glances at her watch. Good housekeeping, Annie thinks, that's all anybody really wants. Shelter. A safe place to raise their kids. The package deal of American life—the way Rockwell had painted it—but there is no package deal, she thinks.

She waits for over an hour. Then one of the nurses calls her name and takes her down to Celina's office. "She'll be right in, Mrs. Knowles."

"Thank you."

Annie likes the office with its cheerful yellow walls and jungle of plants. Celina enters the room wearing her professional smile. "Hi, Annie."

"Hi."

"Sorry to keep you waiting."

Celina sits down behind her desk. They appraise each other coolly. It is obvious to Annie that the woman has never liked her. How ironic that Annie must come to her now, for help. "I like your plants," Annie says to break the ice. "I feel like I'm in the Amazon or something."

"Yeah, this room's my cheap vacation." Celina smiles, shifting gears. "Any news about Michael?"

"No. Nothing. They've got the FBI involved. They're not telling me very much." Her mouth dries up. "He did it for you, you know. He admired you. He respected you."

"I never meant for this to happen, Annie. I hope you understand that."

"But you knew it was possible, didn't you? You knew how awful things could get."

"Yes," Celina admits. "You saw that waiting room. Too many women depend on me. They don't have anywhere else to go. Michael was all I had. I regret it now. You have no idea how much I regret it."

"Oh, I think I do." A familiar envy whirls up inside her and she spits out her awful thought. "It should have been you."

"I wish it had been."

Annie feels a stab of guilt. "I'm sorry."

"Don't apologize." Celina opens Annie's chart. "Are you sure you want to do this?"

Annie nods. "Do you think I'm awful?"

"It's not my business to judge you."

"There's been someone else in my life."

Celina affirms this information with a nod. "Is it his?"

"I don't know. I'm not sure. Anyway, it's over."

"Did you tell Michael?"

"About the pregnancy, yes."

"What did he think?"

"He wanted me to have it. He didn't know, though, that it might not be his."

"Does it even matter?"

Of course it matters, Annie thinks, but the question lingers on Celina's face, and it makes her wonder.

"You've got guilt written all over you, Annie, but let me tell you something. What you did happened for a reason, and Michael played a role in that reason. You don't strike me as the casual type. You needed something that he wasn't giving you and you went and found it. There's no punishment in store for you, honey—the heavens aren't going to open up and shower you with terrible things. You slept with somebody and it took. God gave you a souvenir for your trouble. Now you can pack it away up in the attic, but that doesn't mean you're going to forget it's there." Celina's beeper goes off. "Look. You've been through a lot. I'm not convinced you've had enough time to think this over. I want you to be sure. I don't want you doing this over guilt."

Annie nods and sighs with appreciation. For the first time she understands why Michael liked Celina so much.

"You go home and rest. I can always work you in if you decide you want to go through with it. And if you need someone to talk to, you call me, all right? Anytime, day or night."

Annie nods. "Thank you, Celina."

"Don't you dare mention it."

Driving home, Annie feels numb. She tries calling Simon on her cell phone but there's no answer. She leaves a message on his office machine and even tries calling him at home, to no avail. The last time they spoke, he told her not to call him anymore. Well, she has a damn good reason now.

Her house is dark when she arrives. It has always been a house full of noise and children and music, but now a piercing silence greets her. For a moment she stands in her kitchen, disoriented, as if she has walked into the wrong house, as if she has walked into someone else's life and now faces a whole set of strange problems. A missing husband; an enigmatic lover; an unwanted pregnancy. *It's my life,* she thinks incredulously. Wrapped in a blanket, she roams the rooms as if she is looking for someone, but she encounters only the furniture, inert and indifferent. Still, she can't help feeling that someone's been here. In her bedroom things seem to be missing. Her perfume, her lipstick. Even the bedspread seems rumpled. She searches Michael's drawers, looking for clues, answers, but finds none. Finally exhausted, she lies down on the bed and waits. She waits and waits, for what she does not know.

At dinnertime, Detective Bascombe shows up with a bucket of fried chicken. "It's no good eating alone," he tells her and he's right; she's glad for the company. She likes the way he moves about the house—the burly intrusion of a seasoned cop.

"You okay?" he asks gently.

As if on cue, tears sprout from her eyes, but she ignores them and nods that, yes, she's okay, she's perfectly fine. He takes a folded handkerchief out of his pocket and offers it to her. She cries heartily into it for a while, then hands it back. "Feel better?" he says, refolding it, returning it to his pocket.

"It's a beautiful thing to carry someone's tears in your pocket. Thank you."

"Don't mention it." He smiles almost bashfully. "I have some information for you about your husband's car," he says, getting down to business. "We found his gym bag in the trunk. The bag was pretty much destroyed in the fire, but some of the things survived." He puts a heavy plastic bag on the table. It contains Michael's stethoscope, a pair of sneakers.

"Can I open it?" she asks the detective.

"Please."

Rapaciously, she pulls out Michael's stethoscope and puts it on and listens to her heart as if she might decipher a code that will lead her to him. She thinks about the tiny heart beating deep inside of her and new tears glaze her eyes. She takes off the stethoscope and puts it back in the bag.

"We found this, too," Bascombe says, revealing a gun in his open palms, a little black pistol.

"Is it his? I didn't know he had one."

"Not officially. It's registered to a Marshall Sawyer. Does that name sound familiar?"

"No."

"He's one of the accountants for the hospital, lives a few blocks from it. I sent somebody down there yesterday, but the wife claims he's out of town. Took a week off. We'll keep on it."

"Can I see it? Can I hold it?"

Bascombe hands her the gun. It feels cold in her hand. What else didn't Michael tell her, she wonders. It's clear he was in more danger than he ever let on. "It's so cold," she says.

Cold and small, she thinks, like something dead.

68

SIMON WATCHES HIS WIFE from the bedroom window, loading up the trunk of her car. It is only half past six, a cold, gray morning, and she is up and dressed in jeans and a flannel shirt and rubber boots. The box looks heavy, full of cans of soup and tuna fish, boxes of saltines. And he sees other things, too: shaving cream, disposable razors, toilet paper. What is she doing with it, he wonders. She closes the trunk and hurries into the car and drives away.

Later that morning, he calls McMillan & Taft and asks to speak to his wife. Her supervisor, Martin Banner, gets on the phone and tells him she's been fired. "Fired? Why?"

Banner tells him that she hasn't shown up to work in nearly two weeks.

Troubled by this news, Simon gets into his car and drives to St. Vincent's Hospital to look for Reverend Tim, the one person who might know Lydia's whereabouts. The lobby is crowded, people moving in all directions. "I'm looking for Reverend Tim," he tells the woman at reception.

"He's up in critical care," she says. "You can go on up. Ninth floor."

Simon takes the elevator. He does not like being in the hospital. He remembers the time he brought Lydia into the ER, doped up on pills. They'd made him wait outside while they stuck the tube down her throat. For a month or two after that, she rarely left the house. He'd done several drawings of her during that period, all of which she'd burned in a rage. Reverend Tim had come to town just afterward. Lydia had been vulnerable.

Simon finds the minister with a patient, playing chess. He leans in the doorway and knocks on the door. Reverend Tim squints up. "Can I help you?"

"Where's my wife?"

Reverend Tim excuses himself from the chess game and joins Simon in the hall. With his height and breadth, Simon towers over the disabled minister. "Hello, Mr. Haas. What can I do for you?"

"You can tell me where my wife goes every day."

"Your wife is a committed member of our organization. She's often involved with church events."

"My wife is a troubled woman."

"All of God's creatures have qualities worthy of admiration, no matter how chaotic. Your wife has many. It's a pity you don't see them."

Simon contains the impulse to punch the man's teeth out. "She hasn't been home terribly much. I thought you might know where she is."

"I'm afraid I don't. As a matter of fact, I haven't seen her for over a week."

"I know what you're doing," Simon says. "You don't fool me for a minute."

"Excuse me?"

"You set her up. She's done all your dirty work, hasn't she? And she's still doing it."

Reverend Tim's face reveals nothing. "I don't know what you're talking about."

"You sent her into that clinic with a bomb, didn't you?"

"Do I have to call security, Mr. Haas?"

"Not to mention the other despicable things you did to Dr. Knowles?

Where is he now? Did you kill him? Is that what you did? Or maybe you had my wife do it. Or maybe he's still alive. Maybe you've got him locked up somewhere, is that it?"

"Security!" the chaplain shouts. "I need security!"

"You stay away from my wife, understand?" Simon says, a commotion brewing at the end of the hallway. "You leave her alone or I'll kill you."

69

THROUGHOUT THE DAY, the line of light around the cellar doors indicates the passage of time. Sometimes the shape of light resembles a cathedral and it makes him wonder if there's a God. He admits to himself that he has little faith. His faith has been replaced by a wild terror that astonishes him. He does not know how it will serve him, but he knows, for certain, that it must.

Contrary to his original prognosis, he is beginning to heal. His ribs are less tender and the infection in his eye is beginning to clear up. The cuts and bruises that cover his body don't hurt so much now. Still, he feels weak, listless. Just walking to the toilet and back thoroughly exhausts him.

"I brought you something," she tells him on her next visit.

"What is it?"

She sets a photo album on the ground and shoves it toward him with her foot. "A little present. A tour of your life."

"Where did you get that?"

She holds up his keys. "Where do you think?"

"You have no right. You have no right to do that."

"I can do anything I want," she says. "Don't worry, no one was home. They're off to Grandma's for Thanksgiving."

"Please, just stay away from my family."

"Nice place. All those pretty stone walls. All safe and sound. It must have been terribly comfortable for all of you."

He watches her, amazed.

"In case you haven't guessed, I find you all fascinating. Your house, the way you dress, her fucking gardening clogs. The little pegs in the kitchen where you hang your coats. You're like . . . you're like people on TV. In one of those commercials for laundry detergent."

"Things aren't always what they seem."

She looks down at her hands, suddenly melancholic. Best to keep her talking. "What about your house, Mrs. Haas? What sort of commercial would it make?"

"It's not my house, really, it's *his* house. We're the creepy neighbors everybody avoids. I'm the artist's *mad* wife." She grins diabolically. "It's a reputation to live up to."

And you're doing a splendid job, he thinks.

"*This* is my home. I was happy here once. Before Mama died."

"That must have been very difficult."

"After she died, I used to visit her grave. I was very little. I used to fall asleep in the grass. There was a caretaker; he'd leave me gumdrops. I'd always set the table for meals. Sometimes I'd set a place for Mama. My father didn't like it. Once he pushed all the plates on the floor." She sighs. "I miss her. I thought it would stop. I thought when I grew up . . . but you never stop missing someone. Like a scar on your heart."

"Why don't you pour yourself another drink?"

"She's a ghost now. Upstairs. Sometimes you can hear her walking around. Sometimes I just want to go to her, you know? When I'm driving. Sometimes I just wish . . ."

"No," he insists, thinking of his own predicament. "Death is never the answer." She gathers herself up in her own embrace and rocks back and forth on her haunches. He can't seem to get to her now. "Lydia?"

"People take advantage."

"What?"

"Of family. *Commitment.* People like your wife. People like you."

"Sometimes things change. People grow and change. They go different ways."

"Love doesn't change." She nudges the photo album closer with her foot. "Look. I wanted to remind you."

"I don't need you to remind me! I've got them all right here." He taps his head and grabs the photo album, conscious of the fact that his wife's fingerprints are all over it. He flips through the pictures: Henry's science fair, Rosie's horse shows, school picnics, birthday parties.

"Tell me what you see."

"I see my wife," he says irritably. "My children. Our house. Our dog. All the things you've taken from me."

"Oh, but someone's missing."

Slowly, it dawns on him—it's him.

"Not one picture of Daddy. Now, why is that?"

"You know why."

"Yes, but I want to hear you say it."

"Because I wasn't there!"

"No. You weren't there. And when the cat's away . . ."

"It wasn't like that. Don't make it sound like that."

"Like what?"

"Cheap. Because that's not Annie."

"Oh, yes it is. She's cheap. She's cheap, all right."

"He manipulated her!"

"You're right. He's very good at that. He's relentless when it comes to getting his way. But she took the bait, didn't she? She ate it right out of his hand."

"I can't do anything about that. I can't change the fact that it happened. I gave her everything I could. The house out there. The life. Everything she wanted. But it wasn't enough. It wasn't enough for her."

"No, Michael," she whispers. "*You* weren't enough."

70

THE FACT that Simon has not returned her calls makes her feel unspeakably lonely. She *knows* he loves her on some level, and she wants to tell him that she's pregnant; it's only right to tell him. Unwilling to wait another minute, she drives down to his studio that afternoon. The same men are playing pinochle and drinking beer out front. The lobby stinks of urine and filth. As she climbs the stairs, she hears the other tenants in their apartments, the TVs and radios, and smells their cooking. She knocks on Simon's door, but he doesn't answer. She tries the knob and the door opens. Annie enters the room and finds herself surrounded by a dozen massive paintings, portraits of women in various stages of undress. They are women in uniforms: a waitress, a nurse, a cleaning woman, a nun, a judge, a stripper, a cheerleader. There are name tags and ankle bracelets and deformed pumps, bruised calves, bony ankles, breasts like deflated balloons. The women have homely faces. They have noses and chins and foreheads and ears expatiating with character. There is a pre-dominance of the color yellow, a tawny ocher, and deep rusts and browns. There are windows muddled by dead plants, the gray city beyond, the glowing moon. The women seem to ache for admiration. They beckon the viewer like lovers or thieves. Across the room, separated from the oth-ers, is a painting of her, which startles her. Lured by her image, she wishes to touch it, to run her fingers across the rugged surface of the canvas, but upon closer inspection she sees that it is wet. In it, she is naked, under-water in a kind of starry womb; her hair floats, sinewy as Medusa's. Her body is pale and luminous and utterly exposed. *That's me*, she thinks, transfixed and a little frightened. *That's me.*

The room smolders with Simon's energy. An idea comes to her, a way of letting him know. A tube of yellow paint catches her eye and she squeezes some out on a plate and swirls the brush around in it. With some trepidation, she applies the paint, turning her flat belly into a round globe of light. Surveying her work, she smiles, indulging for the first time in the idea of keeping it, warmed by the prospect of changing shape.

71

THE BAR IS GOOD and quiet and he is glad to be here, away from every-thing, hiding from the world, sitting on the stool near the greasy window. Painting Annie has depressed him and he has been sitting here for the past two hours trying to figure out what to do about her. He is quite cer-tain that if he cannot have her in his life, there is no point in living it. He knows it's melodramatic, but he can't seem to help it. Just being without her for all these days has turned him into a maudlin fool.

Finding Lydia is essential. He needs to get her into his car and drive her straight to Blackwell. Committing her to the hospital is the least he can do, the only way he knows to keep her out of jail because he is fairly certain that's where she's headed.

Hours float by. People come in and out, ordering drinks. They leave him alone. He wants to disappear. He wants to hide somewhere and forget that any of this has happened. He doesn't know why he's been protecting Lydia for so long, and the fact that he's done it makes him uneasy. He knows it comes from the deepest part of him, a desolate place of reckoning, but he cannot do it any longer. He gets up and goes to the phone and dials the police and asks to speak with the detective on the Knowles case. A man comes on the line, his voice gruff. "Bascombe here. What can I do for you?"

"This is Simon Haas," he says. "I have something I'd like to tell you."

72

"TELL ME, LYDIA, what has been keeping you so busy?" Reverend Tim asks her. They're in his car, and he's taking her someplace, he hasn't told her where. She'd been at home in the shower. Drying off, she'd heard someone downstairs, snooping around the house. Glancing through the window, she'd seen his car. His face had blanched when she'd come down in her robe.

"You look—" He studies her savagely. "Tired."

"I haven't been well," she says. "I haven't been myself."

"I'm sorry to hear that."

The bright lights of McDonald's make her squint. He pulls into the drive-through and orders her a Happy Meal. "To cheer you up," he tells her. She's not hungry; she's never hungry anymore, but she realized a long time ago that in the presence of Reverend Tim it is always best to do what he tells her.

"I saw your husband this morning. He came to the hospital. He was very anxious to find you. He told me you haven't been home very much. Now, why is that?"

"We haven't been getting along," she manages. "I've been sleeping in my car."

"Here you go, sir." The boy in the little window hands him the bags of food.

"Thank you, kindly," Reverend Tim says. "And you have a real nice Thanksgiving." He hands her the bag. "What are your plans for tomorrow? Will you be making a feast?"

"Sure," she tells him, although it is the furthest thing from her mind. She sets the bag of food down on the seat. "I don't have much of an appetite now."

"One bite isn't going to kill you, is it?"

Lydia knows he expects her to eat it. He expects her to eat the whole thing. Carefully, she removes the little box from the bag and opens it, admiring the way it all folds together so perfectly. The little toys inside. Somebody took a lot of time thinking about it. Making sure everything fit. And she appreciates that sort of effort in people. For the children of this world. And for the others. The lost ones like her. *I am not afraid of heaven.*

He drinks his coffee, his hands shaking. His face hacked with worry. He looks at her and sighs deeply. "We've got a problem, Lydia."

The interstate is desolate at this hour. They drive through rural towns where dirt roads ramble and converge and wind around in circles. She is completely disoriented. They pass trailers, crooked houses, and tumbledown farms. Finally, he turns into a field of snow, endless, like the ocean. An old barn comes clear in the headlights, lit up inside. Three other cars are already there, two pickup trucks and a station wagon. The sweat is thick down her back, all the way down to her buttocks. She swallows and it hurts and she wonders if she might be sick. "Let's go in," Reverend Tim says. "I've assembled some people."

Frightened, Lydia hurries to get out and then wonders, as she is crossing the field thick with snow, why she is scrambling and rushing. Rushing to her grave. Imagining that they are going to do something awful to her. But inside the others are friendly, standing around in their coats. Patty Tuttle gives her a wave, her eyes twinkling and friendly. Three of the men who captured Michael Knowles are sitting in old chairs with their big arms crossed. All three have been to prison, Reverend Tim's little project in rehabilitation. They take the cause very seriously. They'll do anything for Reverend Tim in the name of Jesus, their arms tattooed with the symbols of their devotion. Marshall Sawyer and Patty Tuttle sit next to each other. Reverend Tim shows Lydia to a chair, and they all look at her. She feels her eyelids fluttering like moths around a bulb. The sweat runs down her back. Even her wrists are wet. She is afraid she is going to be sick.

"I'm sure you've all seen the papers about Dr. Knowles. It seems that somewhere in the midst of all our careful planning a mistake occurred." It's how he talks, she realizes, putting everyone at ease before he uses the knife. Scowling, he condemns her with his suspicion. "You gave him the drug, Lydia. It was morphine, yes? That alone was supposed to kill him."

It was morphine, yes, a lethal dose of it, but it hadn't gone into Michael Knowles. Knowles had gotten a mild sedative. The tainted morphine had gone into Walter Ooms. "Yes, Reverend," she lies, and the memory of that awful night vividly returns.

"Even if the morphine didn't kill him, it's unlikely that he would have survived the crash," Sawyer says, blotting his forehead with a handkerchief.

"Now look, folks. If there's somebody in this room who got emotional over this, I pray they'll let me know. And we can fix what went wrong and go on."

Lydia feels his heavy hand on her shoulder. Nobody moves, and the wind makes the old barn howl.

"He was dead when we left him there," Marshall Sawyer says with grave certainty. Sawyer is a burly man with a beard in a white collared shirt and trousers. One week ago, he had rolled up those sleeves and pounded his respectable fists into Michael Knowles's face.

"Alive or dead, somebody took him. And left another man in his place." Reverend Tim slams his fists down on the table. "Who has betrayed me? Who in this room has deceived me?"

Lydia concentrates on keeping perfectly still, the way she would when she'd sit for one of Simon's paintings. Reverend Tim walks the uneven floor with his crooked leg. "I try so hard to walk in the light of Jesus. He throws us obstacles. Terrible tragedies." He shakes his head. "I will find this person, sooner or later. Jesus has a way of whispering in my ear. And if any of you suspect someone, it's your duty to tell me what you know. Other than that, there's very little I can do but wait and pray for a revelation."

They leave the barn in silence. It has begun to snow, and inside the car the white flakes collect on the cold glass. Lydia feels as though she is inside an hourglass, the sand spilling out so quickly that, before long, there will be no time left. Sitting next to him, her stomach in knots, she does what she knows she has to do. "It may have been Sawyer," she tells him.

Reverend Tim's eyes widen with surprise.

"That night he left his coat in my car. I tried to return it to him the next morning. His wife told me he'd never come home."

Reverend Tim chews on his tongue, shaking his head, his eyes bright with tears. "He's my friend," he says, incredulous, "my best friend. But why?"

"Why don't you ask him."

73

TAKING CELINA'S ADVICE, Annie puts herself to bed and doesn't wake up till the next afternoon. The phone is ringing; it's Henry. "Hi, Mom. It's Thanksgiving."

"Hey, Hen. Have you had your turkey yet?"

"It's still cooking. Wait, Rosie wants to talk to you."

Annie can hear the two of them squabbling: *Don't grab, Rosie!* "Mom? It's me, Rosie. Guess what?"

Henry grabbed the phone back. "Snowflake puked all over Grandma's new carpeting!"

"No!"

"It's okay," Rosie came back on. "Grandma got it all off."

"Thank *God!*" Another call comes through on call waiting. "Rosie, I have to go. Give everyone a kiss for me." She clicks onto the new line. "Hello?"

"You got a paper there?" It's Bascombe.

"I think so. Hold on." She retrieves the paper from the front porch. "Okay?"

"That gun of your husband's. The one registered to Marshall Sawyer?"

"Yes?"

"Turn to the obituaries."

"Hang on." Annie flips anxiously to the obituaries. In the third row down she sees Sawyer's name, dead from a morphine overdose, an apparent suicide. Survived by a wife and daughter.

"Sound familiar?"

"Yes. A little too familiar."

"The wake's tomorrow. I'd like you to go. You may see somebody you recognize."

"Okay. What time?"

"I'll be over at two o'clock. Wear something black."

Manning's Funeral Home is on the corner of St. James and Delaware Avenue, a big white house with three columns in front. The parking lot is packed. Bascombe parks in a tow-away zone and shoves his Official Police Business sticker up on the windshield. "Put this on." He hands her a black hat with a short black veil attached.

"You want me to wear this?"

"Yeah. It's my aunt Lucille's. Go ahead."

Annie puts on the hat with the veil and her dark sunglasses.

"Hey, you look good like that."

"Yeah, right."

Bascombe opens her door and helps her out and escorts her as if they're an old married couple. The chapel is crowded, standing room only. Mourners shuffle past the open casket. "He must've been a hell of a Christian," Bascombe whispers to her as they approach the coffin. "Look where it got him." Sawyer is laid out in splendor, wearing an expensive black suit. His hands are crossed on his chest, a gold ring on his pinky finger. Just beyond the coffin, his wife and daughter receive mourners, their eyes swollen with grief. Annie notices the gold necklace around the daughter's neck. *Theresa.* "You recognize him?" Bascombe asks.

"Never seen him before."

"He's one of them. That group."

A chill rushes through her.

"Look around. See if anyone looks familiar."

Behind her dark glasses, Annie furtively searches the large room. To her surprise she sees Joe Rank slouched in a distant corner next to his wife, who holds a swaddled infant. Annie can tell by some of the white shoes that many of the people have come from work at the hospital. Just as they are about to walk out, a familiar face grabs Annie's eye. "Now, what is she doing here?"

"Who?"

"That woman right there. Lydia Haas."

"You know her?"

"She's the wife of one of my colleagues."

"Strange people. We've been over there from time to time, their house on the lake. Back in the days when he was a big shot. Used to have wild parties. Drugs. We had to get an ambulance once. For the wife. A real nut job. She was all cut up on her legs. All these crosses in blood, you know, crucifixes. Turns out she did it to herself." He shakes his head. "Sick."

Annie's heart turns dully. "I don't know him very well," she hears herself say. "I used to see him at the pool."

"Uh-huh. Well, it appears that Marshall Sawyer knew her. And I have a feeling I know why."

Annie looks at him. "She's one of them, isn't she?"

"I suspect she is. And I intend to find out."

Why hadn't Simon told her, she wonders now. He must have known. Bascombe drives her home through the snow, the sky a pearly violet. The snowflakes are fat and slow. He drops her off and waits while she unlocks the door and steps inside. Waving good-bye, she watches the detective's car pull down the long driveway, out of sight.

A thud on the back porch makes her freeze. Her legs go weak. She stands very still, her ears animal keen, and holds her breath. Soundlessly, she moves into the dark powder room at the back of the house. It's still snowing and there's a wind, the trees bobbing and swaying, obstructing her view of the backyard. Long shadows shift on the snow, but that's not a shadow, it's a person. *There's somebody out there, someone running toward the woods.*

Annie grabs her keys and runs outside to the car, starts the engine, twists on her high beams and drives off the driveway onto the snow, around to the back, roaring over the bumpy field, her headlights bounding after a fleeing jackrabbit, coming up suddenly on the back of the intruder, wiry and agile as a panther in black pants, a black hooded windbreaker, a black wool face mask, nearing the edge of the woods, where the trees stand in solemn unity. Annie's foot hits the floor and she drives as far as she possibly can, coming up against a wall of branches. Leaping out of the car, she scrambles into the woods. The runner trips, enabling Annie to catch up—uncertain and terrified of what she will do when she does. Annie grabs the runner, realizing that it's a woman, and gropes for the mask, tearing it off. She recognizes the girl from the wake. It's the dead man's daughter, Theresa Sawyer.

74

AFTER THE WAKE, Reverend Tim comes up to her and ushers her away from the mourners. "I have some information for you," he tells her. "It's about the Knowles woman."

"What about her?"

"I hear she's expecting."

"What?"

"One of our members is on the inside at the clinic. She happened to see Knowles's name on a urine sample. Of course, we don't know who the father is."

Lydia stands there, feeling the wind on her shoulders. Someone is laughing inside her head, someone is teasing her. *Annie and Simon sitting in a tree, K-I-S-S-I-N-G! First comes love, then comes marriage, then comes baby in a baby carriage.*

Reverend Tim touches her arm. "I thought you should know."

75

"I'M SORRY I RAN like that," Theresa tells Annie, drinking tea at her kitchen table. "I just don't know who to trust anymore. I saw your car. I didn't know it was you. I got scared."

"You can trust me," Annie says.

Theresa has brought her an envelope filled with newspaper clippings. "I've been keeping these just in case," she explains, spreading them out on the kitchen table like a crude collage. "I knew him sort of, your husband. I just wanted to help if I could. My folks don't believe in it. They're part of a group run by our minister. They were very angry at him."

"So you gave him the gun."

"A whole lot of good it did."

"I'm sure he appreciated it."

"They killed my father." She looks down at her hands. "I feel like it's my fault."

"No, that's not true. You had nothing to do with it."

Theresa nods her head gratefully.

"You've done a very impressive job of organizing these," Annie tells her, looking over the articles, many of which pertain to the renovation of the building on South Pearl Street that houses the clinic.

"It used to be a crack house," Theresa says. "I used to run by there sometimes; it was nasty."

Early photographs show the building at its worst, boarded up and swarming with graffiti. Once Celina occupied it, a transformation occurred. Other articles reported on the opening of the clinic, detailing the services it proposed to offer, and the ribbon-cutting ceremonies, where Susan Todd, the sassy head of Planned Parenthood, wielded the scissors. To Annie's surprise, she finds the article she had written about late-term abortion. It was the article, she recalls, that Joe Rank had alluded to that night at the Spaulls' party. Her name, she notices, has been circled in red pen, next to which someone has clarified in the same red ink *the doctor's wife*. Other articles focus on the protestors. A large photo shows the protestors making a human chain in front of the clinic. Even in the grayish blur of the newsprint their rage comes through. Annie opens the junk drawer in the kitchen and gets her magnifying glass. "Maybe you could help me with this," she suggests. "Why don't you circle all the people you recognize from your minister's group."

Theresa takes the pen and studies the photograph and begins circling. She gives the page to Annie, who studies the faces carefully, each one urgent with purpose. A small, shrunken figure stands in the shadows. If it weren't for Theresa's black circle, she might not have even noticed her, but now that she has, everything comes clear.

The woman is Lydia Haas.

76

SUPINE ON THE MATTRESS, Michael hears a familiar sound coming from outside. Two sounds that make a rhythm. Ah, yes, he knows. Someone is digging. He has the distant memory of Annie out in the garden, planting bulbs for spring. A shovel, that's what it is. Going into the soil, then coming out again. Making a great big hole.

He pulls himself up, realizing that his legs have gone aquiver. Holding on to the cold cinder-block wall, dragging the chain behind him, he explores the parameters of the cellar, desperate to find a window. Cobwebs stick to his fingers as he traces the cold walls in the darkness. He discerns the texture of plywood, feels the cold air swarming all around it. A window underneath, he surmises, pulling the wood board off with his bare hands, ignoring the splinters pricking his fingertips. Light streams in and his hands sweep the cold glass; his eyes feast on the outside world, drinking in the colors of the distant trees. He blinks, his eyes stinging and blurred. And then he sees her. She's digging a grave.

"There's no hope for us now," she tells him later in a state of agitation. "Your wife is pregnant."

"Yes, I know."

"You know?"

"I'm her husband. Of course I know. We've been trying to have a third."

"Sorry to disappoint you, but it's not *yours*."

"Of course it's mine," he says, and he believes it.

"Prove it."

"What difference does it make?"

"It makes *all* the difference." Breaking into tears, she drops to the floor and beats her fists into the cement like a small child having a tantrum. "Do you have any idea what it feels like? He doesn't love me anymore."

"I'm sure that's not true," he says, wanting only to placate her.

"What do I have to do?" she shouts. "What do I *fucking* have to do?" Producing a pair of scissors from her apron pocket, she holds it up with menace like a threat, then uses it on herself, slicing off her hair. The locks fall to the floor, ragged as feathers. "There," she says, satisfied, appeased. "Do you like it? Do you think it's pretty?"

Her hair looks haphazard and deranged, but he says, "Yes, I think it's very pretty."

"I don't believe you." She sings the taunt.

"It's very pretty, Lydia."

"I want you to *convince* me." She tugs at the hem of her dress, then turns it up in her fingers. She's showing him her underpants, which are flowered and childish, like Rosie's. "I have an inny."

"A what?"

"My belly button. Do you want to touch it? Do you want to put your finger in it?"

"No." His stomach turns. "I would not."

But she comes nearer. "Don't you want to touch me?"

He is thinking about the scissors in her pocket. Now she is pulling off her dress. "Lydia, what are you doing?"

"I know you want to." Her body is delicate, frail. Nearly emaciated. A girl's body. "Don't lie. Everyone wants to touch me." She runs his hand over her belly, up her torso to her tiny breasts, her neck, the bones of her face. Abruptly, she drops to her knees. Somewhere deep inside his brain he thinks of grabbing the scissors and cutting open her throat, but now she has ventured into his pants and is trying to put his disinterested penis into her mouth. Frustrated, she grins at him imploringly. "No wonder she's fucking him."

"Get out." He shoves her hard away from him and she falls back on the hard cement and bumps her head. She starts to bleed.

She laughs. She laughs and laughs. "Oh, I'll get out," she says, "I'll get out all right. And you'll be lucky if I ever come back!" The lantern swoops in her hand as she flees up the stairs, slamming the door behind her. Then comes the sound of hammering, all around the doorframe, one nail after another while she mutters and curses—a madwoman's harangue. The door quavers with each blow and over the next several minutes of continuous pounding it becomes exceedingly clear to him that she has no intention of coming back.

77

MUDDLED WITH SLEEP, Simon hears a car pulling up the driveway. The rattling diesel tells him it's Lydia. She leaves the engine idling and storms into the house, making a lot of noise. He looks at the clock: three A.M. After so much whiskey, his head feels bruised and dim as a turnip. The smell of cigar smoke floats up into the room. Pulling himself up, he realizes that he's afraid of her. Now she is on the stairs. And now she is in the room, standing at the foot of their bed. He has never seen his wife smoke a cigar before and he doesn't approve of it. Women have no business smoking cigars. "What are you doing? What do you want?" He braces himself for something, he does not know what. And her face breaks open with a smile.

"I hear congratulations are in order." She hurls the lit cigar at his naked chest.

Struck by the burning ash, he jumps and rolls around on the bed, trying to retrieve the cigar. "Jesus fucking Christ! What are you trying to do, burn the house down?" He puts it out in his water glass.

"What do you think I am, *stupid*?"

"What are you talking about?"

"Did you think I wouldn't fucking *know*?"

"I have no idea what—"

"Now everything's ruined," she blubbers. "Ruined!"

Before he can even respond, she's gone, her car racing off down the driveway.

Wearily, he pulls on his trousers, his shirt. What time is it now? Three-twenty. Groggily, he staggers into the bathroom to urinate, wash his face. *I hear congratulations are in order.* What the fuck is she talking about?

He calls the detective and tells him about the visit. Then he gets into his car and drives around looking for her. At a loss, he drives down to his studio. It's not until he's there, standing in front of the painting of Annie, that he realizes what she meant.

78

"I HAVE A GUN," Lydia Haas says, waking Annie out of a deep sleep. The room is dark, splotched with moonlight. Annie sees her standing there in a red wool coat. She sees the gun and her heart lurches and jolts.

"Get up."

"What do you want?" Annie gets out of bed, grateful that she's wearing sweatpants and a T-shirt and Michael's thick socks.

"It makes me sick just to look at you," Lydia says.

Everything slows down. Annie's mouth goes dry.

"Let's go. We're going for a ride." Annie moves into the hall, past the empty rooms of her children, then sinks, on shaking knees, down each step. "I need my shoes," she says haltingly, trying to figure out a plan. "I need my coat."

"Hurry up," Lydia says, moving closer with the gun. Annie pulls on her coat and steps into her winter boots, her mind scrambling. "I'm right here, you feel that? I have a very powerful gun and I'm an excellent shot. I'm especially good with moving targets. Don't tempt me to pull this trigger."

They walk through the dark to Lydia's car. "You're driving. The key's in there." Annie gets behind the wheel. Gravity presses down, her body stiff, rigid. She has never been so terrified in her life. Lydia climbs into the back and puts the gun to the nape of Annie's neck. "Back out. Get on 66 going north."

Annie does what Lydia asks and gets on Route 66. The car reeks of cigarettes. The snow falls heavily, making it hard to see. Up ahead, a group of deer crosses the road and she can feel the tires slipping when she brakes.

"You make me want to puke," Lydia says. "You make me want to throw up."

"Look, obviously you're upset."

"I don't know what he sees in you."

"I can't change what happened. But it's over. It's been over for a long time."

"It's not over! Don't you lie to me! Don't you tell me it's over when I know very well that it's not."

"But it is." Annie can barely get the words out, her voice almost pleading. "I haven't spoken to him in weeks."

"Lies! All lies!"

"Look, look, calm down. Please! This isn't right. You don't have to do this. It happened, I admit it. It just happened."

"Nothing just happens! You thought about it. You made a *decision*. Whatever happened to self-control? It was one of my old shrink's favorite subjects. *Exercises self-control*. You should have tried a little harder, Mrs. Knowles, because fucking my husband was the biggest mistake of your life."

"You're right," Annie says, trying desperately to placate her. "I know. I realize that now."

"Now is too late for you. Jesus is very angry. Turn right onto 20. Go down to the interstate. We're going north."

The highway is open. Annie thinks of pulling over somewhere, but there are few stops on this road, a bleak rural landscape. Lydia smokes continuously, and the smell of it makes Annie sick to her stomach. She is acutely aware of her pregnancy, every inch of her body expressing life.

"Where are we going?" Talking is better than silence.

"To pay someone a visit."

"But it's snowing. The road is very slippery."

"This person is worth the effort. I think you'll want to see him. Unfortunately, he's not himself these days. He's been in a bit of an accident."

"What did you say?"

"There's nothing to worry about. He's recovering nicely. I'm taking very good care of him."

The words suddenly unscramble in her head. She's talking about Michael. *He's alive.*

79

THE WORLD LOOKS DIFFERENT from the backseat, Lydia thinks, holding a handkerchief up to her bleeding nose. Surreal. The way the trees hunker and shimmy. She used to get nosebleeds as a child, she remembers. Her hands filling up with her own blood. It was scary at the time. But not anymore. Now she's a grown woman. She's not afraid of things like that.

No need to feel any pain now, she thinks, the pills blossoming inside her like little buds. Pretty little flowers. No need to feel anything.

She pushes the gun a little harder into the back of Annie's neck. "Turn down that lane. See that house? Park over there. We'll go in the front."

It is amazing to Lydia how much power a gun has. It's a mental thing, what Reverend Tim used to call the Fear Factor. The little movie of premonition the person experiences when they've got a gun at the back of their neck.

"Get out of the car. We're going in."

They walk through the snow, up the front steps, and into the house. The doctor's wife blanches as she reacts to the smell of the trash. *I wasn't expecting company.* "Upstairs. Hurry up." Annie Knowles hesitates at the bottom of the stairs. Lydia nudges her hard with the gun, urging her up to the second floor, into her father's room. "Sit over in that chair. Put on those handcuffs."

Annie pants as if she is trying to formulate a question. Lydia indulges in her terror like a form of entertainment. "W-where is he?" Annie finally stutters. "Is he here in this house?"

"Did I tell you to talk? What were your instructions, Mrs. Knowles?"

"I . . . I can't remember."

"I told you to put those on." Annie takes up the handcuffs reluctantly. "What—you've never played with handcuffs before? I'm *shocked.* It's one of Simon's favorite little games." Annie opens her mouth a little. "Tell me this, Mrs. Knowles, are you ready to be shot?"

"N-no . . . please."

Lydia's tongue swells up on account of the pills, an unfortunate side effect. She imagines that her voice sounds funny, like a record playing at the wrong speed. Just for fun, she aims the gun at Annie and cocks it.

Scrambling, Annie puts on the handcuffs. She sits there, demure as a schoolgirl, her wrists joined in her lap.

"I can do anything I want now," Lydia says. She puts the gun back into her apron pocket. Then she gets the roll of duct tape that she purchased for the occasion and wraps Annie Knowles up like a mummy while Annie whimpers and sweats and bawls like a baby. In no mood for it, Lydia threads the tape through her mouth to shut her up. "Now look," she says. "We *both* know that once something like this happens there's no going back. The fact that my husband made you pregnant is the biggest insult of all. When for years, *years,* we tried and nothing happened. And now you, *you.* Do you know how much that *hurts,* Mrs. Knowles? Do you have any idea the *pain* I'm in?"

She walks to the window and looks out.

"I admit that I've had problems with sex. And my husband, well, you weren't the first. From time to time he'd sleep with a student. Nothing serious. But you. You're different, aren't you? You're like a disease, that's what. You're a fucking plague."

Disgusted now, Lydia gets down real close to her. "Don't think you're *having* that baby."

80

AT DAWN, Simon drives over to Annie's house. It's dark. The door is locked and nobody answers. He checks the garage; her car is there. With growing agitation, he runs around to the sliding doors on the deck. They, too, are locked. He tells himself that her parents came and got her but it doesn't sit well and he has the intolerable instinct that Lydia has done something to Annie. Something awful.

In a fury of desperation, he rips his own house apart, trying to find something that might reveal where Lydia is. After an hour or two of searching, he discovers a receipt in the pocket of a sweater, from a hardware store in Amsterdam, New York, a town near Vanderkill, where his wife grew up. Later that afternoon he hears a car pulling up outside and hurries to the window, hoping it's Lydia, only to see the mailman in his little white jeep.

With a disturbing clatter, the mail drops through the slot in the front door and scatters across the floor.

Simon picks it up and mindlessly flips through it, noting that they've sent the card for his retrospective. It's a four-by-six postcard with a picture of one of his paintings on it. The one he'd taken Annie to see in New York. The one called *Her Father's House.*

81

BOUND TO THE CHAIR, Annie scrutinizes the room. The bed with its bare mattress. The dresser with a picture frame on top. Stuck in the mirror above it is a yellowed snapshot of a woman. Annie somehow knows that the woman is Lydia's dead mother. Annie swallows some more glue from the tape. She does not think she can go much longer without something to drink. The late sun glints off a tiny gold key on the windowsill.

Downstairs, the front door opens and Lydia slams out. Annie hears the car starting up. Now the house is silent. She uses the time to try to get free, but there is no getting out of the tape. The little key will have to wait. Using her hips and legs she gallops the chair across the room. It makes a lot of noise. And then she hears Michael's voice.

"Hello!"

He is down in the cellar.

Her heart beats wildly. She desperately wants to answer him, to call out and tell him she's here, she's right upstairs, but the tape is too tight and her mouth cannot move. She grunts as loud as she can, but she knows he can't hear her. Frustrated, she continues her clumsy gallop until she reaches the door. There is an old-fashioned skeleton keyhole and she peers through it, seeing a narrow hallway and the stairs. Lifting her chin, she sets it down on the top of the knob and tries to make it twist. She attempts this for a while, shifting the position of her chin, pushing the hollow of her cheek into the knob in an effort to make it budge, but she is sweating too hard to get a grip.

"Hello!" he shouts. "I hear you! Who are you?"

She beats her forehead into the door in response.

Silence for a moment.

"If it's someone I know make two beats."

With her head, she makes two beats on the door.

"Where do I know you from? From work?"

She stays quiet.

"Celina James?"

Again she stays quiet.

"You a cop?"

Silence.

For a minute he says nothing, and then he shouts, "Annie?"

Two beats on the door.

"Annie?"

Two beats on the door.

82

THE NARROW ROADS that wind through Vanderkill are slick with ice. It's almost dark, and the temperature has dropped. Simon shivers, remembering his first visit up here. The ramshackle bungalows. The barren fields. At last he comes upon the dirt lane that leads to her father's house, but he does not turn into it. Instead, he drives into a neighbor's cornfield, maneuvering the car through a maze of yellow stalks, deep into its very center. On foot, he runs down the dirt lane. At its narrow end, the old house appears. It is like being inside a dream, he thinks, a fragmented journey into his past.

The place looks deserted. He does not see Lydia's car. Disheartened, he climbs onto the porch and peers into the front windows. The curtains have been drawn, but through a narrow slit in the center he can see inside. Garbage bags line the hall. He tries the door and finds it locked. No matter, he has a key.

During the many days of the doctor's incarceration, the key had been hanging among all the other lost keys of his life on a rack above the washing machine.

He uses it now to open the door and steps inside, instantly encountering the foul odor of garbage. The memory of Lydia's dead father comes back to him. He breaks into a sweat. He glances into the kitchen, noting the empty soup cans in the sink, a dead mouse in one of them. Simon picks up a carving knife, realizing that he is more than prepared to use it.

"Lydia?" he calls out. The silence taunts him. "Lydia, you come out here!"

A thump on the floor upstairs. Simon takes the stairs two at a time and searches the empty rooms, fighting off the ghosts of his memories. In the old man's room he finds Annie. The sight of her bound up like that makes him crazy and he fiercely cuts her free. He pulls her into his arms and she cries with joy. He holds her there tightly, breathing her in. "Annie." Just her name in his mouth makes him weep. "I'm sorry," he whispers into her hair.

Annie cries, holding up her cuffed writsts. "The key's over there."

"Are you all right? Did she hurt you?"

She shakes her head, tears rolling freely down her cheeks. "She's got Michael. He's downstairs."

"We're going to get him out of there."

He takes her hand and they start down the stairs. A car roars up the lane. Through the window he sees Lydia's Mercedes. His wife gets out of the car and slams the door, her hair a wild jagged mess. She is wearing an old red coat and he can see her apron sticking out from under it. In her hand she has a gun.

"In here." Simon shuffles Annie into the pantry in the kitchen. He holds her tight and still, uncertain of what to do next. He can see that his wife has gone completely mad.

Through a crack in the pantry door he watches Lydia enter the kitchen, her keys crashing on the counter. She flashes to and fro, swept up in her jangling quest. Her movements are abrupt, as if she has drunk some diabolical magic potion. He knows there will be no stopping her.

She puts the gun gently in her apron pocket, then empties the contents of a paper bag onto the floor: a tin of gasoline, a box of safety matches, and a plastic Baggie full of bullets.

83

FOR PRACTICAL REASONS, she has decided to shoot them both in the head and set the house on fire. With the house burned down, no one will ever know what has transpired here these past two weeks. It makes perfect sense and she wonders why it has taken her so long to come up with the idea.

All good things must come to an end, she thinks, reaching for a hammer.

The wood is old and dry and she has no trouble breaking it apart. She swings the hammer, savoring the exertion, making guttural sounds in her throat. Her strength is ethereal, goddesslike. The wood splinters and falls, a reckless pile on the kitchen floor. Good kindling, she thinks lightly, wildly anticipating what she has known all along. That it would never work out. That in the end, no matter what, he would have to die.

She breaks through the basement door, a vigorous birth, and kicks the splintered wood out of her way. Everything is going to be fine, she tells herself, slowly descending the stairs. She is in control. Calm. The doctor is lying on the mattress, turned away from her, despondent.

"I've had it with you," she says softly. "You've caused me nothing but trouble."

Darkness drifts throughout the room like smoke, sucking up the last of daylight. "Why did you bring her here?" he says, finally.

"Because it's time for this to end." She takes out her gun. "It could have worked out, but your wife went too far. She took advantage of the situation. I guess she doesn't love you after all."

"Kill me and let her go," he blubbers pathetically, getting onto his knees. "Please. Just let Annie go."

"You know I can't do that." She lifts up the gun, cocks it. Her hand trembles. "Stand up so I can aim better. I don't want to see you suffering. It's not that I don't like you, Michael. The truth is I'm going to miss you."

But what is that? The sound of a car. It pulls up outside and parks. A single door shuts.

Lydia freezes. The tiny hairs on her arms go stiff and prickly. Someone enters the house at the front door and she chides herself for being careless and leaving it unlocked. The irregular footsteps give him away as he limps across the wood floor. "Reverend Tim," she whispers. "He's come to kill me."

It occurs to her that they're trapped. There is no way out of the cellar, not even through the hatch, which is padlocked from the outside. "We're stuck in here."

"Hide," Michael says. "Keep quiet."

"Lydia?" Reverend Tim sings out in a voice one might use to call an animal. "I just want to talk. I know you're here. There's no need to hide, beauty. I understand how you feel. Come on out and we'll have a good, long talk."

Lydia's heart spins like a top. She wishes they *could* talk. She wishes he could help her out of this, the way he used to help her, but now that's not possible. The worst part is how much she loved him once. Yes, it *was* love. The best kind of love, pure and clean. And now he has come to kill her, and even though she deserves to die for all she's done, she feels betrayed.

There is the sudden sound of a scuffling and then a sharp outcry of pain. Lydia wonders if he has stumbled over something. Something heavy falls to the floor.

"What was that?" she whispers to Michael. But he doesn't answer her. She feels cold, terribly cold. Sweat drips down her face as they wait for what will come next. For several minutes it is silent, but then his footsteps resume across the squeaky kitchen floor. At the cellar door he hesitates, kicking the scraps of wood aside. Her head pounds. She can feel her feet pressing into the cold floor, but she does not think she will be able to move. Stuck, she realizes. *Paralyzed with fear.*

"Lydia?" his voice booms, "Lydia!"

The cellar is dark now, the inky moonless night a sign from Jesus that He is here with her, watching over her. Protecting her. Holding out His soft white hand for her. *It won't be long now,* she thinks.

Michael stirs behind her, his breathing hard and jagged like an agitated dog. Her eyes return to the top of the stairs where the minister's monstrous shape fills the doorway. She cannot make out his face but can hear him groping for the light switch, flipping it on and off again in vain. Cutting the wires had been a wise precaution and her heart flutters with pride. He begins his descent and she forces herself to move a little, stepping back an inch or two to prove she can do it. Sweat burns in her eyes, blurs her vision. She blinks. She remembers to breathe. A whining sound curls up out of her ear and she wonders if an insect has crawled down into it and gotten stuck. She wonders if an insect has set up housekeeping inside her ear. An insect or perhaps even a worm. *A bloodsucker.* Shuddering, she looks back up the stairs and watches him slowly sink down into this awful place, this tomb of despair. Clutching the wobbly banister, his hand squeals against the wood. *He's insane,* she thinks. *He will stop at nothing.*

"Please don't," she begs, but it is only a whisper and she doubts he has heard it.

"There's nothing to be afraid of," he says, his voice garbled and slippery. *I'm going to have to kill you is all.*

Her eyes burn and tear, and sweat sprouts from her body like fresh clover, and soon she is a whole wet field of it and it is running out of her, it is running down her back, down her legs to her feet. Everything seems to be moving at once and it is very loud inside her head. It is the volume turned up to maximum on a television game show. It is the sound of her dead mother screaming.

Her hand aches and she remembers that she is holding the gun. Her hand has gone brittle and stiff around the pistol, and it is heavy, impossibly heavy. He has reached the bottom of the staircase and he is moving toward her and she knows that he is going to grab her, he is going to grab her and it is going to hurt and then he is going to kill her. *Please, don't! Please stop!*

"I'm not going to hurt you," he says, but his voice is strange and distant and she does not believe him. *Daddy? Is it you?*

"She has a gun," Michael shouts.

"You *tricked* me," she says.

"I just want to talk."

"You lied to me. You *tricked* me."

"She has a fucking gun!"

The gun is heavier now and her muscles strain to hold it up. "Shut *up!*" she screams. "Don't come any closer! *Don't!*"

"Put down the gun, Lydia."

"You *lied* to me. You . . . you took . . . you took *advantage of me.* I was just . . . I was just a stupid girl. I was stupid . . . I didn't know any better . . . and you put a spell on me. . . . I *trusted* you. . . . I *believed in* you."

Her head throbs and the little slippery worms begin to dance. He comes upon her, his swarming bulk. "Don't come any closer," she warns. "I've asked you nicely. *Please.*" But he refuses to listen to her even now, in the moment of his death, and it insults her profoundly, and she cannot forgive him. "You're not *listening!*" she shouts. "You've never listened to me."

Wait!

No more waiting!

The blast of the gunshot is deafening. The cellar fills with smoke and a hazy, stifling heat. He makes a sound—*pop*—and the air runs out of him. He falls down on the floor.

Everything finally stops. The world stops. The gun simmers in her hand. Pulling the trigger had felt good, and now the gun is clean and hollow, like her heart. Death crowds the room with ghosts and a strange cold glow spreads like mist across the floor. There is her father with his five o'clock stubble. And there. There is Mama. *She shall have music wherever she goes.*

"I think you killed him," Michael says.

"He tricked me," she explains.

"You'd better put on the lamp."

She gropes her way to the oil lamp and lights it, waiting for her eyes to adjust. She looks down at the body on the floor. It quivers a little. An odor rises up to her nostrils. Urine, she thinks, wondering distantly if she has wet her pants. His blood makes a stream across the floor. It collects in a puddle and wets the soles of her boots.

"I think he's dead, Lydia," the doctor informs her.

"My feet," she says softly. "My feet are all wet."

"Michael?" a voice shouts down the stairs. It's a woman. "Michael, are you all right?"

"Annie? Down here!"

Annie Knowles stumbles down the stairs. How she has gotten herself free escapes Lydia. She is holding up Lydia's daddy's ax, the one he always kept on the back porch, and it looks as though she is more than prepared to use it. "Thank God you're all right," she says to her husband, but then she comes upon the puddle of blood, the body on the ground, and lets out a whimper, like she's been hit from behind.

"Check his pulse," Michael says. "I think she killed him."

Lydia blinks and blinks, unable to comprehend how Annie has gotten free. It's a conspiracy, she realizes. Another trick. They've been tricking her all along.

"Look what you've done," Annie says to her, cradling the rusty ax in her arms like a baby.

"What?" Lydia gasps, confused, suddenly terrified.

Annie drops to her knees by the body and sobs, a foul groan curling out of her mouth. "You killed him. You killed your husband!"

Perplexed, Lydia reels unsteadily. "What? I can't hear. . . . I have worms . . . my ears."

"Oh my God! He's *dead!*" Annie whines, doubling over as if she were in pain. "Oh my *God!* Simon! *Simon!*"

Lydia looks down at the dead man. "Simon?" she says, bewildered. "What are you doing down there?"

But he has fallen asleep, and she sees no point in waiting around for him to wake up.

84

"HURRY UP and give me that ax," Michael tells Annie.

"Oh, Michael!" She hands him the ax. "Hurry. She's got a can of gasoline up there."

"Move away." He swings the ax, smacking the chain with its blade. With each strike, the floor vibrates up through his legs. The briny smell of battered cement fills his lungs. After several tries, he feels the chain snap and release. He is free.

Gasoline drips through the floorboards. Michael takes Annie's hand and they climb the stairs. "Lydia!" He searches the first floor and finds the minister out cold on the living room floor. "Lydia!"

The box of matches drops. He finds her in the kitchen on her hands and knees, trying to scoop them up.

"It's over now," he coaxes. "Put the matches down."

"I don't want to go." Lydia shakes her head, an adamant child. "I don't like it there."

Sirens scream up the driveway. There is the sound of feet trampling across the lawn.

"Lydia. Put the matches down."

"Nobody understands me." She picks up a single match. "I'm all alone now," she says.

Just as she is about to strike the match, the room floods with cops. One of them grabs her from behind, but she bites his arm and runs out the door. The cop goes after her. From the window, Michael watches the cops surround her from all directions. He does not want to watch it. He doesn't want to see her being caught. For some reason, he cannot bear it.

"You folks all right?"

"Detective Bascombe," Annie says, tears coming up her throat. "She shot Simon Haas. He's in the cellar. He's dead."

85

SIMON HAAS IS BURIED in the Union Cemetery on Shaker Road. Annie attends the funeral on her own. Lydia Haas is there, handcuffed to Detective Bascombe. She is wearing a black suit and a veil, but Annie can still see her face, her eyes, which are drained of color and dart cautiously about, as though she is in the presence of her enemies.

After the service, people float toward their cars. Annie watches Bascombe lead the widow away. He is exceedingly gentle with her, Annie observes, removing the handcuff from his own wrist and replacing it on hers. Noticing that she is crying, he pulls a handkerchief from his pocket and offers it to her, and she nods and takes it and dabs at her eyes. The gesture seems to comfort her, and Annie finds herself wondering if it is the same handkerchief Bascombe had offered to her, and if he had ever washed it. The idea of their tears mingling on that square of cloth fills her with a strange remorse. Bascombe helps Lydia into the back of his car, then gets in behind the wheel. Annie continues across the grass, but her eyes remain on Lydia in the backseat. She knows that neither of them will fully recover from Simon's death. Lydia takes off her veil, and then as if sensing Annie's gaze, meets her eyes. For a long moment, neither of them moves. Bascombe starts the car and slowly pulls out as Lydia's hand rises up like a flag of surrender and touches the glass.

In the afternoon, Annie and some of the people from the college drive over to Simon's house to take care of the dogs. Over tea in his kitchen, they have a discussion about what to do with them. Annie volunteers to take one, a female named Grace. The remaining Danes will go to other willing faculty members. Outside, the wind comes in gusts. The chimes jangle and spin. The dishes in the cupboard tremble slightly. The door opens suddenly, as if someone has entered. It commands their attention, allows them each a brief and contemplative glimpse of the lake. The door slams shut with finality, and Annie knows—perhaps they all know—that it is Simon's way of saying good-bye.

86

MICHAEL IS KEPT in the hospital for a week and Annie stays with him there, sleeping on a pullout chair in the room. They spend the hours together playing cards, listening to music. She is grateful for this time with him, this time to recover, to reckon somehow with all that's gone on.

The new year promises change, and on a cold winter morning in January the moving truck arrives on schedule. It's hard for Annie to believe the day has finally come. Packing the house has been oddly therapeutic, organizing all of the pieces of their history into boxes, each thing a small token of the life they've shared, both good and bad.

She is ready to move on.

The empty rooms of the house sing with light. It really is a beautiful old place, she thinks, feeling a little sorry now that they have to leave it behind. She walks into her bedroom and takes a last look around. Through the window she sees Henry and Rosie chasing Simon's dog across the field. They are laughing, their breath white as smoke in the cold air.

Standing there, she has the strangest feeling that Simon is in the room with her. She imagines his hand flat on the rise of her belly, weightless as a cloud.

The horn of the moving truck blares and she goes downstairs. Outside, the men are closing up the truck. Michael hands the driver a map. The men get into the truck and the truck pulls away. They stand there with the sun in their eyes, watching it vanish.

"You okay?" Michael asks.

She nods, but she is suddenly choked up. It's harder to leave than she thought.

"Look on the bright side," he says. "We'll have a Blockbuster *and* a Starbucks."

This makes her laugh. She takes a last look around, her eyes sweeping across the open landscape. And then he holds out his hand, and she takes it.

ACKNOWLEDGMENTS

I am profoundly grateful to my editor, Carole DeSanti, for her incisive nurturing of this book and for her generous spirit and patience. Thank you to Karen Murphy, for her clarity and inspiration and kindness. Thank you also to Patty Bozza, Bonnie Thompson, Lexy Bloom, Nancy Sheppard, Carolyn Coleburn, Gretchen Koss, and all of the others at Viking who had a hand in bringing this book into the world. I am indebted to my agent, Linda Chester, for believing in this novel and for fearlessly pushing for it, and also for her friendship and her faith in my work. Thank you also to Gary Jaffe and Laurie Fox of Linda Chester & Associates, for their warmth and assurance whenever needed, and to Kyra Ryan for her excellent advice on early drafts of the book. Thank you to Joe Veltre, Kathy Green, and Michael Carlisle at Carlisle & Co., and Laurie Horowitz at CAA, for their enthusiasm and support.

A very heartfelt thank-you goes to James Michener and the Copernicus Society of America, for granting me a fellowship; and thank you to Frank Conroy, for selecting me. Thanks also to Connie Brothers, for her unflagging compassion and guidance. I'd also like to thank the following editors who have published my work in the past: Constance Warloe, Jim Clark (at *The Greensboro Review*), Peter Stine (at *Witness* magazine), and James McKinley (at *New Letters*).

I owe the following people my deepest gratitude for their unrelenting encouragement: my parents, Joan and Lyle Brundage, for never giving up on me, no matter what; Dorothy Silverherz Rosenberg, for her continued inspiration; Paula Lippman, my soul mate; Beth Abrahms, my surrogate sister; and to all my friends and family who have shown an interest in my career, in particular: Florence and Karel Sokoloff; Millie and Martin Shapiro; Paul Scott; Amy Diamond; Phyllis Abrahms; Sally Abrahms; Betty Sigoloff; Helen Beck and Arnold Abramowitz; Sue Turconi; Richard Morris; John and Lori Rosenberg; Dan and Meg Milsky; Nancy Stone;

Maxine Glassman; Karen Cohen; Joanie Gruen; Pat DuMark and Jamie Grace.

Thank you, Marc and Christine Heller, for sharing your stories. Thank you to all the doctors out there in the world who never stop doing what's necessary, who never stop taking care of strangers.